Where Did Your Heart Go?

AUDRINA LANE

Copyright © 2015 Audrina Lane
All rights reserved.

FIRST EDITION eBook published 2013.

SECOND EDITION published 2015.

ISBN: 150773252X
ISBN-13: 978-1507732526

The moral right of AUDRINA LANE to be identified as author of this Work has been asserted by her in accordance with the Copyright, Designs and Patents Act of 1988.

No part of this publication may be reproduced, stored in a retrieval system, or transmitted in any form or by any means, electronic, mechanical, photocopying, recording or otherwise, without the prior permission of the copyright owner. You must not circulate this book without the authority to do so.

All characters in this book are fictitious, and any resemblance to actual persons living or dead is purely coincidental.

The author acknowledges the trademarked status and trademark owners of various products referenced in this work of fiction, which have been used without permission. The publication/use of these trademarks is not authorised, associated with, or sponsored by the trademark owner.

For more information visit www.audrinalane.co.uk

DEDICATION

I would like to dedicate this book to my fiancé Steve who has allowed me the time and space to write this novel in the first place. I love the way you have put up with my tapping away on the laptop in front of the television or out in the garden.

Also special thanks to my first boyfriend, you know who you are. You have given me some of the memories that I have drawn on when shaping the lives and feelings of my main characters. Also as my first love, which this book is all about, hope I have faithfully re-created those feelings of being a teenager in love.

Finally to George Michael, Rick Astley, A-Ha and Berlin amongst many others for the soundtrack that made up my teenage years and got me through the heartbreak and tears.

THE HEART TRILOGY

Where Did Your Heart Go?
Unbreak My Heart
Closer to the Heart

-1-

I'd been at home for about an hour when my teenage daughter rushed through the front door, tears streaming down her cheeks. Sighing, I realised today was going to be a rough day, despite the lovely winter sun shining through the windows. Turning I pressed the button on the kettle and made us both hot chocolate, sure a cuppa and a chat would cheer her up. I stirred the mixture and left the warmth of the kitchen.

Pausing in the hallway I caught sight of the last photograph I had of my husband Mark. It sat next to our wedding photograph and I saw the faraway look in my eyes, a stark comparison to the warmth radiating from his. His kind, sensitive gaze followed me as I climbed the stairs and knocked on her door.

"Charlotte, are you ok?"

"Go away Mum," I heard her sob.

"Afraid I can't as I'm holding a cup of hot chocolate for you." I waited silently for a few minutes, listening to her sobs. Her cries subsided and slowly the door opened and a tear-stained face with puffy eyes looked at me.

"Can I come in?" I asked

"Suppose."

Charlotte took her mug and cradling it in her cupped hands, sat back down on the bed, sweeping a deluge of tissues onto the floor. I resisted the urge to clear them up into the bin.

"Is there something up with Craig?"

"Yeah, he just dumped me."

"His loss." I hadn't liked him much on the couple of occasions he had been over to the house.

"Guess," Charlotte mumbled before tears started to slide down her cheeks again. I handed her another tissue and remained silent as she sobbed.

"Mum, why does it hurt so much?"

I stood up and closed the gap between us, gently enfolding her in my arms. "Because breaking up is painful. Unfortunately you may go through it a few more times before you meet the right guy for you."

"How do you know Mum, perhaps I might never meet him?"

"Yes, I thought that too when I was your age, but I got through it. A broken heart can take a long time to heal," I said, averting my daughter's enquiring gaze. I didn't want her to see the dark despair clouding my eyes as I was transported back to November 1988 and the day my life ended.

"Craig was perfect, and now it seems I'm not enough for him."

"Perhaps I can give you something that might help you get through this."

I remembered the diary I found a few months ago. It was all that remained of my first love affair. I paused and my hand reached up to my neck where a chain used to lie. I wore the St. Christopher for a while but it was now safely wrapped up in my jewellery box.

"What, Mum?"

"Wait here a moment. I will have to go and look for it."

"Ok," she replied as she reached for her phone and started to tap out a text to her best friend Julia.

I withdrew and crossed the hallway to the small box room that doubled as my office. I opened the bottom drawer of my desk and found what I was looking for; the faded cover of my purple diary dated 1988, the corners bent out of shape, the lock long since broken. I opened it up to see my neat handwriting on the inside:

This book belongs to Stephanie March.

Surrounding this were numerous hearts bearing the initials *SM 4 JC*. Gently I opened the first few pages and skimmed over my childish script. I smiled as I found myself being drawn back to my teenage years. I still didn't understand why I kept this but perhaps it would help my heartbroken daughter cope with her first break-up. Kneeling on the floor of my office, memories from the past swirled around my mind, engulfing me with both intense happiness and devastating despair. Was it the right thing to do, showing my daughter that love could be wonderful and magical, but also destructive and deadly too?

I walked back across the hall and was partly calmed to see Charlotte lounging back against her pillow, phone in hand. She was undoubtedly my daughter with her fair skin, but the blond hair and green eyes she had were inherited from Mark.

"What's that?" she asked, curious.

"It's my diary from when I was your age. It will tell you the story of my first romance and break-up and I hope it might help you through yours."

"Wow, Mum, you've kept this all these years?"

"Yes, I'm not sure why but every time I tried to throw it away, something stopped me."

I remembered how James had thrown my heart away and I turned from my daughter, reminded of the fear and pain I felt. He had taken my heart with him and left a hollow space inside me that still ached.

Standing in the bedroom I looked at Charlotte.

"Well, aren't you the least bit curious?"

Charlotte quirked her eyebrows at my question and started to open the diary.

"Oh so you're waiting for me to leave then?"

Charlotte nodded and I tiptoed out of the room and shut the door.

I returned to the comfort and warmth of the kitchen. Leaning against the island counter, I breathed in and out for a few minutes. Pulling open the junk drawer I rummaged around and found a couple of anti-depressants because I could feel the darkness starting to creep over me. I had been dealing with this feeling for the last twenty-four years. I took them and swilled them down with the remains of my hot chocolate as I crossed the tiles and found my favourite chair in the conservatory. On the table beside me I found an open book and the radio for company.

I worked for the local radio station as a DJ so it was always tuned it to our frequency. Occasionally I would find Radio 1 on if Charlie had been messing around but most of the time she enjoyed listening to the older tracks. She had been brought up on a diet of music, my life having always revolved around it.

It seemed to be an afternoon of memories as dusk started to creep over the ice-blue sky. I thought of all the times as a child she had danced around the kitchen. I would often join in and soon realised she had some talent for performing. She always loved ballet lessons and now at college, she was in a dance group mixing a fusion of street, gymnastics and ballet and I was always eager to see them perform.

As my dark mood slowly passed I went back to the cooker and started to prepare some tea, not sure whether Charlotte would be joining me or not. At least it kept me busy in the meantime and took my mind away from the images starting to seep in.

Dear Diary,

Friday 1st January, 1988
As it's the first day of the year I'm thinking about making some New Year resolutions. Sarah and I went to June's house for a party last night and I danced so much that my feet are still aching now. One of the guys kissed me on the cheek at midnight but I didn't really fancy him so it didn't go any further than that.

I'm laid back against the pillows on my bed, listening to my favourite George Michael album. I need to pass my exams because I want to study media and become a DJ on the radio; it's my dream ambition.

George is singing about sex and I wonder… I'm going to be seventeen in a couple of months and I hope I might be lucky enough to find a boyfriend, someone to love. I have auburn hair that's curly most of the time and sometimes difficult to control. My pale skin is scattered by freckles that fade during the colder weather but they will be back in view when the sunshine returns. I have slim curves but wish my breasts were larger as that's always where boys seem to look first.

My new velvet jeans hug my shapely legs, my best feature. So, although it's not really a resolution, I hope this year will bring love into my life. I turn to look at my ever expanding bookshelves and decide I will read more books. I spot the newest one on my shelf and decide there's no better time than the present, opening the first page of *Carrie* by Stephen King.

Saturday 2nd January, 1988
Sarah phoned and asked if I wanted to go swimming as she needed to get fit. I agreed as it would also be good to get together for a gossip before school.

As we entered the pool area, I stopped in my tracks. Sitting on the lifeguard chair at the deep end was the sexiest guy I ever laid eyes on. I caught Sarah's arm and whispered, "Look at the lifeguard, he's gorgeous."

"Well yeah he's ok I suppose, not really my type," Sarah replied as we walked halfway up the pool and I dived in.

Surfacing I swam to the side and waited for Sarah to take the more leisurely route into the water. We started to swim a couple of lengths together, stopping at each end to gossip and catch our breath. All the time I was surreptitiously checking him out as he monitored the pool.

"I'm going to dive," I said to Sarah, before I swam across the pool and got out to saunter towards the diving board. Inside I felt the nerves kick in as butterflies started to beat against my ribs. Standing on the end of the board I could almost feel his eyes watching me. I jumped and executed the best dive of my life.

Swimming over to Sarah I grabbed the side.

"He was definitely watching you."

"Well, of course he was, it's his job to do that."

"No, I mean really watching," she said, "perhaps he likes you?"

"Doubt it, he looks about nineteen or twenty, guys that age rarely ever like sixteen year olds," I moaned.

We pushed away from the side and swam a couple more lengths together. In my mind I could see him in his shorts and t-shirt. He was quite tall, I guessed about six foot. He was slim but I could imagine the muscles hidden from view. He had blond hair cut short and blue eyes which reflected the colour of the pool. I watched as he jumped down off his chair and started to walk a lap around the edge, carefully watching all the swimmers and ensuring they were safe in the water.

Sunday 3rd January, 1988

I've spent the day tidying my room and getting my bag ready for school. I put my Wham! album on and danced around the room whilst I gathered everything together. As I listened to the melodic voice of George, he sang about staying home instead of going out dancing.

I'm staring now at all the posters I have plastered over my walls, George looking young and gorgeous in his white shorts and *'Choose Life'* t-shirt. There are also some newer photos of him in a leather jacket, stubble on his chin.

I'm still thinking about the guy at the swimming pool, still a mystery with no name. He didn't look anything like George but as I picture him, I feel my heart start to beat faster in my chest. Are these the beginnings of a crush?

Monday 4th January, 1988

First day back today. This morning I hurried to meet Sarah at the corner of the street. I could see her waiting with our other friends, June and Amanda.

"Hi girls," I said, as I fell into step with them.

"Hi Steph, are you ready for study, study and more study," June asked.

"Not really but I guess we need to," I replied, putting my arm through Sarah's.

"So, Sarah says you have a crush on a lifeguard at the pool?" Amanda said, turning to look at me. I blushed and reached out to give her a playful punch.

"Maybe."

"Well, you know Gareth really likes you," June said, naming the guy who kissed me on the cheek at midnight.

"He's not really my type," I replied. I could see my type; it was the guy at the pool.

Walking home in the afternoon, I could hear the conversation surrounding me but I kept drifting off into my fantasy world.

I decided, I will go swimming tomorrow night, on my own. Hoping that if I am alone, and he is there, then he might speak to me?

Tuesday 5th January, 1988
Hurrying home from school, I hugged my secret plan close to my heart. I noticed Sarah giving me a strange look as we said goodbye at the end of her street as usual.

"Is everything ok?" she asked.

"Yes, I'll tell you tomorrow," I replied as I walked until I was out of sight. Then I ran the short distance home so that I had enough time to get ready. I told Mum and Dad I was going to the pool with Sarah as I didn't want to explain why I was going on my own. In my bag I had packed my favourite bikini instead of my swimsuit, hoping it would make an impression. I walked along in the dusk as the streetlights lit the way through Ross-on-Wye to the pool.

Crossing the car park I started to feel nervous and nearly turned around, but it felt as if something was calling me inside, tugging at me to take the chance. Once inside I got changed and then walked out to the poolside. I saw him at the far end of the pool, walking around, so I quickly slipped into the water. The nerves were making my heart pound as I started to swim my first couple of lengths. After ten lengths, I stopped at the deep end. I saw him striding back up to my end of the pool and I could already feel the butterflies starting to flutter.

I watched, transfixed. Before I could quite believe it, he was kneeling down right next to where I was holding onto the side.

"Hi," he said. "Didn't I see you here on Saturday?"

"Um yes," I managed to get out of my stunned mouth. I could feel my skin getting hotter as the redness spread over my face like an embarrassing rash. I wanted to duck under the cool water and hide it from him.

"So I was wondering if you would like to join the lifesaving course I am teaching on Thursday night?" he asked. "I noticed you were a really strong swimmer the other day."

"Yes, that sounds good, how do I enrol?"

"Just pop to reception on your way out and tell Elaine that James sent you."

"Thanks James," I replied, trying out his name on my lips. "I'm Stephanie but most of my friends call me Steph."

"Great, Steph. I look forward to seeing you on Thursday night." For a second he held my gaze and then I watched as he looked up and saw some young lads fooling around on the other side of the pool. He was off, leaving me struggling for air as I slipped beneath the surface to cool my face.

As I left the pool I spoke to Elaine and enrolled. I was about to leave when I turned.

"What is James' surname?"

"Cooke," she replied, watching me blush on my way to the door.

Wednesday 6th January, 1988

Sarah and I had study period so we decided to sneak out of school early, saying that we were going to the library in town. Instead, we went to our favourite café and bought large hot chocolates topped with cream and chocolate sprinkles. Sitting at the table nearest the window, Sarah leaned forward. "You look different today, spill the beans."

"Ok," I said, my grin nearly breaking my face. "I spoke to him and I know his name."

"You mean the lifeguard at the pool? How did you manage that?" Sarah asked, almost dropping the spoon she had been using to scoop cream into her mouth.

"I went to the pool on my own last night and he stopped to speak to me and asked if I wanted to enrol in the lifesaving class that starts on Thursday."

"And, what else?"

"Well, he said he noticed what a strong swimmer I was on Saturday and that he thought I might enjoy it." I took a sip of my drink as I relived the exact words of our conversation. I already knew them by heart as I had been doing the same thing all day.

"So what's his name?"

"James Cooke." I loved the way his name sounded on my lips.

"I'll ask my brother if he knows him. If James is nineteen or twenty, he might have been in the same year as Tom," she said.

"Oh yes, do that," I replied. "Try and find out anything you can"

Thursday 7th January, 1988

I was waiting for Sarah at the corner. June and Amanda had gone on ahead which was good as I didn't want to share any of this with them. Watching my best friend approach, I thought of how long we had known each other. We had been friends since we were four years old and I knew she would always be there for me. She had short brown hair that framed her face. She was taller than me and I envied her fuller figure, but she was always saying that she wished she could swap as she hated the attention it drew from guys in our year.

"So?" I asked, the minute Sarah was by my side.

"Ok, hang on a minute," she replied, putting her arm through mine as we walked along the path together.

"He's a year older than my brother so that makes him twenty or possibly even twenty-one."

"Oh, so I really don't stand a chance and he was just being nice on Tuesday?"

"Tom also said that his last girlfriend was a year younger but he thinks they split up before they finished school."

"Oh," I said again, letting the information sink in.

We had almost caught up with Amanda and June so I quickly said, "Don't tell the others about this yet."

"Ok, it will be our little secret," she replied, as we joined them and walked the rest of the way to school.

The day seemed to drag by so slowly as I watched the clock and waited to escape. Finally, when the evening arrived, I couldn't believe it.

I had persuaded Mum to let me buy a new swimsuit. It was a lovely shade of purple and highlighted my sleek body and long legs. I wore my purple velvet jeans, black jumper and pixie boots and was pleased with the effect as I took one final look in the mirror.

Mum gave me a long look as I pulled my coat on. "You're rather dressed up for the pool?"

"Well, I haven't been out anywhere interesting to wear these yet," I replied, hoping she wouldn't notice my flushed face.

"Are you sure you don't want Dad to drive you there and pick you up afterwards?"

"No Mum, I'll be ok and it's not far to walk."

♪

Charlotte paused reading as she heard Stephanie call from the kitchen. Putting the diary aside, she walked downstairs.

"Did you really buy a new swimsuit just to impress the lifeguard?"

Charlie asked as she sat down for tea. Stephanie nodded and smiled.

"That's so cool, I can't wait to read some more and see if it worked," she giggled.

Her sombre mood started to disperse, despite the continuous beeps through tea as various different friends texted her or messaged her on Facebook regarding the break-up.

Although Charlie answered most of her messages, she felt drawn to the diary lying open on her bed. After clearing all the damp tissues away into the bin, she put her pyjamas on and snuggled under her duvet, preparing for a late night of reading. This diary had her hooked; it was like reading a good book but with the added bonus that you knew the characters.

Dear Diary,

Thursday 7th January, 1988 (continued)

I got changed and saw that there were another couple of girls in the changing room. As I wandered poolside, I watched them emerge from the doorway wearing bikinis. My heart fell as I realised they were both older than me by perhaps a year or two. I didn't think James would notice me now, not with them as competition. A couple of guys appeared from the other changing room and I saw that one of them was in the year above me at school, a boy called Jason. The other guy I later found out was called Matthew and he was twenty and doing the course as part of his lifeguard training.

As I saw James emerge from the poolside office door, I felt my breath leave me. He looked gorgeous.

"Hi, thanks for coming. My name is James and I will be your instructor."

After the introductions, I slipped into the water and we all did a series of lengths in each of the different strokes and James told us we needed to learn side stroke.

"Matthew, can you show everyone?" James asked. Matthew nodded and swam the length of the pool. I tried to watch but I found I kept staring at James to see what he was doing. Then it was my turn and I soon found my rhythm, getting the hang of this new stroke.

After class we went upstairs and James gave out some information for us to learn for the following week. As he passed the sheet to me it shook slightly in his grasp and as my hands were shaking, I dropped it. Kneeling down to pick it up, James did the same thing and I found myself staring into his blue eyes as we both held the opposite edges of the paper in our fingers.

"Sorry," he said as he let go.

"It's ok, my fault," I stuttered. What did that look mean? Crossing the car park I turned to look back and I saw James in the upstairs window, looking out. He raised his hand and waved. I looked around but I was alone so it must have been meant for me. I waved back and hurried home to relive the evening in my dreams.

Friday 8th January, 1988
The alarm dragged me reluctantly from my dreams of swimming pools and James. At least it was the last day of the week and I had a busy weekend planned and also lots to talk about with Sarah. I hurried to catch up as they had already started up the road.

"Hi girls, thank god it's Friday," I said, as I joined them.

"Yes, so much homework to get through already, never mind what they might give us today," Amanda moaned.

"Do any of you fancy going to Gareth's party tomorrow night?" June asked, looking directly at me.

"No thanks," I replied.

"Sarah?"

"Thanks but I'll have to check with my Mum first and let you know tomorrow."

"Ok," June said. "I've got my eye on his best mate John and he's not going to be able to resist me in that new dress I bought yesterday."

"Well, he'll be a guy of strong willpower if he does," Amanda said. "I've seen the dress, well what little there is of it."

When we split into our different groups – Sarah and I to history, Amanda and June to French – Sarah interrogated me as we took our seats. "So, what happened last night?"

"Nothing much really, but it was good and I think we should go swimming again tomorrow evening?"

"Ok, I didn't fancy Gareth's party anyway. Apart from John, some of his friends are such dickheads," Sarah said.

Saturday 9th January, 1988
I arranged to meet Sarah in town at four so we would still have time to look around the shops on our way to the pool. Sarah showed me the dress June had bought from Eclipse at the bottom of town.

"Christ, there's not much of it," I said, looking at it in the window.

"I know, but she does look good in it!" Sarah said.

"I bet. She puts the rest of us in the shade in comparison," I replied, thinking of her long, golden blond hair and fantastic curvy figure.

"Now come on, let's get into that pool before you pull me over in your impatience."

I looked up at the window where James had stood and waved. The memory made me smile as we walked towards the entrance. Once inside,

I put my bikini on and Sarah and I went out into the pool. My heart sank; he was nowhere to be seen as we slipped into the water and started to swim. I was too upset to even say anything. Then while we were resting at the deep end, Sarah nudged me.

"Is that James over there?" she asked, gesturing to the entrance from the male changing room.

"Fuck, it is James," I stammered, suddenly dizzy and faint.

We both watched as he walked up the side of the pool, his trunks hugging his tight ass. I tried to breathe deep, regular breaths. My heart was thumping in my chest so much that I thought I was going to pass out. My knuckles started to turn white as I gripped the side of the pool to stop from going under. My legs beneath me felt like jelly as I tried to keep them moving.

James strode towards the diving board and climbed the steps to take up position. I was transfixed at the sight of him as he took three steps to the edge and dived into the water, hardly even rippling it with his entry. I watched as he swam the entire length beneath the water and then surfaced at the shallow end. He swam a couple more lengths at speed and I watched in slow motion as he came towards us.

"He's coming over."

"I know. What should we do, stay or swim away?" I replied in a panic.

"Stay you idiot, although perhaps I should leave," Sarah said.

"No don't leave," I replied, and then he was holding onto the side just inches away from me. I felt sure he could feel the heat from my body penetrating through the cool water of the pool.

"Hi Steph," he said. "Good to see you again so soon."

"Hi James, this is my best friend Sarah," I replied, before my voice started to shake.

"Hi Sarah, good to meet you," James replied, smiling at her before returning his gaze to me.

"Do you guys fancy a race down the pool? I'll give you a head start." A cheeky grin lit his face.

"Ok," we both said. "You'd better start us off then."

"Ready, steady, go," he said, as we both pushed off against the side and crawled down the pool. I was ahead of Sarah but then as I turned to return to the deep end, I could hear James behind me. I tried to double my efforts but he overtook me by a body length before we reached the edge.

Grabbing the side next to him, I was breathing deeply from the exertions and the closeness of his body. We waited a couple of seconds for Sarah to reach out and take hold.

"I think you'd better give me an extra head start next time," she gasped.

"Can you show us another dive," I asked, as it gave me a chance to admire him from a bit further away.

"Sure," he replied. I watched him pull himself out of the pool and walk towards the board. On the way he stopped to chat to the other lifeguard on duty and whatever was said made them both laugh. I watched as he took to the board and this time lined up with his back towards the pool. The other lifeguard gave him a quick nod which must have been the all-clear signal as he executed a perfect back flip into the pool.

As he swam back towards us, he ducked under the water and I felt a tug on my foot as he dragged me under and started to tickle me. I pulled away, the shock of his touch on my quivering body immense. Returning spluttering to the surface, I waited for James to surface and playfully splashed some water at him. Sarah joined in and we larked around.

"We've got to go now," I said.

"Well, I'll see you again on Thursday night?" James replied, smiling at me.

"Hope to see you again soon," he said to Sarah. "Perhaps I'll bring a friend with me next time I swim. Two against one is an unfair water fight."

"Bye James," I said, as we swam back down to the shallow end to get out. I resisted looking back to see if he was watching but Sarah couldn't.

Giggling we entered the cubicles next to each other.

"He was watching you," she said. I just smiled to myself. We walked home to mine and after tea, headed for my room.

"So what do you think?" I asked Sarah "Do you think he likes me? Do you think I stand a chance?"

♪

Yawning, Charlotte put the diary aside. It felt strange to be reading her mum's thoughts and feelings from when she was sixteen years old, yet at the same time, Charlie knew exactly how her mum felt as it was the same when she had first seen Craig at school.

-4-

Charlotte was startled from sleep by her phone beeping. Through bleary eyes, she saw it was three a.m. She reached for her phone and looked at the screen. It was a number she didn't recognise but she pressed on it and read the message:

Having a great night with Craig, he is one hell of a kisser.

There was no name on the text so she deleted it and tried to forget it as she lay back. The image of Craig with another girl was too much and her chest heaved to release the still simmering heartache. Tears started to slide down her cheeks. Lying in the darkness, thoughts kept tumbling around so she turned her light back on and grabbed the diary. She hoped stories of her mum's life would ease her back to sleep.

Dear Diary,

Monday 11th January, 1988
I woke just before my alarm went off and groaned, it was Monday again. My mind was still on the events of Saturday and the time I had spent in the pool with James. I wondered if Sarah might be right and whether he might fancy me as much as I did him.

As I joined up with Sarah, June and Amanda, the conversation was about the party.

"My dress certainly got tongues wagging," June declared.

"Yeah, the guys just wouldn't leave her alone," Amanda said, smiling.

"But did it work?" I asked.

"Of course. I am now going out with John, in fact he promised to meet me at the gates this morning so let's hurry up as I don't want to keep him waiting."

At the gates we saw John talking to Gareth and they both looked up as we approached.

"Hi John," June purred as he opened his arms to her and she moved into them.

"Hi June, girls," he said, before his lips came down and claimed hers. We all tried not to look.

"Catch you by the lockers," Sarah said.

The day passed slowly but we were soon on our way home. I was about to part from Sarah when we paused for a quick chat.

"So, when will you see James again?" she asked.

"I might go swimming tomorrow night but I'm not sure yet," I replied.

"I really do think he likes you."

"Perhaps he's got a mate he can introduce you to, he did say he would bring someone next time."

"Let's hope so," she said. "I hate playing gooseberry"

I laughed. "I like you being my gooseberry."

Thursday 14th January, 1988

I was eager to get home from school as it was lifesaving night. Packing my bag I decided to wear my bikini instead of my swimsuit. When I arrived at the leisure centre, we went upstairs to the far end of the café as we were going through some of the theory of the course.

James appeared carrying a resuscitation doll that we had to do mouth to mouth on. I felt at a slight advantage as last term at school we had done a basic first aid course and I hadn't forgotten it. As my mouth covered the doll's, I tried not to think about how it would feel to be doing this on James, or for that matter him doing it to me.

Emerging poolside in my bikini, I felt much more at ease. I saw James and felt his gaze run up and down my body. I tried not to tremble and blush as I slid into the cool water. We started with some lengths to warm up until James was happy. Then he gathered us all to the side and explained that we were actually going to try some lifesaving and to pair up. The two girls grabbed the two guys which just left me.

"Don't worry Steph, I'll come in and demonstrate on you and then you can practise on me," he said. I watched in awe as he stripped off his top and shorts and slid into the water beside me.

"So Steph, if you can swim to the deep end and then flail your arms around as if you were drowning."

I crawled up the pool and pretended to drown. I could feel my heart racing as I watched James swimming towards me at speed. Then I felt his hand cup my chin, pulling me back against his chest as his other hand and feet pulled me along and back to the shallow end. The feel of his body behind mine was firm, his muscles rippled as I felt dizzy and light-headed.

"So everyone, your turn now," he said. "We'll do a pair at a time and Steph and I will go last to give her time to watch." He leaned against the side and I tried to catch my breath and slow my speeding heart.

As James swam away from me, I took a deep breath and tried to calm my shaking body as I waited and then swam towards him. I took his chin firmly in my hand and then pulled him back against me as I started to work my way to the side. I felt really pleased with my effort.

"Well done Steph, good work," he said, as we reached the shallow end and I let him go. We ended on that high note and everyone left the pool. Gathering my bag together, my hand still tingled from the feel of his skin under my fingers, his body lying on top of mine in the water.

In the foyer I saw James talking to Elaine. He saw me and walked over. "Are you coming swimming again on Saturday?"

"Yes I think so."

"Cool, I'll be in the pool and I'll bring my best mate Chris," he said. "At least we'll have a more even splash fight, boys against girls."

"Ok, well I'll see you on Saturday then, about five?" I said, just managing to get the words out in the right order.

"Five it is, see you then, Steph."

Walking across the car park I paused and looked back towards the bright lights of the building. He was there in the window again and we both raised our hands and waved. I ran home with all sorts of excitement bubbling away inside of me. In bed that night, I fell into a pool of magical dreams starring James.

Friday 15th January, 1988
I practically skipped down the road towards Sarah as I couldn't wait to tell her the exciting news.

"Are you ok?" she asked, as I linked my arm through hers.

"Oh yes, more than ok."

"Well, share."

"We're going swimming on Saturday with James and he is bringing his friend Chris with him."

"Oh, so things went well in class then?"

"Yeah, he saved me from drowning in the deep end and then I saved him." The image of his semi-naked body filled my mind. My fingertips tingled as if to reinforce the memory.

As we joined the others, I gave Sarah a quick glance so she knew to keep quiet, and we listened to June giving us the low down on John. School passed quickly and as we said goodbye, I arranged to meet Sarah at the end of her road at four the following day.

Now at home in my room, I turn to Rick Astley on the stereo as I try to decide what to wear. I listen intently to the words of 'Whenever You Need Somebody' and as I sing along with Rick, I know the lyrics portray how I feel.

I want it to be love between James and I but at this stage, I would settle for anything and just being a friend is good enough.

♪

Charlotte felt her eyelids getting heavy and looked across at her alarm clock. She had been reading for an hour and needed to get some sleep. She found a bookmark and placed it in the page. Part of her wanted to continue to find out how things went at the pool the next day. Were they going to get together at last? Was the Chris in the diary her Uncle Chris?

I knew Charlotte had missed her alarm as I gave the bedroom door a knock. "Charlotte, are you moving otherwise you'll be late?"

"Yeah Mum, sorry, I overslept," she mumbled from behind the door.

"I'll do you some toast and coffee," I said, going down to the kitchen.

When Charlie emerged I saw more make-up than I would have liked. She was wearing her pale pink jeans and the fluffy white jumper I had bought her for Christmas.

"You look nice."

"Well, I've got to make Craig see what he's missing."

"That's your decision but as I said, there are plenty more guys out there who would be lucky to go out with you," I said, giving her a hug.

"Thanks Mum." She grabbed the thermal mug I had poured her coffee in and opened the door.

I watched her disappear down the driveway and catch up with her friend Julia, who was waiting at the corner. Charlie reminded me of my younger self, except she was much more aware of things that I had largely been innocent to when I was her age. I went upstairs to gather a load of washing before I had to leave for work. My diary lay on her bedside cabinet, a bookmark highlighting her progress. Sitting on the bed I couldn't resist a peek.

Dear Diary,

Saturday 16th January, 1988
It's two weeks since I first saw James and I can't believe I am now lucky enough to call him a friend. However, I still want more – I want to add *boy* to that friend.

Earlier, I met Sarah at the corner of her road and we huddled under my umbrella, sheltering from the rain. After a quick browse around some of the shops, Sarah dragged me to the library so she could hand in her books.

"Look Sarah, they need a Saturday assistant," I said, reading the small advert.

"That sounds good, I'll ask at the desk," she said.

With the application form tucked safely into her bag we walked to the pool. I could hardly wait to see James again.

As we wandered onto the poolside, I saw him up at the deep end, his blond head next to a dark one in conversation. I grabbed Sarah's arm.

"There they are," I said.

"I like a man with dark hair," Sarah replied, squeezing my arm as we slipped into the cool water and started to swim towards them. James moved aside a little so there was space for us to hold onto the side.

"Hi Steph, hi Sarah," he said. "This is Chris," he motioned, who turned and nodded.

We spent an enjoyable hour splashing around together, laughing and joking. James gave me some pointers on my diving technique before showing off with a somersault. Then as we took a breather on the side, he motioned to me.

"Steph, why don't you go under the water and close your eyes."

"Why?"

"It's a surprise," he said, grinning. I smiled back and ducked beneath the surface. As I waited for something to happen, I felt his hands on my waist and I almost opened my eyes. He pulled me closer and I felt his lips on mine in a brief kiss.

Startled, my eyes sprang open and I felt the heat of my skin burning like fire. I looked directly into his eyes for a second and then he pushed up to the surface. I was only moments behind him as I reached out for the side. My heart was pounding and my whole body was trembling as I tried to keep control of my spiralling emotions. I felt faint as I clung to the side, I didn't have the nerve to ask him what this kiss meant. Instead I watched him streak off down the pool and back, racing against Chris.

"So?" she exclaimed.

"He just kissed me," I replied. "I'm still in shock." My lips were engrained with the feel of his lips on them. Everything felt new, exciting and wonderful.

James made no mention of the stolen kiss and I was too nervous in case I had imagined it. As we parted, the guys waved and we waved back, then we walked in different directions. Saying goodbye to Sarah at the end of the road, we paused.

"So what do you think the kiss meant?"

"That he likes you a bit more than just as a friend."

"God, I hope so."

"Chris was nice but a bit quiet."

"You like him?"

"Oh yes, he has something about him."

I'm now lying in bed watching the clock tick away. It's gone midnight and for some reason I can't sleep. I can still feel his lips pressed against mine and the feel of his hands on my waist when they pulled me close enough. His lips on mine were soft and firm against the liquid coolness of the water that surrounded us and held us both. We were suspended in a timeless moment. I'm now going to shut my eyes and dream of kissing James again.

Monday 18th January, 1988
Walking to meet Sarah, June and Amanda, I was looking forward to hearing all the other gossip from the double date of the weekend. As we all fell into step, I gave Sarah a small wink. I loved the fact that James was our secret from the others. Also, I knew how jealous June could be and I didn't need the extra competition for James' affections if she were to suddenly turn up at the pool with us.

"So, how was the date on Saturday?" I asked.

"John was the perfect gentleman and paid for us to go for a meal and then the cinema in Gloucester," June said.

"Not sure how much of the film they watched," Amanda said, laughing.

"Too much kissing going on?" Sarah added.

They both nodded and I watched June clutch at her heart and declare, "Girls, I am in love."

We all smiled at her, and wondered how many times in the past she had said this, only to split up with the guy in question within days.

"For how long?" Amanda asked.

"Forever of course," June said. "He is the one for me."

Thursday 21st January, 1988
As school came to a close, I almost dashed out of the gates at a run. I was eager to get home and do my theory revision for the lifesaving course as it was exam time. Sarah just about managed to catch up with me and we left June and Amanda dawdling near the gates with John and Gareth.

Walking into the leisure centre at around seven, I could tell everyone was as nervous as me. We all shuffled our papers as we waited to take the exam, part of it was theory. Then we had to demonstrate CPR and the recovery position before we went into the pool. Once there, a couple of the lifeguards took turns to be the drowning person and we all had to dive in and save them. I wished it was James I was holding, but I also thought it was probably best it wasn't otherwise I might have been too distracted to concentrate.

Once we had finished, James called us over to the side of the pool.

"Congratulations, you've all passed so your certificates will be waiting for you at reception," he said, smiling. It felt as if his gaze lingered longer on me but perhaps I was imagining it. I walked across to the reception desk and Elaine gave me the certificate. I was about to leave when I heard footsteps behind me.

"Hi Steph, I just wondered if I could walk you home tonight?"

"I'd like that," I replied, smiling shyly at him. He held his hand out.

"I'll carry your bag."

"Are you sure about that?" I replied, handing him my Wham! bag with photos of George and Andrew on each side. I saw James give it a look before he flung it over his shoulder.

"I take it you like Wham! then?" he asked.

We walked in silence across the car park and at the entrance, he hesitated and looked at me.

"Turn left, I'm at the top end of Greytree, second avenue."

"I know where that is, luckily I'm not that far away from you on fourth avenue."

The darkness made me brave and I reached out and placed my hand in his. He didn't let go and as we neared the avenue sign, we stopped.

"Here will be fine," I said. "I'm the third house along"

"Cool," he replied, handing me back my bag.

In the glow of the streetlight, he bent down towards me and gently brushed his lips against my cheek. So soft was the touch, I could hardly feel it. Under the cover of the dark sky he couldn't see the pink blush staining my cheeks. He reached for my other hand and held it in his, passing me a piece of paper before he withdrew.

"Night Steph," he whispered, and I watched him walk on down the road and out of sight.

♬

I carefully unfolded the note that was stapled onto my old diary page; it was ripped and faded in places. How many times had I read this?

Even though I could still remember what the note said, I opened it again and gazed at his words from all those years ago:

Stephanie, I really like you and would love to go out with you, but unfortunately I'm moving away with my parents at the end of January, so it may be best for us to just stay friends. James x

Closing it up I noticed how my hand was shaking. How could I still feel this affected by a note from my past? From the memories streaming into my head that I hadn't thought about for many years?

On the drive into Hereford, I put the radio on and listened to Paul's show. He never failed to cheer me up with his tongue-in-cheek comments between songs. I was looking forward to catching up with the guys at the station. We had been chatting about the possibility of a fundraising event and I had a few ideas I wanted to throw at them.

After a great lunchtime show, I was back in the car driving home. I always enjoyed playing other people's requests and eclectic music made my show what it was. I had been working at the same radio station for twelve years and I loved every minute of it. It also meant that I was always home in time for Charlotte finishing school. In the early years, Sarah and Chris had helped out and were like Charlie's second set of parents. I would never have coped without their help.

Walking through the door I scooped up the post and dropped it on the hallway table before heading into the kitchen. I put the kettle on and made a coffee, taking it into the conservatory. I sat in the chair and picked up the book I was reading. I was so engrossed, I almost didn't register the door open and close until Charlie appeared.

"Hi Mum."

"Hi sweetheart, how was school?"

"It was ok Mum, it was hard seeing Craig with another girl."

"It will get easier."

"I guess, Mum." She filled a mug with coffee.

"I'm going to do some practice now and then I'll be down for tea," she replied, swinging her bag over her shoulder.

I wondered whether practice was code for, *I'm going to read some more of your diary…*

Dear Diary,

Friday 22nd January, 1988
I hardly slept all night, the words from the note echoing around my mind. Why was life so unfair? I had just found a great guy who I knew liked me but it was all for nothing. At the end of January there would be no more swimming, no more walking me home and carrying my bag, no more underwater kisses. Despondently I got up and dressed for school, needing to talk all this through with Sarah.

Luckily I found her waiting alone as the others had gone on ahead. She saw my downcast face and put her arm around me.

"What happened?" she asked, and I passed her the note. She read it and hugged me even tighter.

"I don't know what to say," she said, as we trudged along slowly.

"Do you think I should just tell him how I feel? Or just stay as friends instead?"

"Well, if you talk to him, what have you got to lose? Nothing really as he's going away soon," Sarah replied. I nodded and as the school day drifted by, I went through all the possible scenarios in my head. None of them seemed to bring me any hope.

I'm now back at home in my room, having an early night. My stereo is playing the *'Faith'* album by George Michael. I listen as his soulful voice speaks to me. George's words echo through my heart as I think of James' body and the way it makes me feel whenever I'm close to him. I long to throw myself into his arms and beg him not to leave, not before I have a chance to fall in love with him.

Saturday 23rd January, 1988
I spent all morning reading the note. With Sarah away for the weekend visiting her grandparents, I walked straight to the pool alone. I wished my best friend was with me as I was so nervous approaching James after Thursday night, the note, and the light brush of his soft lips on my cheek in the darkness. Despite this, when I walked poolside and slid into the water, it was as if nothing had changed between us.

"Hi Steph," he said, as I pulled up beside him and hung onto the tiles.

"Hi James," I replied. "It's just the two of us today." He smiled as we swam off down the pool together.

After a great hour I still hadn't decided what to say to James. It seemed as if we had both spent the time avoiding any mention of the note or the kiss from the previous Saturday.

"Would you like to grab a coffee upstairs?" he asked.

"Yes that would be lovely," I replied, smiling back at him. I took a bit longer getting dressed before I couldn't delay anymore. I found him sat at the corner table, coffee waiting.

"You read my note then?" he asked.

"Yes." I lowered my eyes so he wouldn't see the sadness that stained them. I took a deep breath but no words appeared that could portray how I felt.

My courage failed, I just couldn't tell him that I wanted to be in a relationship with him and not just as friends. I wanted more kisses, I wanted to call him my boyfriend and share everything with him. He reached over and took my hand in his, as if knowing that a touch was better than words.

"I'd like to see you next week at the pool. I'm working Tuesday and Thursday evening." His index finger ran over the skin on my knuckles and I found it hard to breathe.

"I'll be here," I whispered.

"Would you like to go out on Saturday? It's my last day in the area."

I paused. Had I heard him right, was this going to be a date?

"Yes, I'd like that."

All I could think about in bed that night was the word goodbye. It sounded so final.

Monday 25th January, 1988

As I trudged along the path towards the end of Sarah's road, I could see all the girls waiting. The grey, overcast sky matched my mood to perfection.

"Are you ok?" June asked me.

"I've got a bit of a headache that's all," I replied. We walked along and I listened as she talked about John.

The lessons kept me occupied and in English, I whispered across to Sarah, "Do you want to come into town on the way home?"

"Sure," she replied.

By the time we left school and walked along the road, I knew what I needed to do.

"So what's the plan?" Sarah asked.

"I'm going to buy James a leaving card and present and suggest that we write to each other once he moves. We're sort of going on a date on Saturday."

"Wow, that's great."

"Well not really, it's just going to mean I fall even more in love with him and then he's just going to leave and I'll never see him again." I was so close to crying but I held it in.

We walked into the card shop and I looked at all the leaving cards but none of them said what I really wanted to say, so in the end I bought a blank one. Then I saw a fluffy elephant holding a heart that said, *'Never Forget'*. It was perfect.

Tuesday 26th January, 1988

After school I hurried home to get ready for swimming. I was determined that James would always remember me with a smile on my face, even though inside, my heart was filled with sorrow. As I walked poolside, he saw me and waved from the chair. I slipped into the shallow end and did a couple of lengths before stopping to the side of the chair at the deep end. He jumped down and knelt to talk to me.

"Hi Steph, good to see you."

"Hi James, how are things?"

"Busy packing at home; I never realised how much stuff I had until now," he said.

"Will you miss Ross?"

"I guess so, it's all I've known since I was born but our new house looks great. It's opposite a large park and not far away from Warwick Castle." I watched him glance up and across the pool, checking everything was fine before returning his attention to me. "I thought I'd take you to Gloucester on Saturday; we can go to the cinema. Dad said I can borrow the car for the evening."

He stood up and motioned that he ought to do a few laps round the pool so I swam a few further lengths and thought about how great it would be to sit next to him in the dark.

Climbing out of the pool, I did a couple of dives and from his chair James gave me a few tips about keeping my feet pointed on entry. I was never going to be as good as he was. As I finished my equivalent of a mile in lengths, I popped out of the water and sat on the side to catch my breath. James was on another lap so I waited until he reached me. As he did he nudged me with his foot and pushed me into the water. I came up laughing and spluttering.

"Hey that's not allowed," I said, pointing at the sign on the wall that said no pushing. Glancing down the list I blushed at the no petting statement and thought again of our kiss.

"It is when I'm in charge," he said, laughing at my comment. Climbing out of the pool I walked towards the chair where he sat.

"I'm off now, see you Thursday," I said. I pulled my hair back from my face and looked up into his beautiful blue eyes.

"See you then Steph," he replied.

Wednesday 27th January, 1988
I am listening to 'A Different Corner' by George Michael; the lyrics are making me cry.

Thursday 28th January, 1988
As we walked home from school, Sarah turned to me to ask, "Is it ok if I come swimming with you tonight?"

"Yes sure, that would be great. I'll meet you back at the corner at around 6.30?"

"Yes, great, as I need to talk to you and school is definitely not the place."

"Ok, see you later," I said, wondering what secret Sarah needed to share with me.

"So what's the secret?" I asked, when we met up later.

"Well, I really like Chris but if James leaves, how will I get the chance to see him again?"

"I'll try and talk to James and find out for you. Maybe this evening, but for certain on Saturday," I replied, happy to help my best friend if I could.

Poolside, we saw James leaning down to talk to someone in the water. As he pulled up, Sarah grabbed my arm because we saw it was Chris.

"It's your lucky day," I said, as we wandered up to the deep end and James raised his hand.

"Do I look ok?" she asked

"Of course, you look lovely. Dive in, impress him."

Then as I turned to James, Sarah did a lovely dive off the edge and swam back towards the side to wait for me.

"Hi Steph, is that a new bikini?"

"No, just one I haven't worn for a while," I said, blushing as always at his compliment.

"It suits you. Now stop distracting me from work and do some swimming."

I nodded and sauntered towards the diving board, producing a pretty good dive into the cool, blue waters beneath me. Chris had noticed us but I guessed he was shy as he continued to swim lengths with just the occasional glance in our direction. We did the same until James motioned me over to the side.

"I'm just about to finish my shift so I'll come and join you."

"Ok, any chance you can drag Chris over, Sarah really likes him?"

"Sure, he is a bit shy, not a bit like me," he said, grinning.

After another spectacular entrance into the pool from the diving board, he swam over and disappearing beneath the water, he grabbed my foot. Pulling me under he tried to drag me away from the side but I scrambled against his grip until he released me.

"I'll tickle you next time," he said.

"You'd better not, I hate being tickled."

Chris swam over to us and joined in the general laughter. Once again I waited for James to make a move but he didn't. Whilst the guys raced each other up and down, Sarah pulled me close.

"Why don't you kiss James? It's almost your last chance."

As I pondered this, we swam a couple of lengths and I decided that Sarah was right. So when James was alone with me in the deep end, I took the chance.

"I've got a surprise for you, but you need to go underwater and keep your eyes closed," I told him. James looked shocked at my request but he did as I asked. Taking a deep breath, I disappeared under the water and swam towards him.

I reached out and as I did, he opened his eyes and caught my hands in his. He pulled me close and our lips found each other's. This time, my eyes were open and we gazed. I felt such love for him already, looking into his eyes, sparkling and blue. I couldn't hope to guess what he was thinking as we broke the surface together, our hands still clasped. We didn't need to say anything as we parted and swam the short distance to the poolside. Running my hand up to catch some loose hair back into my ponytail, James reached out and tucked a tendril behind my ear. Just that slight touch had me reeling and struggling to catch my breath, my heart racing.

♪

Dragging her eyes away from the words on the page, Charlotte realised it was much later than she had planned. She was so caught up in her mother's story. Part of her wanted to turn to the back and see how it ended but she didn't want to miss any of this enthralling romance as it had started to get really good. Underwater kisses! It was years since she had been to the swimming pool; perhaps that was the place to go to find a gorgeous guy? Or perhaps her mum and Aunt Sarah had just been extremely lucky that year?

"Bye Mum," Charlie yelled as she raced out of the door, ready to begin a new day.

"Bye Charlie. Have you got dance practice tonight?"

"Yes, so I will be later than usual," she replied, as the front door swung shut.

I tidied up in the kitchen and pulled my laptop out so I could prepare for my lunchtime show. As the screen came up I found myself looking into the green eyes of my husband, whose picture I had as a screensaver. I closed my eyes tight for a moment and as the world swirled around me, I remembered the evening that had crushed my world...

I had just settled Charlotte down to sleep. Luckily she was a fairly content baby and once she had eaten, she was out like a light for a couple of hours. I had poured myself a glass of wine and glanced at the clock to check the time. Mark was on the late shift but I had promised to try and stay awake for his arrival home.

As the hours ticked by, the wine and the warmth of the house lulled me into a light sleep so when a knock on the door came, I was startled. Thinking that Mark had forgotten his key I jumped up to find a policeman and woman standing there. They told me Mark had been found barely alive in the hospital car park, with stab wounds. Grabbing Charlie from her cot I bundled her up in blankets as they escorted me to a police car. As the scenery passed by at speed I could only hope that this was all a big mistake. Looking down at my child, I remembered my own scars and a time when I had been rushed to hospital. Blackness started to creep over me, filling me with dread.

It was like I had never been away as the artificially bright light hurt my eyes and the disinfectant smell hit my nostrils. The nurse took Charlotte from me as they ushered me through to the window that looked over the operating table. There under the lights, I watched the team try and fail to revive him. His life seeped away and all I did was stare, my hand placed on the glass.

Shaking my head to try and clear the recollection away, I flicked open a word document and started to type. All the while my memories crowded me, hemming me in with their tight claws. In the end I closed it down and went upstairs to get ready for work. I avoided looking at the photographs lining the wall. Why had life been so cruel to me? Who had I upset? What had I done wrong? These questions frequently accosted me and I had no answers. I also felt guilty for not loving Mark as much as I could have. My heart died, long before I met my husband.

Walking past Charlie's room, I saw the diary lying face up on the bed, as if abandoned in a moment of haste. I crossed the room to close it but as I glanced at the entry, I noticed the date. Happy memories of my youth fought against the darkness and won. I sat down and picked it up, the worn cover comforting under my fingertips.

Dear Diary,

Friday 29th January, 1988
Sarah was staying over so we blitzed my wardrobe until a suitable outfit was found. It was to be my black velvet trousers, black ankle boots and a fluffy purple jumper. I decided that as I always wore my hair up for swimming, I would keep it loose instead.

As I gave Sarah a twirl she said, "You look fantastic, he'll never be able to resist you."

"I hope so, not that it will do much good with him leaving on Sunday," I said, my smile fading.

"Well, at least you tried." She put her arm around me and pulled me close. "You'll still have me."

I looked at my best friend and smiled. "Thanks."

Saturday 30th January, 1988
The day dawned bright but cold. Sarah left for home at eleven, giving me ample time to write the card and wrap the present. I scanned all my favourite songs for some suitable lyrics and found a small verse from the song 'Somewhere Out There'.

Dear James,
And even though I know how very far apart we are,
It helps to think we might be wishing on the same bright star.
I hope that we can write and stay friends and if you are ever
back in Ross that we can meet again.
Love Steph (your new pen-pal)

James arranged to meet me outside the pool at four. As I waited on the steps, I watched a car pull up and James got out and walked towards me. He was wearing ripped jeans and a shirt. He literally took my breath away.

"Hi Steph, you look fantastic," he said.

I walked towards the car and with a flourish he held open the passenger door for me. I climbed in. As we negotiated the streets of Ross before heading out on the A40 towards Gloucester, all was silent.

"Shall I put some music on?" he asked. "I've put some songs on a tape especially for the drive over." Then the upbeat sound of 'Wake Me Up Before You Go-Go' filled the silence between us.

"Wham!" I exclaimed over the music. "My favourite."

"Thought so," he said. "Go ahead, sing if you want, I don't mind." Various other tracks filled the journey and I found out that his favourite group was Madness.

Throughout the drive to Gloucester we chatted easily about all the songs we both liked. Once we arrived, James bought popcorn and coke for us to share and we walked into the darkness of the theatre.

Sitting together in the dim lights as we waited for the adverts to finish, James turned to me.

"So what's your favourite film?"

"I love so many but it has to be *Star Wars*."

"Good choice for a girl, most don't like that sort of thing," he said, surprise in his eyes.

"Well I guess I'm not like most girls."

"Have you seen *Top Gun*, that's my favourite film."

"Not yet but I'll call in and see if the video shop has a copy."

"I'm sure they do, Chris works there so just go in and ask him."

The lights dimmed and we sat in the darkness. Our hands occasionally brushed as we reached for popcorn at the same time and I felt jolts of electricity race through my skin every time.

As we came out of the cinema, I saw June and John in the queue waiting to go into the next screening. I could see she was surprised to see me there with James because although I had mentioned him in passing, I was sure she thought I was lying. Walking towards McDonalds, James reached out and took my hand and I didn't want to let it go. We found a quiet table and ordered burgers, fries and chocolate milkshakes. While we waited, James reached into his jacket pocket and pulled out a small parcel.

"I got you a present to remember me by."

"Thanks, I've got you one too," I said, reaching into my handbag and passing him his present and card.

I watched as he unwrapped the cuddly toy elephant and smiled at the sentiment expressed by the flower it was holding.

"I doubt I could forget you," he murmured. He looked at the card and read the inscription. "Did you write the words?"

"I pinched them from a song called 'Somewhere Out There'."

A slight stain of colour tinted his cheeks.

"I think I may have to listen to that song," James replied, smiling at me. He watched as I unwrapped the small parcel to find a mix tape of songs.

"It's the same as the one in the car," James said. "Hope you like it."

Realising I didn't have his address, he borrowed a pen off one of the staff and scribbled it down on the envelope his card had been in, pushing it back across to me.

At the corner of the street he stopped the car. "Well, I guess it's goodbye then," he said as he leaned over and placed his finger under my chin, lifting it so he was staring into my eyes. I nodded, words failing me. I squeezed my eyes shut, trying to blink back tears forming beneath my lids, like cold drops of ice, a shiver spreading to my body. James pressed his lips gently to mine and pulled me into a hug before I got out of the car.

I watched as he drove away and turned to wave, shouting out of the window, "Write soon, I'm looking forward to your first letter!"

Tears fell down my cheeks as I waited until he was out of sight. I really wanted to run after him and beg him not to go, fling myself back into his arms and kiss him again.

♪

Putting the diary back in place, I tried to remember all the songs that had been on the mix tape. There were so many special songs with so many memories and firsts connected to them. Even as I played different songs on the radio, sometimes one would catch me by surprise and spring me back to a moment in my life. Music was such a powerful memory tool and one I could never silence, no matter the pain it brought.

Charlotte arrived home from dance practice and flopped onto a chair in the kitchen.

"Good day?" I asked.

"Ok. Practice was good. We're working on a dance to the Rihanna song 'Umbrella'."

"I'll look forward to seeing it at some point."

"Mrs. Grantley has entered us into a competition and we should know soon if we have made it to the heats for the Midlands area."

Over tea, we discussed the dance competition a little more and I told Charlie about the event we were hoping to put on in the summer called Rock On the River with various local bands and performers to help raise money for the hospital.

"That sounds good, can our group dance at it?" Charlie asked.

"Don't see why not."

"Well, I'd better go and finish my homework," she said, leaving the table.

I suspected Charlie didn't have any work to do and I wondered whether the diary was calling for her to read more…

Dear Diary,

Sunday 31st January, 1988
The rain beating on the window pane woke me and I thought how apt it was, the weather matching my mood. The only thing I had to look forward to was giving Sarah a call to let her know how yesterday had gone, plus I had the mix tape to listen to I supposed.

It was certainly an eclectic mixture of songs. I loved the upbeat sound of Madness and Baggy Trousers, but there was some Wham! and George Michael tracks on there, too. Finally there were a few songs that were taken from the *Top Gun* soundtrack, including the slow ballad 'Take My Breath Away' which I played a few times to allow the words to sink in.

I remembered James had possibly not left yet and could still be just down the road. Leaping off the bed I pulled on my shoes and hurried out of the door.

"Just off for a walk, Mum," I shouted, grabbing my handbag. I knew the video shop would be open at noon so I could also call in and see if they had a copy of *Top Gun*. I ran the short distance downhill to the entrance of the avenue and then paused. Would he still be there? Would he want to see me again this morning after saying goodbye last night?

Walking slowly into the road I couldn't see any sign of movement but as I neared the end, I saw a couple of large removal vans. I could feel my heart beating in my chest at the thought of seeing James for one, final time. I walked closer, paused as my nerve failed me, and turned around. Slowly I sauntered back along the pavement but then I heard footsteps running behind me and I turned to see James.

"Steph, fancy seeing you here," he exclaimed.

I blushed and tried to look away from his gaze but he reached out and grabbed my hand.

"Don't run off, it's great to see you before we leave," he said.

"How's it going?" I asked, motioning at the large vans.

"Just putting the last few things in now," he said, glancing down at his watch. "We're hoping to leave in about ten minutes."

"I'd better go then and let you get finished," I said trying to pull away, but his hand held mine tight.

"I'm glad you came," he said, taking my other hand in his, stepping closer to me. I briefly closed my eyes as I started to feel dizzy, my heart pounding. Letting go of my hands, his arms wrapped around my trembling body and held me close for what seemed like an age. I laid my head on his chest, smelling his deodorant and aftershave. I was certain he could feel me shaking in his embrace. I felt his hand run up my spine and to my neck, then round to my chin to tilt my face towards him. Opening my eyes I watched as he bent down, his lips touching mine for a final kiss. It didn't feel like a goodbye kiss even though I knew it was.

"James, James, we're leaving now," his Mum shouted. We broke apart and I took one last look at him, filling my mind with his image.

"I'll write soon."

"Bye Steph."

"Bye James," I whispered, even though I didn't want to say it, let alone think about it.

I watched him run back down the road and jump into a car. I waited as the two vans pulled off down the street, followed by the car. James was in the front passenger seat, next to his dad. He waved as they passed me. Then the heavens opened and it started to rain hard. I didn't pull my hood up as it splashed onto my hair and ran down my face. It helped to hide the tears falling as I waved until the car turned out of sight. Looking back down the road at his empty house, it mirrored the empty feeling within me. Rain trickled down my spine between my clothes, tracing the line his hand had just taken.

Walking down the road I turned in the opposite direction and walked into town. It stopped raining so I wiped the mixture of rain and tears from my face as I neared the video shop. Inside I saw Chris standing at the counter and went straight over.

"Hi Chris, do you have a copy of *Top Gun*?"

"Hi Steph, yes of course I do," he said. He walked out from behind the counter and straight to the exact shelf where the box was. Returning to the counter he found the video tape and placed it inside.

"Membership number?"

"Eight-zero-eight," I replied as he tapped it in and scanned the video out to me.

"You do know that's James' favourite film?"

"Yes." I nodded, feeling fresh tears rise in my throat, just at the mention of his name. I looked away quickly before Chris could see them.

"I'll miss him," Chris said. I nodded and fled.

Back at home I wandered into the kitchen where Mum was preparing dinner for later.

"Is it ok for me to watch a video?"

"Yes sure, I think Dad's in his office so the room's all yours."

Grabbing a glass of lemonade I shrugged off my wet coat and shoes and raced into the lounge. Placing the tape into the machine I waited for the film to begin. It started with lots of military planes flying around and I wondered if I was going to enjoy it at all. As Maverick filled the screen and started to flirt with Charlie at the bar, I was hooked. Hugging a pillow on the sofa, I studied the love scene and wondered how it would be between James and I. Then I cried along with Maverick as Goose died. As the end screen faded, I almost pressed rewind to watch it again but I didn't have time.

All night my mind ran through the time I had spent with James, every word he had ever said to me, every time he had touched me and of course all the kisses. It was like watching my own film reel.

Monday 1st February, 1988

As I walked to meet Sarah, June and Amanda, I could see they were already deep in conversation. With June seeing me on Saturday night I guessed I was going to be the main talking point.

"Hi girls," I said, watching them all turn to look at me.

"Well aren't you the dark horse," June said. "Do tell us all the gossip." Her blue eyes stared me down and I could see the glint of anger there because she had not known anything about James.

"There's not much to tell really," I began. "I met James at the swimming pool a couple of weeks ago but he has just moved away with his parents."

"But I saw you together at the cinema?" June pouted.

"Yes, as friends, spending some time together before he left on Sunday." I could already feel tears trying to escape from the corners of my eyes and I hastily blinked them back.

"We are going to stay friends and write to each other," I said, hoping this was enough to satisfy them all.

"So nothing happened between the two of you?" Amanda asked, joining in with the interrogation.

"Not really. He kissed me when he said goodbye on Saturday and he gave me a mix tape," I said, not wanting to share anything more with them.

"That's a shame as he was gorgeous," June gushed.

"Yes it is," I replied, nearing the school gates. John was waiting for June so she switched her attention to him and left me alone. Sarah tucked her arm through mine.

"Come on," she said softly. She had obviously noticed my trembling lips and sore, red eyes as she steered me in the direction of the nearest toilets.

After school we walked into town. I needed to buy some writing paper, envelopes, stamps and for good measure, a new pen. I was on a mission to write and post my first letter to James that evening. Once in my room I took out the first sheet and paused. What should I write? Lacking inspiration I turned to my stereo and put in the mix tape he had given me.

Dear James,
I will start by thanking you for the lovely time we spent together on Saturday night. The film was really good but the company was excellent.

I hope you didn't mind me coming down to see you off on Sunday? I'm sorry if it was inappropriate but I just had to see you one, last time.

How is the unpacking going? Have you settled into your new house ok? Please write and tell me what it's like there. Have you managed to get a job yet?

School is ok. June wanted to know all about you after seeing us together on Saturday night. I told her little bits but not much as she is a terrible gossip and I don't need anything spreading round school. I am studying hard as it is exam year and I want to continue afterwards and do a media course. I have a mad ambition to work on radio as a DJ but we'll have to wait and see if anything progresses on that front.

The mix tape is fantastic, I have been playing it non-stop since you left as it reminds me of you.

Anyway, take care and write back soon. Your pen-pal, Stephanie x

Tuesday 2nd February, 1988
On my way to meet Sarah, I posted my first letter. I kept it friendly and chatty when really what I wanted to write was how much I loved him, how much I missed him. How I had been crying myself to sleep every night listening to the mix tape and wishing he still lived down the road.

Catching up with Sarah, we arranged to walk into town together after school because I had to return *Top Gun* to the video shop. On the way I turned to Sarah.

"I've had an idea," I said.

"Go on then, I'm guessing it's about James?"

"Yes, I'm going to tell him how I feel when I send him a Valentine's Day card and present. After all, what's the worst thing that could happen? He is miles away anyway so if he never wants to see or speak to me again, it won't matter."

"That's brave of you," Sarah said. "Are you sure?"

"Not really but when I saw him again briefly on Sunday, it was as though I could feel something between us. Something unspoken but at the same time, real."

Nearing the video shop I turned Sarah towards me and passed her my lipstick.

"You might need this," I said.

"Why?"

"Chris works here, you want to make a good impression?"

"Why didn't you tell me earlier, like last night? I would have done my hair better. Trying to look good in this uniform is impossible," she sighed.

We walked in and saw him talking to a guy at the back of the shop. We headed to the counter with the video and he turned and saw us. He waved but remained in conversation, so we left.

"I knew it, he doesn't like me," Sarah moaned, slumped against the wall.

"Don't give up yet. James did tell me he was shy."

Friday 5th February, 1988
Why was the post taking so long?

After school I met Sarah and we walked to the pool. It would be my first visit there since the last time I had seen James. Walking poolside, I tried to stop myself looking directly at the lifeguard chair at the deep end. It was filled with someone new. We walked up the side and I looked across at the diving board. So many memories tumbled off it, disappearing into thin air.

The noise of everyone else's happiness echoed around the place but I couldn't share in it. There was no one to grab our feet and drag us beneath the surface, no one to chase and no one to laugh with. However in some ways it did make me feel closer to James again. I swam underwater and paused in the spot where he first kissed me and where I had kissed him back. Was I imagining it or did the water feel slightly warmer there, or was it just the blush of my memories?

Saturday 6th February, 1988
The postman brought me an envelope and my first letter from James. It's lunchtime and I have already read it a thousand times and I have just written my reply.

Dear Steph,
How nice to get such a long letter from you so soon. Sorry about my handwriting. I hope you can manage to read it ok?
The move went well and I have managed to get a job straight away at the local swimming pool as a lifeguard. I have made a couple of friends at the pool but I am missing all of you so much. The pool is much larger than the one in Ross-on-Wye and has a separate diving pool which is fantastic, although you might be a bit scared at the top of the high board!
I am glad you are enjoying the mix tape; I have been listening to my copy even though the Wham! song makes me cringe slightly, it also reminds me of you. I am hoping to sort out enough money to buy a car soon and then I will be able to head back and see you all again and catch up with Chris too. He phoned me the other day and said you had been in the video shop to hire Top Gun. *Did you enjoy it? I would love to fly a plane like that but America is a long way to go!!!*
Anyway, I hope you are studying hard for your exams as they are so important for the future. I have just sent my CV to the Fire and Rescue Service as I am sure you remember me telling you, I always wanted to be a fireman. I am going to try and get in up here, so I will keep you up to date with any progress in that direction.
Well, got to go now but just wanted you to know that your elephant has pride of place on my book shelf above the bed. I will send you a picture soon.
Fondest regards,
James

In the afternoon I walked down to Sarah's house as I was staying over.
"What shall we do this evening?" I asked.
"Let's get a video or two in. My parents are going out so we can slob out on the sofa in the lounge." She looked at me and asked, "So, have

you got a letter then?"

"Yes," I said, showing it to her as it didn't really say anything that I couldn't share with my best friend.

"I've already replied and posted it on my way here."

We walked into town and went to the library first as Sarah wanted to hand in her application for the Saturday job. Then we were on our way to the video shop. I noticed Sarah had made an extra effort with her hair and make-up as we walked inside. Sarah started to scan the shelves but I went straight to the counter and spoke to Chris.

"Can you recommend a good film for us to watch," I asked.

"How about *Stand by Me*," he said, pulling it out from behind the counter. "It's based on a short story by Stephen King."

"Great. Have you found anything else?" I called to Sarah. She came over with a romantic comedy and handed it over. I watched them both smile shyly at each other before we left.

♪

"Charlotte, I've brought you up a hot chocolate," I said, meeting Charlie on the landing.

"Thanks Mum," she replied, taking the mug.

"It's almost eleven so I'm going to bed shortly."

"Don't worry Mum, I won't be long," she replied. "You must explain what a tape is to me as it's obviously like a CD."

I laughed and nodded my head at the memory of the mix tape.

"Night sweetheart."

"Night Mum," she replied. "Thanks again for giving me your diary, it's great reading."

It was Friday at last. Charlie left for school and I could see her heartbreak hadn't lasted long. My daughter was obviously made of stronger stuff or perhaps she hadn't really been in love with Craig as deeply as I had been with James. Driving into Hereford for work, I heard my phone beep. I parked and glanced at the screen; it was Sarah.

Hi Steph, are you doing anything tonight as Chris is away and I need a good gossip and a glass of wine or two?

I quickly replied:

Sure, head over whenever you like later, probably going to get a takeaway in for Charlie and I so you're more than welcome to join us.

Sauntering into the studio I waved through the glass at Paul and he waved back, then held his mug up. I nodded knowing this was the sign for coffee. I read my emails and noticed how many replies we had already received from local bands and performers interested in our Rock On the River event in the summer. I quickly tapped out a couple of replies and sent them off. I hoped it was going to be a great experience helping to organise something so huge for such a small place like Ross. As I passed Paul on the way into the studio, we exchanged a quick couple of words whilst the news played in the background.

"Have you seen all the replies we're getting for the event?" he said.

"Yes, it's great. By the way my daughter's college dance group would like to perform."

"Great, the more the merrier." He stopped to think. "Is Charlie that old already?"

"She'll be seventeen this year, I can't believe it myself," I replied.

"You'll have to bring her into the studio sometime."

"Don't think she'd be interested in seeing where her boring, old Mum works."

Getting home later, I went straight upstairs and pulled open the loft door and the extending ladder. I had been thinking about James and my diary all day and I wanted to see if I could find more of his letters. I knew I had kept them; it was just a case of locating the right box amongst all the other junk I thought it necessary to keep. After a few boxes yielded nothing, I pulled another towards me and sat down on the floor. Inside were a number of photo albums and I skimmed through the ones from my early childhood. I loved reminiscing but now was not the time as I only had a short window of opportunity before Charlotte returned home.

I was about to close the box back up when I saw my pink photo album right near the bottom. I was about to pull the other albums aside when I heard the front door bang closed. Having wasted a couple of hours surrounded by more memories of times past, I quickly started to descend the loft ladder and she appeared on the landing.

"Hi Mum, what are you doing?" Charlotte asked.

"How was college?"

"Ok. Managed to avoid Craig all day, so was cool."

"I've just been up in the attic looking for something," I responded, hoping she wouldn't spot the lie, "but I'd better get on with some food, if you're hungry?"

"Can you leave the ladder down, I've got some stuff I want to put up there," Charlotte asked. "And yes, I'm starving... can we have Chinese like usual?"

"Yes, sounds good to me. Oh, and Auntie Rah is probably going to come over as Uncle Chris is still away." I loved reminding Charlie of her aunt's nickname from childhood.

♪

Charlotte didn't really have any stuff she needed to put up in the loft, she really wanted to have a hunt around and see if she could find any old photo albums. After going through a couple of different boxes, she spied a tatty looking pink photo album, underneath some old birthday and Christmas cards. Then she found a pile of letters tied together with a red ribbon underneath the photo album. A quick look inside the album confirmed it belonged to her mum. Charlotte gathered up her finds and went back to her room before her mother wondered what was taking so long.

Charlotte was just about to open up the photo album when she heard the doorbell sound.

"I'll get it," Charlie shouted, racing down the stairs and skidding across the wooden floor in her socks.

♪

I stood in the kitchen doorway watching as Charlotte greeted Sarah, "Hi, Auntie Rah."

"Hi Sarah," I added.

"Hi guys, glad to have an invite for this evening, my house was feeling a bit empty without Chris." Charlie wrapped her arms around

Sarah's waist and they walked towards me.

"I've already ordered our usual set meal from the Chinese," I announced, "should be here soon." I crossed to the fridge and pulled out the chilled bottle of rose wine.

"Charlie, can you grab some glasses?" I asked.

"So long as I can have one?" Charlie replied, a cheeky glint in her eye.

Sarah settled down opposite me at the island unit and smiled.

"You're looking well," she said. "What's been going on in your exciting world of radio? I've been working most lunchtimes this week so I haven't had chance to hear your voice."

She picked up the glass of wine and clinked it against mine. Charlie was busy getting plates and cutlery out.

"Good thanks; we're planning an event for Ross in the summer called Rock On the River. It's to raise money for the hospital."

"Perhaps you'd better include libraries in that fundraising; things are not looking good with us at the moment," Sarah told us, looking downcast.

"Why?"

"Well there's hardly any money left in the council reserves and since the government is cutting back, we'll have less money to run the service. I should know a little more in a couple of weeks but I believe we may have a fight on our hands. Anyway… enough about work. How is my favourite god-daughter?" she said to Charlie.

"Ok, thanks," Charlie replied. "Craig finished with me on Tuesday but I think I'm getting over him already." I saw her smile across at me, as if to acknowledge my diary as part of the quick-healing process.

"Mum gave me her diary from 1988… I'm reading about when you were both my age."

Sarah looked across at me with a worried look on her face. She didn't say anything and the moment was interrupted by the doorbell again. This time it was the takeaway. Silence reigned as we laid all the food out and tucked into it. I hadn't realised quite how hungry I was.

While Charlie went upstairs to her room, Sarah and I adjourned to the lounge and I put some music on low.

"Don't you ever get tired of George?" Sarah sighed.

"Nope," I replied, curling up in the armchair opposite and taking a sip of my wine.

"Is it wise giving Charlotte your diary from 1988?"

"I don't know but as I have never thrown it away, I knew I must have kept it for some reason and this seemed like it."

"Well ok then, but if you need me for anything you know you only have to ask." She took a sip of wine and sank back against the pillows.

"So how long will Chris be away this time?" I asked.

"Until July," Sarah said. "I never get used to him being away. I always feel lonely even though we keep in touch every day."

"Well you are always welcome here. I know that all too soon Charlie will find another guy and be out of the house most evenings."

"She looks so much like you."

"Yes, except for her eyes, they are definitely her dad's."

"Do you miss Mark?"

"Of course I do, he was a great father."

"Yes... and husband to you?"

I nodded and managed a weak smile.

"It's ok, it's me. I know you never really loved Mark. I could see it all the times the four of us were together. You always looked distant."

Standing up, I walked back into the kitchen to get a breather from my best friend's interrogation. It was all true and even admitting it made me upset and angry. Perhaps it was time I tried harder to move on with my life. Grabbing the wine, I went back into the lounge and refilled our glasses.

"It's a good job I'm within walking distance," Sarah giggled. "This wine is going straight to my head!"

"Just let it, the spare room is always available."

"Have you seen Jack recently?" she asked.

"No, but he's forever emailing me with news of his latest romance."

"He needs to find a guy to settle down with, he's too old to still be flirting around." We both giggled some more and then once the wine was finished, Sarah stood up.

"I'm going to get home now," Sarah said, swaying slightly.

"Ok hun, thanks for coming over." I stood up and pulled her into my arms for a hug.

"Charlotte, Sarah is going now," I shouted. We waited and saw her appear at the top of the stairs. She was already in her pyjamas but hurried down to fling her arms around Sarah.

"Night Rah, it was great to see you tonight."

"And you Charlie," Sarah responded, dropping a kiss on her forehead. "Keep up the dancing, I'm looking forward to your next performance."

"I will," Charlie replied. "I'm off to bed now."

On the doorstep I watched Sarah walk down the drive.

"Give me three rings when you get in, just so I know you're home safely," I shouted. Sarah turned and smirked.

"Who do you think you are... my mother?" she shouted back and started to giggle again. It was infectious as I stood on the doorstep. It was a cold, clear night and I looked up into the dark sky. The moon was almost full and the stars twinkled brightly, making dot-to-dot patterns. Once again I remembered a time in my life when the sky meant so much, the words to a certain song springing to mind. I sighed and shut the door on the memories that had returned unbidden to haunt me.

The following evening after tea, Charlotte excused herself to finish her homework and then to start the investigation of her finds from the attic, along with some more of the diary if she had time. The photo album was fun – the first few pictures were of her mum and Sarah at primary school and various birthday party pictures showing her mum wearing some pretty rank clothes, including brown, flared cords and an orange jumpsuit… yuck! Some photographs from secondary school included some awful shots in a drab, grey uniform.

As Charlotte neared the end of the album she wondered if there were any photos of her mum and James. Perhaps she had removed them or hidden them? But there on the very back page, was a photograph of her mum wearing a gorgeous black and white prom-style dress, with hundreds of petticoats underneath, her curly ginger hair piled up on her head, a few tendrils escaping. She looked breathtaking and next to her stood a tall, slim, sexy blond guy wearing a full suit and tie, his arm protectively round her waist. They looked perfect together.

Charlotte looked in the mirror and pushed her hands through her light, sandy blond hair, wondering whether she should colour it red for a change. After all, it suited her mum back then and it would be good to have a fresh start since her break-up with Craig. She wished she had a photograph of herself with Craig but she had pressed delete on her phone and all those pictures had disappeared.

Closing the album she pushed it underneath her bed along with the letters. She reached for the diary and turning her iPod on low, she started to read again.

Dear Diary,

Monday 8th February, 1988
School is getting tough; the teachers seem to be piling us up with so much coursework to finish. We also have lots to get through during half term too, but at least it's keeping me busy. James has also sent me another letter, much like the first.

Dear Steph,
Thanks for your quick reply to my letter. It is so lovely to hear what you are doing in Ross. I was quite excited about moving to a larger place when my mum initially told me but I have to admit that I do miss Ross a

lot more than I thought I would, especially my friends there. Although, the guys at work are great fun, so it's not as if I have no-one to talk to. The boss at the pool is awful though so I have to stay on my toes every second when I am at work.

I hope they have not given you too much coursework to do over the half term holiday as it might mean you don't reply so quickly to my letters.

Anyway, I'm pleased that you enjoyed watching Top Gun. I try never to let a week go by in between watching it as the film is excellent and so is all the music. That's why I put a couple of the tracks onto the mix tape that I gave you. I also grabbed the chance to watch Star Wars the original film again and it made me think of you and all your comments from our night out!! It's funny how different things remind you of different moments in your life?

Well enough from me for now, I'm going to the gym before I start work so I'll finish and wait for the postman to bring me another letter from you.

Fondest regards
James x

My reply letter will be going with his Valentine card which I chose on the way home from school. It is a fantastic card where I get to choose the message on the outside by placing stickers on the relevant spaces shaped like love-heart sweets.

Tuesday 9th February, 1988
I have found the perfect present for James for Valentine's Day, one I will be able to post to him. It's a kit to make a model fire engine! I just hope he will love it as I wrap it up along with the card and letter:

Dear James,
I am writing this letter to tell you how I really feel about you. I am hoping that you will read it and perhaps, you might decide that what you have read is what you might want. If not then I am sorry if this will spoil our friendship and hope that perhaps it won't.

Ever since I first saw you at the swimming pool, I knew I fancied you. When we started to become friends, I started to feel it was even more than just a crush. Then when you kissed me for the first time under the water, I didn't know what to feel. I could only hope you felt more than just friendship for me.

Now that you have gone, I just seem to miss you more and more. Your letters are great but I want more than friendship. I want love. I want to be your girlfriend. I know that I am only sixteen but don't let that be the barrier between us trying to have a relationship that is more than just friendship. I also know that it will be harder due to the distance between us but I hope that we can work it out somehow.

Well, that's all I can say and I am just wishing and praying that you might feel the same way too.

I hope you like the present?
Love Stephanie x

Wednesday 10th February, 1988
After school I rushed into town and posted the parcel first class just to make sure. I hoped James might send me something in return, even if it was only a card. Another letter was waiting for me when I got home, telling me about work and about the area where he now lived. Apparently there was a great park nearby for roller skating. He asked if I could skate and I smiled and thought about what it would be like to skate along next to James, holding onto his hand tightly – knowing it would probably never happen. He told me he bought a car and was just waiting until he could pick it up. He would arrange to come down and see me. Inside the envelope was a photograph of his room, and I could see the elephant on the shelf above his bed.

Thursday 11th February, 1988
At school today, Sarah and I grabbed a quiet spot away from the others to eat our lunch. I showed her the last letter James sent me.

"I've already posted the Valentine card and present and letter," I said, between crisps.

"Here's the card I bought for Chris," Sarah said, checking first before she pulled it out of her bag. I smiled. It said *'Guess Who'* on the front.

"So what shall I write inside?" she asked me.

"I think you should put something about him making a splash in your life as it might make him think about the swimming pool."

"Do you think it will?"

"Well, you do want him to guess who sent it, don't you?"

She nodded as she wrote the message.

"So, should I post it to the video shop or do you want to drop it off there?"

"I think we should both drop it off on Saturday, either before or after we go swimming," I said, making the decision for her.

Saturday 13th February, 1988
I woke up and was disappointed I had not received a Valentine card.

Perhaps I was hoping for too much, or it was still in the post and I would just have to wait until Monday instead. Sarah tried her best to cheer me up, but not even a swim at the pool could lift my mood. Was I setting my sights too high? Were we only destined to be friends until he met the right girl for him and abandoned me completely??

We just managed to get to the video store before it closed and I found the copy of *Top Gun*. Taking it to the counter I couldn't see Chris anywhere.

"I don't think Chris is here."

"What should I do with the card then?" she asked.

"Leave it in their post box for returned cassettes, no one will look in there until tomorrow morning now." We slipped the red envelope in through the slot on our way out.

"I'm sure James will send you something, you might just have to wait until Monday," Sarah said, as she hugged me on the corner of the street.

"I hope so, but I'm trying not to hold my breath. After all, we're only friends."

"Well, I have my fingers crossed for you."

"And I'll cross mine for you then."

I sat in the lounge and watched *Top Gun* later that night, trying not to cry when I watched the love scene. How I wanted that to be me and James! How I longed for him so much, my heart seemed to ache. In bed that night I put my stereo on low and played the mix tape and cried in the darkness until sleep claimed me.

Sunday 14th February, 1988 (Valentine's Day)
I woke up and went down for breakfast and saw my mum seemed to be acting slightly strange. Had Dad forgotten to give her a card?

I went back upstairs to shower and then to tidy my room and try to forget about not receiving a Valentine card. I put my favourite Wham! album on full blast and danced around the room. I heard a car pull up in the driveway outside and peered out of the window to see a lovely red Mini. Then I heard the doorbell go.

"Stephanie, there's someone here to see you," Mum called.

I rushed downstairs, which seemed to take me ages, but it was worth it when I saw James standing there, smiling shyly and holding a single red rose and card in his hand.

"Hi Steph, I thought I would surprise you."

As the blood rushed to my head I almost fainted. I smiled and wished I had the nerve to run into his arms.

"Hi James, it's a lovely surprise," I said as I took the gifts and he kissed me on the cheek before accepting Mum's offer of a coffee. We sat together in the kitchen and chatted with my parents.

"Would you like to come into town with me as I have to see Chris?"

"Yes that's great as I have to take my video back to the shop," I replied.

Sitting next to him in his car was fantastic, especially when he turned the stereo on and all the tunes were from the mix tape.

"So I'm going to be around until Tuesday. Would you like to go swimming on Monday night?"

"Yes, so long as Chris and Sarah can come," I replied. James nodded and smiled across at me, knowing I was trying hard to play matchmaker.

We spent an hour in the video shop and Chris agreed to come swimming.

Then we drove back to my house and I made us both a cold drink.

"Mum, is it ok for James to come up to my room before dinner?"

"Yes that's fine," Mum said.

James followed me up the two flights of stairs to my attic room. By the time we reached the door, I was shaking with nerves. Had he received my card and letter? What did he think of my proposal? He sat down on my bed and kicked off his trainers as I walked across the room and put my stereo on. Only George Michael would do at this moment. I turned and stared at him, unsure what I should do next as George started to strum the guitar and sing *'cos you gotta have faith'*. How true! James beckoned me over to him and before I knew what was happening, he pulled me into his arms and said, "The answer is yes."

My heart was beating so hard I could hear it drumming in my ears as I trembled in his arms and waited for his lips to reach mine.

He pulled me onto his lap, his hands pulling my hair loose so he could run his gentle fingers through it, making even my scalp tingle from his touch. His lips on mine were infinitely gentle and then growing bolder, his mouth opened and mine matched his as our tongues explored. My whole being was rocked by the new sensations coursing through it. It felt exhilarating and scary so I pushed James away and he pulled back.

"What's wrong?" he asked.

"I need to breathe," I managed as I opened my eyes. "Am I doing it right? I've never kissed anyone this way before."

"You're doing fine, but we can practise some more if you like?"

As he inclined his head towards me and our lips met again, all too soon the album came to an end and I untangled myself to turn it over. We spent the rest of the afternoon just lying together on the bed, talking and of course kissing. All the time I was thinking, *He's my boyfriend, he's my boyfriend, this gorgeous, handsome guy is my boyfriend.*

James had to drive over to Chris's place but as we lingered on the doorstep saying goodbye, I didn't really want him to go and felt sure James felt the same as he held me in his arms and kissed me one, last time.

"Until tomorrow, Steph," he whispered as he walked to his car and then drove away.

♫

Charlotte rubbed her eyes. Her mum definitely had a way with words because she felt the same emotions her mum had, all those years ago. Charlotte remembered the feelings of elation when Craig had asked her out and also the scary but delicious feelings of their first kiss six months ago.

-11-

While Charlotte was at school I went to the loft to search for the letters, but came down empty-handed. My pink photo album had also disappeared and I guessed my daughter found them when she had been up there the other day. Anyway, I was way past mooning over my first boyfriend, especially when I remembered how it had ended. I wondered if James still thought of me, but dismissed that idea. After all, he had ended it and broken my heart.

Charlotte came racing in through the door later that evening, full of excitement.
"Mum can I go to Birmingham this weekend?"
"Well if you explain why, then perhaps I can answer that."
"Our dance troop have been picked for that competition I was telling you about. It's at the LG Arena in Birmingham. There's a minibus going so you'll just need to do me a packed lunch and make sure I don't miss the bus as it leaves at seven a.m."
"Yes, sounds great," I replied, knowing how much Charlotte enjoyed her class. We both liked to watch all the dance programmes on the television together; it was our favourite girly time, generally curled up on the sofa, eating popcorn or crisps.
"Going to go and practise some more straight away," Charlotte said.

♪

Up in her room, Charlotte turned some music on and did half an hour, then decided to check out the internet site for the competition and see who their rivals were going to be. Watching the small video clips of some of the other groups, Charlotte knew it was going to be hard to get through with that much talent. Then Charlotte reached for the diary, eager to see how the next few days went with her mum and James, now they were a couple.

Dear Diary,

Monday 15th February, 1988
I woke up early and gave Sarah a ring. "You'll never believe what happened yesterday!"
"I'm not even going to try, so tell me."

"James turned up in his new car and he's staying with Chris until Tuesday. We're all going swimming later," I said, stopping to take a breath.

"Ok, I think I'd better come over to your place then to get ready."

"Definitely, as I have even more exciting news but I'll tell you when you get here."

Sarah soon arrived.

"You look different somehow," she said.

"That's because I now have a boyfriend," I replied. We fell into each other's arms and squealed in excitement before falling back onto my bed, where the previous afternoon I had spent hours kissing James. I hoped there would be many more hours like that to come, preferably before he went back home on Tuesday.

Our visit to the pool was great fun, just like old days, except that James kept motioning to me to go underwater so he could kiss me without getting told off. Sarah and Chris laughed at us both and I could see that Sarah kept shyly looking at him when he was not looking. We had coffee upstairs in the café afterwards and James asked if he could walk me home.

Then it was just the two of us and this time, I didn't hesitate in putting my hand in his as he squeezed it. I let us both in and made hot chocolate before I let my parents know we were going upstairs. It took so much self control for me to actually put some music on before I found myself stretched out on the bed.

"I don't want to rush things," he murmured between kisses, "so you must tell me what you are happy with and we will stick to those limits. After all you are only sixteen."

I agreed as we kissed and talked before he went back to Chris's around midnight. Lingering on the doorstep, I could still feel the heat of his lips on mine.

Tuesday 16th February, 1988
I woke up early so I had plenty of time to get ready. James had not told me what we would be doing but he did say to wear something warm and sensible as it would involve being outside. James arrived early and we had a quick coffee before he whisked me out to his car.

"Are we going far?" I asked as we drove out of town.

"No, not far," he replied as we drove towards the Forest of Dean and stopped outside a bike hire centre.

"We're going to cycle round the ponds and then when we get back, I have a small picnic in the boot, so if it stays dry we'll eat outside, but if not then we will eat in the car."

The scenery was spectacular as we rode along the path beside the ponds.

"Dad used to bring me here when I was a kid, normally on a Sunday to get us out of the way of Mum cooking lunch," James said.

"It's beautiful," I breathed.

It obviously held a special place in James' memories, so I was pleased he had shared it with me. I struggled to keep up with James on some of the uphill parts, but he was always waiting for me. At the bridge over the weir, we stopped and leaned the bikes against a nearby tree.

"Have you ever played Pooh sticks?" I asked James.

"I can't say I have even heard of it, but go on and explain. I'm all ears," he said, leaning against the railings of the bridge.

Quickly I found two sticks that were about the same size and passed one to James.

"It's from the *Winnie the Pooh* books and the aim is to drop the sticks over the edge of the bridge and see whose stick reaches the bottom of the weir first."

"And what's the prize for the winner?" he asked.

"Loser kisses the winner."

James grinned as he held his stick over the edge of the railings before we both dropped them into the water and watched to see whose would reach the bottom first. It was a dead heat as James pulled me close and our lips touched.

"I don't want today to ever end," I said, as we went back to the car.

"I don't either, but I promise you there will be many more days like this."

He pulled me close and we looked out across the lake that seemed to stretch into infinity and beyond. The weak sunlight touched the ripples at the shore as I felt my own ripples of emotion spreading out within me. In James' arms I felt happy, content and completely and utterly in love with him.

Back at my place he stayed for an hour but then wanted to get back before it was too late. I stood on the doorstep watching him wave as he drove away, tears already forming beneath my eyelids, ready to fall in the privacy of my room.

Saturday 20th February, 1988

I realised our letters must have crossed over in the post as I hurried to open his latest one to me…

Dear Steph,

This Valentine's Day was the best one I ever had. Thank you again for my model kit, it is already assembled and sitting next to the elephant on the shelf. I am so happy you are now my girlfriend. As soon as I left Ross, I realised how much I missed seeing you at the pool. I am glad you had the courage to tell me that you felt the same and I am sure we can make this long-distance relationship work if we both try.

I promise I will not try and rush things but I will admit that I am looking forward to your birthday in March as I am planning something very special.

Keep your letters coming, they really brighten my day and perhaps we can call each other on the phone every Friday evening if that's ok with your parents? I have to let you know that my folks are really looking forward to meeting you at some point soon and I would love to show you around Leamington Spa and Warwick.

Fondest regards
James

I asked Mum and Dad if this was ok and then replied to James, asking who would phone first, counting down the days until Friday evening.

Friday 26th February, 1988
I sat in the lounge with my parents and waited for the phone to ring. Sure enough at seven, it did.

"Hi Steph," he said, and in that instance of hearing his voice, I felt my heart yearn for him.

"Hi James, how are you?"

"Missing you."

"Me too," I sighed, cradling the receiver as if it were his hand in mine. We chatted for half an hour and then rang off so I could phone him back.

"So will it be ok for you to come and stay at my place for your birthday?" he asked.

"I asked my parents and they said yes as long as your parents will be there."

"Yes they will be here, they are looking forward to meeting you."

It felt good to have something to look forward to as well as our letters and phone calls.

Tuesday 8th March, 1988
Grabbing Sarah after school, we made our apologies to June and Amanda and walked through town to the doctor's surgery. Sitting in the waiting

room, I chewed my nails.

"Are you nervous?" Sarah asked.

"Yes, what if they won't give me any pills?"

"I'm sure they will, after all they would rather you are protected than pregnant," Sarah said.

Clutching my prescription, Sarah and I walked home.

"Was it ok?" she asked.

"Yes, I was a bit embarrassed but they won't start working for a month."

"So do you think you might?" she asked, curious.

"Not yet, and I don't think James will push me," I replied.

In my mind I knew I was not ready to take the next step yet. In fact I worried I might never be ready; all I knew about sex was the factual biology lessons and what I had seen on films or read in books.

"Do you think he's had sex before?" Sarah asked.

"I'm sure he must have, we haven't really talked about that yet. I'm just enjoying all the kissing."

Thursday 10th March, 1988

Once in my room, I put the mix tape on the stereo and Sarah pulled open my wardrobe doors.

"So what do you think you'll be doing at James' place?" she asked.

"Probably going swimming," I said, finding my favourite bikini. "Hopefully he's taking me out for a meal for my birthday, too."

Sarah pulled out two of my dresses. I stared at both of them and chose the newer one, carefully folding it into my bag. With jumpers, t-shirts and a couple of skirts following the dress into the bag, it was soon full.

"What about underwear?" she said. I blushed and opened my drawer, wishing I had more sophisticated underwear to choose from instead of just my plain black and white sets.

I couldn't wait to share such a special occasion with my boyfriend, my first boyfriend.

Friday 11th March, 1988

Mum and Dad gave me some money for my birthday and some clothes, so I crammed them into my bag before I left for school. Sarah bought me some body spray, June and Amanda the usual bubble bath and a book voucher. They had been so jealous when I told them what I was doing for my seventeenth birthday.

I was standing with the others by the gates when I saw a familiar red Mini pelting up the road.

"Do I look ok?" I asked, "as it appears James has come to fetch me."

June and Amanda's jaws dropped as the Mini came to a halt right in front of the gates. In fact most of the school crowd had done the same and they were all staring at the red Mini and the gorgeous guy getting out of the driver's seat. I ran the short distance separating us and he pulled me into his arms, seemingly not worried that hundreds of kids were watching as he kissed me. Then all I could hear were whoops and cheers and the weight of jealous stares from some of the other girls in my year as they passed by.

"So how did you manage this?" I asked, as we drove back to my house.

"I got here early and called in to ask your mum if I could come and pick you up," he said, grinning. "I just couldn't wait any longer to see you."

At my place I left him downstairs, talking to my parents as I quickly changed and grabbed my bag for the weekend. As he drove he rested his hand on my leg when he wasn't changing gear or I would rest mine on his knee, all the while we talked about plans for the weekend.

The nerves kicked in as we pulled up on the driveway. Would his parents like me and think I was good enough to be going out with their son? James pulled open the door and helped me out, giving me a quick hug and kiss. As we walked in I found myself enveloped in a motherly hug.

"Hi, I'm Pam and this is Peter," she said, motioning to an older version of James. "It's lovely to meet you, James is always talking about you."

We sat and had coffee in the kitchen before his mum looked at the clock.

"You might want to start getting ready as I'm sure you don't want to be late for dinner."

"Follow me Steph, and I'll show you the spare room," James said.

He picked up my bag and I followed him upstairs.

"This is your room, the bathroom is across the hall and my room is here," James said, pointing at the door.

"Great, I think I'll have a quick shower," I said.

When I returned to the spare room I found a card and a present on the bed. Still in my towel, I opened the card which was beautiful. It was fantastic to see 'girlfriend' written on the front of it. Then I opened the present and inside was a lovely set of white underwear covered in small black hearts. The bra was my size and I put it on under my dress for the evening.

I struggled with the suspender belt and stockings but surveying the results in the bedroom mirror, I was shocked at how sexy the whole thing looked. They accentuated my long legs and I found myself blushing at the sight. Was this what guys wanted to see when they undressed a girl? I smoothed my dress down and heard a knock on the bedroom door.

"Are you ready?"

"Almost," I replied as I sat down on the bed and slipped my feet into some heels. When I stood up, James helped me into my bolero jacket. At the same time he brushed his lips over the nape of my neck which got my pulse racing and made me blush all over again.

"Thanks for the present, it's beautiful and just the right size, how did you manage that?"

"I sneaked a look in your cupboard at home when I was over, but I did cheat a bit and got my mum to choose and buy it for me."

The restaurant was fantastic. I felt a bit overwhelmed by it all as we were shown to our table. Once we ordered, I started to relax as we drank orange juice. We had white wine with the meal, and as I was only used to drinking white wine and lemonade mixed on special occasions, I found that it was going to my head a bit. However we soon finished our sumptuous chocolate dessert and it was time to go home.

After wishing his parents goodnight, we headed upstairs.

"Would you like to come and listen to some music in my room?"

I smiled when I saw the elephant next to the fire engine model on his shelf.

"I like your display," I said, motioning to the shelf above his bed. I shrugged off my jacket and stepped out of my shoes.

Pulling me into his arms his lips came down to meet mine and we kissed for ages. I felt his hands running up my stocking-clad legs but only to the hem of my dress, although this seemed to be higher than usual.

"Shall I take my stockings off?" I asked.

"Let me," James said, as he found the catches on the belt and then rolled them to the floor. His hands slid over my smooth skin, once more pulling me into his embrace.

We heard his parents heading to bed and we stopped kissing.

"I guess I'd better go to bed now," I said in a breathless voice

"I guess so," James replied, reluctant to let me go. Standing up I smoothed down my dress.

"Goodnight James. Thank you for a wonderful birthday."

"It was my pleasure, night Stephanie," he said, as he watched me leave.

Alone in the spare room I undressed and thought about how daring I had been to let James remove my stockings. I left my knickers on and then pulled out my nightshirt and snuggled under the duvet. I saw the door slowly open and James crept in.

"I was cold and missing you," he whispered.

Surprised but happy to see him, I pulled aside the duvet and he jumped in next to me. We cuddled up and started to kiss again, slowly at first but then more urgent. I pulled back a bit, afraid of this going too far, too quickly. We curled up together and I was very aware of his body pressed against mine. I trembled. This was the first time I had ever shared a bed with a man but as our breathing slowed, we fell asleep in each other's arms.

♪

Charlotte was amazed at her mum's self-restraint and also that of James. What a cool guy, she thought. Craig had been eager to go straight from kissing to sex and in a way, Charlotte knew that it was her saying no the last time they were together that had probably triggered the split. Although many of her friends had already lost their virginity as young as fourteen, she was not as eager. She wanted love as well as sex and that was hard to find. Closing the diary she heard her phone ping and a text was there from Craig. He wanted to make things up to her and was sorry for dumping her. Charlotte deleted it and turned her phone off, her mind already made up that she was not prepared to settle for second best. She wanted the works.

-12-

I gathered up the laundry from Charlotte's room; a typical teenager, her stuff lay strewn all over the floor. I noticed my diary lying open on her pillow so I went over to see how far she had got. Once again the words of my teenage years sucked me back into a past I had tried so hard to forget – but somehow couldn't.

Dear Diary,

Saturday 12th March, 1988
I woke to an empty bed; James had snuck out early to make sure his parents didn't find out we had shared a bed that night. I was just about to get up when the door opened and James appeared with a tray.
"I thought I would bring you breakfast in bed," he said, putting the tray on the bedside table, bearing coffee and hot, buttered toast.
"Looks lovely," I replied, drinking in his tousled blond hair and blue eyes. I watched as he shrugged his way out of his dressing gown and was stood there just in his boxer shorts.
He jumped into bed beside me and I was enfolded in his arms for a good morning kiss and cuddle that seemed to last for ages. The spell was broken when we heard his mum shout upstairs that they were off out to do the shopping and would be back later. We were all alone and James grinned at me, lying back on the pillows.
"Well, what are you waiting for?" he asked me. I reached across him to the tray and grabbed a piece of toast and put it in his mouth.
"That's not what I meant," he mumbled between mouthfuls of toast, "you are in serious trouble now."
He grabbed me and started to tickle. I was soon pinned down beneath him, gasping for breath between my giggles as I tried to push him off. Then he leant down and kissed me long and deep and I felt my body arch to meet and mould with his.
His hands ran through my hair and down my face, then my neck, along my sides and to the hem of my nightshirt.
"Can I?" he asked, looking into my eyes.
I nodded, feeling the cool air catch my skin as he pulled it up and then over my head. As he pulled back to look at my body I quickly covered my breasts with my hands, suddenly shy and afraid that he would find me lacking.
"Do you trust me?"

"Yes." I breathed quietly as his hands covered mine and then gently moved them away so they rested on his hips. I felt the soft smoothness of his skin under my fingertips which were just above the waistband of his boxer shorts.

I shut my eyes as I felt his fingers run over my breasts for the very first time, my nipples springing to life as he gently ran his fingers around them.

"You are so beautiful," he murmured as his lips came back down to mine and my skin touched his. It was magical as all my nerve endings tingled in response. Time ticked by slowly as we kissed and talked and then kissed some more, my fingers running over the smooth skin of his back, his in my hair.

Eventually we drew apart and noticed it was almost noon so we decided we had better do something for the day. A trip to the pool was in order, then perhaps the water would cool the heat flaming through my blood. The pool was fantastic, much bigger than the one in Ross – and the diving board was so high. I watched with huge admiration as James climbed right to the top and executed a wonderful dive. He introduced me to Ian who was working that shift and also Michael, who was in the office.

As we were about to leave I heard a female voice shout his name. James stiffened and turned to see his boss walking towards us. She wore a short skirt suit and looked amazing as she extended her hand to me.

"I'm Felicity, you must be Stephanie," she said.

She was a little older than James but not by much. Under her piercing gaze I felt like a mouse caught in the gaze of a hungry cat.

"We are a bit short-staffed on Sunday, is there any chance you can fill in?" she asked.

"I can only do the evening as I have to take Stephanie home that day."

"Great, see you tomorrow at six then," she responded and promptly turned, clicking her way back to her office.

James seemed subdued as we drove back to his place.

"Sorry about Felicity. I think I did mention how awful our boss was in one of my letters."

"It's ok," I said as I tried to cheer him up by running my hand up and down his leg.

Dinner that evening was great. His parents asked me about school and my plans for the future before we excused ourselves and headed for James' room, where we rediscovered the taste of each other's lips and the feel of each other's skin. We dived under James' duvet, once again curling up together to sleep, just my knickers and his boxers between us.

Sunday 13th March, 1988
We awoke with a start at a knock on the door and his mum popped her head round.

"Morning James, Stephanie, would you like a coffee?"

"Thanks Mum, we'll be down in a bit," James replied. I tried to hide behind James but it was no good. James turned to see me burning with mortification.

"Don't worry about my mum. She's cool about this and I will speak to her and let her know that nothing happened, if that will ease your mind?"

"Yes, please," I replied, just before he pulled me into his arms for a good morning kiss.

After breakfast we grabbed our roller skates and walked to the park. James showed off his immense skills on the wheels while I tried to keep up and stay upright as he kept whizzing away and hiding behind trees, jumping out just as I was going past. It was such good fun and took my mind off the fact that very shortly, we would be driving back to my place and then not seeing each other for a while.

After Sunday lunch I packed and we were soon in the Mini, driving to Ross.

"It's been a wonderful weekend," James said, as his hand captured mine.

"The best birthday I have ever had," I replied, smiling over at him.

"When I'm in at work later, I'll check my shifts and see when I can see you again."

"I'll ask my parents if it's ok for you to stay at ours?" I didn't want him to have to come down to Ross and stay with Chris. I wanted to share a bed with him once more, feel his skin on mine as we shared our dreams together. All the way home I kept my hand firmly on his knee or his on mine, not wanting to break the physical connection that the weekend had only served to make stronger.

James managed a quick coffee before he had to be back for work, so once again I found myself standing on the doorstep staring into the red rear lights of his car, wishing he was not leaving. Once in my room I hugged the pillow and relived the magical firsts I had just shared with James.

♫

I carefully put the diary back down. My hands were shaking, remembering all those details from the happiest days of my life. I couldn't deny that having Charlotte was a happy time too but when my husband Mark had been killed only three months after the birth, even that was tinged with sadness. Since then I had decided it was better to be alone than to risk heartbreak for a third time and as Charlotte grew up, we became almost as close as sisters. Perhaps she would realise now why I had never jumped back onto the dating bandwagon all the years that she had been growing up. I had placed what was left of my heart in a sealed box, afraid to love again, because all it seemed to bring me was heartache and pain.

-13-

Charlotte had been practising her routine almost non-stop since her dance teacher told them about the competition in Birmingham. The troupe was twelve girls, including her best friend Julia, and they were going to be doing their most difficult routine for the competition to the song 'Umbrella' by Rihanna. It meant they had to use umbrellas as props. What was even better was that Charlotte had been chosen to perform the small solo section in the middle of the song. While she spent time rehearsing, I noticed the diary remained unread for a few days.

"Good luck, sweetheart," I said as she boarded the coach at seven a.m. on Saturday morning, her nerves evident. I knew she would be fine.

Having the day ahead without any interruptions was a luxury, so I gave Sarah a call and we headed for the health spa for a day of pampering.

"You know I gave Charlie my diary to read?"

"Yes, is something wrong?" Sarah asked.

"Well, every time I go into her room I find that I have to keep reading it myself, and my mind is a mess of memories," I explained. "I'm not sure I've done the right thing."

Sarah reached out and patted my arm.

"I'm sure you've done the right thing and I'm sure she's strong enough to cope with everything you've written," Sarah said, looking down as we both remembered New Year's Eve.

"After all, it was because of James that you got together with Mark." I nodded and smiled again, although deep in my heart I knew that Mark had always been the consolation prize.

I smiled and remembered the significant part I had played in getting Sarah and Chris together. I was amazed they had come through the years together and still looked as much in love as they did at our school leaver's dance twenty-four years ago. Their only heartbreak had been the realisation they were never going to be able to have children, but they had helped me so much when Charlotte had been born and Mark had gone, they were almost like surrogate parents to her and she always knew she could turn to them as well as me in times of need.

"Thanks for a lovely afternoon," Sarah said as I dropped her off at home. "I hope Charlotte's group has got through."

"Me too, otherwise there'll be tears before bedtime," I groaned and Sarah giggled.

"Well you know where I am if you need to escape."

♪

As the coach pulled into the large arena car park, Charlotte started to feel the nerves. However once she was in the large auditorium with all the other dance groups, the excited noise of teenage voices was calming, although she had already thrown up after breakfast that morning. Julia and Charlotte went for a quick walk around to check out all the competition but secretly they wanted to check out all the guys that were there as some of the groups were from colleges.

Each troupe watched all the others dance their routines and Charlotte was glad she wasn't a judge as the competition was fierce. Charlotte was particularly impressed with the group of guys from a college in Rugby as their acrobatics took an amazing amount of skill. In particular one guy stood out from the rest. He was tall with dark hair and a fantastic muscular physique. She guessed he was around twenty years old.

"Come on Julia, let's go and congratulate them," Charlie said and they sauntered over to the side of the stage.

"I'm at the mercy of your hormones," Julia sighed.

"Hi, great routine," Charlie said as she stuck out her hand at the dark-haired guy.

"Hi there, thanks," he said. "My name's Mitchell by the way."

"Pleased to meet you, Mitchell. I'm Charlotte and this is Julia."

As she shook his hand she felt a shock of desire spike through her body and blushed as he smiled, his green eyes drinking her in.

"Come on Charlie, we've got to warm up before our routine," Julia said, trying to drag her mesmerised friend away from the gaze of Mitchell.

"I'll look forward to seeing you dance," Mitch said, walking away with the guys from his group.

Their routine was as tight as they had ever performed it and with applause ringing in their ears, they left the stage. She glanced around for Mitchell and spotted him with his mates, smiling and waving. At the end the groups all assembled around the stage to hear the results. Only six would go through to the final and Charlotte grabbed Julia's hand as they waited for what seemed like an age before their names were called out and they were through. Then she waited and sure enough, the college from Rugby also went through which was good news.

As they were waiting outside for their minibus, Mitchell rushed over to Charlotte and handed her a scrap of paper. It had his mobile phone number and just the words, Text me, Mitch.

All the way home Charlotte debated how soon she should text him. Should she do it now or later tonight or tomorrow morning? In the end she decided that a short text tonight when she got home didn't look too eager but also didn't look like she was not interested at all.

Charlotte told her mum the great news when she got home, describing the event and everything that happened in great detail. She was so excited. Once in her room alone, Charlotte reached for her phone and typed in Mitch's number and then paused. What should she write? In the end she decided to keep it simple and wrote: **It was great to meet you today. Hope we can stay in touch between now and the next round? Charlie x**

Then she turned to her mum's diary for a few pages before sleeping. Still so hyped up from the competition and Mitchell, she didn't know if she would sleep at all.

Dear Diary,

Friday 19th March, 1988
It was James' turn to phone and I could hardly wait to hear his voice again.

"Hi James," I answered, his deep voice filling my ears at the same time, sending a tingle down my spine.

"How's your week been?"

"Ok, so much coursework to get finished."

"Keep at it, I know I was pretty lax at school except in subjects that I liked," he replied. "So... my next free weekend is the Easter one."

"That's great news, only two weeks to wait until we see each other again!" I was positive he could hear the happiness in my voice. "My mum says it's ok for you to stay at ours. You'll be in my room and I'll be in the spare room."

"It will save me sharing with Chris, I'd much rather share with you," James said, his voice low so his parents wouldn't hear him. I was lucky to have the phone in my room now so I could talk more freely.

"I loved sharing a bed with you," I replied, feeling heat in my cheeks as I remembered all that had taken place. It seemed so distant now.

"I've got an interview for the fire brigade next Tuesday," James said.

"Wow, that's great news. You'd better let me know how it goes. I'll be keeping my fingers crossed for you."

A vision of James in uniform filled my thoughts and I sighed.

"What's the sigh for?"

"Just imagining you in your uniform. You can save me any day."

"Well I may need to practise my fireman's lift next time I see you." He laughed.

Friday 1st April, 1988

I woke early and after breakfast, I got the spare bedroom ready. I told Mum I would sleep on the small pullout bed and let James have my room. Also I knew that I could probably sneak up the flight of stairs once my parents had gone to bed without stepping on any creaky floorboards. I had arranged with Sarah that we would meet and go swimming on Saturday and she hoped that Chris would come again. Since Valentine's Day, she had not even managed to pluck up the courage to go into the video shop. After that I was not sure what we could do but I was sure that between us we could think of some way to pass the time.

Just after ten I heard a car pull into the driveway and quickly dashed downstairs to open the door. I ran into his arms as he held me close and breathed in the scent of my freshly washed hair.

"Aren't you a sight for sore eyes?" He bent down for a quick kiss, aware that my parents might see us.

"You too."

We wasted some time over coffee and then eagerly went to my room. He pulled me into his arms and we had a proper hello kiss that literally left me gasping and shaking in his arms as we moved the few yards to the bed and sank onto the duvet. Oh, the feel of his touch after a fortnight apart felt like heaven as my body pressed against his in such a way that we felt like one.

"Lunch is ready!" Mum shouted, so we went downstairs and afterwards, walked into town to meet Chris at the video shop.

"Can you invite Chris to come swimming tomorrow as Sarah wants to come," I said, walking along together, our hands tightly clasped.

"Sure I can, I like matchmaking." He grinned.

"Hi Chris," James said as I wandered over to the shelves to give them some space to catch up. As I joined the conversation, Chris smiled at me.

"We've decided to go to the cinema afterwards," James said, pulling me close.

"Sounds great, I'll give Sarah a quick call later and check she is free all evening."

♪

Charlotte was startled when her phone beeped and there was a message from Mitchell: **It was great to meet you too, are you on Facebook? We can talk through that as well as with text. I want to get to know you a bit more, Mitch x**

He had signed his with a kiss too, what did that mean? She replied immediately with her Facebook username and wished him goodnight.

-14-

The following morning Charlotte woke late, immediately reaching for her mobile phone to check Facebook. There blinking at her was a friend request from Mitchell Cooke accompanied by a small picture of him looking gorgeous. She accepted the request and while she tidied her room and finished her homework, she waited for the beeps alerting her to messages. There was still nothing when she went down for a sandwich at lunchtime so she quickly phoned Julia, who told her to calm down and just be patient. She was rewarded by a message on Facebook later that afternoon saying, 'Hello' and a link to a video clip he had recorded of her group's dance routine from yesterday. She was impressed he'd filmed it and wished she had filmed his.

Lying on her bed Charlotte responded to the message and then settled down to an afternoon of her mum's diary. Now even more so, she needed to know what older guys did differently so that she could learn to read between the lines of her messages from Mitch.

Dear Diary,

Saturday 2nd April, 1988
Creeping up to my room at around midnight, I was rewarded when James pulled the duvet aside and I squeezed into my single bed next to him. Once I had set my alarm for six a.m., James pulled me close and we shared some extremely long, devouring kisses before he pulled my nightshirt away from my body. I let his hands wander down to gently brush over my erect nipples. Then we moved so that I lay beneath him as he ran a trail of kisses down my neck, and lower. Glancing up at me in the semi-darkness, I nodded my consent as I stretched out under his expert touch. As his lips moved softly over my breasts, I ran my fingers through his short hair and held him there so that he would continue with his kisses. His tongue licked over them as my body melted into hot, burning liquid, on fire beneath his touch.

James headed lower to my belly button and I tried to stifle my laughter as it tickled. When his lips returned to mine I felt his weight crushing me into the mattress. I didn't mind this as I always seemed to find it hard to breathe easily, even when we were not touching. Then we curled up tightly together.

"Sorry I laughed when you kissed my belly button," I whispered.
"At least I know where it is now, in case of emergency."

"What emergencies?"

"The tickling kind," he said as he pulled me into his arms.

His breathing slowed and I enjoyed the feel of his taut muscles around me. I didn't want to sleep and lose the opportunity to drink in everything I was feeling in the moment. Before drifting off I vowed that tomorrow night it would be my turn to explore.

When the alarm sounded at six, I kissed James goodbye and left the room.

"I'll give you a shout when I wake up," I said.

"I'd prefer a wake-up kiss." He watched me creep out of the room.

In the spare room sleep eluded me so I ran my hands over my body trying to recreate the feel of his touch. I knew how responsive my nipples were under his fingertips and tongue. I could only guess how good it would be when I let him explore further.

I must have slept because the sound of voices downstairs woke me up. I quickly got dressed in my leggings and long jumper and went down. James smiled when I entered the room and I sat down next to him as he continued to talk to my dad about the training involved in becoming a fireman.

"Morning Mum, Dad, James," I said, as Mum passed me a mug of coffee.

After breakfast we drove over to see Chris.

Arriving at the pool I saw Sarah waiting for us.

"Hi Sarah," I said, linking my arm through hers on the way into the changing room.

"So what's the gossip?"

"Your Valentine card is still on the mantelpiece at Chris's flat," I said, as we started to get changed.

"Really, don't tell me surrounded by lots of other cards?"

"No it's the only one. James told me that Chris likes you." I straightened my ponytail and waited for Sarah to emerge from her cubicle. "Come on then, let's go and have some fun," I said and we walked out poolside and spotted the guys already in the water at the deep end.

James and I spent our time in the pool larking around and trying to get Sarah and Chris to talk by leaving them alone and swimming in other areas of the pool. It did seem to be working and as we walked to the burger restaurant later, I watched them taking secret glances at each other. Perhaps the cinema would help.

Beetlejuice was a fantastic film. I loved every minute of it as we shared popcorn and a drink. It was just a shame when the lights came on. As we drove home I saw Sarah was holding hands with Chris the same as I was with James. This was a definite result and I couldn't wait to talk to her after the weekend. Once James and I were home, we went straight upstairs to my bedroom and put some music on.

"So how do you think that went?" I asked.

"I think it went very well, just call me cupid." James laughed, stretching out on the bed, and I followed suit.

"So how was your interview?"

"Good I think; I'm just waiting for a letter to confirm the next stage," he said, casually stroking my arm. "Now, radio DJ? Is that even a proper job?" James asked off the cuff, smiling at me.

"A very important job, entertaining people," I retorted. "I'm hoping to get some practice in by applying for some work experience at Hereford Hospital."

What I really wished I could say was that I just wanted to be with him forever and I loved him so much, it hurt when we were apart. In the pause I crawled onto his lap and started to kiss him, my hands entwining in his hair as he lay back so that I was on top.

Sitting astride him, I was filled with a desire and longing so strong that I was brave enough to run my hands down and then unbutton his shirt so that I could feel skin on skin, running my hands over his smooth chest.

"Do you like having your nipples kissed?" I asked.

"I don't know, no one has ever tried it before," he replied, "so you will be the first."

With a smile I dipped my head and cautiously kissed his nipple and then the other before I looked up.

"Feels great," he breathed as he reached up and pulled my jumper over my head. His eyes drank in my body and his hands reached around to try and find the catch on my bra. He looked at me puzzled as the strap was smooth, and I giggled and reached up to release the front catch. As it slipped from my shoulders, his hands explored.

He worked his belt buckle free and I helped pull his jeans down, trying not to notice the bulge in his boxer shorts that literally terrified me. As he did this I wriggled out of my leggings and then I laughed out loud.

"What's so funny?" James said.

"Us in just our underwear and socks."

We took off our socks and ducked under the duvet together as our hands and tongues took turns to explore, avoiding all tickly areas. I heard my parents head up to bed as we paused but then instead of heading down to the spare room, I stayed with James. Luckily my alarm was still set for six as I struggled to leave James and head for the spare bed.

Sunday 3rd April, 1988
I was awake before James and we spent the morning lazing around. My grandparents were coming over for dinner that night and James had been drafted in as a substitute for the local six-aside football tournament with Chris. I wrapped up and went with him to watch. It was quite a game and I enjoyed gazing at James in his shorts and t-shirt. The home team won and afterwards, we went to the local pub for a drink. Some of the other guys in the team had girlfriends the same age as them. I noticed them looking at me and wondering why James was with me. He noticed I was feeling uncomfortable under their gaze and put his arm protectively around my shoulders.

We shared a portion of chips while we were there before we walked back to mine. After a shower we sat and chatted to my parents and my nan and granddad. I think James was a little nervous at meeting them but he soon settled into the conversation and answered all their questions, complimenting my nan on her hairstyle. I thought I saw her blush but she gave me a smile and I could tell she approved of my choice.

Then we excused ourselves and went to my room to listen to some music and do some more exploring. I was officially addicted to the feelings coursing through my body every time we touched. James started at my feet and after removing my shoes, he reached up and pulled off my jeans and socks. He ran his hands up my long legs and his fingers touched the lace of my knickers but as I stiffened, he continued upwards and I was able to breathe again. As his fingers took in the familiar warmth of my breasts and the tight bud of my nipples, his lips followed his hands, whilst mine entangled in his blond hair. He pulled back to look at me once more as he peeled off his clothes and my hands felt the solidness of his muscles beneath his smooth skin.

Once we were under the duvet he reached for my hand in his and then slowly took it down over his chest to the point where the waistband of his boxer shorts lay. All the while his eyes held my gaze and his lips touched mine with such longing and need that my whole being melted away.

"Will you?" he asked me, as he pushed his hands down further to remove his boxers. I was about to touch him, all of him, but I didn't know if I was brave enough.

I stroked my finger down through his curly hair to a point and hesitated.

"What do I do?" I mumbled, embarrassed by my lack of experience.

"Do whatever feels right," he breathed, his lips capturing mine.

Ever so gently I touched the whole shaft, which seemed to spring up even larger. I stroked up and down with my fingers, taking in the feel of it. All I could think was how huge it was, it was never going to fit inside me. I felt the immense power that my touch seemed to have on James as his breathing increased and his kisses became longer and deeper. I withdrew my fingers and paused for breath. Was he disappointed that I had stopped? I couldn't tell as I pushed my body tightly into his embrace.

"Not bad for a first go." He smiled at me; it was almost like he could tell what I was thinking and how nervous I was. His arms wrapped around me as we drifted off to sleep. I felt even more aware of his whole body pushed up against my back, separated by only my thin piece of fabric.

♪

Charlotte breathed out, only just aware she had been holding her breath as she read that last entry. Her mum had been scared, just like she had when she had touched Craig for the first time. He had been pushing her hard at that point and she remembered how she had pushed him away from her body and he had turned away, angry she had not been ready for anything further. What a difference having an older guy made. Or perhaps James was just a rare gentleman and her mum had been extremely lucky to have found a guy who was happy to take things at her pace and not his own?

♪

Monday 4th April, 1988
The alarm didn't need to sound this morning as I was already awake and just happy to drink in the sight of James. He stirred slightly as I trailed my fingers over his cheek and leaned down to kiss him, before I reluctantly crept back to the spare room. Without his arms around me the bed felt cold and empty, pretty much like my life when we were apart. Over breakfast we tried to decide what to spend our last few hours together doing. As it was a nice bright, spring day we decided to go for a walk along by the river. Holding hands with James as we wandered along, we talked about my impending exams and his interview (avoiding the inevitable parting that loomed like a black cloud).

Sitting on a bench we watched the swans sail by.

"I hate having to leave you all the time. I wish I still lived here."

"I do too," I agreed. "Then we could see each other every day."

"Yeah, that would be great," he replied as his finger traced a heart on the palm of my hand.

"I think I'm falling in love with you," he whispered as his arms wrapped themselves around me. Had I heard him right? I stopped breathing and my heart was pumping so fast, it was all I could hear in my ears.

"Me too," was all I could respond with before my lips touched his in a long and lingering kiss.

"Do you have a pen in your bag?" James asked as our lips parted. I found a black marker and handed it to him.

"What do you want that for?" He removed the lid and we looked at the back of the wooden bench where others before us had left their mark.

There was a blank space in the corner so James drew a heart and put our initials inside it: *JC 4 SM*. He handed me back the pen and then we kissed for a final time before we wandered back to my place. He had to be home for his shift at the pool so once he had packed his bag, in between long bouts of kissing, I found myself standing in the driveway. Alone and forlorn I watched him leave, my heart ripped from my body to follow him as he drove home.

I wandered back down to the river and sat again on the bench we had shared only a few hours earlier. It still felt warm, but probably from the sun shining down. In my heart it was raining as I leaned back and remembered his words. He was falling in love with me. I had fallen for him from the first moment he had spoken to me at the pool in January. After a last look at the heart, now dry and sealed within the bench – our bench – I hurried back home. I knew I had time to write him a letter and get it in the post box for the early morning collection at six tomorrow.

Dear James,
I am already missing you loads since you left about an hour ago, so I've decided to write to you straight away. This weekend has been amazing as is usual when we are together. After you drove off I walked back to our bench and sat there for a while and thought about what you said to me. I think I started to fall in love with you the first time that you spoke to me at the swimming pool. I could hardly believe that you even noticed me!!

This weekend has been full of firsts for me. I'm sorry if I'm not going fast enough for you? I hope you are ok waiting for me to catch up (I'm learning all the time but then you are a good teacher). Don't forget you are my first ever boyfriend. I'm sure you have had a few girlfriends (don't tell me about them otherwise I will get jealous)!!

Anyway, I can't wait to see you again as I am addicted to your kisses.
Already in love with you,
Stephanie x

I'm in bed now, writing this diary entry, inhaling the faint scent of him lingering on my pillow. I really hope it won't be too long before we see each other again.

-15-

Walking past the door of Charlotte's bedroom on Sunday, I listened to the music floating through. I had to admit that a lot of the music in the charts left me cold and Charlotte was forever teasing me when I professed not to know who certain rap artists were. I paused as Adele's 'Skyfall' came on. She had been listening to this almost non-stop since she returned from the dance competition because it was the music for the new dance they were practising for the final. If they were lucky to be the top two chosen acts, then the grand final was a weekend affair in London and I was hoping for some time away in the capital.

"Charlie, are you hungry yet?" I turned the doorknob and pulled it open, watching silently as the last few chords faded and my daughter sank down on the floor in the perfect splits.

"Does it look ok?" she asked, through her gasps.

"Well from the last few moments that I saw, it looks fabulous. You'll be on *Strictly Come Dancing* before long," I teased.

"Mum, that's totally different dancing to this," she retorted and I threw her the towel that was draped over the end of her bed.

She rubbed sweat away from her face and tucked a few tendrils of hair back over her ear. I saw my diary still on the bedside cabinet and had to admit she looked even more like me after recently colouring her hair red.

"Come down when you're ready and we'll see what's in the cupboard."

"Sure," she replied as I spotted her reach for her phone, a smile spreading over her face.

"Julia?" I asked.

"No Mum, a guy I met at the dance competition... don't worry we are just texting and friends on Facebook." I watched a slight blush spread up her neck. I had learned when to push and when to just wait for her to tell me and this was a waiting moment. At least she was no longer upset about Craig. I hoped my diary was teaching her to wait for the right guy and the right moment because that was what really mattered.

The next morning Charlotte raced out of the house to meet Julia. As I was not due to be at work until lunchtime, I found myself sneaking into Charlie's room so that I could reclaim my diaries for another trip down memory lane. I scanned through a couple of weeks as it appeared I was in the midst of revision and the entries were short, each ending with sentiments about missing James. I stopped and pulled out some of the letters that were still stuck between the pages of the diary. James' handwriting was distinctive as I smiled at all the strange things we used to talk about on paper. It was strange to think how different things might have been if we had mobile phones like my daughter did now. In some ways this would have been great, but looking at the faded and torn pages of the letters meant so much more than text on a small screen.

After all, if that had been the case the messages would have long since been deleted, lost forever. I held one letter up to my nose as I remembered James used to spray them with aftershave after I had sent my letters sprayed with perfume. Perhaps I imagined that I could still smell the faint scent of him and with it, my memories. Then I found the next dates when I had been lucky enough to escape for a long weekend with James. As I started to read I realised it was the weekend when his parents had gone away, so I carried the diary and retired to my favourite rocking chair.

Dear Diary,

Friday 29th April, 1988
We were spending another weekend at his parent's house but the most exciting part of this was that his parents were not going to be there so it would just be the two of us, alone. The weather turned warm so I packed some of my mini skirts and dresses to allow my legs to see some sunshine. Also I knew that James loved my legs, every single inch of them. He told me so the last time we were together, as he snaked a trail of kisses up and down them. I blushed just remembering those sensations, hoping for more to come.

Hearing his car pull onto the drive I waited in my room, knowing Mum would shout and then tell James to head on up. It was always going to be a much better hello kiss when my parents were not in sight. I listened to his steps taking forever on the stairs, then the door opened and a furry face appeared followed by James.

"I bought you a cuddly present for when I'm not here," he said, and I took the pink elephant. This one had a flower saying 'I'm Yours'. Then I was in his arms before I could even say thank you, showering him with enthusiastic kisses.

Following him back downstairs James carried my bag.

"Would you like a coffee?" Mum asked as we entered the kitchen, on our way to the car.

"Thanks but I think we'll get going," James said.

"Ok have a good weekend and give my regards to Pam and Peter."

I nodded and tried not to blush and give away the fact that they were not going to be there.

"Bye Mrs. M., see you on Sunday evening," James said.

Driving off, I started to laugh. "You don't think she's guessed?"

"Well, you do need to learn to control your blushing," James said. He reached across and squeezed my knee.

As the music played in the car, we sang along, talked some more and took it in turns to stroke each other's legs or just hold hands. When we arrived in his driveway I felt suddenly nervous. James hurried round to open my car door and my nerves dispersed as I knew that I was with the man I loved. The house felt quiet with just the two of us but once I had dropped my bag in the hall, we walked into the kitchen. I hopped up onto the worktop whilst we waited for the kettle to boil. My blood reached boiling point far quicker than the kettle as James took my head in his hands and fitting his body between my dangling legs. We kissed long, hard and deep.

He lifted me up and carried me into the lounge where we settled on the sofa, drinks forgotten in the heat of our embrace.

"I love this skirt," he said, as it rode up my legs revealing more and more skin. I sat astride him and his fingers trailed their way up and down my smooth skin. The hours ticked by as we rediscovered each other. However my stomach soon started to growl with hunger of a different kind.

"Shall we order takeaway?" James asked.

"Yes, please," I sighed as we managed to pull our lips away from each other's.

As James grabbed the phone to order, I went upstairs and placed my bag in James' room. I loved that he had cleaned his room as it smelt of polish more than of him and I noticed he had a copy of *Top Gun* on video, lying on the shelf. I picked it up and returned to the lounge.

"Can we watch this?"

James smiled and grabbed it from my hands.

"Yes, so long as you don't drool over Tom all night."

"Deal," I replied. "Anyway, I don't want to let you out of my sight now that we are together."

The pizza arrived and we settled onto the sofa and watched the film together for the first time. It was his favourite film and fast becoming mine. When the love scene started and the familiar lilting melody of 'Take My Breath Away' began, I looked at James just as he glanced over at me.

"Shall we?" he asked as he pulled me into his arms. The rest of the film played on in the background as we kissed and then let our hands wander. Firstly over our clothes but then as the intensity increased, my top was on the floor, followed shortly by my bra and James' t-shirt and jeans, lastly my skirt which hadn't been covering much anyway.

Then feeling incredibly confident, I pulled away and leapt off the sofa.

"Come and catch me." I giggled as I quickly ran through the door and upstairs. I only just made it to his room before he grabbed me from behind and started tickling me like crazy, pinning me down on his bed, the tickles becoming caresses. We disappeared underneath the duvet and continued to explore. I took the initiative and removed his boxer shorts so that I could stroke him again. I was so caught up in the moment that I almost didn't feel his fingers as they ran over the lace of my knickers.

"Can I?" he asked, cautious. Oh my god, half of me wanted to say yes but the other half was terrified. "It's ok if you don't want me to," James breathed, running his hands through my hair.

"I'm sorry, I'm letting you down," I mumbled as tears started to fall down my cheeks. I tried to turn away from him, but he wiped the tears away and kissed me so that I soon forgot.

"I love you Stephanie and I will wait for as long as it takes."

"I love you too, James and I want to experience this with you but I'm scared as I've never done this before. What if I disappoint you?"

"Believe me, you could never disappoint me."

Happy again, I relaxed back into his embrace and as it was late, we fell asleep, curled up together.

Saturday 30th April, 1988
The sun shining through the window woke us and after a few good morning kisses, James hopped out of bed. Wrapped in his dressing gown, he went and made us some coffee and toast. While he was gone I took the chance to have a better look around his room and when he came back in, he was greeted by the sight of me, kneeling up on his bed looking at all his albums lined up on the shelf.

"Any you want to hear?" he asked, putting the tray down.

"Lots, I want to know everything about you."

"Everything?" He arched his eyebrows, a grin spreading across his face. I loved this man so much it hurt and he had told me that he loved me last night for the very first time. It was such a special moment. I turned to fall into his awaiting arms again, knowing this was where I belonged.

After a very pleasurable morning in bed, I pulled away from him and went for a shower. As the warm water played over my skin it felt like heaven as I had the chance to replay the events of last night in my mind. Had I been wrong to deny him? Even though he had said it was ok and that he would wait, where would I find the courage from to take the next step? Lost in my thoughts I didn't hear the bathroom door open until a draught of cold air hit my skin and I turned to find James standing there, completely naked and holding a sponge.

"Thought I would wash your back for you." He grinned, stepping under the water.

I loved the feel of his fingers on my wet skin as he poured shower gel onto my back and slowly rubbed it in, the sponge forgotten on the floor. It felt heavenly as I languished under his expert touch, letting his hands wander down my back and over my bum, then my legs, slowly climbing back up. Turning around I offered to do the same for him and after a quick kiss, he turned away from me and I got to work with the shower gel, my hands marvelling over his taut muscles. I still could not believe that this gorgeous man was with me and I loved it. When I had finished he turned around and poured some more gel into the palm of his hand.

"I'll do your front now." Slowly, he massaged my shoulders first and then my breasts.

His hands ran down my stomach and I shut my eyes, trying to control my slightly panicky breathing as he knelt down and ran them over my legs and slowly back up. He was seeing all of me for the first time and I heard his breath shorten as his hands steadied themselves on my upper thighs. When we heard the phone ringing, this seemed to break the spell as James ran downstairs to answer it.

I breathed out slowly and turned the shower off, so that by the time James had returned, I was already wrapped in a towel.

"Who was it?"

"Felicity asking if I could work this evening... I told her no." He reached for me and I entered the circle of his arms.

"Have I told you how beautiful you are recently?" he murmured.

"Yes, but you can tell me again if you like," I sighed, his lips meeting mine again.

We spent the day shopping in nearby Warwick and I bought him some more shower gel as we had almost emptied the bottle that morning. I didn't notice that James had picked up a bottle of baby oil until he dropped it into my bag.

"What's that for?"

"Later."

We went to the supermarket because James was going to cook for me when we got back – spaghetti Bolognese, along with a bottle of wine.

"Are you trying to get me drunk later?" I giggled, holding hands at the checkout. I could see the girl serving us was impressed by James. I couldn't help the smug smile that crept over my face.

Back at home I helped in the kitchen before going upstairs to get changed. I had a new lilac dress and it was quite short and very figure hugging. I wanted to see what James thought of it. I piled my hair up in a loose ponytail and applied a slick of lipstick, which was hardly on for two seconds as I entered the dining room and James took in the effort I had made for him.

"We're not going out with you in that outfit. I would never stop all the other guys staring at you!" he said, planting kisses on the back of my neck.

The food was lovely, the wine made me dizzy and the company was superb. When we finished James grabbed my hand and we disappeared upstairs.

"I am going to give you a massage this evening," he declared, pulling me close. I abandoned myself to his kisses as he removed my clothes and I caught his smile when he noticed my underwear was the set he had bought me for my birthday (soon discarded). I lay on the bed face down so he could do my back first, closing my eyes. I had never had a massage before so I couldn't comment as to whether it was good or not – all I knew was that I felt relaxed and aroused at the same time.

"Turn over," he commanded. As the room was lit by a small, bedside lamp I breathed in and turned over, allowing James access to the whole of my body. I was naked under his gaze, totally aware of the blush spreading all over my skin.

"Close your eyes if it helps," he whispered, his lips kissing my forehead. "Just say stop at any moment, you know I won't mind."

He tipped more oil onto my skin. I was on fire, trembling and breathless under his touch, his fingers sliding everywhere. I didn't care, I was his, he was mine. I was falling, drowning, floating – words could not begin to describe it. This felt better than any of the books I had read or any of the films I had seen. My mind rested on the lyrics from my favourite George Michael song, 'Father Figure'.

"What are you smiling at in that strange way?"

"I've been singing 'Father Figure' in my head."

"Shall I put it on the stereo?"

"Yes, please," I replied, suddenly shy beneath his gaze, quickly pulling the duvet over me. He reached for his copy of 'Faith' and placed the needle over the second track as the melody in my head filled the room.

Cuddling up to me we listened in silence, but I could see a slow smile spreading over James' lips as he said in time with the song, *"I will be the one who loves you till the end of time."* It was a perfect moment, the best of my whole life in fact.

♪

My older self wiped tears away that were shamelessly falling down my cheeks. What had happened to the end of time? Our love affair had finished far too early and I could never move on. I was trapped again in that exquisite moment, knowing about the joys that were to come further in the diary, followed by the horrific aftermath that had changed my life forever.

-16-

It was the weekend of the Midland dance finals and Charlotte was a bundle of nerves as Stephanie helped her gather her outfit together so that she wouldn't miss the bus.

"I shall keep my fingers crossed for you," Steph said before Charlie went to catch up with Julia and get their seats on the bus.

"God I am so excited," Charlotte said in a breathy voice, sitting down next to Julia.

"Mitchell?" Julia replied.

"Yes, I've already texted him today saying I am looking forward to seeing him again at the competition."

"You have got it bad," Julia laughed, watching Charlie get her mirror out of her bag and check her make-up. "You look fine."

"Fine's not good enough, I want to bowl him over the first moment he sees me," Charlie replied, smiling back at her reflection.

The bus journey seemed to drag but soon they were outside the grandeur of the LG Arena. There seemed to be a heightened level of excitement and nerves buzzing around the whole place. This time they had to perform two dances, a repeat of their winning dance from the heats followed in the afternoon by their new dance. As Charlotte wandered around with Julia, she was suddenly startled to hear her name being called.

"Charlie… Charlie?" She turned to see Mitchell running down the corridor.

"Mitch," she replied out of breath, feeling a blush spread over her face, desperately hoping he wouldn't notice it.

He stopped in front of the two of them and there was an awkward silence.

"I'll go get us a bottle of water?" Julia said. "Nice to meet you again."

"How are you?" they both said at almost the same time. They laughed and looked away. Charlotte was shaking with nerves.

"Fine, bit nervous though," Mitch said as they walked along towards the café area.

"Me too," responded Charlotte. "Thanks for sending me the clip of my dance, it looked great."

"You are one hell of a dancer."

"You're not bad yourself," Charlie replied, too shy to notice he was looking back at her.

"What are you dancing to later?"

"'Skyfall'. So you had better be warned, I have a gun and am armed for most of the routine."

"Cool... I'll try not to get shaken or stirred," he laughed, using the famous punch line.

"Well, I had better go," Charlotte said, seeing Julia beckoning for her.

"Yes, me too, shall we met up at lunchtime?"

"Yes, I'd like that," Charlotte replied.

"I'll bring my mate, he says he fancies your mate Julia so it would be a shame not to introduce them." He laughed and before she knew it, he leaned down and dropped a light kiss on her cheek, adding, "Catch you later."

"Later," Charlotte said in a husky voice, revelling in the feel of his lips on her hot skin.

The morning flew by and as Charlotte and Julia hurried to the canteen, they could hardly contain their excitement at meeting the two guys. The lunch hour was too short because they all needed to get back for the second part of the competition. The guys were the first onstage and this time Charlotte remembered to record their routine on her phone. It was breathtaking to watch Mitchell move across the floor or fly through the air in a series of somersaults. Then it was their turn and as they walked towards the stage, she saw Mitch raise his hand to her. She smiled and aimed her fake gun at him, making Mitch laugh at the gesture.

When Charlotte dropped into the splits at the end of their routine, all she could hear was a wave of applause hitting the stage as she remained still for a few seconds to gather her breath. They had absolutely stormed it; all they needed now was for the judges to put them in the top two. Who would go through to the London final and get to compete against the rest of the country? All she hoped was that Mitchell and his friends would be the other team, then it would be perfect. After a break to freshen up, the groups all assembled for the decision to be made. Charlotte almost failed to hear their name being called over the beating of her heart in her chest. They had made it and so had Mitchell's group! It was fate, it was destiny and now she had a weekend in London to look forward to, as well as countless more texts and messages.

As they started to gather up their bags for the journey home, Charlotte found Mitchell and wandered over to him.

"I can't believe we both made it," she said, looking up into his green eyes.

"Fantastic," he replied. "You looked amazing up there, I loved the outfit."

"You too! How do you get so high in the air with your somersaults?"

"I learnt at the swimming pool. Dad was a good diver and he taught me, then I just transferred it to dry land. What about you?"

"Ballet and gymnastics when I was younger. Mum let me do whatever I wanted. I think she knows it has paid off. She will be well pleased to hear she can spend a weekend in London for the finals."

"Yes, I think my dad is going to come and watch. I don't see my mum much; my parents split up when I was two and Mum didn't want to look after me so it's just been me, Dad and my older brother, Darren."

"Yes, I saw your brother's name on your Facebook."

"I showed him your picture, he thinks you look nice... I think you look gorgeous, especially with your new red hair."

"Thanks, you're pretty fit yourself," Charlie replied. "I hope we can stay in touch between now and the final?"

"Yes, perhaps your mum might let you meet me sometime, maybe for a wander around the Bullring shopping centre?"

"Is that a date?"

"Yeah, I really like you Charlie and want to spend some more time getting to know you if it's ok?"

Breathing slowly Charlotte could hardly believe the way this conversation was going. He liked her enough to want to spend some more time with her and she just hoped her mum would say yes.

"Yes, I'd love to," Charlie replied in a daze. "I'll ask my mum when I get home and drop you a text later this evening so we can arrange a date."

There was a pause and before she could say anything else, he caught her hand in his and pulled her into his arms.

"You definitely stirred me earlier," he murmured into her ear. Ever so slowly his lips came down to hers and they kissed, a kiss so seductive and sensual that Charlotte could feel her legs trembling.

"Don't forget my text later," he said as he pulled away, starting back towards his rehearsal room.

"I won't," Charlotte replied, unable to move as she watched him walk away.

She now knew exactly how her mum had felt when James had walked away – a pull, a longing in her heart for more. Would there be more? She really hoped so. He turned and waved just before she had chance to move. She waved back and smiled as she turned and ran back to where Julia was waiting for her. Today was the best day of her life so far. Craig just a long-distant memory, she relived the feel of being in Mitch's arms and his kiss on her lips. What a kiss! On the way home she thought of the way Mitchell made her feel.

As the coach pulled in she saw her mum waiting and quickly raced over to tell her the good news – they were through to the finals!

Over Chinese takeaway later, Charlie was waiting for the best moment to say something.
"What's eating you?" Steph asked.
"Can I go shopping in Birmingham for the day?"
"With Julia?"
"Well, not exactly, but Julia can come if you would rather I didn't go on my own," Charlie blurted out, a blush rising up her neck.
"Go on..."
"Mum, I met a guy at the last dance competition and I met him again today and he's going to be at the finals and he asked if I would like to go on a date with him as long as it is ok with you?" she said, hardly stopping for breath.
"Well, perhaps if Sarah and I decide we would like a day out in Birmingham then you can go, so long as I can meet him at the same time?"
"Uh... ok, but you'll have to be cool. I don't want you or Aunt Sarah to embarrass me in front of him."
"Would we?" Steph laughed.
"Yes, you know you would," Charlie laughed, relieved her secret had been sprung and a positive outcome reached.
"What's his name?"
"Mitchell, or Mitch for short. Mum he's gorgeous," Charlie sighed.
"How old?"
"I think he's twenty... this is what he looks like," she said, pushing her phone across the table, "he's the one that does all the somersaults."
Steph watched the video with admiration, mesmerised by the wonderful dance routine that unfolded.
"Fantastic dancer," Steph replied, handing the phone back to her daughter. "I can see why you fancy him."
"Mum!" Charlie blushed and disappeared up to her room to let Mitchell know they could meet, so long as he didn't mind meeting her mother at the same time.
Inside, Charlotte danced with joy. She was going to see Mitch again and hoped the fact her mum would be there when they arrived would not put him off. What would she wear? What would they talk about all day? Would he still like her at the end of the day? So much to think about, she stretched out on the bed and after sending Mitch a text, she settled down to more of her mum's diaries. She wanted to know how long they waited before sex and who made the first move? Was sex as wonderful as she imagined it to be when you were deeply in love with someone?

-17-

Dear Diary,

Sunday 1st May, 1988
Waking up early I decided to surprise James and make him breakfast in bed. I pulled on my knickers and James' discarded t-shirt from the night before, padding down to the kitchen. Once the coffee and toast were ready I decided to finish the washing up from our meal last night. I washed up imagining this was our house, wondering if living with James would be as magical as the times we had already spent together.

I was so engrossed in my daydream about the future, I didn't hear James creep up behind me. When his arms wrapped around me, I jumped a mile.

"You scared me!" I laughed and turned, trying not to drip water or bubbles on the floor, leaning in for a welcome kiss.

"You look lovely in my t-shirt."

"What, even with my hands covered in soap suds?"

"Definitely," he murmured as his hands wandered down to the hem of the t-shirt and then disappeared beneath it. I was helpless as I couldn't reach the nearest towel, so instead I placed my hands on James' bare back, this time making him jump as water droplets ran down his spine.

"You are wicked," he whispered. "I think I need to take you upstairs."

Then before I could say another word, he hoisted me over his shoulder in the traditional fireman's lift and I was back in his bed, where we spent an enjoyable couple of hours enjoying each other's company and bodies. For once, I took the lead and removed his boxer shorts.

"Show me how to make you come," I asked, blushing.

"Even better, I will help you do it," he replied. "Are you sure about this?"

"Not really but sort of, if that makes any sense?"

"No," he laughed and then before I could say anything more, he started to kiss me as we lay down together and he slowly moved my hand in his.

Reaching over he grabbed the bottle of baby oil from the night before and dropped some onto my palm.

"You might need this," he said in a breathy voice, guiding my hand down. Then with his hand, he wrapped my hand around him, and we started a slow, sweeping up and down motion.

As I did this we continued to kiss as his free hand moved up and into my hair, gently pulling me closer and tighter into his embrace, the rhythm getting faster and faster before he shuddered.

"Stephanie," he whispered in my ear as he went still in my embrace.

After a few minutes he reached for some tissues before lying back in my embrace.

"That was beautiful," he murmured, kissing me slowly.

"Are you sure?"

"Absolutely. But I'm a bit hungry now and could do with a shower. Care to join me?"

"I would love to."

After another dreamy session of bubbles in the shower, we reached the kitchen, where we had started.

"It's a bit late for toast now, how about fish finger sandwiches?"

"Sounds great, I've never had one of those before," I replied. "Shall I butter the bread then?"

As we got on with the task in hand I caught myself glancing at James and felt his stare on me. This felt so right, it was amazing.

"There's a fun fair on and a band playing later in the park if you fancy going?" James asked.

"Sounds great."

"Some of the guys are going from work so I said we would meet them there."

"But what shall we do between now and then?" I asked.

"Well, I could help you with your revision if you want?"

Later on we walked over to the park which was buzzing with people and the sounds and sights of the fairground rides and games. We headed for the waltzers first. I loved being spun around at high speed, feeling James' arm around me as we laughed out loud. James drove me around on the dodgems and then I drove him around as he covered his eyes at my appalling driving skills.

Feeling hungry, we ate hotdogs piled high with onions, mustard and sauce, also sharing a bottle of beer.

We wandered towards the stage area as the band started to warm up and James saw Ian and another guy called Sean from work, so we went over to where they were standing.

"Do you want any popcorn?" I asked, craving some sweetness.

"Yes, sounds good… want me to come with you?"

"No it's fine."

Turning around from the stand with my box of popcorn, I almost bumped into the back of a dark-haired woman.

"Hi Felicity."

"Hi… um, what's your name again?"

"Steph, I'm James' girlfriend."

"Oh yes, how could I forget? Can't understand what James sees in a girl like you… he really needs a woman in his life."

I stared at her open-mouthed, wondering what I should say back, but she continued, "I see James almost every day and when he's not poolside, he's in the gym working out like a maniac, which is normally a sign of sexual frustration. Oh but you wouldn't know anything about that I guess, at your age."

"James loves me, he told me," I retorted, my face red with rage and upset at her remarks.

"Well, we'll see about that. I should keep a close eye on him if I were you. He's a good-looking guy and there are a lot of distractions at the pool." She flicked her hair and strolled off.

I took a few steps and found a park bench to sit down on, tears springing to my eyes. I held them back but I couldn't help but worry about what she said and what those words implied. After all, I had seen the way she looked at me the first time we met. Composing myself, I was determined to put this behind me because she was obviously just jealous of what James and I shared. I was soon stood back next to him and with his arms around me, we enjoyed the music as I tried to forget the words swimming round in my head, bringing doubts and fears with them.

After the music finished, we walked back home for our last night together. I tried not to let my run-in with Felicity spoil those precious moments we had left. In bed later I told James what had happened with Felicity. I could tell he was angry I hadn't told him earlier but in the end, he said the words that more than made up for it:

"It's you I am with, you are my girlfriend and you are the one I love."

Then he pulled me into his arms and kissed me with such tenderness and longing, I almost cried with joy.

Monday 2nd May, 1988
As our last morning together dawned, I reached for James as soon as I was awake and started to kiss him with a passion and fierceness I had never felt before, determined to dispel those last few nagging doubts that Felicity had placed in my mind. I trailed my hands down his chest and felt his hardness spring up under my touch. Then feeling very brave indeed, I let my mouth follow and decided that I would approach my first ever blowjob without fear. I gently ran my tongue down his length and then up again gently to the tip. I did the same thing again as I felt James stroking my hair in a way that told me to continue.

Tentatively I opened my mouth and took the whole of the tip in and swirled my tongue over it, testing and tasting the whole of him. I heard

James groan and push slightly on my head so I took more in and then almost choked myself as it hit the back of my throat. This was going to need more practise, I thought, as I came up from under the duvet and replaced my tongue with my hand, remembering the way I had done this yesterday. James kissed me, his eyes hooked onto mine in a gaze that was hard to fathom; I thought it was the look of love – pure and good and true.

Then he shuddered and sighed as he came in my hand. I felt good, I felt naughty, I felt powerful and at the same time scared of the impact I had on James – more importantly, that he had on me.

"That was amazing," he caught his breath, "I want to do the same for you, show me how."

Oh my god, I had only ever had orgasms in the shower so how was I going to show James how to do this with his fingers?

"I don't know how," I mumbled, so embarrassed by my omission. "I have never done it with my fingers, only with the showerhead jet."

"Ok then, shower it is and you can show me there."

"I'll try," I said, so shy and nervous he must have felt me tremble in his arms.

Under the warming jets of the shower we spent ages kissing and stroking each other, before James took the showerhead off its hook and placed my hand with his onto it.

"I can't," I whispered, turning away from him.

"Ok," he responded as he turned me around towards him again, "I can wait as long as it takes because I love you."

"I love you."

Arriving back home, I didn't want to get out of the car but James had to get back for his afternoon shift. He carried my bag back upstairs and we shared one last, long, lingering kiss as he held me tight in his arms. How I was going to miss the feel of them! It was as though he could read my mind.

"I'll miss you and will be back down to see you as soon as I have a free weekend, so long as it doesn't clash with your exam dates."

I nodded, unable to speak, choking back the sobs forming at his imminent departure.

"I love you," I said into his chest, where my head was resting.

"I love you too, Stephanie."

I walked with him back to his car and watched as his tail lights disappeared from view, his car turning the corner at the end of the road. I ran back to my room and threw myself on the bed, crying until my eyes were red and sore.

-18-

Charlotte put the diary aside and checked Facebook, downloading her clip from the dance finals for Mitch to see. It was a lovely surprise to see a message already waiting for her from him, along with a clip of their dance routine to 'Skyfall' and the comment *nice legs*. She responded with a comment on his routine saying *nice ass* and a smiley face. Almost immediately a response came back asking if she could talk if he gave her a call. Lying back against her pillows, Charlotte took a deep breath and then typed *yes*, waiting for her phone to ring to hear his deep voice.

"Hi Charlie."

"Mitch."

"So, did you get chance to speak to your mum yet?"

"Yes she said yes, but she is going to come up to Birmingham for the day with my Aunt Sarah... she says she wants to meet you."

"Ok, I can go with that," he replied. "If it means I get to spend the rest of the day alone with you."

"Yes... my mum is cool. I've told her not to embarrass me when she meets you."

"Well, if she is half as nice as you, it won't be too bad. Does she work?"

"Yeah, she's a DJ for a local radio station."

"Wow, that's cool."

"Yeah... cool if you like old music," Charlotte replied, laughing and settling into the conversation, like she had known Mitch for a lot longer than a few weeks. He was easy to talk to and listened instead of just talking about himself.

"What about your dad?"

"He died when I was three months old, so I never really knew him."

"Oh, that's awful, so no step dad then?"

"No, my mum hasn't even been on a date as far as I can remember. I think she misses my dad. He was a doctor and he got stabbed in the car park at the end of his shift... drug addict or something. It must have been awful for her."

"Gosh, that's one hell of a thing to have to go through. I know my dad comes home from work sometimes and can hardly speak after some of the fires he has attended. He's a fireman."

"That's a cool job," Charlotte replied.

"So how about next weekend?" Mitch said.

"I'll ask Mum later and drop you a text if that's ok?"

"Sure, hope it will be, as I can't wait to see you again. You looked fine in those tight dance pants you wore for 'Skyfall'."

It was a good job Mitch couldn't see the blush spreading over her cheeks.

"Thanks," she mumbled, suddenly shy at the compliment.

"I've gotta go now but will look forward to your text later. I really hope we can get together."

"Catch you later then, Mitch."

She couldn't believe the grin spreading over her face. He was so nice and gorgeous and seemed to think she was too. Today had been a very good day.

Luckily her mum had already spoken to Aunt Sarah, so by the time Charlotte went to bed, she was able to tell Mitch they were all set.

Monday dawned and Charlotte couldn't wait to tell Julia about her weekend, the phone call from Mitch and the date.

♬

When Charlotte returned home that evening, she rushed through the house like a whirlwind.

"What's wrong?" I asked.

"We need to find a song from the Eighties to dance to! The stipulation for the grand finals in London is that on the Saturday we dance our two previous dances and then on Sunday, we dance the new one. To make it easier for the judges we all have to choose music from the Eighties so, any chance we can go through your music?"

"Yes, I'm sure I can help you with this."

"My dance teacher thought you might be able to come up with a couple of suggestions that I can take along with me to practice on Thursday?"

"Well, we had better get started," I said. "Do you want something fast or slow?" We both sat cross-legged on the floor in front of the record collection.

"Slow is better for us but I don't really mind."

Eventually we had a choice of four different songs, 'Hunting High and Low' by A-Ha, 'Billie Jean' by Michael Jackson, 'I Wanna Dance with Somebody' by Whitney Houston and 'Take My Breath Away' by Berlin. Strangely out of the four songs, Charlie liked 'Take My Breath Away' the most. She looked up the video on YouTube and I could see Charlie was taken in by the strong images of the woman with her singed, black-tipped hair, standing on the broken fuselage of the plane.

"This song is from that film you and James liked?"

"Yes, it is, it still reminds me of our time together."

"You really loved him didn't you Mum?"

"Yes, you never forget your first love. He will always have a special place in my heart."

"Do you have a copy of the film? I'd like to watch it with you," Charlie asked.

"Yes, I think so," I replied. "But I'll have to go and look for it."

"Ok Mum, I'll go put some popcorn in the microwave then."

When Charlie returned, I placed the DVD in the machine and we settled back. Charlie stretched out on the sofa and I took the armchair. As the film started and the planes streaked across the screen, Charlotte was soon sucked into the story of Maverick and Goose.

"Mum, did you name me after Charlie on the film?"

"Yes."

As the love scene between Charlie and Maverick filled the screen, I had to excuse myself from the room and went to the kitchen to make drinks – unable to process the jumbled memories it evoked.

The credits rolled at the end and Charlotte decided, "Great film. I think our group should choose that song. I think we can come up with something spectacular."

"Well, I will look forward to the final even more if you do this song, it would make me so proud."

Charlie walked to me, giving me a hug. "Do you miss Dad?"

"Yes, he would have been so proud of you, you were his princess."

"I wish I had known him," she sniffed, wiping tears from her eyes, partly from the film but I guessed, also partly from not knowing or having a father in her life.

"He would have been a fantastic dad," I assured her, handing Charlie a tissue and also wiping my own eyes, the emotions of the evening almost too much for us to handle.

As we both went up to bed, Charlotte turned to me.

"Thanks Mum."

"What for?"

"Everything, you're the best."

"Night, sweetheart."

-19-

Dear Diary,

Friday 1st July, 1988
At last my exams were over and I could breathe a sigh of relief and just wait for the results. Still, I had more pressing things to worry about. James was coming down and taking me to our end of year dance. It had taken me weeks to find the perfect dress. I had been to the hairdresser's for the occasion and my hair was piled high on my head, curled to perfection, tendrils escaping down my cheeks. I just had my make-up to do and my dress to put on before James came to collect me. He had been working today so was just able to get away in time to drive down and pick me up before the dance.

Sarah was just as excited as me. She had been dating Chris since our weekend together in April and they made such a cute couple. I had even bought new underwear as the dress was strapless; a black satin strapless bra, French knickers, suspender belt and stockings. I couldn't wait for James to see the whole ensemble later when he undressed me. Tonight was going to be the night and I couldn't wait to feel that magical feeling as our two bodies became one.

I was so caught up in my daydreams, I never heard his car pull into the drive and was startled as James walked in and quickly drew breath.

"Wow, you look amazing." He crossed the room and paused to take all of me in. Then I walked into his arms and we kissed so much that when I drew away, I couldn't help but laugh at my lipstick on his lips.

"Is your bag ready?"

I nodded. After the ball, we were driving back to his parents for a whole week.

At the bottom of the stairs my parents were waiting, Dad with his camera poised.

"I have to get a photograph of you looking so beautiful," he said. "My little girl looks all grown up tonight."

James stood aside as my dad snapped away.

"Can you take one of us together?" I asked. He nodded as James came and joined me, putting his arm around my waist. He looked so gorgeous in his suit and tie, he literally took my breath away that evening. Once we picked up Sarah and Chris, we arrived at the hotel where the dance was being held. I felt so smug when we all entered the room and quite a few heads swivelled to stare at us.

After getting drinks, we got on the dance floor. I had never seen

James move before but he was good, then later in the evening they started on the slow songs and the lights were dimmed. The lilting melody of 'Take My Breath Away' came through the speakers with a dedication.

"To the most beautiful girl in the world, you know who you are."

I stared up at James and he grinned down at me.

"It's for you, baby," he said as he took me in his arms and we moved slowly to the rhythm, feeling as if we were the only two people in the world.

As it was getting late we said goodbye to Sarah and Chris. Once in the car James turned to me and said, "We're not going to my parent's place, we are going somewhere special instead."

"Where?"

"It's a surprise."

I must have drifted off as the sudden stop of the car woke me up and I saw we were outside a large hotel.

"Wow. This looks posh."

"You deserve it," James replied and helped me out of the car, travelling up the steps to the door. Once James had signed us in, we headed for our room. Opening the door I wandered in and once again, I was speechless.

"This looks lovely, I bet it was expensive."

"Well, we have lots to celebrate but as it's late, I'll explain in the morning," he said as he put our bags down and looked at the large four-poster bed.

"I think you are wearing far too many clothes for the occasion," he murmured and I was back in his arms. Slowly he untied my dress at the back and then as it fell to the floor, he drew in breath once more as he removed the petticoat and drank in the sight of my new underwear.

"You look amazing," he said, as I grabbed his tie and pulled him close.

Before I knew it we were lying on the bed and I was naked in his arms, his lips travelling down my body. They didn't stop as they passed my belly button and soon, he was kissing me in a place where he had never kissed me before. I gasped at the sensations rising through my body; this was much better than the shower head. Then he kissed back up my body to capture my lips in his.

"Are you ready?" he whispered in my ear.

"Yes," I murmured as he moved over me and slipped a condom on.

I arched my body beneath him as he slowly pushed into me for the very first time. I caught my breath, pain shooting through me. I didn't let it show as James continued to kiss me and slowly move inside of me, the pressure building. Then I felt him shudder and slow as he held me close. Where were the fireworks? The symphony of music that many books had led me to believe would happen at this very moment? Perhaps I had done it wrong?

James pulled me into his arms and kissed me again.

"That was wonderful baby, I love you," he sighed.

"I love you too," I replied, hoping he wouldn't catch the slight tinge of disappointment in my voice – but he was too sharp not to notice and he leaned up.

"Are you ok? Did I hurt you?"

"No, it was fine but where were the fireworks I read about?" I asked, trying to sound sensitive.

"I think the first time is always like that, I know mine was," he replied, "but then I wasn't with a girl I loved as much as I love you."

"Will it get better?"

"Yes, I will make sure it does," James promised. He was so solemn I couldn't help but start to giggle.

"I love you James, with all my heart and soul," I said as I kissed him and then snuggled up into his awaiting arms.

"I love you too, Steph," he told me in a raspy voice, as sleep took us and we drifted away.

Saturday 2nd July, 1988

We awoke to a knock on the door. I watched as James sprang out of bed and grabbing one of the hotel robes, opened the door. It was room service with breakfast on a tray, which the waitress left on a small table next to some French doors. Rubbing my eyes I smiled at the opulence and James carried over two glasses of orange juice. After putting them on the bedside table, he slipped back into bed beside me.

"Morning baby," he murmured. I pulled him into my arms and passion overtook us. This time James took much longer kissing and caressing me so that by the time he slipped in, I was weak with longing and my whole body was on fire under his touch. We moved together, our hearts beating as one and I flew, high on this fantastic feeling of being with James.

Floating back down to earth together, we must have slept a bit more, lying sated in each other's arms. By the time we reached the breakfast tray the coffee had gone cold, but we enjoyed the croissants and orange juice as we sat at the table together in our dressing gowns, staring out at the blue sky and sea of the horizon.

"So, where are we?" I asked between mouthfuls.

"Lytham St. Anne's. It's the town just next to Blackpool."

Opening the French doors I stepped out onto the small balcony and smiled as the heat of the midday sun warmed my skin.

"It's a fabulous day, shall we hit the beach?"

James slid his arms around me and rested his chin on my head. "Sounds good to me. I'm sure I packed some towels for the beach, hope you have your bikini?"

"Yes." I turned around and on tiptoes, I reached up and kissed James again.

"If you keep doing that I don't think I'm going to leave this room," James groaned, his hands beneath my dressing gown.

"Come on." I dragged him into the bathroom and after showering together, we packed a bag and dressed for the beach.

We sauntered along the promenade until we found a secluded spot. Lying on a towel, it was a rare, hot summer's day. I thought nothing could beat this feeling, especially as we were staying until James' 21st birthday on the Tuesday, before driving home for a family meal and then a party at the weekend.

"What shall we do with our time?" I asked, looking into his blue eyes and revelling in his hot gaze and cheeky smile.

"Obviously more time in the bedroom," he laughed, a wicked gleam in his eye. "We could go clubbing in Blackpool tonight and then there is the Pleasure Beach on Sunday and a nice meal on either Sunday or Monday, what do you think?"

"That sounds like a great plan, how about a dip in the sea?"

"Race you." We both ran down to the shoreline and into the rather cold waves.

We soon warmed up again on the beach before returning to the hotel.

"How did you manage to afford all this?" I asked, cuddled up on the bed, watching a spot of television.

"Mum and Dad offered me some money for my birthday so I asked if I could have an early loan and I've spent it on us."

We were soon changed and waiting for our taxi to pick us up and take us out nightclubbing. However, we nearly didn't go out when James realised I was wearing my lilac dress, almost taking me back to bed there and then. I had never been to a nightclub before and I was overawed by the sights and sounds as we queued to get in. I gazed around me. Wow it was fantastic, and the sort of club I wanted to work in as a DJ when I finished school.

James had already told me it was the best in the area.

We danced so much and by the time the taxi arrived to collect us, I had removed my heels as my feet were hurting. When we got back to the hotel James picked me up and carried me through the door so I didn't have to put my shoes back on. Once in our room the bed beckoned and after making love again, we both slept, holding each other, our breathing in time with the beat of our hearts.

Sunday 3rd July, 1988
It was another fabulous, sunny day so we went out in the car and drove to Blackpool to enjoy its many daytime delights. It was the tower first and well worth the long climb up the stairs for the views at the top. On the way back down we took in the ballroom and watched couples gliding gracefully around the polished wooden floor, the fantastic organ rising up from below the stage. As we watched, an elderly couple saw us and persuaded us into a short, easy waltz lesson, taking each of us and going through the steps. Then they let us have a go together. It was great fun, especially when James lifted me up at the end of the song and kissed me.

After lunch of fish and chips we made our way into the bustle of the Pleasure Beach and all the rides it had in store. We loved the old-fashioned Grand National rollercoaster and got soaked on the log flume, and also in the Tunnel of Love. Candyfloss and hot dogs later we were pleased to be returning to the hotel for a rest. Pulling me into his arms, James waltzed me towards the bed and we collapsed together in a pile of arms and legs as our lips found each other and our clothes were soon discarded on the floor.

As we moved into the usual position I pulled back and looked into James' eyes. "Can I try going on top this time?" I asked, feeling slightly nervous but willing to give it a go.

"Sure," James replied as he swung me over so that I was lying on top of him.

Our hands took in the shape and feel of each other's bodies, never tiring of the wonder it all brought. Carefully I positioned myself and then lowered onto him. It felt so different and fantastic. Perched astride him, I felt powerful and sexy as hell. I shook my hair loose from its ponytail and started to move up and down, realising that this position was bringing me to my very first, real orgasm. As it hit me I shuddered in James' arms, gasped and kissed him so deeply, the rhythms moving through my body overlapped with his in a personal symphony of pleasure.

"I love you," I gasped, a huge smile breaking over my face at the feelings still coursing through my body. It was spectacular, wonderful and everything I had read and dreamed about. More than that, it was ours.

"I love you too," James grinned back at me. "You were fantastic up there."

We stayed joined together, reluctant to part after what we had shared.

That evening we wandered through the town and found an Italian restaurant. The food was excellent and I couldn't stop grinning all the way through as I remembered our earlier moment together. On the way back we stopped to watch the sunset and taking our shoes off, we walked along the beach together. I found a stick and drew a heart in the sand and inside it *SM 4 JC*, just like the heart we had left on the bench in Ross. We left it there for the world to see before the tide gently swept it away.

Monday 4th July, 1988
It was James' 21st birthday so I made sure I was awake before he was and found his present hidden at the bottom of my case.

I placed it on the bedside cabinet and snuggled back into bed and started to kiss him until he woke up and joined in.

"Happy birthday James."

"I could get used to this," James replied as we moved together, gently at first but then with more urgency until we both cried out in ecstasy. It was true that the more we made love, the better it felt.

I saw him look over at his present and card.

"Go on, open them," I implored, eager to see his reaction.

"Ok," he replied, picking up the card. He loved it, especially as I had written some words from 'Take My Breath Away' inside.

He knew they were from his favourite film because he kissed me with such longing that he did literally take my breath away. Then he opened his present to find some black silk boxer shorts and a tiny box wrapped inside them. Opening this, he pulled out a St. Christopher I had saved up for and even had engraved with the words, *JC till the end of time, SM.*

"It's perfect," he replied as I helped him with the clasp. "I will never take it off as it will be a constant reminder of you when we are apart."

I grinned at him, so full of love, I thought I would burst with all the joy and happiness that having James in my life brought.

♪

Charlotte sighed as she scanned through the next few entries. Feeling tired, she put the diary aside. This is what she longed for; to feel what her mum had felt all those years ago.

-20-

Charlotte was pleased that the weekend seemed to come round quickly. At dance practice on Thursday night, her teacher agreed they were going to be dancing to 'Take My Breath Away' for the finals in London. She showed the other girls the video for the song and they decided they would copy the tattered jumpsuit and hairstyle from the video. Julia suggested they ask the art department to do them a backdrop and for the students that did their lighting to recreate a war-torn feel.

As the sunshine shone through the window, Charlie pulled open her wardrobe and scanned through her clothes. After an hour of trying different things on, she plumped for her favourite dress and flat ballet pumps. With her hair pinned up and a minimal amount of make-up on, she appeared for breakfast, although her stomach was so full of butterflies she could hardly eat.

After picking up Aunt Sarah, they parked at Ledbury Station and then as her Mum and Sarah chatted, she texted Mitch to say she was on her way. He replied saying he would be standing outside Top Shop. As they all walked into the Bullring, Charlie felt her temperature rise and the nerves make her hands shake.

"Are you ok?" her mum asked, as they all walked towards the map to find out where Top Shop was located.

"Yes, Mum," Charlie replied, smiling nervously.

Then she spotted him and as he scanned the crowds in her direction, she waved her hand and he started to walk towards them.

"He looks lovely," Sarah said, giving her shoulder a squeeze as they got closer.

"Hi Charlie," he said, standing nervously in front of them all.

"Hi Mitch," she breathed, almost unable to get the words out with him standing so close. "This is my mum, Stephanie and my aunt, Sarah."

"What are your plans then?" he asked. "So we can arrange to meet up later?"

"How about we meet for food outside Nando's," Steph suggested. "You are more than welcome to join us if you like, Mitchell?" Steph's eyes were locked on Mitchell, wondering what it was about him that seemed so familiar.

"Thanks, that would be lovely," the youngster replied.

"Good, well look after her and we'll see you later at around five," Steph warned, watching as they walked away.

He reached out for Charlotte's hand and she took it, smiling at him.

"So what do you want to do then?" Mitch asked Charlie as they slowed and then stopped, sitting down in one of the many seating areas.

"I don't mind really," Charlie responded. "Perhaps a coffee would be nice first?" She gazed up into his green eyes, suddenly shy in his presence.

"That sounds like a plan," he replied. "By the way, you look fantastic."

"Thanks, you too."

They sat and talked for over an hour about work, school, music and of course, the dance competition.

"I know a great club, not far from here where they play music all day and we can dance," he said, "and all I really want to do is dance with you."

"Cool," Charlie replied, being swept up in his plans and feeling just a bit wicked that they were leaving the shopping centre.

They walked through the streets before turning into a small side alley and walking through a door, into a salsa club. The music was provided by a live band and after a quick drink, Mitch turned to her and said, "Can I have this dance?"

"Certainly sir, I would love to."

In the middle of the dance floor, she marvelled at the way their bodies fitted together as they moved in time with the music. She had done some salsa over the last few years and knowing that Mitch was training to be a dance teacher, it made perfect sense that he could teach her a few moves, too. This whole date was perfect. He twirled her around and they lost themselves in the rhythms of the Latin-American vibe.

All too soon, it turned four and they left the dance floor, knowing they had to be back in an hour. On their way back through the streets, she felt his arm around her shoulders and looking up into his eyes, she smiled. Before she could express how much fun she was having, his lips came down to meet hers and they kissed. Pulling her closer the intensity increased and she relaxed into his embrace, feeling as though she had known him for a lifetime.

"You are so special," he breathed into her ear when they pulled apart.

"You are too," she mirrored, wanting to say much, much more but feeling overwhelmed by the situation and the magic they had shared on the dance floor as well as with the kiss.

"Come on," he said as they ran back to the centre. "We need to buy something so it looks like we've been shopping all afternoon and not dancing."

"Don't worry, Mum won't mind if we tell her," Charlie replied.

♪

Sarah and I stood waiting outside Nando's. The young lovers were late, but I soon saw them running towards us, and decided fifteen minutes late was not too bad. I noticed the bright glow on their skin and the smiles lighting up their faces; it was lovely to see my daughter like this again.

"Hungry?" I asked as we were seated in the restaurant.

"Famished," Charlie and Mitch said in unison. They looked at each other and laughed.

"Shopping is hungry work," Mitch said, as I spotted a secret look pass between the two of them. I didn't say anything, not wanting to spoil the happy atmosphere surrounding us.

"You didn't buy much?" I replied, noticing there were no shopping bags in comparison to the stack Sarah and I had accumulated.

"Nothing I liked," Charlie said.

"Me neither," Mitch added.

They turned to each other and that secret smile flitted between them again.

Eventually it was time for us to catch the train. Sarah and I gave them space to say goodbye while we waited out of sight, round a corner of the entrance hall. Luckily, we could still hear everything they were saying.

"I had a fantastic day with you," he enthused.

"It was wonderful," she said, out of breath as he pulled her close.

"Hope we can do it again soon?"

"Yes, you can always come and visit me, although we don't have any salsa clubs in Ross-on-Wye."

"I'd like that, I'm sure we can find something other than dancing to fill the time." He leaned down and their lips were joined together again. Before they parted, he handed her a disc.

"It's got some salsa music on it; I picked it up at the club," he explained, "I hope it will remind you of today."

"Thanks, you didn't have to get me anything, just spending time and dancing with you was more than enough!"

"Same here," he grinned, looking awkward when he realised I was peering round the corner.

"Text me later," he said, "I'll be waiting."

"I will," Charlie assured him, and reluctantly pulled herself away from him, heading to us. She turned around and saw he was still watching. They waved, and he was gone.

On the train journey I noticed my daughter's dreamy, far-off look.

"So what did you do all day?" I asked.

"Well, we went to this salsa club and danced for hours. Did I tell you he's training to be a dance instructor?"

"So that's why you didn't end up with any shopping?" I laughed.

"Is he a good dancer?" Sarah butted in.

"The best," Charlie sighed. "He wants to come and visit me in Ross."

"Well I can't see any reason why not. You did tell him there are no salsa clubs here?"

"Yes, of course I did," Charlotte retorted.

"So what song from the Eighties are his group dancing to?" I asked.

"'Thriller' by Michael Jackson, he said it's great. Apparently he's never heard our song so he's going home to look it up on the internet. I might just send him it online later."

"An interesting choice as the dance in the video is so well-known, it will be good to see something completely different to it," Sarah contemplated. "Any chance I can come with Uncle Chris?"

"Yes, everyone in the group has four tickets for family so that will be three of mine filled, instead of just the one," Charlotte grinned. "I'd like you both to come."

I passed Charlie's bedroom door and caught muffled giggles so I knew she was chatting to Julia. Once I was alone in my room, I pulled out the diary I had removed from Charlie's room that morning. I knew she wouldn't miss it that night, not with thoughts of Mitch consuming her, and for some reason I needed it, to relive and remember how good first love felt and how easily it might also fall apart. I flicked forward to where I had last finished reading.

Dear Diary,

Tuesday 5th July, 1988
Waking up together for the last time in the hotel room, I didn't really want to leave as I had spent the most magical time with James. Still, it wasn't too bad as I was going back to James' house and there was going to be a party on the Saturday night. I was going to meet loads of his family which was a bit scary. We made love for a final time in the sumptuous four-poster bed and then after a shower and breakfast, we packed our bags.

On the drive back to James' place, we talked. I told James I had an interview the following week for a holiday job at the local hospital, working on their radio station. I was hoping to impress them as it would really help with my future career plans. James had also been for an initial interview with the Fire Service and was just waiting to hear if he had got to the medical and physical test stage. It felt strange discussing our futures when all I really hoped was that we had a long-term future together. I felt that now we had made love, James would no longer feel frustrated when we were not together (the words of Felicity still plaguing me).

As we pulled up in the driveway, birthday balloons and banners welcomed James home. Once inside he opened cards and presents from family and friends, including one from Chris saying that he was hoping to come up for the party and would it be ok for him to bring Sarah. I couldn't wait to see her again and tell her all that had happened since I said goodbye to her at the school dance. We had Chinese takeaway for tea and all sat round talking about the party and who was coming.

Wednesday 6th July, 1988
I still can't get to grips with James' mum waking us up with cups of

coffee in bed. I could never imagine my mum even getting to the stage of allowing me to share the same bed with James. We decided to head off to Warwick Castle that afternoon. I had always wanted to go there and since moving to the area, James had never been.

It was breathtaking looking at the castle and we enjoyed watching the re-enactments of jousting and falconry. It felt good to wander around hand in hand, making and sharing memories together. In the evening we went to the cinema as there was a new Tom Cruise film out called *Cocktail*. It was great, especially when they were making love under the waterfall and on the beach.

"I wish we could do that," I whispered.

"One day, baby."

That night as we made love, I imagined us together under a waterfall, droplets falling on our bodies, kissing our hot skin with their coolness.

Thursday 7th July, 1988
James was working the lunchtime shift at the pool so I said I would go with him. I sat on the balcony area with my book. It was taking me a long time to get through 'Riders' by Jilly Cooper, but it was a more enjoyable read now that I had experienced the high of making love. Every few minutes I looked up from the page to watch as James walked around the pool or sat in his chair. When our eyes met, his face would light up with a smile. I still couldn't quite believe he was mine.

I saw Felicity stalking around the pool to where James was standing. She looked fabulous in her tight red shorts and white t-shirt. I could see the eyes of all the men in the pool drinking her in but what really worried me was her gaze that had settled well and truly on my boyfriend. She hadn't realised that I was in the building and I watched her stand close to James. From the angle I was at, I could see everything as she leaned in to ask or tell him something. I watched as her hand moved around and down across James' bum. He flinched slightly from the touch and looked up to where I was sat, so I quickly looked back into my book, pretending I hadn't noticed what was going on down there.

Then as she walked away she squeezed his arm and for some reason, she looked up to where I was sat. Spotting me she smiled and gave me a small wave. She looked so smug and self-satisfied. I wanted to kill her there and then as jealousy bubbled inside of me. When James gave me the nod I went downstairs and emerged poolside, looking radiant in my bikini. The time on the beach had given my pale skin a sun-kissed look. I soon saw James in the water and I dived in and swam over to join him. He pulled me under the water and planted a long kiss on my lips before we surfaced.

"I will always remember that kiss," I said as we stopped for a breather on the poolside.

"Me too. I think I knew then that I wanted to spend more time with you."

"That was my first ever kiss you know," I replied. "I'll never forget it for the rest of my life."

Before I could say another word he quickly swam away. Managing to grab his ankle, I pulled him under so that I could kiss him again. I wanted him to know he was mine; I wanted to dispel any worries I had that he could possibly like or want Felicity more than me.

Saturday 9th July, 1988
The day dawned bright and sunny so we spent the morning sunbathing in the garden and relaxing before we had to go and get the venue ready for the party. I giggled at all the photographs his mum had put up around the place, of James when he was a baby and a young boy. He looked cute even then. His cake was shaped like a fire engine and looked fantastic. I watched with interest the DJ setting up his decks and equipment, even showing me how it all worked when he did the sound check.

Back at home we got ready and I definitely looked different and felt different now I had taken the step from girl to woman. Turning, I saw James looking at me from where he was sat on his bed and I gave him a twirl.

"You look wonderful," he said as I walked over to him and he held me in his arms. I reached down and placed a careful kiss on his lips so I didn't ruin my lipstick or get too much on him.

"You look gorgeous and I love you more than ever."

"I love you till the end of time," he murmured, planting small light kisses down my throat as his hands took in the curve of my waist and hips.

"Are you ready?" his dad shouted from the bottom of the stairs.

"Yes, coming now," he replied as I took his hand in mine.

"You look beautiful Stephanie," his dad said. "I may have to whisk you off for a dance later."

"Join the queue Dad," James said, giving him a playful punch on the arm.

After being introduced to all his relatives by his mum and dad, I was able to escape and join James who was catching up with Chris and Sarah.

It seemed like ages since I last saw my best friend so we grabbed a table together.

"So how has your week been?" she asked.

"Fabulous, you'll never believe it but James took me straight from the dance to a posh hotel near Blackpool and we stayed there until Tuesday morning!"

"And?"

"We made love, it was fantastic," I said, feeling a blush creep up my cheeks at even the thought of all the times we had shared in that hotel room. "What about you and Chris?"

"Well, he walked me home after the dance and we kissed loads and when he hasn't been at work, we've been spending time together. He's lovely," she replied, looking dreamily over at Chris. He noticed and gave her a smile.

After the food and the cake cutting, the party really began to rock. I was pleased to notice that Felicity (although invited) had not turned up so I was able to relax without her spectre looming over me. Then the music stopped and everyone turned to look at the DJ but he seemed to have disappeared. James tried the men's loos and found him slumped over in one of the cubicles throwing up. With some help from his dad and Chris, they managed to get him out and gave him a glass of water but he was in no fit state to continue so I went over.

"I'll play the music," I said. "John showed me earlier how the equipment works so I should be ok."

"That's great Steph, you're a lifesaver," James replied, squeezing my hand.

Walking behind the decks I took a few moments to familiarise myself with the layout and all the records I had to choose from, then I got started. It felt fantastic to be in control of a crowd as they laughed and cheered and the dance floor filled up to overflowing. At the end of the night John had sobered up enough to take back the turn tables so I slipped off the stage and into James' waiting arms for the slow songs.

Luckily I had already lined up 'Father Figure' and 'Take My Breath Away' just for the two of us. Hidden by the darkness on the dance floor, James held me close and kissed me as we moved together.

"I am so lucky to have you as my girlfriend, not just beautiful and sexy as fuck, but a cracking DJ."

Then as John lit us up with the spotlight, James swept me into a waltz and finished by lifting me up, reminding me of our time in Blackpool. All his family and friends cheered and clapped.

Chris and Sarah were staying at James' parents house so after we had all mucked in to tidy up the venue, the four of us decided to walk the short distance back, the moon bright in the sky and the night warm.

"That was one hell of a party," Chris said. "You were great on the decks."

"Thanks, I loved it," I replied, as James gently squeezed my hand in his. I noticed Sarah was quiet and realised that they would be sharing a bed for the first time and she was probably suffering from nerves. I looked over and smiled at her, mouthing, *it will be ok.*

James showed them into the spare room and then came back downstairs to allow them access to the bathroom.

I removed my shoes and was standing on the patio, gazing up at the stars.

"It's beautiful," I said in a raspy voice, as I felt his arms coil around my waist, joining me to look up into the sky.

"Not as beautiful as you." He turned me around and his lips met mine in a kiss that literally left me gasping.

"I have an idea," he said, grinning. Taking my hand in his, we wandered across the garden to where the fruit trees were.

Before I could complain, he started to undress me, my body glowing in the moonlight as I stood bold and naked before him. I unbuttoned his shirt and removed his trousers to find my silk boxer shorts which I slid down his legs.

Lying on the soft grass he trailed kisses over my body, making me shiver in delight as my body arched to meet his so we fit together. He made love to me slowly at first but then as the urgency grew, our breath became faster and faster, until we cried out each other's names at almost the same point. Our orgasms joined us together even stronger than before, as we lay in each other's arms and stared at the endless expanse of stars above.

"I would give you the world," he breathed.

"I don't need the world, just you," I replied, grinning at him before I started to gather my clothes.

Before the spell was broken James turned to me. "If you are ever lonely when we are apart, just look up at the stars and know that I will be looking up at them too." His words were so beautiful, I had to gulp back the lump forming in my throat. How had I been this lucky to find him? I truly felt as if we were soul mates at that moment in the moonlit garden together.

♪

I reached for the tissues on my bedside table and let myself cry at the sentiments I had written down twenty-four years ago, when James and I were at the height of our passion. How the mighty fell and how my world had changed when the mirror splintered.

-22-

Dear Diary,

Sunday 10th July, 1988

We surfaced in the kitchen at around ten, the smell of bacon too much for us to resist. I wandered over and sat next to Sarah and although we couldn't talk, I could see from the twinkle in her eyes that something had gone on between her and Chris. I think James realised as he clapped Chris on the back and they exchanged a secret look. All was absolute happiness in my world as I glanced around at my boyfriend, best friend, Chris, Pam and Peter. The only problem was leaving James behind yet again as I was going home. Chris had offered to drive me back to save James a journey in his car and although I was disappointed to not be sharing the return drive with him, it did make the most sense.

"Shall we have a barbecue?" Peter suggested.

"That sounds good Dad," James replied as we all went into the garden. Sitting outside I looked down towards the apple trees and the place we had made love only hours earlier. James saw me looking and gave me his wicked grin to say without words that he was thinking about exactly the same thing.

Later, as James loaded my bag into the boot of Chris's car, I felt my face fall. Hugging his mum and dad goodbye, they went back indoors and Chris and Sarah jumped in the car, leaving me with the back seat.

"Thank you again for a fabulous time," I murmured into James' chest as he held my trembling body.

"Thank you for making my 21st birthday the best it could possibly have been," he said, his finger lifting my chin. As tears rolled down my cheeks, he kissed them away, one by one. "Don't cry. I want to only have happy memories of you when we are apart."

I sniffed and smiled between tears.

"Sorry, it hurts so much when I have to leave you. I miss you so much. I love you so much." I cried as I kissed him back with a fierce longing rising up like flames in my chest.

"Look at the stars later, baby," he crooned, his hand on my cheek getting covered in tears.

When we drew apart, he passed me his hankie. "For the journey home," he said, smiling, but I could detect the pain in his heart as it matched mine.

"See you soon," I sniffed.

"As soon as I can get away, I will be down to see you."

"I'll write as soon as I get home."

"I'll be waiting."

As we finally let go of each other, I stared out of the back window of the car. I didn't turn away until he was out of sight.

Sarah looked over from the front seat. "Are you ok?"

"Yes, I guess," I replied, wiping my eyes for a final time with James' hankie.

Breathing in, I realised it smelt of him and holding it tight in my hand, I closed my eyes and spent the rest of the journey replaying all the events of the last week.

When we reached home Chris helped me carry my bag to the door.

"Shall we meet up tomorrow?" I asked Sarah.

"Yes, I'll come over at around ten."

"See you tomorrow, thanks for the lift home." I watched them drive away, jealous that they were still together and James and I were miles apart.

Remembering his words from earlier, I crossed to my window seat and stared out at the moonlit night and the millions of stars that littered the black velvet.

"Goodnight James," I breathed silently into the night.

Monday 11th July, 1988

"So," Sarah said. "Spill the beans and I mean everything."

"Ok, I'll tell you as much as I can but some of it's personal and I want to keep it between James and myself," I replied, as we settled in the garden.

"That's cool, I understand," she replied. "So did it hurt?"

"A bit, but it was just kind of strange really, especially when he was inside me. The first time was ok but it just gets better the more you do it," I said, feeling my face flush at the garden experience. "Anyway, the whole time we spent together was fabulous, we went to the beach, swam in the sea, dinner out and room service!"

"You lucky thing," she replied, envious.

"We also went up the Blackpool Tower and then had a ballroom dancing lesson with this elderly couple called Jack and May who showed us how to waltz."

"I thought you both looked a bit professional at the end of James' party the other night."

"What about you and Chris?"

"He was a gentleman because I had never shared a bed with him before Saturday night."

"And?"

"Nothing much really, we just kissed lots… as we don't want to rush things."

"Cool. Isn't it great when you get to go to sleep and then wake up next to them?"

"Yes, it's the best feeling in the world," Sarah replied, as we both lay back and enjoyed the sunshine.

"When's your interview for the hospital radio job?" she asked.

"Tomorrow, so I'm going to dust off my records this evening and take them for a spin."

"Well, if you can get a party jumping like on Saturday night then you'll have no problem amusing kids stuck in hospital," she said, giving me a hug.

"See you Wednesday… shopping?"

"Yep, definitely," she replied as she walked down the drive.

Tuesday 12th July, 1988

I woke early and full of nerves. I had retyped my CV and found a sensible looking skirt and top to wear. As Mum dropped me off at the reception area, she wished me luck before I walked in.

"Can I speak to Mr. Ford?" I asked the girl on the desk, and she quickly buzzed his extension number.

"He will be with you shortly," she replied.

Sitting there I felt nervous and wished James was next to me, his hand in mine would have helped. Instead I shut my eyes and thought of his smiling face. I opened my eyes just in time to look up and see a guy in a suit approaching.

"Are you Stephanie March?"

"Yes," I replied, standing up to shake his proffered hand.

"If you'd like to follow me we'll go and have a quick chat about things and then I can introduce you to the guys who run the radio station here?"

"Ok," I replied as I grabbed my bag and followed him down the seemingly endless maze of white corridors.

I could hear the tunes over the corridor speakers and realised that the music they were playing was more like the stuff my parents enjoyed.

Once in his office I told him all about the type of music I liked and what kids would be more interested in, along with some ideas for competitions we could run to get some more involvement. I watched as he smiled and wrote some notes.

"Well, I think you've got yourself a job," he said, smiling as he stood up. "But I guess you'd better meet your radio colleagues and decide if you want it before you say yes?"

I grinned in amazement as we set off along some more corridors, eventually reaching a room that said *Radio* above. The green light was illuminated which generally meant it was ok to head on in. He pushed open the heavy door and the music hit me at full blast.

"Gerry, Vic, this is Stephanie, your newest DJ," Mr. Ford said, and I shook hands with two middle-aged guys who looked rather amused. "Is Jack around?"

"Nope, he'll be here in an hour," Gerry said. "We'll look after Stephanie until then."

I spent the next hour being shown the music system before a young guy breezed in.

"Hi guys," he said, before he stopped in his tracks and stared at me. "Who's this then?" he asked with a grin on his face.

"Hi I'm Stephanie, but you can call me Steph," I replied. "And you are?"

"Jack," he replied, and we shook hands

"Steph here is going to be helping you with some of the kid's programmes as she wants to do this full-time and needs some experience before she starts her college course," Vic explained.

"Cool, I have a partner in crime at last," he grinned and I was immediately caught up in his enthusiasm.

"Well, while these two oldies finish their shows, shall I take you on a visit to the kid's ward to meet your audience?"

"That sounds great," I agreed, following Jack through the corridors.

"I think I'm going to need a map," I said, feeling totally disorientated with all the corridors looking so similar.

"I'll get you one," Jack replied, "but just ask someone if you're not sure... well, avoid asking the surgeons as they are always too busy."

Once we reached the ward I took a deep breath and lots of young faces looked up expectantly at the new arrivals. It only took a second before a couple of girls walked over to Jack and each took one of his hands.

"Jack you're back," the blond girl said. "Come and sit on my bed," said the other girl, both vying for his attention.

"Why don't you say hi to my new friend, Stephanie, she is going to be doing some radio shows with me and she needs to know what you like to listen to the most."

Kneeling down I stuck out my hands and sure enough they decided I was more interesting. Soon I was surrounded by young expectant faces as I heard them asking for all the usual favourites – A-Ha, Rick Astley, Sonia, Sinitta, Kylie Minogue. It was great fun as I wandered around the ward and spoke to those that were unable to get out of bed, still smiling despite the pain they were in. The hours flew by until it was time to head back to the studio so I could sit in on one of Jack's shows. As he showed me again how it all worked, I settled in and helped out where I could, but also took notes as I had a week to learn before I launched my own show.

Leaving Jack to his show, I walked off down the corridors, trying to read my map and locate the way out. I bumped into a doctor hurrying the other way as I dropped my map and he dropped all his notes.

"I'm sorry," I said, as I quickly knelt down and started to help him gather up his paperwork.

"My fault, I should have been looking where I was going," he replied, kneeling beside me. Looking up into his face I smiled and blushed.

"My name's Stephanie," I said to break the silence.

"Mark," he replied. "Nice to meet you."

Standing up, he took a better look at me. "So are you new here, I don't think I've seen you around before?"

"Yes, I'm going to be working on the radio to help with my media course at college in September," I replied, taking in his blond hair and startling green eyes.

"Well, Stephanie, I will look forward to hearing your show as I do my rounds. I'm a junior doctor, still in training."

"Nice to meet you. Am I going in the right direction for reception?"

"Yes, just keep going down this corridor and it's through the double doors on your right."

Friday 15th July, 1988

I couldn't wait to speak to James on the phone, even though we had exchanged letters that week. I told him all about the hospital radio job and about all the stuff I had to learn before my first show the following Friday. Then he told me he had been accepted into the Fire Service but just had to complete his physical and medical in August – so if that went well, he would be able to start in September.

Then we reminisced about our week. "Are you still wearing your St. Christopher?" I asked.

"Yes, I never take it off," he said, as I imagined his fingers wrapped around it and wished that they were wrapped around me instead.

"I look at the stars every night."

"Same here," he said. "When I hear certain songs I think of you, at night I dream of you."

"Me too, when will I see you again?"

"I can get down to yours for the weekend of the fifth of August. Sorry it's not sooner but other staff are away on holiday so there are not many breaks in the shifts."

Thursday 21st July, 1988
I woke up with nerves again as it was my big day at work. James had sent me a good luck card so I packed it in my bag. Just as I was about to leave to catch the bus to Hereford, the phone rang and it was James.
"Hi babe, just wanted to wish you good luck for today, you'll be great!"
"Thanks James, it was good of you to give me a call."
"Sorry it's a quick one but I'm just on my way out to work."
"Me too, but I'll phone you later and let you know how I get on."
"Love you, loads."

I had never been so pleased, having Jack help me out with my first show. It was only two hours long but felt like five and it was really tricky to get the music queued up and answer the phone at the same time. I was shattered by the end of it but overjoyed, especially when Jack gave me a hug.
"That was great, you have a real flair for music," he said.
"Thanks, I loved the whole buzz of it," I said feeling euphoric.
"Are you going straight home or do you want to come out for a burger with me and some of the other guys at the hospital?"
"Yes that sounds good," I replied.
There was a group of people waiting and I watched shyly as Jack introduced them all to me. The only one I knew was Mark who I had bumped into the other day.
"Hi Mark, nice to see you again."
"Hi Stephanie, great show, loved the music you played and the kids in the ward appreciated it, I could tell by the smiles on their faces."
It was great to make so many new friends but all I really wanted to do was go home and speak to James.

Once I got home, I chatted with my parents and then up in my room, I called the number I knew by heart and lying back on the bed, I waited to hear James' voice once more.
"Hi James," I said, when he answered on the second ring.
"Hi Steph, how did it go?"
"It was brilliant, but much harder than I thought it would be. You almost have to do three things all at once, play music, answer phone calls and talk."
"Well I've got some great news. I have my physical test on the first of August so I might know if I get through ok when I next see you." I could

hear the excitement in his voice as his dream job appeared to be within reach at last.

"Only two weeks until I see you again," I said, breathing softly down the line.

"I know baby, I hope the time flies. I'm missing you so much."

"Me too, my bed is empty without you."

♪

I remembered how things had moved on in both of our lives that summer, taking us closer to the careers we craved but at the same time driving a wedge between us. Lying back on my pillow I wondered whether James was still a fireman. Was he still married to *her*? Was he happy?

-23-

I woke up to music coming from Charlie's room. Looking at my clock it was only 6.30a.m. I had to admit she was dedicated to her dancing as I realised that it was 'Take My Breath Away' that was on continuous loop. By 7.30, she was finished and polishing off some toast.

"How are things going?"

"Great, the song is amazing."

"Well, you know there will be at least three people in the audience who will think it's fantastic."

"Mum, would it be ok for Mitchell to come and visit this weekend?"

"Yes, is he coming on the train as I don't mind picking him up?"

"I'll find out," Charlie replied, reaching for her phone.

"He's got a motorbike so he's going to come down on that, he just needs to know where we live," Charlie replied, almost instantly. I watched as she tapped away again and everything was organised for the weekend.

"We have practice after school again tonight so I'll be home later. Is it ok for Julia to come over and stay?" she asked, picking up her bag.

"Yes, that's fine. I'll pick up some stuff for tea then."

Once she had left, I went back to my room to retrieve the diary and was about to set it down on her bedside table when I decided I needed one more trip down memory lane.

Dear Diary,

Friday 5th August, 1988

I was sunbathing in the garden when I heard the sound of an engine pulling into the drive and realised James had arrived at last. He had ended up working the morning shift from seven till two so it was already late afternoon. I quickly stood up and ran towards him. He swept me up into his arms and I kissed him for all I was worth.

"It's been too long," he said, breathing in my hair and at the same time, sending shivers down my spine.

"I've missed you," I said, trailing small kisses over his face and neck.

"Steady now, remember what happened the last time we were in a garden?"

"How could I forget?" I blushed at the memories we had made in the moonlight on his parent's lawn.

"I forgot to say... Dad found one of your stockings draped over the apple tree the following day."

"Oh god!" I replied, blushing like mad.

"It's ok, he just gave it back to me with a rather knowing look on his face. Anyway, he thinks you're great."

"I'll still feel embarrassed when I see them next! Dad's cooking barbecue later and I'll warn you now, it's normally burnt offerings." I gathered my book and my empty glass and we walked back towards the house.

"When will you get your exam results?" he asked as we sat in the kitchen with another cold drink.

"Next week. I'm a bit nervous but I've already got a place at college so I don't mind as long as they aren't dreadful. Anyhow, what about you?" I asked, watching a huge grin light up his face.

"I'll be a fireman in September. I've already handed my notice in at work so my last day will be at the end of August and then I start properly on Monday the fifth of September!"

Catching his hand in mine, I pulled him close and gave him a long kiss, until we were interrupted by Mum heading through to the garden with plates and cutlery.

"We'll be eating soon. Would you like a cold beer or wine?"

"Beer will be great Mrs. M," he told my mum.

"We're just going to go upstairs and get changed," I announced.

In the bedroom I changed into my sundress and let my hair out of my ponytail so it dropped down over my neck and back. James pulled me close and breathed in. "You smell gorgeous, coconut suntan cream."

"I can't wait to see you in your uniform. You can be my hero anytime."

James laughed as we heard Mum shouting for us so he caught me up in his arms and slung me over his shoulder.

"Fireman's lift for you, young lady."

The evening flew by in the garden. Mum and Dad were eager to hear about James' new job and then I started talking about Hospital Radio. They left us in the garden and went inside. A half moon lit the sky and the two of us as I crawled onto James' lap, kissing him until I shivered with longing for more.

"Let's go in," I asked softly, nibbling his ear and neck.

Once in my room, we soon lost our clothes and were naked on my bed, pressed tightly together in our embrace. I guess we had both been apart for too long as our lovemaking was urgent and quick, but still satisfying as we lay lost in the moment, linked together.

After hearing my parents go to bed we dozed for a bit, then I woke up and decided to wake James up. I crawled under the duvet and found what I was looking for, running my tongue over his length. James stirred but lay still so I continued and took him all into my mouth. This time I didn't stop until I had the warmth and taste of him sliding down my throat and sticky on my lips.

James pulled me up into his arms and the look in his eyes said it all.

"That was the best," he murmured as he kissed me. "You taste salty."

"No, I taste of you and it's wonderful," I replied, grinning at him, my eyes sparkling with the feelings of love I felt.

"Well, I believe it's my turn now," he responded. He made me lie down, trailing kisses over my already quivering body, his lips heading between my legs. Breathing in I closed my eyes and gave myself completely to the sensations his lips and tongue were creating. From the centre of me, sensations radiated out in ripples that grew stronger and stronger until I arched my back. Holding his head in my hands I came, shuddering under his touch.

"I love you till the end of time," I said as we curled up together.

"I love you."

Saturday 6th August, 1988
It was carnival day in town. We had arranged to meet Sarah and Chris at his flat and after we had caught up on each other's news, we took the short walk into town which was buzzing with people. We were able to find a good vantage point near the Market House to view the parade as we waited for the sound of the first marching band. It was a corny spectacle of tacky flower-covered lorries and plenty of children dressed in various outfits, waving and throwing sweets out to the crowds. Some of them had water pistols and we tried to avoid the water arches but failed and it didn't matter as the atmosphere of the day was so full of fun, it was infectious.

We followed the crowd towards the riverbank and the small array of fun fair rides that were set up on the one side. On the other side of the road were traders selling and the usual fairground stalls. Being with Chris and Sarah meant that the guys got incredibly competitive at the various games. Sarah and I soon held an assortment of cuddly animals they had won for us. After hot dogs and doughnuts, we wandered along to the Hope & Anchor. James fetched us all a drink and we sat and talked. Chris had applied to join the Army and was off for an interview shortly. If he got in, he would have to go for training in Colchester so I understood completely the look of sorrow that flashed over Sarah's eyes. As the sun sunk and showered red and gold over the placid, winding river, we walked home.

"This reminds me of the first time you walked me home from the swimming pool," I said, looking up at James and seeing his smile.

"Do you know how much courage it took for me to ask you? I was so worried that you wouldn't like me?"

"Not like you! I was already in love with you at that point," I replied. "Or at least I thought I was, but I know I am now, one hundred per cent, prime-time in love with you," I said, quoting some lines from *Top Gun*.

"Show me the way home," James laughed as he pulled me into his arms and we stopped for a kiss.

Sunday 7th August, 1988
I was awake before James and decided to take him up toast and coffee as we had the house to ourselves. It meant that we had the chance to make love at leisure and without having to worry about being quiet. James suggested that we tried it standing up but it became a bit of a strain on his knees so we then tried doggy style, which was different but I hated not seeing James' face so we reverted back to our usual two positions and just enjoyed the time that we had together.

For lunch I cooked us fish finger sandwiches and we went outside for the afternoon as the sun had decided to come back out. With the radio on the table, we spread a blanket out on the lawn and lay down together.

"I'm worried about you being a fireman," I said looking into his eyes.

"Why?"

"Well, so many get hurt. It's on the news, some even die."

"I guess I can't give you any promises but I will take as much care as I can," he murmured. "But enough worrying, I haven't even started yet!"

"I know, but if you are at any big fires, you will ring me as soon as you can and let me know that you are safe," I said, reaching over and kissing him gently on his shoulder.

"Well, don't you think I worry about you in that hospital with all those young doctors looking at you?"

"You're jealous?" I said, surprised by this.

"Yes I am." He returned the kiss with one on my neck that just turned into a string of them as his lips found mine.

"Don't worry, it's you I love," I murmured, as the strains of 'Together Forever' by Rick Astley floated out of the radio. Perfect timing.

Monday 8th August, 1988
It was our last day together and I woke with a heavy heart at the thought of saying goodbye later in the day. We decided to drive into Hereford so I could show James the studio where I worked in the hospital and he could meet some of my work colleagues as I had done at the pool. After

parking near the town centre, we walked to the hospital and after signing James in at reception, we wandered down the now familiar corridors to the radio station room.

Jack was doing his afternoon show so in between songs, I introduced him to James and they were soon laughing away as if they were old friends. Then we went back into town and after some lunch, we wandered around the shops. We decided to visit the cathedral because despite always living in the county, I had never been there before so we took the time and climbed to the top.

The views were spectacular and as it was quiet, James took the opportunity to pull me into his arms and kissed me.

"I have to say we have kissed in some different places."

"Yes, but my favourite is still the swimming pool, it is engraved upon my heart," I said, smiling again before his lips reached mine and we were soaring away, lost in the moment. A noise interrupted us as we looked up and watched as a hot air balloon took off from the side of the riverbank, steadily rising up above us.

"I would love to do that," I gasped, waving at the people in the basket.

"Yes, me too, there are so many things I'd like to do with my life."

"I hope we get to do some of them together?" I whispered, but he didn't hear me.

Saying goodbye, again, we lingered on the driveway for one, last moment. The feelings of emptiness filled my whole body as he held me close.

"I'm off to write that letter now," I said, leaning in through the car window for another kiss.

"I'm already waiting for it," he said, smiling and reaching up to wipe the solitary tear snaking its way down my cheek.

Then he was gone, his tail lights disappearing into the darkness. I looked up at the stars and more tears started to spill out. This was only ever going to get worse. The more time we spent together, the deeper I fell in love with James.

♪

I shook myself from my reverie and closed the diary, placing it back on my daughter's dressing table. That was enough emotion for the day. I needed to get on with my life and not keep dwelling on what could have been. I remembered all the plans I had made in my mind before that day in November. I was going to move to Warwickshire once I finished my course and get a job there on a local radio station or in a club. We would buy a house and then get married and live happily ever after. I never knew then that fairytales rarely came true and mine certainly didn't.

It turned into a nightmare.

-24-

I could tell Charlotte was both excited and nervous as I made her breakfast on Saturday. Between checking her watch and her phone, she barely ate any of her cereal and I kept re-heating her coffee in the microwave.

"What time did he say he would get here?" I asked her, watching her flushed face and bright eyes with amusement.

"He said he would leave at 8.30 and it would take him about an hour or so depending on the traffic," she replied, the time having just turned 9.30.

"What if he's had an accident?" she said, worry tingeing her voice.

"I'm sure he will be fine. Remember he has never been here before and the one-way system round Ross can baffle anyone, even with a sat-nav."

"Where was the place you went in the forest with the bike hire when you were with James?" she asked.

"I'll find the details for you, if you like," I replied, as I fired up the laptop and tapped in *Speech House*.

"I'm just going to brush my teeth," Charlie said, jumping up and racing for the stairs. I knew she would check her make-up and hair at the same time. God she was so nervous, even more than the last time they met. I wondered whether it was because he was going to be staying over.

I was just jotting the details down on a piece of paper when I heard an engine roar up the drive.

"He's here!" I shouted up the stairs at Charlie.

I walked over to the front door and then nearly got knocked over as the whirlwind that was my daughter rushed past me. I watched as she raced over to him and as he removed his helmet, she smiled so broadly I thought her face would break. Turning away I went back to the kitchen to put the kettle on.

Through the window I saw Charlotte jump into his arms as he held them open for her.

She gave him a quick peck on the cheek but moving his head, her next kiss met his lips. When he put her down, she was flushed from head to foot and I sniggered, watching her try to steady herself.

She pulled him indoors with her hand in his whilst he carried his bag and helmet.

"Hi Mitchell," I said. "Coffee ok?"

"Hi Mrs.–"

"Oh just call me Stephanie, Mrs. Eden makes me sound ancient and I hope I'm not there yet," I laughed, instantly liking this nice young man.

"Oh, no you could almost pass as Charlie's older sister," he said, a grin on his face. Charlie looked over and grinned at me, before her gaze returned to Mitchell. She was besotted already, I could tell.

"Go on," I responded, as they sat down and tucked into the biscuits with their coffee, my daughter's appetite returning.

"I've got that information for you," I said to Charlie. "Are you thinking of going there today?" I asked, as I pushed the tablet PC across the table and the piece of paper with the address and postcode on it.

"Mitch, I thought we could go for a bike ride in the forest as Mum went there when she was younger," Charlie said. I watched as he leaned over and looked at the pictures.

"Yes it looks great, my dad said the scenery around here was fantastic."

"Oh, has he been here then?" I asked, my curiosity piqued by this comment.

"Yes, when he was younger and at school, I think he wanted to drive me down just for the trip down memory lane but he's at work today."

"I'll drive you both there if you want?" I offered.

"Oh, I wanted to go on the motorbike," Charlotte said. "Please let me Mum, please."

I looked at both of them, waiting with eagerness for my answer. I remembered how my mum had been when I was younger and also how James' mum had been much more lenient and trusting – that was how I wanted to be.

"I can take you for a spin up the road first Mrs. Eden... I mean, Stephanie, so you can check I'm a careful biker?"

"Thanks but I'll pass and yes you can go with Mitch on the bike," I told my daughter. Looking at Mitch, I asked, "I assume you have a spare helmet she can borrow?"

"Yes, I had to go and buy one yesterday." He leaned down to his bag and pulled out another black and red helmet that matched his but was smaller. He handed it to Charlotte, who grinned and tried it on for size. She pulled the visor up and said, "Hey, I look like the Stig off *Top Gear*."

"You look much better than him," Mitch replied, and I watched his eyes roam over my daughter from head to foot, appreciating her figure.

"You're the best, Mum," Charlie said.

"Please don't worry. I'll take care on the road," Mitch reassured. "In fact we'll have a quick spin up and down the road first as a practice."

Standing on the doorstep, I watched as he made sure her helmet was secure and then she swung her leg over the bike and held onto his waist tightly. I guessed she was a bit scared but didn't want to show it in case I changed my mind and got the car out. Then with a roar, the engine burst into life and he pulled out of the driveway and rode slowly up the road, turned and then returned to the end of the drive. He pulled up his visor to ask, "Everything ok with you?"

"Yes," I replied. "See you both later, we'll order takeaway for tea."

They both nodded and then before I could say another word, they made it down to the end of the road and were gone.

I walked into the house and it felt empty without their joy and laughter.

♫

As she held onto Mitch's waist and zipped along the road, Charlie felt free. They soon reached the site of the bike hire company but sadly it had gone out of business so they climbed off the bike for a discussion.

"We could still go to the lakes and walk round them instead?" Mitch suggested.

"Ok," Charlie replied, hoping that when she was with Mitch holding hands, her legs would not turn to jelly from all the sensations swirling around inside of her at this moment.

After a few minutes on the bike, they came into a parking area and parked up between some cars.

"So why here?" Mitch asked her as they locked up the bike and their helmets, walking to the pathway that meandered around the lakeside.

"My mum came here on a date when she was my age. Well, except they did hire bikes and it sounded really romantic so that's why I wanted to come."

"You mean your mum has never brought you here?"

"No, not that I can remember, unless I was very small at the time."

"So I'm guessing this date was not with the guy who became your dad then?"

"No, I'll tell you about it all as we walk if you like?"

With her hand firmly in his, they set off towards the bridge over the weir on the far side of the water.

As they walked she told him about breaking up with Craig and how her mum had given her the diaries from 1988 to read about the story of her first love James. When she had finished telling Mitch, they reached the bridge.

"Sorry, I should just shut up for a while," Charlie said.

"No, that was an amazing story, so what happened to them?"

"I don't know yet, I haven't got that far but I guess it finished badly.

Although… my dad has been mentioned in the diaries so I think she falls for him at some point." She turned to him and asked, "Do you believe in true love?"

"Yes, I do," Mitch replied. "I know for a fact my parents were not in love and I occasionally catch him with a wistful look on his face. He told me he had only been in love once and it all went wrong. I pushed him for more details but he just clammed up and said it was all his fault." Mitch reached for Charlie's other hand and pulled her close. "Well, enough about our parents, I think it's time we concentrated on us."

"Us?" Charlie squeaked.

"Well, yes, that's if you want there to be?" he replied, gazing into her eyes with a longing she had never seen before.

"Yes," she finally managed as she watched his lips come down to graze hers, gently at first, but then they opened and the passion took over as she leaned back against the railings on the bridge.

When they broke apart Charlie couldn't stop smiling. She had got herself an amazing boyfriend and she couldn't wait for the future times they would spend together.

"Let's play Pooh sticks," she exclaimed, noticing some sticks nearby.

"I don't think I know what that is," Mitch said, looking puzzled.

"My mum described this in her diary. Apparently you throw the sticks in at the same time and then watch to see whose stick reaches the bottom of the weir first. It's from the books about *Winnie the Pooh*," Charlie revealed, passing him one of the sticks.

"And the winner gets what?" he asked.

"A kiss from the loser."

"Ok, I'm in," he said as they let the sticks fall.

In the end Charlie's stick won so Mitch grabbed her and picking her up, kissed her a million times all over her face and neck. It was heaven.

"So, what's your favourite dance film?" Mitch asked, between bites of lunch at the picnic benches.

"*Dirty Dancing*. I know it's old but it's still a classic."

"Snap! Even though as a guy I shouldn't like girly dance films, it was what made me decide to learn to dance and ultimately my training now as a dance instructor."

"Yes, it was so sad when Patrick Swayze died but I loved last year's *Strictly Come Dancing* show when they recreated the lift."

"Hey, we should try it," Mitch said.

"What, the lift?"

"Yes, why not, there's no one around!"

"Well, we could I suppose," Charlie replied.

He stood up and extended his arm in the style of Swayze, moving his finger to coax her to him. Charlie needed no further prompt as she stood up and he pulled her into his arms. She could almost hear the music in her head, just louder than the beating of her heart as they moved together in perfect synchronicity.

"Perhaps we'll change it a bit for our first attempt," Mitch said, as he lifted her up and placed her on the picnic table. "You can jump from here and I promise I will catch and lift you."

Charlie smiled at him. "I trust you," she said, leaping into his arms.

In the lifted position, she gazed out over the lake and trees for what seemed like minutes, her arms outstretched, feeling so secure in his strong grasp. Then as she slid down his body they heard clapping and cheering, realising a small audience had gathered and witnessed much of their routine while they had been in their own private dance world.

"Wow," she said, breathless, and he pulled her back into his arms.

"We make a great team," Mitchell murmured. "But I think that's enough impromptu public dance demonstrations for one day."

"Me too, shall we go home?" In her head she was still dancing on the wave of applause and the natural high it produced.

"Sounds like a plan."

On the way home Mitch opened up the throttle as the landscape sped past them and Charlie held on tighter, liking the way their bodies fitted together perfectly.

When they climbed off, Charlie was still buzzing from the high of the day's revelations, dancing and of course the bike ride.

"Hi Mum, we're back," she shouted.

"Have you had a good day?" Steph asked, poking her head out of the lounge.

"Yeah, the bike place has closed down so we just walked around the lakes instead. It was a lovely day," she said, smiling over at Mitch.

"Chinese or Indian takeaway for tea?"

"I don't mind," Mitch said, "I like both."

"Indian please Mum."

"Is it ok for us to go up to my room and I can show Mitchell the spare room," Charlie asked.

"Sure, I'll shout you when the food arrives," Steph said.

As Charlie walked up the stairs, she felt Mitchell behind her, watching her. His gaze was heated, she could feel it all the time. It made her feel shy as they crossed the landing and she showed him to the spare room. "You'll be sleeping in here tonight if you want to put your bag down," she said.

"That's cool, I hope the bed is comfy."

"Anyway, let's go to my room instead and we can put some music on." Charlie was pleased she had taken the time to do a proper clean and as she put some music on and kicked off her trainers, she realised he was having a good look around.

"Who's this?" he asked as he picked up one of the photographs on her dressing table. She wandered over and realised he was looking at a small frame and a picture of her in a pink tutu.

"That's when I passed my Grade One, with distinction," she said, remembering the moment proudly.

"Let's see," he asked, and he watched her perform a pirouette and then dip into a graceful curtsey.

"You are good. But I prefer something a bit less controlled than ballet." He pointed at the CD he had given her from the salsa club. "You like it then?"

"Oh yes," she replied.

He grabbed her around the waist and spun her away from him before pulling her back in. With his hand on the small of her back, they moved together.

-25-

After dinner and some lively conversation about dancing with Charlie and Mitchell, I was amused to find they wanted the lounge so they could watch *Dirty Dancing* together. Obviously, music was proving to be the strongest bond between them and I was pleased that dancing had played a huge part in Charlie growing up. Although Charlie had other career ambitions, dancing was the favourite by miles.

I retreated to the conservatory even though they suggested I watch it with them, not wanting to cramp their style. Later in the evening I walked past the door and looking through the glass, noticed they were dancing along to the images on the screen and making such a good job of it. I was mesmerised, as if the film had come to life in my own front room. I snuck away and put the kettle on for some hot chocolate.

When I pushed the door open and saw they were sat hot and sweaty on the sofa, I just couldn't help but smile.

"What's so funny?" Charlie asked.

"Looking at you two on the sofa! If I hadn't known you had been dancing, I would be thinking lots of other things." I laughed again. "By the way you both looked fabulous dancing together. I saw you as I passed by the door."

"You really think so?" Charlie asked.

"Yes," I said, handing them the mugs. "Well, I'm off to bed now so I'll leave you to clear up your own mugs."

♫

"Well, what shall we do now?" Mitch murmured, placing his mug down and reaching to take Charlie's from her. Charlie gazed up into his eyes and smiled as she watched his lips capture hers in a kiss that was by far the most earth-shattering yet. She let herself go with the flow as they both started to explore each other's bodies through their clothes. Even though they had danced closely with each other earlier, this was much more intense. However, Charlie remembered her mum's diaries and pulled back enough for Mitch to stop and give her a puzzled look.

"What's wrong?"

"Can we go slowly? I don't want to rush things even though it feels amazing," she asked, hoping he wouldn't reject her like Craig.

"Sure, I've no problem with that, even though I'm going to find it hard to keep my hands off you," he grinned.

On the landing he pulled her into his arms for one, last embrace.

"Come wake me up in the morning?" he said.

"It's morning now."

"So it is," he agreed, drawing her close for a goodnight and good-morning kiss.

"Later Mitchell," Charlie whispered as she left his arms.

"Later Charlie, I'll be dreaming about you."

She blew him a kiss and entered her room. Lying there in the darkness she struggled to drift off, hoping he might try and sneak into her room. Being a true man of his words, he didn't appear. Even though she was disappointed, she was also pleased he was willing to wait for her despite the physical attraction between them. She found him waiting in her dreams as they danced together, surrounded by golden leaves that were gently falling as he lifted her and she glided towards the warmth of the sun.

♪

I woke up first and crept downstairs to put some coffee on. I had slept fitfully, worried Charlie and Mitchell had spent the night together. After a coffee, I dismissed those thoughts. I decided I had to trust Charlie; after all she had read the diaries and knew what I used to get up to. If this relationship continued, I would allow them to share a bedroom together and would treat them like the adults they were.

In the next moment, I was startled from my thoughts as Mitchell entered the kitchen and perched on the nearby stool.

"Morning Stephanie. Is Charlie not up yet?"

"Afraid not, she's not known for early mornings at the weekend, however if I turn the radio up she might hear it and come down."

I poured Mitch a mug of coffee and turned up the radio. It was tuned to Love Shack Radio, so a mixture of hits bounced around ranging from the Sixties through to the Nineties.

"I love this group," Mitch said, as the distinctive bass of 'Our House' by Madness filled the room. "I saw them on the television for the Golden Jubilee celebrations."

"Yeah, they're great. I remember dancing to their hits when I was young."

"They are one of my dad's favourite groups. He looks so funny when he jumps around to this, telling me that is how dancing was in the Eighties."

"We weren't as sophisticated in those days as you are today but maybe that's how music and dancing progress?"

"Charlie tells me you're a DJ. That is such a cool job, playing music all day and chatting."

"Yes it is, it keeps me sane and allows me to play music I love. So, you had to choose Eighties tracks for the final of the dance competition?"

"Yes that was a bit of fun, I love Michael Jackson but thought it would be great to reinterpret something different, especially as the dance for 'Thriller' is so well-known," he said.

We both turned around to see Charlie had arrived, dressed in her pyjamas and fluffy slippers.

"Morning sleepyhead," I said, turning to pour my daughter a mug of coffee as she took the stool next to Mitchell.

"Yeah, I've been up for ages," Mitch said, giving her a quick peck on the cheek.

"You could have shouted me. What have I missed?"

"Oh, I've been telling Mitchell all about your annoying habits." I laughed as Charlie turned to look at Mitch with horror on her face, until she realised I was teasing her and gave me a look that said it all.

"We've been talking about music and dancing," Mitchell said, "although I would love to hear about your annoying habits."

"So what are your plans for the day?" I asked the loved-up pair.

"Thought we might go round the town and Mitch can see what a boring place we live in, then I have dance practice this afternoon for a couple of hours so Mitch can come along if he wants."

"Is that wise? He is your rival in the dance competition."

"Yes, but I trust him not to steal our routine, anyway I may have a plan for him to help us out," Charlie said, being cryptic.

"Oh yes?" said Mitch. "And when were you going to tell me about this?"

"Well later when we're out," she replied, smiling shyly at him.

"Bacon sandwiches then?" I asked. "Since you will need to eat to give you some energy for later?"

They both nodded as I set to work at the stove.

"What time are you heading home Mitchell?" I asked.

"I promised I would be home by nine so as long as I leave here about eight, that should be fine."

"Ok, I'm doing lasagne for tea so I'll feed you before you head off."

♫

Walking into town Charlie knew it would be pretty deserted on a Sunday but it was nice to just walk around together as she shared her knowledge of the different places. They walked through the car park towards the swimming pool so that they could cut through to the riverbank.

"My dad used to work there," Mitchell said, looking at the tired façade of the leisure centre.

"Really?" Charlie looked amazed. "My mum met her first boyfriend there, isn't that strange?"

"Yes. What was his name again?"

"James," she replied, as the sudden realisation hit her. "What's your Dad's name?" she asked, holding her breath.

"James," Mitchell replied.

"Do you think my mum's James is your dad?" Charlie exclaimed.

"That's just what I was thinking, how weird if it was!"

"I know a way we can check," Charlie revealed. "We'll need to go home though as I have a photograph of the two of them together."

Grabbing his hand, they turned and quickly walked back to the house.

Carrying cold drinks they went upstairs. Her mum had gone shopping so the house was deserted. As Mitch sat down on her bed, Charlie pulled the photo album out from under it and turned to the back page before handing it to Mitchell.

"Oh my god, it is my dad!" Mitch exclaimed, almost dropping the album from the shock of this realisation. "This is so mad!"

"So do you think my mum was his true love then?" Charlie said, sitting down beside him and gazing at the now familiar photography.

"I guess so as my brother Darren is twenty-three and the diaries are from 1988. He was born in 1989 and I was born in 1991 before Mum left us." Charlie watched the shock in his eyes; this was a massive discovery for both of them.

"I think I need to read some more of Mum's diaries to see what happened between them before we dare mention this?" Charlie tried to gather herself together. "I haven't got that far yet and it's such a compelling story that I don't want to spoil it by just turning to the end pages."

"Ok, but I think you had better start reading faster as the dance competition is not far away and my dad is coming to watch."

"Yes, so is my mum!"

Looking at the clock Charlie realised it was time to head over for her dance session and she hadn't even talked to Mitch about what she was planning. Grabbing her dance bag and Mitch's hand, they started back down the stairs.

"Can we go on the bike?" she asked.

"Sure, is it far?"

"No but I want to be there before anyone else so I can talk to Mrs.

Grantley about what I am planning."

"Yes, and I would quite like to know what I'm letting myself in for," Mitch reminded her, grabbing their helmets.

Once they arrived at the school and were walking towards the entrance for the main hall, Charlie turned to Mitchell.

"Ok, what I want to do as part of our dance is to fall from a fair height and have someone catch me... but as we are a group of girls, there is no one who would have the strength to do this so I wondered if you might step in?"

"I would catch you any day," Mitch replied, and they both thought back to yesterday's visit to the lakes. "I would love to."

Inside Mrs. Grantley was already there so she looked startled to see Charlie heading through the door accompanied by a tall young man who looked vaguely familiar.

"Hi Charlie, you're early?"

"Hi Mrs. Grantley, this is Mitchell," she said, introducing them.

"I've had an idea about our dance to 'Take My Breath Away' and I want Mitchell to help us with it. By the way, he is in the dance group from the college in Rugby who are also in the finals."

"Ah, that's where I recognise you from," Mrs. Grantley said smiling. "Ok, tell me what you are thinking then."

Putting the CD in the system, Charlie found the music and played the song, highlighting the section at the end where she thought the drop would fit in.

"I like your idea," Mrs. Grantley decided. "It will certainly give our dance a dramatic ending."

"I'll just go and change into my dance clothes and we can have a couple of tries before anyone else turns up." Charlie was eager to put her idea into practise.

When she returned, Charlie explained that they may require some stage props at the London venue and then the music started. Charlie couldn't help but run through the first part of the routine as she built up to the point where the drop would come in. She flitted up the steps at the side of the stage area, and taking this as a cue, Mitchell went to the point below Charlie on the floor.

Mrs. Grantley paused the music and then walked over as Charlie explained she would launch herself backwards off the stage. Then Mitchell would catch her, lift her above his head whilst she was still in that position, her arms outstretched. Then slowly, she would slide down his body and finish wrapped around Mitchell's feet.

"Ok... I'm ready," Mitch said, glad he had taken his trainers and socks off and could plant himself firmly on the wooden flooring.

He watched as Charlotte very gracefully, with arms outstretched, fell into his arms. Holding her around the waist, he lifted her directly above his head. She could feel the full strength of his body as it trembled slightly underneath her but she remained still and started to slide down his body. However, she never reached the original ending spot on the floor as suddenly, she was being cradled in Mitchell's strong arms. He knelt down and she was draped over his knee, his one arm holding the top of her thigh, the other cradled under her head. All this time Mrs. Grantley had been both holding her breath and marvelling at this young man's strength and skill on the dance floor as well as how wonderfully fluent the two of them looked together.

Charlotte brought her head up and looked straight into Mitchell's eyes, her breathing ragged and quick.

"That felt fantastic," she gasped. Mitch carefully placed her down so she was sat on the floor, him joining her there.

"Beautiful," was all Mrs. Grantley could exclaim. "You two look fantastic together. I was so carried away with it all."

They tried it a couple more times and then Mitchell went to find some water as they waited for the rest of the class to turn up.

Mitchell sat at the back as the girls all got together at the front and Mrs. Grantley explained that the dance would change slightly at the end. Then she introduced Mitchell to them. Julia recognised him and a few of the other girls just drew in a sharp breath at the sight of him. Charlie held his hand tightly and smiled. They all knew she was the exceptional dancer so after going through the dance as a group a couple of times, they all sat back and watched the proposed new ending. Before Charlotte took up position on the stage, Mitchell gave her hand a squeeze.

Then once more she was dropping, then soaring. As their bodies connected, he slowly lowered her to the ground, stealing a kiss on her cheek as he finished the move to a resounding applause from the small audience.

"It's brilliant!" Julia said, over the clapping.

"So are we all agreed on including this for the final?" Mrs. Grantley asked.

"Yes!" came the response as all the girls were eager to have one more dance-through before they finished.

-26-

After having a quick chat with Julia at the end, Charlotte grabbed Mitch's hand and they took the short ride home. As they opened the front door they were hit with the wonderful smell of home-cooked lasagne and realised they were starving.

"Hi guys," Steph said, as they both appeared in the kitchen. "How was your day?"

"Great thanks," Mitch said.

"Fantastic," said Charlotte, moving to the fridge to reach for a cold drink.

"How was dance practice, did they like your idea?"

"Oh yes it looks amazing apparently," Charlie replied.

"Yes it is a great routine, they might even beat our group," he said, grinning at Charlie.

"Oh I doubt it, your other routines are far more technical than ours so you might end up winning!"

The trio ate dinner and then Charlie and Mitch went upstairs for an hour before he had to leave. Once in the bedroom, he pulled her to him and they kissed as they lay on her bed.

"So bearing in mind we have only six weeks until the dance competition, do you think you might like to come up to mine for a weekend?" he murmured between kisses.

"That would be great, as we can always practise the lift at yours," Charlie replied, returning his kisses with enthusiasm.

"I'll check with my dad when I get home and then drop you a text so you can ask your mum."

"Talking of my mum and your dad, I'll try and get on a bit further with the diaries as it's no good us trying to introduce them again if it sounds like the parting was really bad," Charlie said. "I would hate to cause a scene at the dance competition in London."

"Yeah, it's a tricky one, but I will see if I can find out anything more from my dad."

"Deal, but enough talking, I need some more kisses before you have to leave."

Mitchell didn't get a chance to reply as she pushed him back and jumping on top of him, brought her lips down to meet his in a kiss so sensual, it made her feel light-headed.

Then all too soon she was standing on the doorstep watching him climb on his bike, feeling a strange mix of emotions flowing through her

– part happiness that he was well and truly hers, while also wondering how she was going to get through the time they were apart.

Charlie wandered into the lounge and plonked herself down on the sofa next to her mother.

"You ok?" Steph asked, concerned.

"Yes Mum, a bit tired, so I'm going to call it a night," she said, reaching over to give her mum a quick kiss on the cheek. "Night Mum."

"Night, Charlie"

Once she was in her room, Charlie took another look at the photograph and shook her head at the enormity of the situation, wondering how something like this could have happened. Then she slipped under the duvet, which still felt warm from the hour she had just spent with Mitchell. Opening the diary, she kept her phone close as Mitch had promised he would drop her a text when he reached home. She flicked through another couple of weeks of entries which described her mum's work experience at the hospital. Tempted to linger whenever she spotted her dad's name (but realising she needed to know how things ended as soon as possible), she skipped to the next weekend when her mum was with James again.

Dear Diary,

Friday 19th August, 1988
As I was working the afternoon shift on the radio, I had taken my weekend bag with me so that James could just pick me up from there. By the end of the show I was so excited to be seeing him that I positively ran down the corridors and almost floored Mark again, who shouted, "Hi," to me as I passed by in a blur. Outside I scanned the parking area and soon saw James standing by his red Mini. I ran over to be enveloped in a huge hug.

"Aren't you a sight for sore eyes?"

"You too," I replied, reaching up so that my lips could meet his.

"How was your day?" he asked as he grabbed my bag.

"Great, the show is such fun and I'm getting loads of requests so it makes it all worthwhile when the kids phone in or want me to go and visit them on the ward. What about you?" I asked.

"Felicity is making my last month hell. I had to beg and plead for this weekend off so I could see you."

Why did he have to mention her? I thought, but I let it go as he grabbed my hand and placed it on his knee.

"Anyway, I only have another twelve days to go so I couldn't care less," he said as we sped off up the road, Madness playing on the stereo as we sang along to, 'House of Fun'.

When we reached home it was time for dinner and I enjoyed telling Peter and Pam about my radio show. Then as soon as we could, we went upstairs to James' bedroom and at last I could relax into his embrace. I reached for him as he pulled me close and our lips met slowly at first but then with more urgency as James started to remove my clothes. With every layer that fell, the more turned on my body was under his caress. Then when I was naked he lifted me up and carried me the short distance to his bed. Once he slipped out of his jeans, t-shirt and boxer shorts, he joined me. I revelled in the feel of his touch as he gently trailed kisses down my throat and then to my nipples, taking each of them in turn. I felt as if I would come just from the sensations running through my veins.

His tongue went lower and his head was between my thighs. I sighed and felt his hot kiss followed by the coolness as he blew gently in between every lick. It was mind-blowing as my body arched to meet his finger, plunging into my wetness.

"Please, now," I whimpered softly, as his finger withdrew. He moved up to kiss me and plunged into me. Within a single breath, I was coming so much that I felt as though I was floating on a cloud, weightless and out of control. All I felt were the convulsions through my body, spreading like ripples on a pool, widening from the core of me to the tips of my fingers.

"I love you," I gasped, as I felt James join me in this bubble of sensations that made up both of our bodies.

"I love you too," he replied, both of us dropping back down to earth. Still in his arms, he hugged me tighter and feeling so content with my world, I fell asleep.

Saturday 20th August, 1988
I woke up before James and revelled in the time I had to gaze at him as he slept. I decided I needed action as I ran my fingers down his chest, encountering his erection which had sprung up from nowhere. Taking it in my hand I stroked him and manoeuvred myself so that I was straddling James. Looking down into his face I saw a smile spreading over his lips but he remained still and kept his eyes closed. Feeling this empowered only enhanced my own feelings as my body responded and I slowly lowered myself onto him and started to move. Leaning forward I kissed him but as small butterfly kisses rained all over his face, he could lie still no longer and his arms reached up to run through my hair, bringing me closer so that his lips could capture mine.

"Keep riding," he murmured in my ear, before he exploded inside of me as I joined him a few moments later.

"I wish you were here to wake me up every morning," James said as I lay in his arms.

"I wish I was with you every day," I replied, snuggling closer to him.

"What would you like to do today?"

"Staying in bed with you would be nice, but I don't mind."

"Ever been ice skating?"

"No, have you?"

"No, so we can both have a go together then," James said, as he bounded out of bed.

"First we need a shower." He grabbed my hand and pulled me out of bed. We snuck into the bathroom together and trying to keep the giggles to a minimum, we shared a long, indulgent shower.

After brunch we drove to the ice rink and once we had our skates on, we both staggered out onto the ice. It was quite tricky at first to keep our balance and we both howled with laughter as each of us took it in turns to fall over before we found our flow on the thin blade. Then there was no stopping us as we glided around the rink. Overhead the music played and in my heart, I was as one with James.

We headed into town for some late lunch and ended up bumping into his mate Ian from the pool and his girlfriend, April. They asked if we were going out that night with the rest of the gang.

"Not sure," James replied.

"Oh go on," said Ian. "I haven't had the chance to talk to your wonderful girlfriend who we hear so much about at the pool."

I blushed when he said this.

"Can we go?" I asked

"We'll see you both later."

Luckily I had brought a couple of dresses, one of which was brand-new so when we got ready to go out, I spun around so that James could take in the view.

"You look gorgeous. I'm going to have to keep my eyes on you this evening," he murmured. Stooping and catching my hand in his, he brought it up to his lips.

"You don't need to worry, I am completely and utterly hooked on you," I whispered. "Together, forever, remember?"

"Till the end of time."

The club was busy but James soon found Ian and April, Graham and Lizzie, and unfortunately Felicity and a guy, Jason. As we reached the group I squeezed his hand, suddenly shy and unsure of myself. He squeezed back and as I looked up, he smiled at me. Once the introductions were over, Felicity turned her attention to Jason who was enjoying it as she kissed and touched him in front of us all.

"Shall we hit the dance floor?" James asked

"Sure," I replied, feeling the beat of the music invading my body like a drug.

We found a spot and James held me close as we moved together in time to the rhythms. It was hard to have a conversation over the loudness but I didn't mind so long as I was with James. After a while we headed for the table where the others sat and I stayed there while James got a round of drinks at the bar. Felicity had disappeared so I turned to include Jason in the conversation and we were soon chatting away about music. I didn't notice Felicity's return until she was stood in front of me, her eyes blazing.

"What do you think you are doing?" she snarled.

"Just chatting about music," I answered, my stomach flipping over as I quickly glanced around for James.

"You leave Jason alone," she growled. "He's mine."

Ian suddenly piped up. "You should leave Stephanie alone, they were only talking."

"And you should remember who your boss is before you speak," she retorted.

I noticed Graham had started to move away as had Jason, an embarrassed look on his face. At that moment James returned and the mood turned icy as her gaze swept to him.

"I think I will need you to work tomorrow afternoon," she said. "And in future, could you tell your schoolgirl here to leave my man alone otherwise there will be trouble."

By this point I was seriously shaking and as James was about to say something, she promptly picked up her glass of wine and emptied it over the front of my dress before stalking away, grabbing Jason by the arm and propelling him to the door. For what seemed like minutes but was probably just seconds, we remained shell-shocked.

"Sorry," everyone said at once as they turned to me, April passing me some tissues.

"It's ok," I stammered, still in shock.

"She's a bitch," Graham said. "You are so lucky to be leaving," he asserted, looking at James who was standing there holding a tray of drinks.

"Can we go home?" I pleaded.

"Sure," he replied, as he took my hand and said goodbye.

Just feeling James' arms around me was a comfort on the short walk home.

"Why does she hate me so much?" I asked.

"She hates everyone, but when I first started at the pool she asked me out and I said no. Even though we weren't together then, I had strong feelings for you," James replied, hugging me tighter to him. "She's been awful ever since."

Once home and in the safety of James' room, he peeled my dress off and then my underwear. It seemed we were both keen to rid ourselves of the unpleasant scene as we dived for the comfort of the duvet and held each other tight, each lost in our own thoughts, or bodies together as one.

♪

Her phone beeped and Charlotte grabbed it to find a message from Mitchell.

Thanks for a wonderful weekend, I am home safe and sound but missing someone to hold me tonight. Wish you were here because when I am with you, I have the time of my life and I've never felt this way before. Sleep well my baby and keep in touch, Mitchell x

Charlie smiled at the reference to the lyrics from *Dirty Dancing*.

Mitchell, you're like the wind, you've taken my heart and you don't know what you've done, missing you too and can't wait until we are dancing together again, your Charlie x

Charlie knew she was falling hopelessly in love with Mitchell and there was nothing that could stop her. She put the diary aside and fell asleep, her dreams a muddle of wishes and desires, held together by music and dance.

-27-

School seemed to pass so slowly for Charlie as she finished lessons and then more rehearsals with the group. Every time they danced their way through the routine, she missed Mitch for the fall at the end. Mitchell could not get away that weekend but had invited her to stay the following weekend. Although it seemed an age away, they continued to text and chat to each other almost as constantly as they could, depending on college.

Charlie spent the weekend practising and in between texts from Mitch, reading the diaries so that she could let him know what had happened twenty-four years ago that was as much a part of his life as hers.

Dear Diary,

Friday 2nd September, 1988
James was coming over and I couldn't wait to see him again. While cleaning my room, I danced along to Rick Astley and was so lost in the music, I failed to hear his car pull onto the driveway. The first thing I knew was someone clapping from the doorway and as I spun round, I saw a smile that lit up my day.

"Nice moves," he said. "Now get over here and give me a kiss, it's been a long haul."

I needed no further prompting as I ran the short distance into his arms and felt my body curve into his. Like a final piece of a jigsaw, we were complete again.

The first kiss we shared was always the best but as our lips came together, I sensed a small moment of hesitation from James. It was so slight that I soon forgot as he responded to my touch in the usual way. We staggered over to the bed and fell together onto the softness of the duvet. When we parted, we were both hot and breathless.

"Shall we go and grab some cold drinks?" I said.

Sitting in the kitchen he told me about his last few days at work and his leaving party. Looking into his eyes I noticed a strange sadness lurking there beneath the calm blue.

"Do you miss working at the pool?"

"Nah, will miss the guys, you know Ian and Graham, but definitely not Felicity."

"So, big day on Monday when you start at the fire station?" I responded, a smile creeping over my features as I imagined what James looked like in his uniform.

"What's the smile for?"

"Just thinking about how good you will look in your uniform."

"You can see it next time you come and visit."

"Mmmmh that sounds like an offer I can't refuse," I replied, fluttering my eyelashes and going into a fake swoon.

"You can do more than see it, you can remove it if you want," he suggested. James was enjoying the undercurrent of sexual tension running through our conversation.

He leaned across the table and kissed me, before my mum interrupted us.

"So what are you two planning for this weekend?" she asked.

"We're meeting Chris and Sarah at the pool in an hour and going for a swim, then bowling later at the new alley that has opened in Gloucester," I told her.

"Would you like some sandwiches before you head off?"

"That would be great Mrs. M," James replied, as I nodded and jumped up to grab us some crisps and another drink.

We drove down to the pool and spied Sarah and Chris immediately. They were locked in a passionate embrace just to the side of the entrance. James tooted the horn of the car and we laughed as they jumped and then realised it was us. Once in the pool, it felt like old times as we swam, laughed and mucked around. Then in a quiet moment, James motioned for me to go under the water and close my eyes. He gently pulled me close and kissed me, recreating our first ever kiss in exactly the same spot. It was beautiful. As we broke the surface together, I mouthed *I love you* to him. James responded with, *Till the end of time* back at me.

After we dried off, the four of us piled into James' car. I let Chris sit in the passenger seat as there was more leg room and I didn't mind having the chance of a gossip with Sarah in the back. Bowling was good fun even though the guys wanted to make it a competition. It was funnier when they decided to do boys against girls because Sarah and I somehow beat them by two points.

Saturday 3rd September, 1988
I forgot to set my alarm and woke in a panic when I heard footsteps below us. I extricated myself from James' arms and, grabbing my dressing gown, headed silently down the stairs to where they met the open landing. Waiting in silence, I decided it was safe, but just as I stepped round the corner onto the landing, my mum appeared from her

bedroom doorway.

"Hi Mum," I stammered, knowing there was no way I was going to be able to lie and say I was on my way to the bathroom.

"I'll talk to you later once James has left," she warned.

In the safety of the spare bedroom I took some deep breaths. I was in trouble and I just hoped she wouldn't tell Dad as I would be grounded for years. I had just finished getting dressed when I heard James' footsteps on the stairs. I was able to catch him on the landing and pull him into the spare room.

"Mum caught me coming down the stairs this morning as I forgot to set the alarm. She's going to talk to me once you leave on Sunday," I said.

"Do you want me to talk to her?" James asked.

"No, it's ok, but I just wanted to let you know as I might get grounded and not be able to come to yours when you next have a weekend off."

He put his arms around me and hugged me close.

We went downstairs for breakfast and I knew that Mum had not said anything to Dad as he greeted us both.

"What would you like to do today?" I asked James.

"Not sure."

My dad said, "You can always help me in the garage as I'm going to sort through all the records and disco equipment, try weed some of them out that we don't need anymore."

"Sounds like a plan," I replied. "Are the decks still set up in there?"

"Yes, why don't you go ahead and do the music and I'll go to the shed and do the lights," Dad suggested.

Once in the garage I switched the decks on and started to open all the cases. James soon had his head buried in the different sections, lifting out singles as I gave them a spin on the decks.

"I love this song," he told me, pulling out 'You've Lost That Loving Feeling' which I recognised from *Top Gun*. Pulling me away from behind the deck, the empty garage acted like our private dance floor as he pulled me into his arms.

"Since we never got to slow dance in the club when you were up at mine," he murmured as I laid my head on his chest. We moved together before he spun me round and we started to waltz like we had been taught in Blackpool. As the music faded I heard clapping in the background and turned to see my dad standing in the doorway.

"I liked your Waltz," he said. "Who taught you?"

"My dad taught me," James quickly replied, knowing that my parents had no idea about our long weekend in Lytham St. Anne's.

"Well, he did a good job. I'll leave you to finish off."

When he had gone, I started to giggle.

"That was a close one. Nearly got in trouble for two things instead of just the bedroom." I breathed deep, relief washing over me.

"How about we put on something a bit faster? I have some sexual energy I need to release and it won't wait until later," James said, as he found an album of dance music.

Although we started out with good intentions, the dancing slipped into an extended foreplay session that soon had my blood boiling as James slipped his hands beneath my loose top and realised with a start that I had no bra on. His fingers stroked my nipples and I felt my body start to soar. Pushing up my top I stood there as James' lips and tongue took over. I hardly dared to breathe at the sheer wickedness of doing this in the garage when only moments before, my dad had appeared at the door. It had only served to heighten my senses.

Running his hands over the outside of my skirt, he reached the hem and then explored beneath. I heard him gasp even louder when he found I wore no knickers. His warm hands touched my burning skin and ran down to my feet, then back up my legs to the centre of all my nerve endings. His fingers delved into my wetness and then kneeling down, his tongue tasted me, drinking me in like I was a fine wine to be enjoyed with care. I grabbed his shoulders and hung on as he pulled up and released himself from his jeans. He lifted me up and pushed me against the rough garage wall so that he could plunge into me without a moment's hesitation.

My body exploded in his strong arms as I came with such abandon, I cried out and had to smoother the sound into his chest as he joined me. Our bodies felt like one shimmering, shining sun at the centre of our own private universe. I think if the wall hadn't been behind us we would have fallen to the floor in happy exhaustion. Instead with shaking hands, James lowered me to my feet and we both just stood there, overwhelmed by the experience.

We heard a shout from outside, "Lunch is ready," followed by my mum's footsteps. I straightened my clothes just in time for Mum to appear through the garage door as she pulled it open.

"I wasn't sure you could hear me over the music," she said, looking slightly bemused at the sight of the two of us stood in the garage and no doubt looking slightly dishevelled.

"Thanks Mum, we'll be in shortly," I replied, feeling the heat of my blush and the remnants of our activity still on my skin.

"Thanks Mrs. M, all this work has made me hungry," he said, looking over at the pile of records we had sorted.

After lunch we went to the video shop and rented a couple of films for the evening, what with my mum and dad going out. We ended up with *Ferris Bueller's Day Off* and *Mannequin* to watch. Both were good but in the end we finished up with another viewing of *Top Gun*, making out on the sofa to the soundtrack that had pretty much made up our whole relationship to date.

"Do you know, if I ever had a daughter, I would call her Charlotte," I sighed. "Yes, Charlotte Cooke has a great ring to it."

"Hey that's a bit far ahead of you," James responded. "I'm too young to think about responsibilities like that just yet… I have a life to live."

"Yes and fires to put out, people to save and cats to rescue from trees," I replied as I thought of him rescuing me in the pool.

"I can't wait to get started on Monday, they are even training me to drive the fire engine… now that will be a buzz!" He grinned. I hoped our careers would not create a barrier between us. I just needed him to give me another year so I could do my course and learn to drive and then our relationship would move forward in the direction I wanted; the direction I had dreamt about for the last eight months – that I would be his forever.

Sunday 4th September, 1988

After getting caught yesterday, I set my alarm an extra hour early so that I could creep from James' warm arms and into the cold spare room. As I lay there I considered our conversation from last night. Did James not think the same as me, did he not want to make the ultimate commitment a couple could make? I tried not to let it worry me, but it lurked there at the back of my mind, along with Felicity's threat and the strange, far-off look I had noticed fleetingly in James' eyes.

After breakfast we returned to my room so that James could pack. He was leaving after lunch so that he had enough time to prepare for tomorrow. I knew I had preparation to do too as it was my first day of college and the nerves had started to kick in. Even though Sarah was going to be there, we were studying different courses. Also, I had to face my mum and hope that I wouldn't get grounded. I put my stereo system on and selected 'Hunting High and Low' by A-Ha. James pulled me into his arms and as the delicate strains of the title track poured over us, I melted once more. Our kisses were gentle, loving and ultimately meant to see us through our next stretch apart. Every touch of our fingers created an indentation, a shadow in our memories of how our bodies fitted together.

I stared into James' blue eyes, like sinking into a beautiful calm pool where I drowned. His hands in my hair as his fingers tangled through it and pulled me even closer, I didn't want him to ever let me go as my pulse raced. With my head on his chest I listened to his heart beat, which drummed in time with mine. He was my guide and every twist and turn, I longed to share with him. Every hope, fear and dream I had was linked to our future.

I watched him leave and I stood there for some time, waiting for the pain to pass but it didn't, even when my tears stopped falling. I walked into the house feeling numb and saw that Mum was waiting for me. I sat down at the kitchen table and after I wiped away the last solitary tear, I looked at her.

"It's not what you think," I said, believing attack was the best form of defence in this matter. "I was up there and we just fell asleep and before I knew it, it was morning."

"Do you think I was born yesterday?" my mother spluttered.

"No, but it's the truth," I replied, hoping my lie was convincing enough for her to drop it.

"I just need to know one thing, are you being safe?" she said, her anger dissipating as she sat down opposite me.

I felt the blush creeping up my cheeks as I thought of all that I had done with James, especially when the image of the garage appeared.

"Yes Mum," I replied. "We are… we are in love."

"I know all about that," Mum replied. "Just try and protect yourself as it may not last with James living so far away."

I desperately wanted to defend my feelings to her but I decided against it, so I just nodded and started to stand up.

"I don't want you spending the night in your room with James. My house, my rules," Mum finished. Relieved that I had got off so lightly, I walked up to my room where I lay down on my bed and breathed in the scent that still lingered there from James.

-28-

Charlotte wondered how her mum had got off so lightly but vowed to remember this should she ever say anything in the future about her and Mitchell. As she thought of Mitchell, a text came through on her phone:

Check your emails, I have a proposal for you x

She laid down the diary and fired up her laptop. As she read and re-read his email, she hugged herself excitedly and then she pressed *call* on her phone and waited for Mitch to answer. The organisers of the dance competition wanted submissions for a group or individuals to dance whilst the judges made their final decision and Mitchell wanted the two of them to dance together.

"Hi Mitch," Charlie said.

"Hi Charlie, it's lovely to speak to you," he said, and she went weak at the knees just listening to the deep softness of his voice and the way her name sounded when he said it.

"So what do you think?" he asked.

"It's a yes, definitely yes, we can start practising when I come over to yours on Saturday?"

"It's going to be tough; they want a recorded submission by the end of next week so we probably only have this weekend to do it. I'll get my brother Darren to film it for us. Are you up for some hard work?"

"Definitely, as long as you don't shout at me too much!"

"I'll try not to. I have been told I can be a bit of a hard taskmaster."

Charlotte blushed, her mind stirring up other images his words suggested. "So what shall we dance, so I can start to practise now?" she asked, eager to hear what he had in mind.

"I thought we could do the routine from *Dirty Dancing* and of course that lift."

Charlotte's whole body tingled with the anticipation of being in Mitch's arms again, lifted into the air, soaring weightless above him and the world below.

"Great, I would love to dance that with you!"

"Hey, if they pick us we could always tip the wink to my group and yours and see if they want to join in at the end, just like the film," he replied, the eagerness in his voice matched by Charlie's reply.

"Oh yes, I'm sure they would, but we need to get picked first before we fly off with more plans like that!"

"Great, I am really looking forward to seeing you at the weekend. Is there any chance your mum will let you come up on Friday night instead, as I can come and fetch you then instead of Saturday morning?"

"I'll ask her later and let you know."
"Cool, I'll be waiting."

Rushing downstairs Charlotte almost slipped over as she slid into the kitchen.

"Mum, is it ok for me to go to Mitchell's on Friday night instead of Saturday?"

Steph stood there and let her daughter stew for a few minutes as she pretended to contemplate her request.

"Of course you can," she replied, watching her tap out a text to Mitchell. A few minutes later a beep returned the reply and Charlie's face broke into a broad grin.

"So what's the secret?"

"I can't say but it's to do with the dance competition and I need to go and start practising now, ready for Friday. Is it ok for me to use the lounge as it's bigger than my bedroom?"

Charlie found the *Dirty Dancing* DVD and located the end of the film as she sat cross-legged on the floor. She studied the routine intently three or four times before she put her iPod in the docking station and the familiar strains of '(I've Had) The Time of My Life' started. Kicking off her slippers, she closed her eyes and started to run through the basics of the dance in her mind, her feet and body feeling the music as the beat bounced through the room and into her pores. Then with the film on at the same time, Charlie opened her eyes and began to practise the basic samba steps, her arms outstretched and holding the invisible body of Mitch.

♪

Charlotte rushed home from college on Friday evening. She couldn't wait to see Mitchell and was shocked to see his bike already in the driveway as she turned the corner, immediately quickening her pace.

"Hi Mum, hi Mitch," Charlie said as she entered the house.

"Hi Charlie," they both responded and Steph asked, "How was college?"

"Good thanks," Charlie replied before turning her attention to Mitchell.

"You're early?"

"Yeah, I thought we needed to get started," he replied. "I've just been telling Stephanie what we are planning to do."

"Yes, it sounds ambitious but from what I saw of the two of you the other week, I'm positive you can both do it," Steph said, encouraging them.

"I'll go and get changed and grab my bag," Charlotte said, walking towards the door.

"I think you might need this," Mitch said, reaching down and producing a parcel. "I believe it's your birthday next week." He smiled as he passed it over.

Charlie undid the ribbon and paper to reveal a set of motorbike leathers in black and red. She held them up against her as Mitchell said, "I hope they fit ok? If not I can take them back and exchange them."

"I'll go and try them on," Charlotte replied, quickly giving Mitch a kiss on the cheek before running upstairs.

Ten minutes later Charlotte appeared in the doorway looking like a real biker chick, beaming from ear to ear.

"How do I look?" she asked, her gaze falling to Mitchell who could hardly speak as he took in the tight leather trousers and jacket that hugged her curves in all the right places.

"Like you're ready to go," he said, a noticeable catch in his voice.

"You look great, Charlie," Steph enthused. "And at least I know you'll be safe on the journey to Mitchell's. But you must give me a call when you get there?"

"Ok Mum, I will." Charlie struggled to put her rucksack on her back, so Mitch gave her a helping hand. Steph waved them off the drive and then they were gone.

As they flew along the roads and motorways towards the Midlands, Charlotte hung on tightly to Mitchell's waist and marvelled at the way her body fitted to his, both of them moving as one with the bike. When they pulled into the driveway, she was quite pleased to get off as her body had just started to stiffen up. Mitchell helped her and then as she removed her helmet, he reached for it and put it aside so he could pull her into his arms.

"I have wanted to do this ever since you walked through the door of your house," he murmured. "But even more so when you came down in your leathers." His lips came down and met hers.

Just as Charlie was relaxing into his embrace, they were interrupted by a loud voice.

"Will you put her down?" someone exclaimed, and they both turned to see Darren standing at the door.

"Hi bro," Mitchell said. "This is Charlotte... Charlotte, this is Darren."

All of a sudden barks started to echo around the hallway and a huge black Labrador came bounding towards them, stopping and lying down directly in front of Charlotte for a belly rub. She knelt down and ran her hands over his warm fur.

"Who's this then?" she asked.

"Jester," Mitch said as he bent down next to her, their fingertips touching as Jester got twice the attention.

"Is Dad around?" Mitch asked.

"No, he's still out but he mentioned getting some fish and chips in for supper," Darren said as they all entered the kitchen and he flicked the switch on the kettle.

"What are you doing later?" Darren asked as he lounged back against the worktop.

"We have an appointment with a DVD and then an early night as we will be dancing tomorrow," Mitch replied. They picked up their coffee mugs.

"Come on, let me show you around," Mitch said to Charlie.

She followed Mitch and Jester down the hallway and into the lounge and dining room before he opened the patio door and they stepped out into the garden. Jester bounded on ahead of them seeming to know exactly where they were going.

"Come on, I promised Nan and Gramps that I would introduce you to them," he said.

They walked down the garden and through some apple trees to find a small chalet-style house nestling at the bottom of the garden.

"The main house used to be theirs but when my parents split up, we came to live with them and then they built this a few years ago," Mitch said.

"Mitchell?" his Nan exclaimed as they got closer to the chalet.

"Nan, this is Charlotte," he said, as Charlie extended her hand only to find herself pulled into an embrace.

"Call me Pam," she asked as she stepped away. "This is Peter."

An older version of her mum's ex-boyfriend stepped forward and shook her hand. "It's great to meet you. Mitchell has been talking about you non-stop," he said, as Charlie blushed and looked over to Mitch who was smiling back at her.

"I can see the likeness to Stephanie," Pam said, looking Charlotte up and down.

"You told them?" Charlotte exclaimed.

"Yes, I was trying to do some research. Hope you don't mind?"

"We loved Stephanie, we were heartbroken when James told us they had split up. How is your mum?" Peter asked.

"Fine thanks," Charlie replied, unsure what else she could say as she wondered if her mum was still heartbroken about the whole affair.

As they walked back up the garden, Charlotte turned to Mitchell.

"Have you said anything to your dad?" she asked.

"No not yet, I thought I would wait until you had got a bit further with the diaries."

"Ok, that's a plan. I am up to the September entries so based on your brother's birth, I must be getting closer?"

"Well, enough speculation. Let's get your bag upstairs and much as I love you in the leathers, they aren't the most comfortable things to stay in," Mitchell grinned, and Charlie followed him back in the house and upstairs.

Once again déjà vu hit her as she stepped into Mitchell's room and spotted the same shelf arrangement above the bed (as described in her mum's diaries). It seemed it was just the décor had changed.

"You're in here with me, unless you would rather go in the spare room?" he asked, placing her rucksack on the floor. He started to unzip her jacket so his hands could reach around and pull her close.

"Now, where were we?" he breathed, his lips brushing her cheek, on the way to meeting her lips.

"Here is perfect," she breathed in between kisses, running her hands over his chest and then wrapping them around his neck. When they parted she reached down to undo the leather trousers and started to wriggle out of them.

"Lie on the bed and I'll pull them off," Mitchell said, laughing at her struggles.

"Ok." Charlie lay back on the soft duvet and tried not to get distracted by the scent of him wafting up from the pillow, a scent that was hard to mistake.

He pulled them off but before she could sit up, he pinned her down, staring into her eyes.

"You are so fucking sexy," he murmured, his voice so low it was like a rumble.

She lowered her eyelashes and at the same time she parted her lips slightly. Mitch needed no invitation and his lips greeted hers, his tongue probing her mouth as she reciprocated. It felt like heaven.

Before any more clothes could come off, they heard a door shut downstairs and further barking from Jester. Mitchell reluctantly pulled back and they both sat up. She looked at his hair all tousled from her fingers raking through it while they kissed, his bright green eyes staring at her, mirroring her own feelings of lust.

"Darren, Mitchell, are you home?" came a voice, sounding like

Mitchell but slightly lighter in timbre.

"Yes Dad," they heard Darren reply.

"Yes Dad, be down in a moment," Mitchell shouted, pulling Charlie off the bed, helping her straighten the t-shirt that had ridden up over her stomach. As he did this, he lightly ran his finger along the waistband of her leggings and pulled her to him for a last kiss that left Charlotte reeling from the heat racing through her nerve endings.

"Do I look ok?" she asked him, when he let her go.

"You look fab–u–lous darling," he intoned, doing his best impression of Craig Revel Horwood from *Strictly Come Dancing*. This made Charlie laugh and lightened the mood from serious to fun.

"Come on, let's go as I'm starving."

Downstairs she was confronted by a sight that made her inhale sharply. He still looked almost the same as he did in the photo her mum had of him from twenty-four years ago, hair short and still blond, plus a slim, muscular physique. Apart from some wrinkles around the eyes she could see why her mum had fallen for him in the first place and why she had fallen for his son.

"Dad, this is Charlotte… Charlotte, my dad James," Mitchell said, stepping aside so his dad could see her standing in the doorway. James did a double take and she noticed his quick intake of breath. Had he guessed who she was? She wondered as he reached out and shook her hand. She felt it shake slightly under her grasp as he looked her up and down once more.

"So you're the dancer from Ross that Mitchell has been talking about? You really remind me of someone I used to know," he said, his voice trailing off as his mind seemed taken by memories lurking there.

Charlotte looked across at Mitchell and shook her head; luckily he understood perfectly that now was not the right time to say anything more. They were startled by Charlie's phone as she pulled it from her pocket. It was her mum. She ducked into the hallway and quickly apologised before saying goodbye and returning to the kitchen, the smell of fish and chips irresistible as James plated them up and they sat down at the kitchen table.

After nearly two hours I started to worry and kept checking my phone in case I had missed a text instead of a call. Eventually I gave in and rang her mobile number.

"Hi Charlie?"

"Hi Mum, sorry I forgot, I'm ok but I have been busy meeting all of Mitchell's family," Charlotte gushed.

"That's ok, I just needed to check you had arrived," I said, pleased to hear from her voice that everything was going well.

"We're just about to have some tea," Charlie said. "So I'd better go."

"Sure, sweetheart, just let me know when you are coming home on Sunday. Have a good time and don't forget to say thank you to Mitchell's dad for letting you stay," I gently reminded.

"I won't. Bye Mum."

"Bye Charlotte."

The house always felt empty when I was alone so I wandered into the lounge with my solitary meal and a bottle of wine. I called Sarah but Chris was taking her out for a meal and although they had invited me to join them, I declined. The television was dire so I gave in to my misgivings and located my worn copy of *Top Gun*, slotting it into the machine. At the same time I picked up my diary and opened it up to the bookmarked page, settling in for a night of memories.

Dear Diary,

Friday 30th September, 1988

It had been a long time since I last packed my bag for a weekend in Warwickshire with James. However it also felt quite quick as college had been really interesting in most parts and I had managed to keep a couple of my shows going at the hospital at the same time. Also on a Saturday night I would go out dancing with Jack, Mark and some of the nurses Caroline, Catherine and Melanie. It was always a laugh but would leave me feeling sad when the slow songs heralded the end of the night and people paired off while I was left to miss the comfort of James' arms holding me. I sat on my window seat and scanned the road until I heard the familiar roar of an engine and the Mini came into sight.

By the time he stepped out of the car, I had reached the ground floor and was waiting to jump into his arms. He spun me round and kissed me before we broke apart so that he could say hello to my parents. After a quick coffee, I was soon in the car.

"So how's the job then?" I asked, even though his letters had been full of the fire station.

"Amazing. Driving the fire engine is something else, especially when you hear the siren and see cars part in front of you."

I could tell from the excitement in his voice and the sparkle in his eyes that this was what he really loved.

"My course is going well and I've still got a couple of hospital radio shifts to keep me busy in between time."

"Are the kids enjoying your talents?"

"Yeah, I get mobbed as soon as I enter the ward," I revealed. Smiling, I thought of Lisa, Jenny, Sam and Ben who were always the first ones to call the show.

I didn't tell him how much my heart ached when we were apart, how empty my arms felt without him filling them. I saw the chain of his St. Christopher tucked into his jumper and I smiled. We held hands for most of the journey and by the time we pulled into his drive, I was ready to fall into his arms again.

After an evening of catching up with Peter and Pam, we made our excuses and went upstairs. James put the mix tape into his stereo and as the now-familiar tunes swirled around the room, he walked the short distance that separated us and pulled me into his arms. My body meeting his, revelling in the feel of his strong muscles that rippled under his clothes, my hands crept under his jumper to touch his skin.

Even after all this time, being with him was exciting and thrilling, his lips catching mine in a long, slow kiss. Our lips yielded to each other and opened so that our tongues could slip past and explore. I couldn't wait to pull his jumper off so that I could see what my fingertips had already felt and I started to tackle the belt buckle on his jeans. Soon he stood before me in all his glory, whilst surprisingly I was still semi-dressed in the underwear he had bought me for my birthday. Kneeling in front of me he unclipped the suspender belt attachments and rolled down the stockings, his hands smoothly caressing my legs. Kissing his way back up, his hands unclasped my bra and as it fell from my body, his fingers caught my nipples and ignited the flames inside.

James had brought up a glass of iced water and I watched as he took a sip and then brought his mouth down onto my nipple. I jumped from the shock of the cold ice cube that tumbled against my warm skin, the feeling intense. The pinpricks of ice hitting my warm skin created a delicious feeling of both heat and cold and droplets of water trailed down my breast and along the valley in between.

"Fuck, that feels fantastic," I gasped when James surfaced.
"You liked it then?"
"Yes, mind-blowing, where did you find out about this?"
"Graham at the pool told me about it as his girlfriend tried it on him."
"Can I have a go?" I asked, grinning up at James as he lay down on the bed.

Popping an ice cube into my mouth, I headed for James' nipples and ran the cube over the surface of his skin. I felt him flinch before he pulled me closer. Every so often I would glance up and watch his face. Once the ice melted, I trailed my fingertip down the route of the water as it pooled in his belly button and then licked it up. I watched as James reached for the glass again.

"My turn again," he decided. "And this time I'm going lower."

I watched as his head disappeared between my legs and then I closed my eyes as the first rivulet of icy water trickled down and failed to cool the heat of my body. Soon I couldn't contain myself any longer as I gasped.

"Fuck me now, I can't wait any longer." My orgasm was already on the brink of breaking me wide open.

As I came I grabbed James' shoulders and to stop myself from screaming, I kissed him deeply as I felt his orgasm fill me and join with the ripples of mine that were more like waves crashing around us. The drumming of my heart so loud in my ears, it was like a violent thunderstorm had erupted around us. Afterwards, we lay together and stared at each other with new eyes, neither of us wanting to break the spell surrounding us at that moment in time. Love was perfect.

Saturday 1st October, 1988
I awoke to the sound of rain drumming on the window pane as I leaned over and gently kissed James on the lips. It was all I needed to do to wake him up.

"Morning babe," he murmured between kisses. "This is the best way to wake up," he said as he held me close.

"What are we doing today?" I asked.

"I thought we could go into town, maybe see a film if there is anything good on?"

"Can I see where you work?"

"Sure, I will warn you the guys are full of banter and I may have to rescue you from them." His kisses started to drift down my ever eager body.

"Isn't that what they teach you to do?" I giggled. James silenced me with his lips. After last night's wildness, that morning it was all about just being together and sharing our love in the gentleness of touch. My heart reached out and surrendered to his.

As it was still raining we took the car and parked up before looking around the shops. James dragged me into Ann Summers and I felt faintly embarrassed as he wandered around showing me things he wanted to see me in. In the end I found a set that we both liked and bought it for later. After lunch we drove to the fire station and James showed me around, much to the amusement of the other lads. They all seemed like a friendly bunch and I was just pleased that Felicity was no longer on the scene.

"We're going clubbing tonight, do you want to come?" Michael asked us. James looked across at me and I nodded.

"Yeah, why not," he replied. "We'll meet you there around ten."

Getting ready to go out I tried not to think about what happened the last time we hit the town. James just pulled me to him.

"You're quiet, what's wrong?" he asked.

"Nothing, just remembering last time we went out. I hope we don't see Felicity."

"Well, you will be well protected this time with all of us strong fireman to look after you," James replied, kissing me lightly on the tip of my nose. "Anyway we may not be there long as you look so sexy tonight," he said, letting his eyes and hands wander over my curves.

The club seemed to attract the more sophisticated crowd and I noticed that James had made an effort to wear a tie with his suit. He looked so handsome that I was sure I wouldn't want to let go of him all night.

The crowd of fireman were great fun, some had girlfriends and some were very much single and on the pull. All in all I felt comfortable in their midst and I didn't mind when James went off to the bar later in the evening. However after nearly twenty minutes of him being gone, I started to get worried and left the group to do a quick wander, seeing if I could find him.

Looking back, I wish now that I hadn't gone looking for him as I saw him in the entrance with his arms around a girl. Even though I could only see the back of her, I knew it was Felicity.

As my eyes filled with tears, James saw me and quickly withdrew his arms and tried to step into my path as I took flight and ran past them, out of the club. I ran until I reached the corner of the street and then I wandered down the next street until I came to a park I recognised. I didn't notice the tears rolling down my cheeks as the rain was beating down on me too and when I found a bench, I just sat down and let the rain continue its stream down and through my dress. I was soaked to the skin but I didn't care as I wondered, why? Why was James hugging Felicity? What was she doing there? Why had he betrayed me? I started to shiver from the cold as I held my head in my hands, my mind a maze of emotions.

I heard running footsteps and James calling my name. I stayed hunched over but he found me and carefully draped my coat over my shoulders. I couldn't speak; I didn't know what to start with but in the end I didn't need to as James broke the silence

"It's not what you think," he mumbled.

"What am I supposed to think when I see my boyfriend with his arms around another woman?" I spat back.

"Felicity has just broken up with Jason and needed a friendly shoulder to cry on," James replied. "And I just happened to be there to provide that."

"So when did the two of you become good friends?" I retorted.

"Well, she was a lot better once I handed in my notice at work," he replied, slowly reaching out to take my hand in his. He rubbed it between the two of his as it was numb from the cold.

"Please believe me Steph, I would never lie to you or hurt you. I love you… till the end of time…" his words trailed off, as I heard the catch of a sob in his voice. Even though my mind was still lost in confusion, I leaned into his arms. I wasn't ready to give up on him as he held my heart and soul and I knew I couldn't wrench them away.

I can't remember how long we sat on the bench in the rain but I started to shiver, even with my coat on, so we walked back to the house. There were no stars in the sky that night, our way was lit only by the artificial streetlights along the path. James never took his arms from around me and although we didn't talk, the silence was safe. As it was late we tiptoed upstairs and into the bathroom. James gently peeled my clothes away from my frozen body and started up the shower, joining me under the hot stream of water. With care he ran the sponge over me as I clung to him. When we were under the comfort of the duvet, I kissed him.

"I love you, I believe you," I whispered as I looked into his eyes. All I could see was love burning brightly.

As James drifted into sleep I lay there awake for a while before I drifted off. However I only found nightmares when my eyes were closed. Felicity had hold of James and was taunting me with the words *he's mine now, he's mine now*. I woke up sweating and pulled James' arms around me as I tried to dispel the awful scene I had just seen in my dreams.

♪

I reached for the tissues as I mirrored the tears of Maverick onscreen as he cried over the death of Goose. I cried for all the good times I had shared with James, and all the love he had given me which I had reciprocated for that short period of time. I cried as I recalled the hurt he had caused me and it felt as though my wounds deliberately started to throb with every beat.

-30-

After tea, Mitch and Charlie went upstairs to his room to watch *Dirty Dancing* again and to really analyse the routine at the end. As the storyline unfolded on screen, Charlotte was transported into the scenes, except that Johnny looked more like Mitch and she was Baby. He reached over and grasped her hand in his as they watched the romance unfold and all the dances in between. They both leaned forward at the end from the point where Johnny says, *Nobody puts Baby in the corner* – the action launching into the final dance of the film.

"I want to start now," Charlie said at the end, wiping away tears.

"Me too, but I think we should wait until tomorrow as I still have to show you my studio."

"What, you have your own studio? Where is it? Can't I see it now?" Charlie begged. "Is it far away?"

Mitch paused for a moment and then relented, grabbing her hand. "It's not far at all," he replied as he pulled her off the bed.

"What about shoes?" she said as they left the bedroom.

"You won't need them," he replied as they walked through the kitchen and to a door that linked to the garage. Opening it Mitchell flicked the switch and Charlie was confronted by a wooden floor, wall to ceiling mirrors along the one side and even a bar. Speakers hung from the ceiling and a top of the range music centre was in the far corner.

"Wow," she said, astonished as she stepped into her perfect world.

"Welcome to my studio. Hope you like it?"

"I love it, it's fantastic," Charlie replied, and he pulled her further into the room, spinning her around before bringing her close for a kiss.

"Come on then," she said, in between kisses. "Let's get started"

"You are an eager pupil," Mitch remarked as he let her go and crossed the room to the stereo.

"I might just need to go and get my dance pumps," she said.

"Well, I need to get out of my jeans so I'll bring them down with me, anything else you need?"

"No, I think I'm ok with my leggings and t-shirt thanks," she said smiling as the music from the film started to pour out of the speakers and into her soul.

"Back in five," Mitchell said. "I'll leave you to start warming up"

She watched him leave before walking over to the bar, starting to bend and stretch to warm up her muscles. Then as the music surrounded her, she closed her eyes and started to dance around the room. Her feet no longer felt cold against the wood as she imagined she was Baby. She was so wrapped up in her movements, she failed to hear Mitchell return until she felt his firm hands on her waist. She didn't need to open her eyes or stop moving as his hands held her firmly and his body brushed hers. Instinctively they moved together in time with the music. The song ended and Charlie opened her eyes to find she was staring up into Mitchell's.

"That was great," he said, taking deep breaths, "we really work well together."

"Yeah," Charlie replied. "So where shall we start then?"

"Here I think," Mitch said as his lips found hers. "I'm sure I saw some kissing in their routine."

However before they could get carried away, the next song started and they decided that dancing was what they wanted to do. After another warm-up session to the next song, Charlie put her pumps on and they forwarded the tracks to the one they really needed to work on. Grabbing his phone, Mitchell pulled up the video clip from the film and they had a quick watch before they began. Most of the steps were fairly easy but it was getting them in time with the music that would take more practise and also the lift was going to take trust and judgement.

They had just finished the song for the sixth time when the door opened and in bounded Jester followed by James.

"I'm just off to bed you guys, it's gone one," he said.

"Night Dad," Mitch replied. "We're about to call it quits anyway."

"Night, Mr. Cooke," Charlotte said, smiling whilst wiping the sweat out of her eyes.

"Just call me Jim."

Charlotte sank to the floor and Jester padded over and put his head in her lap.

"He likes you," Mitch said, sitting on her other side, resting his head on her shoulder.

"What, Jester?"

"No, my dad, well… and Jester… and I really like you," he said in a husky tone, as she turned to him and his lips came down to meet hers.

"Shall we head up?" Mitch asked. "We are going to have a long day of this tomorrow."

"Yeah," replied Charlotte, suddenly realising how exhausted she was now that she had stopped moving.

"Is it ok for me to have a quick shower?" Charlotte asked.

"Sure I'll have one after you," he replied as they separated on the landing.

Charlie quickly located a towel in the airing cupboard and stripped off her sweaty clothes. Under the warm stream of water, she thought about how far they had managed to get in only a few hours. It was as if their bodies had been made to dance with one another. She lathered up well with her new vanilla shower gel and then cleaned her teeth, hoping more kissing would take place. As she dried off and wrapped the towel around her she thought about the sleeping arrangements. She had never shared a bed with a guy before, let alone one she fancied like crazy. Would she be able to resist going further than she wanted to at this stage?

Mitch was wearing his dressing gown when she returned and after a quick peck on the lips as they passed one another, he headed for the bathroom. Charlotte had packed her shorts and vest set so she put them on, sprayed liberally with deodorant and some perfume, and then dived under the duvet. Which side should she be on? Which side would he want to sleep? What would he wear? Yawning she closed her eyes while she waited for him to return from the bathroom and within a couple of seconds, she had fallen asleep.

The next thing Charlotte was aware of was sunlight flooding through the curtains and a heavy arm draped over her. It startled her at first but then she remembered where she was and as she relaxed back, she felt the firmness of Mitch's body curled up behind her. She was still wearing her night clothes and although Mitch's chest was bare she could feel his pyjama bottoms. How could she have fallen asleep on him? Well not even on him, but before he returned from the shower? He must have felt her stirring because his arm tightened around her and she felt his soft breath on the nape of her neck as he kissed her, her body leaping into life.

"Morning sleepyhead," he murmured.

"Morning Mitch, sorry about last night. I didn't mean to fall asleep," she replied, as she wiggled round so that she lay facing him.

"It's ok, you looked so sweet last night, snoring softly. I just curled up next to you."

"I was not snoring," she retorted, punching him lightly on the arm.

"I think you were," he replied, looking smug as he pulled her close. "I'll record it on my phone next time so there'll be no arguments." He laughed and then before she could say anything more, his lips claimed hers in what could only be described as the best morning kiss she had ever experienced. When they pulled apart she was breathless from the force of his kisses, her lips bruised, the rest of her burning with desire.

They heard sounds from the landing and realised that the rest of the household were awake so they got up. Charlie felt suddenly shy in the presence of such male nakedness.

"Coffee?" he asked.

"Yeah, I'll be down in a bit," she replied, as she watched him leave, tipping her a cheeky wink.

She smiled as she found her leotard and footless tights and slipped them on, shrugging on her long woolly jumper before heading down to the kitchen. She paused at the door because this whole thing felt so strange, yet so right. To be standing and walking in all the places where her mum had been twenty-four years ago made her mind flip out and she couldn't help but believe that somehow, this was meant to be. She was meant to bring her mum back to the person who had loved her all those years ago.

The kitchen was a hive of industry as she sat down next to Mitch whilst his dad fed the toaster with a mountain of bread.

"Hope you are hungry?" he asked them all, as Darren sat down opposite them.

"What were you two up to last night?" Darren grinned.

"Just dancing," Mitch assured his brother, reaching over to squeeze Charlotte's hand beneath the table.

"Yeah right," he smirked, "when will you be needing a cameraman then?"

"Probably not until this evening and maybe not until tomorrow morning, depends on how things go today," Mitch replied, reaching for a piece of toast.

"You must try and get some fresh air and show Charlotte our town," James said, sat opposite Charlie. She didn't fail to notice James' stare and the slight shake of his head. It was pretty obvious he was reminded of Steph while looking at her, his expression one of guilt and regret.

-31-

As I climbed the stairs to bed holding the diary in my hands, part of me wanted to put it back in my daughter's room, but in the end I kept it with me and once I was under the covers, I continued to read. I wondered what Charlie was doing at Mitchell's house? Was she being sensible with her heart? I read on, trying to forget the dangers of falling in love.

Dear Diary,

Sunday 2nd October, 1988
After a sleepless night filled with worries and despair, I awoke to a kiss from James and immediately felt better as my hands pulled him close and our tongues collided hungrily. I wanted him to know that I loved him with every inch of my body and mind. I manoeuvred into place on top of him and as I could feel he was already hard and I was most definitely wet, I lowered myself down on him and started to ride. Slowly at first but then faster and faster, until neither of us was in control of our bodies, they were in control of us. His finger reached down and found my clit and he started to stroke it slowly as I ground myself harder onto him. I was pulsing as I bit my lip to stop myself from screaming, the sensations starting to become almost too much to bear, pushing us harder and faster to the point of no return. I had read about multiple orgasms but knowing how difficult it was to experience just one, I was sure they didn't exist – until that moment of pure pleasure.

Our worlds collided and spun us out of control into a space filled with love, lust and desire, all rolled into a ball of light. I let myself surrender to the waves that crashed through my body over and over again, leaving me a wreck in his arms. We lay there not able to move or even speak but with his arms wrapped tightly around me, I again felt safe and secure in our love. Pushing the covers off our hot and sweaty bodies, the coolness enveloped our skin and helped us return to earth.

"Till the end of time," James murmured as we drifted together.

"You take my breath away," I replied, grazing his lips with mine. I could still taste the faint tang of blood from where I had bitten down earlier.

We spent a lazy day around the house as the weather was still wet and wild. After Sunday lunch with Peter and Pam, I reluctantly packed my bag and we drove back to my place. Although I always enjoyed any drive sat next to James, I also hated the ones that tore us apart at the end. Why was life so unfair to have separated us all those months ago, so we had to take the pleasure when we could and deal with the pain for the rest of the time in between? After spending a final couple of hours together in my room, just smooching, we had to say goodbye. How I hated goodbyes as I stood once more on the doorstep of my home, watching the red of his tail lights disappear into the darkness of the night.

I returned to my room and buried my head in the pillow, crying once again. How many tears of pain had fallen from them? How many more were to come before I could at last claim my life as my own and be with James forever? Rick Astley's voice through my speakers both calmed and consoled me as I vowed that my life would be as wonderful as music proclaimed it to be.

♬

I sat back and closed the diary to consider the lines I had written. How naive I had been, so full of certainty that my life would work out as I had planned it in my dreams. I thought about my daughter Charlotte and hoped she would not be the same, although first love was an extremely powerful drug to resist.

I remembered back to the night Mark had proposed to me. We had been on holiday together in France, strolling along a moonlit beach when he had dropped to his knees in front of me and popped the ultimate question. I had said yes, even though my heart had dredged up memories of another beach, in another time and place. I had left my heart drawn there in the sand, but it had been swept away even though I had tried to reclaim it – the tides relentless.

Mark had been a kind and caring friend. He had always wanted more, I had seen it in his eyes. Eyes were like the windows of a person's soul and if you looked close enough, you could see what they were thinking and feeling deep down. My eyes had been like that until the moment my world had almost ended, and then they became hazy and dark. I shaded my thoughts and smothered my feelings to keep the pain away. It was as though my world had been in colour and then faded into black and white. There had been no way to save myself from this fear that invaded my every waking moment.

We hung out with Sarah and Chris and I guessed that to all eyes, Mark and me looked like the perfect couple. We had been joined together in the one act that I had committed after the bells had chimed in the start of 1989. None of us had ever talked about it much since then, yet it had hung between us. Even now I would catch Sarah's gaze at my scars and see her shudder from the memories. I had side-stepped questions from my curious daughter over the years, yet if I let her read this diary, she would soon know what I had done. Would it upset her to know how I had really felt about her father? Would it save her from falling too deeply or was that just a risk that everyone took in their lives?

Turning off the lights I lay there and wondered if my life would have been different if I hadn't fallen in love at sixteen, if I had somehow waited until I was older. Would it have felt better or different? Then as sleep claimed me, I was once again on the beach in the sun, James beside me as I laughed and drew the heart in the sand. My body tingled slightly as I remembered our time together in the hotel room and then in the moonlit garden for his 21st birthday. As my dream continued I was back in that garden, searching through the leaves of the apple trees, searching for a man of forty-five who held my heart. This man would always have a part of me with him and I would always be searching for it. My bare feet crept between the shards of broken mirror that littered the lawn and lay intermingled with droplets of blood and a ripped-up invitation.

Even in sleep I couldn't escape my memories as they fell like grains of sand through the hourglass of my life, tears falling and staining my pillow.

When I woke up the next morning I noticed my scar was red and angry; I must have been rubbing it whilst I slept. Pulling on my jeans and jumper, I decided to go out for a walk and a swim to clear my head of all the dreams and nightmares of last night. It would serve me right for drinking a whole bottle of wine alone!

Once in town I bought a bottle of water from the supermarket and then wandered into the leisure centre car park and walked towards the faded façade of the pool, realising that it looked like I felt – unloved. As I climbed the steps and entered the doors, I realised I hadn't been there for ages. It had always been the one place where I felt calm. As I changed into my swimsuit I heard voices laughing from the poolside and spotted a couple of girls about seventeen or eighteen chatting to the lifeguard as he tried to remain alert despite the distraction. I grinned as I dived into the cool water and ploughed up and down between the other swimmers.

The monotony of the task in hand helped to soothe my mind and I pulled into the side, relaxing before I did the final length to get out. As I did this I dived under at a particular spot and closing my eyes, remembering my first kiss, the sweetest kiss of all. First love never died, it was just supposed to fade happily into people's memories.

Leaving the pool car park I turned and looked back at the point where James used to stand and wave when we had first met. Smiling I returned home to change and drove into work, suddenly feeling that life was not too bad after all. I had the whole day ahead of me, a couple of hours doing the Saturday Request Fest on Love Shack Radio and then out to the local Chinese with Jack, Paul and Ian, who I worked with. I grabbed my phone and dropped Charlie a text asking if she was ok and what time would she be home on Sunday. I put the phone away in my bag knowing that I would be lucky to get a reply until evening. There was definitely something about Mitchell that was so familiar and safe. Perhaps it was because he reminded me of James.

After my radio show I arranged to meet the guys outside the restaurant at seven. The meal was fantastic and the company even better as we laughed about all the strange requests that found their way to air. We discussed the Rock On the River event at length and surrounded by my friends, I felt that life was worth living again. This project was just what I needed and perhaps if I could move on, then I could find happiness again. Jack kissed me goodbye before I went home.

"Are you ok?" he asked. "You seemed a little quiet tonight."

"Yeah, think so, it's just been strange in the house without Charlie around."

"Where is she?"

"Up in Warwickshire with her new boyfriend Mitchell."

"Don't you like him? Or trust her?"

"No it's not that, he's a lovely guy, but he really reminds me of James, you remember James, don't you?" I asked.

"Yeah, that hot guy you were dating when we first worked together?" Jack replied. "Is that a bad thing then?"

"No, but it's bringing back all these memories that I thought I had left behind," I sighed, as Jack pulled me in for a hug.

"It will be ok, you're a great woman and if I wasn't gay, I'd fancy you. You should get back on the dating scene again, you shouldn't be alone."

"Well, maybe I will, but the main thing is working on our fundraising event, it's going to be huge."

"Sure will," Jack replied. "Now get going and I'll see you soon. You should pop in the hospital sometime."

"Yeah," I said, realising I hadn't been back there since Mark was stabbed in the car park. That was another ghost I had to lay to rest in order to move on with my life.

-32-

In the studio Mitchell put the stereo on and they started to warm up.

"How are we going to practise the lift?" Charlie asked, remembering the last time they had tried it, when she had been stood on a park bench.

"I'm not sure, we may have to bring a mattress down here for any unforced landings," he replied, arching his eyebrows. "Although my dad might wonder what it's for."

"We need a lake like they had in the film."

"Well, the duck pond is in the next park but it's only two inches deep," Mitch laughed.

"Bit cold and shallow for that," Charlie responded. "I will just have to get it right first time then."

"Yes, you will otherwise we might both be out of the competition if we break anything," Mitch said. "But that's not going to happen so we had best get started."

"Can we also do a few practises of the fall from my routine?" Charlie asked. "I saw a table in the garden so we can use that."

As the music flowed they danced, and every time they moved through the routine, they got a bit farther and a bit surer of the steps and the way they worked together. Once or twice Mitch shouted when Charlie went wrong but it was all in good fun and eventually they sank to the floor, just the lift left to perfect.

"Shall we grab a drink?" Mitch asked. He threw her a towel so she could wipe off the sweat that was dripping from her body.

"Yeah, great."

They realised it was already two in the afternoon and Charlie's stomach let out a small rumble as she gulped down a pint of water.

"I'm hungry," she said. "Is there any food around?"

Mitchell checked the fridge and found a couple of slices of cold pizza.

She finished off the slice and gave her crust to Jester who had sat down next to her.

As they started work on the lift, Charlie knew that it was up to her to launch herself at Mitch with both power and control, then trust him to lift her up high so she could float above him. After a few half attempts, they managed to nail the first full lift and as she slid down his body, their emotions were so high that she pulled his lips down to meet hers. Although they were both breathless, they were even more so when they pulled apart and slouched against the wall.

"Come on, let's do that again," Mitch said.

Charlie wiped her brow and retied her hair, determined that this time it was going to be perfect. As she leapt and rose into the air above Mitch, his strong hands held her solid as her arms stretched out to the side and for those few seconds, she closed her eyes and believed that she was Baby. In reality she didn't want to be Baby, she wanted to be exactly who she was – Charlotte Eden in complete and utter love with Mitchell Cooke.

Deciding to finish on a high note and go back to it for a final run-through in the morning, Charlie grabbed her 'Take My Breath Away' CD and inserted it into the music system. Mitch stood aside and watched as Charlie flowed with the music as it carried her to that deserted airfield from the video. He studied the emotions that crossed her face, perfectly in line with the poignant lyrics of the song. The girls had sorted out their costumes and apart from the fall at the end, they were almost perfect. Mitchell was amazed by her fluidity and style as he watched her bend and leap until the end part.

♫

James returned from the shops and stopped in his tracks when he recognised the music bleeding out from the studio next door. He leaned against the counter and allowed the familiar melody to wash over him. Closing his eyes he was a young man again and in his arms he held the love of his life once more. This was an omen if ever he needed one – it was the wake-up call he needed. He had to speak to Mitchell and ask him the all-important question about his new girlfriend and her family. It was time to open up about the past in order to move into the future.

James was startled when the studio door opened and after a quick, "Hi," from both of them, he watched as they ran into the garden. He crossed to the sink so that he could watch as they danced across the lawn together towards the garden table. He wondered what they were up to as Charlotte climbed onto the table and then launched herself backwards into Mitchell's waiting arms. His son moved Charlotte down to finish with her outstretched across his knee. She climbed off and they went through the whole thing again until on the last one, he bent down at the end and his lips brushed her throat, creeping up until they captured her lips. James stood mesmerised as his son laid his girlfriend out on the grass, her hands scraping through his hair, him holding her close.

James looked away not wanting to spoil their moment but at the same time, he blinked back the memory of a moonlit night in the very same garden, the stars shining brightly in the velvet darkness. The glow from the moon lit up the sun-kissed skin of Steph's slender body as they came together.

Quickly he shook off those memories and emotions and started to prepare tea. Darren appeared, saying he was off to see Sophie and wouldn't need any so it would just be himself, Mitch and Charlie for tea – and some all-important questions that were burning inside him. Part of him wanted to wait until he could just talk to Mitch but another part wanted answers from Charlotte directly. She could answer his questions for sure, but was he ready to hear the truth?

Charlie and Mitch walked back into the kitchen, Mitchell brushing the grass from Charlotte's back as she picked some out of her hair and retied it in a ponytail.

"Hope you are both hungry. I'm doing spaghetti Bolognese for tea."

"Oh yes," Charlotte replied. "I'm starving."

"Me too," echoed Mitchell as he poured them both a drink and they sat down at the kitchen table, their breath ragged from the exertions.

"Should be ready in about an hour," James said, pouring himself a glass of red wine and looking at the two of them. "Good practice? I recognised the last song that was playing when I came in, it was one of my favourites from the film *Top Gun*."

Charlotte looked startled and James grew ever more worried he was right. This was Steph's daughter.

"It's my group's entry song for the dance final," Charlie elaborated, "Mum helped me choose the song and Mitch is helping at the end as we don't have any guys in our group."

"Charlie's group are probably going to win in a couple of week's time," Mitch claimed.

"No, Mitchell's group will and I can't wait to see his take on 'Thriller'," she enthused as she smiled over at him, their eyes locked, betraying the strength of their true feelings.

"We're going to go up and have a shower now before dinner," Mitch said standing up, his hand still firmly in Charlotte's. James didn't fail to notice the lust the pair betrayed with their eyes and hoped they hadn't got too carried away yet.

"Tea's ready," James shouted, and Charlie and Mitch soon joined him downstairs.

James had laid the table in the dining room and as they entered, he passed Mitch a bottle of beer and then turned to Charlotte.

"Wine or beer?" he asked.

"White wine and lemonade if you have it," Charlie replied.

The music playing on the stereo was from *Top Gun*. Sitting down for dinner, the food was excellent and the three of them just sat and ate to start with until 'Take My Breath Away' flowed from the speakers.

Mitchell looked up and across at his dad.

"I didn't know you had a copy of this song?" Mitch exclaimed, and his father reached over and turned the stereo up slightly.

"Yes, it was a favourite of mine back in the day when I was in love with a girl called Stephanie March," James explained, turning his gaze to watch Charlotte's reaction. "I think you might know her?"

Charlie glanced at Mitchell but he just nodded.

"Yes, she's my mum."

The three of them sat in a moment's silence that seemed to stretch a lifetime. Charlie and Mitch cast anxious glances at each other and then at James, who visibly turned pale and closed his eyes, his hands gripping the edge of the table, the knuckles white.

-33-

It was Mitchell who broke the silence. "I was going to tell you who Charlie was; I was just waiting for the right moment."

"Well, it was not hard to guess when I saw Charlotte yesterday," James replied as he opened his eyes and shook his head slowly. "It was only the eye colour that had me puzzled, but the hair colour and skin tone and build," James continued. "It's pretty remarkable that the two of you happened to meet?"

"Yes, we didn't know until the weekend that Mitch came to visit me and I was showing him the sites of Ross. He told me you had worked at the swimming pool and I said my mum had met her first boyfriend at the same place and we were hit by this realisation."

"Yes, then Charlie had a photo back at her place of the two of you at that time and I recognised you instantly Dad," Mitch answered, joining in with the story.

"You looked very handsome in your suit," Charlie said, smiling at James across the table. There was no mistaking her smile, it was the mirror image of Stephanie's.

"How is Steph... your mum?" James said, his words catching on the lump that had formed in his throat.

"She's well thanks," Charlie replied.

James wondered if Charlie knew what had happened between him and Steph. He felt so ashamed and remorseful. How would Steph react to this? Did she still love him like he still loved her?

James could see Charlie shaking, the enormity of this unreal. Mitch tried to comfort her but it would take some getting used to. The youngsters both waited as they looked at each other again and then back at James.

"And your father?" James managed.

"My dad died when I was a baby," Charlie replied. "I never really knew him but Mum is always telling me that I have his eyes so it's just the two of us."

She squeezed Mitch's hand as a small tear slipped down her cheek and he gently wiped it away with his spare hand.

"I'm sorry," James said softly. He stood up and headed for the kitchen to regain his composure and to give Charlotte some space.

Alone, James leaned against the kitchen counter and breathed in and out as he considered this information. Most important was the knowledge that Stephanie was single and so was he. Could he dare hope that he might win her back? Would she want him after the way he had finished things? How would this affect Mitchell and Charlotte's relationship? He had so many considerations, his mind awash with all the possibilities. However the most urgent one was the slim chance that Stephanie might forgive him and possibly end up back in his arms.

Mitch walked into the kitchen and found his dad leaning against the worktop, tears clouding his normally clear eyes.

"Are you alright Dad?"

"Yes, thanks Mitch, I just need a moment," James replied as he turned to rinse his face at the sink, trying to clear the jumble of thoughts in his mind.

"Have we got any ice cream?"

"Better look in the fridge, you might be lucky."

As his son walked past him, James tapped him on his shoulder. "Look after Charlotte, if you really like her, don't fuck it up."

Mitchell nodded at his dad's advice and then pulled open the fridge door, finding what he was looking for – a tub of chocolate ice cream.

"You ok if we go upstairs to my room and listen to music?" Mitch asked, as he opened a drawer and found two spoons.

"Ok but just one thing. How does Stephanie look now?"

"Like Charlie's older sister," Mitch replied, watching a grin spread over his dad's face that made him look years younger, a sparkle in his eyes.

"Are you going to be alright Dad?"

"Yes, I have a date with a DVD and some memories. I'll share them with you another day, you don't want to keep the lady waiting too long," James laughed, watching Mitchell return to the dining room, the subsequent sound of feet on stairs telling him they were heading up to Mitch's room.

As James cleared up, he turned the stereo on and flicked back to their song. He was finally able to listen to this tune again without feeling despair, now he had hope to cling to.

♪

Upstairs, Charlotte turned to Mitchell. "So, how do you think that went?"

"As well as could be expected. I think Dad is still very much in love with your mum or at least his memories of your mum," Mitchell decided. "So, we just need to know how things finished between them and how your mum might feel about my dad now."

"Let's hope the diaries will tell us and that I can finish them before the dance competition, otherwise we might end up witnesses at the worst reunion in history," Charlotte sighed.

"Now what's that behind your back?" she grinned, as she tried to duck behind him to see.

"A treat, but it's only for girls who are incredibly nice to me," Mitch replied, a naughty glint in his eyes.

"Oh Mitch, I can be very nice indeed," Charlie purred. "And I have the added advantage in that I am the only girl here."

"Well, I can always give the others a call," he smirked.

"Don't you dare Mitchell, I want you all to myself," Charlie said as she edged closer to him. She reached out and started to tickle him. As he laughed he had to reveal the tub of ice cream so that he could free his hands to retaliate.

"You do know how to make a girl happy," Charlie said.

"Just you wait and see," Mitchell joked. "But first, let's get comfy so we can really enjoy this."

They both curled up on the bed and Mitch flicked the switch on his music system.

Pulling Charlie close, he opened the tub and ran the spoon through its smooth silky surface. Carefully he placed the spoon against her lips and watched as her tongue licked it off. She took the other spoon and did the same to him and considered how erotic this whole thing felt as the coolness of the ice cream slid down their throats and met the heat that was pulsing within their bodies. By the fourth spoonful Charlie was already breathing heavily as her pulse raced.

Then as Mitchell took his next mouthful from her spoon, he pulled her to him and pressed his cold lips on hers. They opened under the light pressure and they shared the cold ice cream as it swirled around between their tongues and melted with the heat. Mitch managed to place the tub and spoons on the bedside table as they continued to kiss and he laid her down on the soft duvet beneath him. His lips travelled down to the neckline of her dress, his hands running down her body to the hemline and slipping underneath, finding the bare skin of her thighs. Charlotte trembled in his embrace as she felt his cool fingers on her hot skin; she was burning up beneath him, flying so near to the centre of his sun. He glanced over her silky knickers and upwards to the wire of her bra and as she arched to his touch, he slipped up and under to take his first caress of her nipples, springing into life under the palms of his hands.

Looking up into her beautiful green eyes, he smiled softly.

"Keep going," she whispered as her lips came down and met his again, holding his head in her hands. Then somehow she wriggled out from beneath him. She pushed him back and straddled him. Staring down, she smiled before she slipped her dress over her head and then unfastened her bra. Mitch stared in admiration at her fantastic body as she tugged his t-shirt over his head so that she could press her naked skin onto his. Heat met heat as they burned together, kissing and exploring each other with sheer abandon.

They swapped positions once more as Mitchell's tongue travelled down her body and encircled her nipples. Charlie felt as if she was going to float away on the sheer bliss of what Mitchell was doing to her body. As they parted for air they gazed at each other in amazement. It was far more than enough for one night and although they both would have liked to have gone further, he held back, happy not to rush things.

Charlotte wanted to throw caution to the wind and just experience everything but she knew from friends in the past that had done the very same thing, it rarely worked out. She would wait, just like her mum had done before her; waiting meant it would keep getting better and better.

-34-

Mitchell was the first awake as the sun glinted on the duvet cover. He could hear his dad was already awake so he carefully moved out from under Charlie's arm that had been flung over his chest for most of the night. He dropped the whisper of a kiss on her forehead and then put his dressing gown on and went downstairs.

"Morning Dad."

He sauntered into the room and nearly tripped over Jester who was lying in the centre of the floor. He grabbed a cup of coffee and sat down opposite.

"How are you?" Mitch asked.

"Well, my mind's a bit all over the place. It all feels a little weird."

"Yes, Charlie and I thought that when we realised."

"So tell me more about Stephanie," James asked, leaning forward.

"Well, she's single and she's a DJ on a local radio station in Hereford. I think it's called Love Shack."

"Ok, anything else?"

"Well Charlie is reading Stephanie's diaries from 1988 at the moment which is the year you two were together but she hasn't got to the part where you split up yet," Mitch said, as he took a sip of coffee and wondered if he should be telling his dad all of this.

"So why did you split up with Stephanie and end up with Mum?" Mitch asked.

"Well, that's a long story."

"I have time."

After a few moments of silence James began to talk. "I fucked things up with Stephanie in a big way and I was too weak to make the right decision at the time. I was working at a leisure centre in Warwick before I became a fireman and your mum, Felicity was the manager there," James paused, clearing his throat. "So when I had my leaving do I kind of got drunk and she offered to drive me home so I agreed. Then before I knew it she pulled into a lay-by and jumped on me. I had a moment of weakness and allowed it to happen and then next thing I know, she's pregnant with Darren and demanding we get married."

Mitchell watched as his dad put his head in his hands, red shame rushing over his cheeks.

"I tried to tell her that I would support her but that I didn't love her and that was when she threatened to tell Stephanie that we had been having an affair for months. That would have destroyed Steph! Felicity was just intent on breaking us apart. She also threatened to let me have no access to Darren if I decided to stay with Stephanie, so I was stuck between a rock and a hard place and couldn't win either way. So I made the hard decision of breaking up with Stephanie, but I didn't tell her the real reason, I tried to let her down gently."

A sob rose in James' throat and he choked it back quickly.

"Then Steph begged me to visit her one, last time and I did. I left early as I just couldn't stay and lie to her as she tried to change my mind. I almost told her the truth then as it would have made me feel better. Perhaps I should have but she was so young, only seventeen," James said, taking a gulp of his coffee and looking up at his son.

"You were fucked, Dad," Mitch said, as he stood up and poured a coffee for Charlotte.

"That's why I said what I did to you last night. If you have strong feelings for Charlotte and she has the same for you, you must keep them safe as whatever you do in the future you may regret what happens. Be honest with each other, completely honest, even if it ends up hurting one or both of you. I have had to live with these lies for nearly twenty-five years and I don't know now if I will ever get through them but I'm going to try to make amends."

"I'm going to take this up to Charlie, it's about time we got started for the day," Mitchell said, the mood around them lightened.

"Shall I do some bacon sandwiches for you?" James asked.

"Yeah that would be great and Dad, don't beat yourself up about what you did back then, we might be able to help you fix it," he said, pushing open the door and carrying the mugs upstairs.

As Mitch stepped into the room Charlie was just opening her eyes and he felt his heart leap at the sight of her dishevelled hair and sleepy eyes. He was pretty certain he loved her but having never been in love before he wasn't sure. He knew he desired her and after last night, it was apparent that she felt the same as he remembered the feel of her skin on his.

"Morning baby," Mitchell said. He crossed the room and put the mugs down next to the half-finished, melted tub of ice cream. Charlie reached for him and pulled him into her arms for a kiss.

"How long have you been awake?" she asked, when they pulled apart. He shrugged off his dressing gown and got back under the covers.

"About an hour," Mitch replied. "I've been downstairs having a chat with Dad."

"Tell me," Charlotte replied, sitting up to cradle her cup of coffee.

"Well, Dad told me that he broke it off with your mum because he had a drunken one-night stand with my mum, Felicity. She got pregnant with my brother Darren and blackmailed Dad into either breaking up with your mum or not having any contact with his son. So I don't think he would have won whichever choice he had made," Mitch paused, watching the information sink in with Charlie.

"The problem is that Dad tried to let your mum down gently and didn't tell her the truth about the situation. He really regrets that now."

"Fuck," Charlotte replied. "This might make it harder for us to resolve, especially if Mum is still heartbroken over the whole thing."

"I know, even Dad believes he will have a hard job convincing her that he is truly sorry," Mitchell sighed, reaching over to pull Charlie into his embrace as silence reigned over them.

"You still need to get the diaries finished before the competition in a fortnight, as we need to know if them meeting will be for the best or to be avoided."

"Yes, I will get back onto it this evening," Charlie said. "Now, we'd better get up and started as we don't have long left to practise."

"Just one more kiss," he cajoled. He pulled her onto him and wrapped his arms tightly around her as their lips met in a kiss that seemed to portray not just their love, but the lost love of their parents.

♪

"Morning Charlotte," James said, looking up from the frying pan. "Bacon sandwich ok for you?"

"Yes please Jim, can you make it crispy?" she asked, as she sat down and realised that they were listening to Love Shack Radio.

Charlotte finished her sandwich and listened as 'Father Figure' started to play in the background. She knew it was one of her mum's favourite tracks. She looked over at James, who had paused and reached to turn it up, a smile playing over his features. Mitchell looked between the two of them and then smiled too.

"That was especially for our very own DJ Stephanie from a secret admirer," Paul announced at the end of the track.

Would her mother have heard the tune and dedication, she wondered.

"Come on," Mitch said to Charlie. "Let's get some more work done before Darren gets home."

"Ok, slave driver."

-35-

In the studio as Charlotte warmed up, Mitchell sent his brother a text to see what time he would be back home.

"We've got until noon to get it perfect before Darren gets back here," Mitchell said, as he watched Charlie stretch her leg high in the air.

"Ok let's get started." She took a minute to stretch her other leg, whilst giving Mitch her best pout. He crossed the room and started up the music to 'Love Is Strange' and immediately Charlotte was transported to the moment in the film. Charlie pulled Mitchell into her arms and they started to dance together, sexual tension surrounding them. She watched as Mitch dropped to the floor and then gazed as she wiggled away from him, dropping to her knees and crawling back to his arms, melting there as his lips touched hers.

As the song ended they realised where they were and slowly pulled apart.

"There's time for that later," Mitch murmured. "It's time to work that butt." He gave her ass a cheeky slap and pulled her back to her feet.

"Ok bossy boots, let's do it then," Charlotte replied, taking up the starting position and waiting for the music. Mitchell walked towards her and beckoned her with his finger as they started to dance. The lift was like magic as she flew above his head, tight and secure in his strong hands, sliding down his body for the final moves of the routine. When they finished they held each other tight, huge grins plastering their faces.

After a couple more attempts Charlie sagged against the floor in the corner, out of breath, sweaty but overjoyed at what they had achieved together.

"I'll get us a drink," Mitchell said. "And then I'll show you 'Thriller' if you like?"

"Yes, please to both," Charlie replied.

After handing Charlie a glass of water, he sank down next to her on the floor.

"You were fantastic," he said, dropping a light kiss on her cheek.

"You were too, I couldn't have done it without you," Charlie assured him, reaching out and taking his hand in hers. After five minutes he stood up and changed the music to 'Thriller', dancing for Charlotte, her own private show of his skill, strength and acrobatic abilities.

She watched in admiration the sinews of his muscles, highlighted in every stretch and leap he took to the music. Charlie was mesmerised by the whole spectacle as the song finished and as she clapped, the sound was joined by another set.

They turned to see Darren stood in the doorway.

"Well, bro I'm sorry I ever called dancing sissy... that was amazing."

Charlotte just couldn't speak so she got up and walked straight into his arms and on tiptoes, she kissed him softly on the lips.

"Ok lovebirds the camera is ready whenever you are," Darren said.

Mitchell looked down at Charlie. "I forgot to ask, do you have a dress to wear?"

"Yes, I have just the thing."

"I'll be right behind you," Mitch said, "just going to talk everything through with Darren first."

Upstairs, Charlie took a quick rinse in the shower and then headed into the bedroom. She hadn't told Mitchell but, she bought a dress a year ago that reminded her of the one from the film. Now she was going to get to dance in it, instead of just looking at it hanging in her wardrobe. She grabbed her brush and combed out her hair, fastening it up in a thin hair band before she put on a small amount of make-up, just enough to look natural and glowing. Staring in the mirror she was pleased with the effect as she perched on the bed to fasten her silver heels. Mitchell appeared and breathed in slowly at the sight that met him.

"You look wonderful," he said. "Perfect in fact."

She stood up and gave him a twirl, the black dress fanning out around her. Mitchell admired her legs and then his eyes followed the dress up and over her curves. Her eyes wide and lips gently parted, they were slicked with a pale gloss he just wanted to lick off.

She watched as he started to remove his jogging trousers and vest top, his body rippling as he bent and stretched. Charlotte longed to reach out for him. He pulled on his black trousers and shirt which looked remarkably similar to those worn in the film, plus his Cuban-heeled shoes. He ran his hands through his hair and then looked across to Charlie.

"Very sexy, very sexy indeed," she said as they stood only inches apart, each running their eyes over the other, desire making their pupils dilate.

"Let's get this dance nailed for film," Mitchell said, "I have a great feeling about it."

"Yes I have a great feeling about you too," Charlie murmured, her breath coming in short staccato moments as her heart seemed to drum away in her chest. The butterfly nerves in her stomach fluttered against her rising ribcage and she followed Mitchell back downstairs and into the studio.

She noticed Darren give her a good, long look, his video camera set up on a tripod in the far corner.

"Darren works for our local television station as a cameraman so it's going to be so professional," Mitchell said proudly, "and his girlfriend Sophie works in the costume department so they make a good team."

"It's you guys that have to do all the work here," Darren replied. "Do you want to have a rehearsal first and I'll test the camera at the same time?"

They both nodded as Mitchell strolled over to the stereo to set up the music and Charlotte took up position.

As the music flowed Charlie tried not to think about the camera but as the melody entered her body, nerves faded away as she became part of the dance. The song seemed to fly by as they moved together, perfecting the lift and then finishing with a kiss.

"Cut," shouted Darren. "That just blew me away," he said shaking his head as Mitchell and Charlotte broke apart and went over to look at the playback on the small screen. They watched and Darren suggested a few changes to the angles and Mitch as always found the smallest fault in one of his steps. Charlotte gazed in amazement at the sight of the two of them together. It was magical, the chemistry tangible even on this small screen.

"Let's go again," Mitchell said, taking Charlie's hand and leading her back to the starting point. Then the music filled the room once more.

It took four more attempts before Mitchell was satisfied with the results and with some clever editing by Darren, they would have the finished film ready for submission on Monday evening, just before the deadline.

"Pleased?" Mitchell asked.

"More than, blown away is more accurate," she said in a breathless whisper, as he held her trembling body in his arms.

"Come on, Darren can play it on the television for us to watch," he said, looking over at his brother who gave them the thumbs up.

"Thanks Darren," Charlie said, as she walked over and gave him a hug.

"Mitch thinks a lot of you, you know, so look after my baby brother," he said, as he kissed her on the cheek.

They all wandered into the kitchen to find James sat there, still listening to the radio as if in a trance. Charlotte looked at the clock and realised it was her mum's programme playing.

"Dad, would you like to see what we've been working on?" Mitchell asked.

"Yes. Drinks first though, you look like you need them." He crossed to the cupboard and handed them all some bottles of coke before they went to the lounge.

James sat on a chair and Charlie snuggled up to Mitchell on the sofa as they waited for Darren to plug in the necessary cables. When he did, he sat back on the floor and Mitchell immediately leaned forward, ever the critic. As their images appeared onscreen, Charlotte sucked in breath and then slowly breathed out again. They looked beautiful together as they danced their way through the routine perfectly in sync with the music. The emotions on their faces matched the mood of the dance and as she watched Mitchell lift her above his head, she smiled broadly and looked at him, finding he was looking at her. When the music faded and the screen went blank there was a moment of silence.

"Amazing," was all James could say as he looked at them.

"Exactly what I thought," agreed Darren. They all turned to look at Mitchell who was silent as he tried to dislodge the lump that had formed in his throat.

"Well there were a few bits I could have done better but Charlotte was perfect all the way through."

"What bits, I thought you were wonderful," she replied, beaming back at him. "Better than Patrick Swayze." She gently kissed him on the cheek.

"Well, we just need to keep our fingers crossed that they choose it and we can dance it again at the competition," Mitchell replied.

"Talking of that, do you know which hotel you will be staying at yet?" Charlotte asked. "So I can make sure Mum books us into the same one."

"We haven't decided but I am sure we can discuss it all next weekend when I can come down to yours, if you like?"

"Cool... Talking of home, I guess we'd better start getting ready to leave?" Charlie asked.

"Lunch first?" James asked, even though it was nearly two in the afternoon.

"Yes please."

"Will Pizza do?"

Darren and Mitchell had a quick chat about the editing and then Darren left to get started on it, leaving the two of them on the sofa.

"Can you email me a copy," Charlie asked, "I would love to watch it again and show Mum."

"Of course I will," Mitch promised, and moved so that he could wrap her in his arms, his lips meeting hers. The adrenaline from dancing had now been replaced by a different sort of physical pull. He ran his hand through her hair and pulled the hair band out so that it was loose and free flowing between his fingertips. He trailed one hand down her cheek and neck to her shoulder line and the strap of her dress, following the line of fabric as it ran down between her breasts.

Charlotte arched towards him, her body ultra responsive under his touch, her nipples already rubbing in a tantalising way against the soft fabric.

He must have been able to read her mind as he eased her back against the arm of the sofa so that he could cover her body with his, pushing her into the softness of the fabric beneath. It was easy for his hands to slip beneath the fabric of her dress and take her nipples in his fingertips as Charlotte slipped hers beneath his shirt so that she could feel the smooth skin of his back.

"I want you so much," he breathed, his lips capturing hers once more as his one hand moved down over the outside of her skirt and then disappeared under the hemline. His hand felt the hot smooth skin of her naked legs as he ran it steadily upwards. Charlie breathed in slightly as his fingers glanced over the outside of her knickers. Part of her wanted to continue to feel everything in this wonderful, post-dance, adrenaline-fuelled moment but she wiggled slightly and moved her lips to whisper in his ear, "Not here, not yet, I want it to be special."

Mitchell paused, looking down into her sparkling green eyes that matched his for colouring and shade. Charlotte felt his pause and wondered if she had said the wrong thing. Would he get tired of waiting for her? She looked into his hungry eyes, full of desire for her, and knew that her eyes matched his in intensity. They were perfect together on the dance floor, she felt certain they would be perfect together entwined in bed.

"Ok," he replied, reluctantly removing his hands from her skin as they both sat up.

"Sorry Mitch," she murmured, missing the feel of his touch. "Part of me really wants to just throw caution to the wind because when you touch me it feels so right but I'm scared," she admitted, hoping this would not put him off.

Mitchell pulled her back into his arms and gently stroked her arm. "I should be saying sorry. You are the first girl to say no to me and I guess I'm not used to it."

"So how many girls have you been out with then?" Charlotte asked, sort of wanting to know even though she knew she would feel jealous of them.

"You're number four," he replied. "I did play the field when I was younger but that's the number I've slept with."

"Oh," she replied.

"But you are the only one I have ever danced with." He pulled her closer to him and their lips came back together again, the tense mood dispelled. Charlotte hugged this information, being his first dancing partner was special and different from the rest.

"What about you?" he asked. "Since we are on this delicate subject."

"You are my second boyfriend but I am still a virgin," she replied, feeling nervous admitting to her lack of experience. "I hope you don't mind," she whispered, shyly looking away from his gaze.

"Don't be sorry, I love your honesty," he replied. "I also love dancing with you, the way you look and of course the way you feel when I have you in my arms." He tilted her face back so he could once again look into her eyes and show her the strength of his feelings.

"I'm finding it hard not to push you too far, too fast, you are so fucking hot and I'm just a horny guy," he said, grinning at her in such a sexy way she couldn't resist. "But I can try and wait."

Charlie didn't really know how to respond to such an honest statement so she just pulled him close. They were about to kiss again when they heard the door swing open, the smell of hot pizza wafting through.

-36-

After they had eaten they went upstairs so that Charlotte could pack her bag and get her leathers back on for the ride home. Mitchell took great care in zipping up the jacket for her before he pulled her into his arms.

"You're like a magnet, I just keep getting pulled towards you."

Charlie smiled up at him. "I could get used to being your magnet," she replied, parting her lips slightly so she could run her tongue over them before his lips came down to capture hers.

When they reached the hallway Jester came bounding over and poked his nose into her hand for a stroke, as if he somehow knew she was going. James appeared in the kitchen doorway.

"Are you taking Charlotte home now?"

"Yes Dad, I'll be back later."

"Thanks for letting me stay Jim," Charlotte said. "It was nice to meet you."

She extended her hand to him but James had other thoughts and pulled her into his arms.

"Thank you Charlotte, you don't know how much Mitchell meeting you may have helped me get my life back on track," he said, dropping a kiss on her forehead.

They were about to leave when Jester started to bark and they saw Pam and Peter in the hallway.

"We didn't want to miss saying goodbye to Charlotte," Pam said, pulling Charlie in for another embrace.

"We are both looking forward to the dance competition. We caught a glimpse of the two of you in the garden yesterday," Peter said, reaching out to also hug Charlie. Shaking his head he turned to James. "So like her Mum," he murmured, and Charlie smiled at the compliment.

"Please give her our love," Pam said.

"Come on Charlie, we'd better get going," Mitch said, taking her hand.

Charlotte climbed on the motorcycle behind him and held tight as the engine shuddered beneath them. Charlie thought Mitch was showing off as he put his foot down, confident in the feel of the bike beneath him. Charlie's hands wrapped tighter round his torso and he almost felt her heart beating in time as they sped along the roads.

Pulling onto the driveway of Charlie's home, they both dismounted and Mitch helped Charlie remove her helmet – at the same time taking the opportunity to kiss her. She held it out for him but he shook his head.

"You keep it here; it matches your leathers."

"Thank you," Charlie replied, realising what this symbolised – Mitch had no intention of asking anyone else to ride pillion with him. It was a small statement of his claim upon her and Charlie loved it, smiling up at him, drowning a little further in his eyes.

The door was unlocked so they went in and breathed in the smell of stew.

"Mum, we're home," shouted Charlie, dumping her bag and helmet at the bottom of the stairs as they entered the kitchen.

"Hi Charlie, hi Mitchell," Steph said, turning from the counter to see their smiling faces. "How was the weekend?"

"Great thanks, Stephanie," Mitchell replied, removing his jacket and then turning to watch Charlie unzipping hers, desire burning in his eyes. Charlie poured them both a drink as they sat down on the stools by the island unit.

"How did the routine go?" Charlie's mum asked. Curious to hear about it all, she took the stool opposite, cup of tea in hand.

"It was amazing, Mum. Mitchell got his brother to film it and then we watched it on the television and it looked almost like the real thing." Charlie gushed, glancing over at Mitchell, eyes just as hungry for him.

"Oh and I met Mitchell's dad and his grandparents and Jester the dog," she said, careful to avoid saying their names in case her mum guessed.

"My brother should finish editing the recording tomorrow, ready to send off, so I'll email a copy to you as soon as possible," Mitch said.

"Are you staying for tea?" Steph asked. "I've made a pot of stew so there's plenty."

"That sounds great," Mitchell said.

"It will be ready in about an hour."

"Ok Mum, we'll be upstairs."

Upstairs Charlie dumped her bag and carefully placed the helmet on her stool under the window. She put the samba music on from the club, turning towards Mitchell.

"I think I may need your help with these leathers again?" she said, breathless with anticipation for the feel of his hands on her body.

"Now that I am happy to do," Mitch replied. "So long as you'll help me with mine?"

"Deal."

Mitchell put one hand firmly on the waistband of her leathers as he located the zip and started to pull it down. Kneeling in front of her, he managed to get them to her ankles and as she steadied herself by holding onto his shoulder, he was able to pull them over her feet, each in turn. Then he slowly ran his hands back up her legs over her jeans and then to the hemline of her t-shirt. His hands touched the skin of her belly as they ran to discover that she wore no bra, his fingers encountering her already erect nipples. She ran her fingers through his hair and then slowly stretched them above her head so that he took the hint and pulled it over her head.

Then it was her turn. She reached down and undid the button on his leathers and slowly bent down, easing them off and throwing them aside. Her hands travelled up over the outside of his jeans and then on up and under his t-shirt. She mirrored his moves from minutes before but as she was shorter than him, she struggled to get the t-shirt all the way up. With a quick move he helped her with this and then ran his hands down her back, revelling in the feel of her smooth skin as he reached her bum. In a swift move, he picked her up and walked easily with her in his grasp to the bed. He laid her down on the soft covers and paused for a moment to drink in the sight of Charlie beneath him.

Charlie lay there beneath his hot gaze, his pupils burning an invisible path over her skin, deciding where they would touch first. She reached up to him.

"I'm getting cold," she warned, even though that was the furthest thing from the truth.

"Are you?" he said softly, leaning down to blow on her nipples.

"Are you getting warmer?" he asked. She shook her head but grinned up at him at the same time. He watched her pupils widen as he gently blew on the other nipple and her body arched to get closer to his mouth.

"And now?" he teased. Charlie loved his wicked grin, deliberately licking her lips before her arms reached out, drawing his body onto hers.

The buckles on their belts hit and rubbed against each other, metal on metal as Mitchell and Charlie pressed hot skin onto hot skin. Charlie writhed beneath Mitchell's weight. Her hands ran over all the muscles of his back as the beat from the Latin music seemed to make the atmosphere grow warmer. They paused and looked into each other's eyes, green pools of desire rippling and spreading between them.

"I think I'm in love with you," Charlotte said, looking directly at him. She trembled feeling both certain and afraid of what he would say in reply.

"I think I'm in love with you," he said, his gaze telling her no lies. It was a wondrous moment as time seemed to stand still.

"Tea's ready!" Charlie's mum shouted from downstairs, interrupting the moment.

"We'll be down in a minute!" Charlie replied, though not wanting to move from where she lay.

Charlie and Mitchell's hearts were beating in perfect time, their eyes locked onto each other. It felt strange to have to stand up again. Charlie's legs were still shaking as Mitchell threw her the t-shirt he had removed earlier, also pulling his back on. With shaking fingers Charlotte tried to do the same but in the end Mitch took it from her and placed it over her head, as if she were a small child.

Sitting down for dinner, Charlie noticed there was something different about her mum, who seemed happier.

"Are you ok Mum, you look sort of different?"

"Yes fine honey, I had a good weekend while you were away."

"Is it ok for Mitch to come down next weekend?" Charlie asked, not wanting to waste her mother's obvious good mood.

"Yes that's fine," Steph replied, watching the two young lovers exchange looks and smiles.

After dinner Steph retired to the conservatory with her laptop to continue working on the Rock On the River event while Charlie and Mitch cleared up in the kitchen.

Bubbles overflowed in the sink and some got lodged in some strange places. The happiness was infectious as Steph went to investigate the screams coming from the kitchen. Scooping up a handful and lobbing them at Charlie, they landed in her hair and Mitch squashed them and then added his own handful.

"Next time you want to play with bubbles do it in the garden," Steph joked. Charlie stopped after a final handful had been placed down the back of Mitch's shirt and patted in.

"Well, I guess I'd better get going," Mitch said, as the clock showed it was nearly nine. Charlie's face fell as she realised this was the moment for goodbye.

"Bye Mitchell, see you again next weekend," Steph said, pulling him into a quick hug. Steph still couldn't help but compare his body to how James' used to feel at that age.

"I'll walk you out," Charlie said, taking his hand in hers.

Before he put his helmet on, Mitchell pulled Charlotte into his arms for one, last time, enfolding her tight against his body.

"Until next Friday," he murmured.

"I'll miss you," Charlotte replied, her voice soft and soothing.

"I'll miss you too, but at least we can text and call each other and I'll drop you the film file when I send it off on Tuesday morning."

"I'll be keeping my fingers crossed," she replied, laying her cheek against the cool, smooth leather of his jacket. Charlie breathed in and out, trying to savour the intoxicating scent of Mitchell that lay just beneath the surface. She didn't want to let him go, not after this evening and the precious exchange of love.

As he slipped from her grasp, she watched as he mounted the bike and turned on the engine. The last thing she saw were his beautiful green eyes before he flipped down the visor and then rode off down the road. She hugged herself tight as she wandered back into the house. She was too happy to cry and after all, it would only be a week before she would see him again.

"Are you ok?" Charlie's mum asked, poking her head back into the kitchen.

"Yes Mum," Charlie said, perching on a stool.

"There is definitely something different about you Mum," she said, reaching over to turn on the radio.

"Perhaps there is," Steph replied. "The plans for Rock On the River are going really well and I was wondering if you wanted a time slot for your group to dance?" Steph asked, putting the kettle on.

"Yes please Mum, that would be great. Can I see if Mitchell's group want to take part too? I saw what they are planning to do for 'Thriller' and it's amazing," she gushed, her mind drifting off for a split second.

"Yes, you can ask him next weekend when he's here."

"Mum?"

"Yes, Charlie?"

"When Mitch stays next weekend, can he share my room?" she asked, uncertainty in her voice.

"Yes of course he can, I trust you both," Steph replied. "I'm guessing it's getting serious between you two?"

"Yes, Mum and... thanks."

"Shall I make us a hot chocolate?"

"Sounds good to me."

Charlie wrestled with her conscience, desperate to tell her mum all about James and Mitchell being his son. She wondered whether her mum had been listening to the radio when James put out the dedication – something had definitely put a spring in Stephanie's step.

"Something you want to tell me?" Steph asked, watching her daughter.

"No. I'm off to bed," she replied, taking her hot chocolate with her.

"Ok, night sweetheart," Steph said, watching her daughter head for the stairs, Charlie's pale skin seeming to glow in the evening light as her curls bounced on her shoulders.

-37-

When Charlotte stepped into her room she looked over at the new additions to her wardrobe. The helmet shone in the moonlight as she crossed to draw the curtains, pausing for a second to take in the stars that speckled the sky. She jumped into bed and detected the faint scent of Mitchell's aftershave on her pillow. She decided to read until he dropped her a text saying he was home. Reaching for the diary, she knew it was important to finish it before the dance competition in a fortnight. She had wanted to say something to her mum earlier – just ask her what had happened – but it was easier to read the words before that conversation.

Charlie flicked through six weeks' worth of entries to get to the next time her mum saw James. Was this when it all came to an end?

Dear Diary,

Friday 11th November, 1988
College really dragged but I was soon home and in the shower. I ran the shaver over my legs and underarms as usual, pausing for a moment as water trickled over my body, its caress waking up my dormant desires. As I absently moved the showerhead over my body, I closed my eyes and remembered all the times James and I had been together in some form of water. All of them were happy memories.

I turned the water off and walked to my room in a towel, almost dropping it in shock when I found James already sitting on my bed. I rubbed my eyes just to make sure I wasn't dreaming but he was very real as he stood up and closed the distance between us.

"Aren't you a beautiful sight for sore eyes?" he murmured, his hands in my wet hair.

"How did you get in without me hearing?" I asked, laying my head on his chest so I could hear his heart beating.

"Your mum let me in and said you were in your room and to go on up," he said, grinning. "But much better to find you in just a towel." His hand running along the top of the towel, he pulled it off in one swift tug.

He stood back and allowed his gaze to run down my body, like the water had just moments earlier, some of the droplets still hanging there. I felt his hands gently slide over my shoulders and down to my breasts as he gently tugged each nipple between his fingers. I held my breath as he leaned down and took each into his mouth. The hotness of his tongue met the coolness of my skin in an explosion of sensations. I felt my legs start to quiver and James did too because he steered me over towards the bed and pushed me down onto the covers.

"This is definitely my favourite way to start the weekend," he murmured, his lips nuzzling my earlobes and a whole set of nerve endings starting to tingle even more than before.

"I agree," I said, breathless as I lay pinned to the bed under his weight, extremely aware of his cock nudging my thigh.

"Would you like a drink?" my mum shouted up the stairs from the landing below. We both froze as I managed to get enough breath to respond.

"We'll be down in a minute Mum, coffee please."

As we listened in silence to her footsteps on the stairs, I looked up at James. "We'll have to finish this later."

"Oh, yes. There will be no distractions or interruptions at my place as my parents are away," he said, and after one, long kiss he pulled away from me and I stood up. As James lounged on the bed, he watched me pull on some jeans and a jumper and pack the last few items for the weekend.

"Do I need to bring anything special?" I asked.

"No just you," he replied. "Now we'd better get our arses downstairs before your mother gets suspicious about why our minute takes ten."

James picked up my bag and I grabbed my coat, following him down to the kitchen.

"I was just about to send a search party up for you two," my mum said, passing us our coffee.

"I just had to finish my packing," I replied, glancing over at James who was looking amused as he bit into a biscuit. I blushed just thinking about what we had been doing upstairs and I couldn't wait until we got going.

"How's the job?" Mum asked, sitting down with her cup.

"Great, loving every moment of it," James replied. "It's hard work but on the whole it's fantastic."

The drive was good and we were soon at my favourite place in the world. James raced round the car and as always, opened the door for me, another of the little things I loved about him. Once inside the house, he turned to me and said, "So, what shall we do tonight?"

"Did you have anything in mind?"

"I have plenty of things I want to do," he said, grinning at me with a wicked glint in his eyes, "but first off I think we need to finish what we started in your bedroom." He picked me up and carried me to his bedroom.

Placing me on the bed and starting to slowly remove all my clothes, he paused to admire the new baby pink underwear I had picked up the previous week. His hands slid over the silk and lace before they lay on the floor. Lying naked in front of him, I watched as he removed his jeans and jumper and I spied the silk boxer shorts from his birthday. Even after all the time we had spent together, I still felt shocked that someone so gorgeous was actually in love with me. Before we could continue, James flicked the switch on the radio and the sound of 'Waiting For a Star to Fall' swirled around the room. James' lips captured mine and our tongues started to explore as I let the lyrics into my mind, shocked at how apt they were.

The music faded as the beating of my heart increased with every touch on my skin. James indulged both him and me with the sensations his caresses bought to us both. As he entered me, I pulled him close.

"I love you more than you'll ever really know or understand," I whispered as I closed my eyes and let the gentle ripples turn to breaking waves crashing on rocks. I was shaking when he finally withdrew and curled up beside me. Finally he turned and said, "Till the end of time," his eyes closed as he slept beside me, while I gazed at him in awe.

I heard the phone ring and as James remained asleep, I crept out from under his arms and padded downstairs to answer it. When I did I just heard silence and the faint sound of someone breathing before the line went dead. Shaking my head I stepped into the kitchen and searched in the fridge for some cold drinks. I found a half open bottle of white wine so I poured that into a glass before I grabbed a bottle of beer for James and returned back upstairs. He opened his eyes just as I walked through the door

"What a fucking hot sight you are. You should always be naked." He sat up and I handed him the beer.

"The phone rang but when I answered it, there was just breathing on the other end before whoever it was rang off."

"That's strange," James replied but as I watched him, he took a long gulp of beer and seemed nervous.

"Shall we order takeaway for tea?" he asked.

"Yeah that will be lovely, I'm starving."

We enjoyed an evening of food and television, only interrupted by the phone ringing again. The first call was his parents letting James know they had arrived safely in Scotland and giving him the number for the hotel should he need it. The second call was just as we were heading upstairs to bed, so I continued on as James answered it. I lay in bed wondering who it was and why the conversation seemed to be taking a long time. I was almost on the verge of going back down when I heard footsteps on the stairs followed by the usual sounds from the bathroom.

When James entered the room he looked slightly different, his usual smile replaced by a more sombre look.

"Is everything ok?" I asked.

"Yes, just some stuff from work, nothing to worry about," he replied, seeming to quickly switch on a forced smile.

I opened my arms to him as he undressed and we embraced. Our lips came together and I took the lead, trailing kisses over his face and neck and chest, heading down his body. However his usual response to my touch never happened and he remained soft in my hands and mouth before he pulled me up and nuzzled his face into my neck.

"I think I'm just tired," he murmured, pulling me close. "Sorry sweetheart."

I smiled softly in the darkness and we settled down to sleep. It eluded me as I lay there worrying about the phone call and his lack of response to my touch, but I knew there was something wrong and I didn't know how to ask him about it.

Saturday 12th November, 1988
When we awoke, I looked through the crack in the curtains to find snow falling on the ground. Snow always excited me and appealed to my inner child so I moved to the bottom of the bed and pulled the curtains wide, revealing a white wonderland below. All of a sudden I felt hands grab me around the waist as James pulled me into his arms, all trace of last night's failure erased as I felt his cock nudging my thigh.

"You're awake this morning," I said, as I twisted round so that I could kiss him.

"Definitely, awake and raring to go."

"Best be quick then as it's snowing outside and I want to go and play in it," I replied, turning in his embrace so that I was on top of him. Playfully I eased myself down on him and James ran his hands up my body to find my nipples with his fingers.

As we moved together I stared into his eyes and tried to see the shadow that had been there the night before. It had disappeared and I abandoned my body to the feelings of love and desire that coursed through my hot skin. I decided I had been worrying about nothing as he flooded into me, his orgasm mingling with the sweet wetness of mine. Lying in each other's arms I felt so secure in my feelings for James, so sure he was truly the love of my life.

"Come on, the snow might melt," I said, pulling off the covers.

"You're just like a little kid," James said, laughing as my enthusiasm infected him. "But I think we should have breakfast first."

"Ok," I relented as I pulled my jeans and t-shirt on, followed by my thick jumper. After toast and coffee we pulled on our coats and gloves and entered the garden. I spun around looking up to the sky, flakes continuing to fall and kiss my face with their coldness, hanging in my hair. I didn't notice that James had bent down and shaped a snow ball until it flew and hit me on my back.

"Snowball fight," he shouted, scooping up more snow. I dodged behind one of the apple trees so that I had the chance to start an arsenal to attack.

We played a stealthy game of cat and mouse between the trees, each getting some good shots in and also receiving some in return. Then I decided to make a run for it back towards the house as more snowballs pelted my behind. I eventually collapsed in the snow, laughter shaking my body and making my sides ache.

"I surrender," I called out, as I could see James advancing towards me with two final snowballs, one in each hand.

"Are you sure?" he said.

I looked up into his face, excitement glittering in his eyes.

"Yes, please put down those balls, I'm defenceless," I replied, surreptitiously scooping up some snow in the hand furthest away from him.

"Ok," James replied as he dropped his to the ground and then bent down to pull me up.

It was then I struck and landed mine straight in his face.

"That's so fucking naughty," he spluttered through the mouthful of snow.

"Sorry, I'll make it up to you," I murmured, and he stopped trying to pull me up and sank down on top of me, a blanket of snow beneath us.

"You are a cheeky minx," he murmured, his lips reaching down to capture mine.

"I think we should call it a draw," I replied, suddenly not feeling so cold even though the snow surrounded me and started to soak into my jeans. I couldn't deny the feel of his hot kisses on my cold face and neck. His fingers slid down and opened the zip on my coat so that he could run his hands down my jumper and then up and under it too. I jumped when his icy touch seemed to burn into my skin and made it to my already rock hard nipples that tingled even more. My hands found their way round his back and then under his coat and jumper, James shuddering as my fingers touched the skin of his back.

When we broke apart and without his body close to mine, I felt an icy chill spread through my bones and I started to shiver from the cold instead of the passion. James pulled me up and brushed the snow from my body as we walked together back into the warmth of the house. My fingers were so numb that I struggled to remove my clothes but James covered that and soon had me naked. He wrapped me in his dressing gown and then started to fill the bath.

When the bath was full I broke the bubbles on top and dived into the comforting heat. James eased in behind me so that I was able to lie back in his arms. It felt as though we were lying in heaven as the chill from the snow melted away into the scent of the bubbles surrounding us. James rested his chin on my shoulder as my hands entwined in his beneath the surface.

"Kiss me," I requested, turning slightly so that our lips could meet and benefit from the heat rising in our bodies. I melted further into his embrace and as the numbness was released from our fingers, we began to re-awake the frozen nerves with each caress.

Turning around carefully so the water remained below the rim, I was soon looking into my favourite blue eyes. They seemed brighter than ever as my lips captured him and I poured my very essence into our kiss. Our hearts began to beat faster but still in time as his one hand ran through my hair and kept me close, the other travelling down my hips and then parting my sex.

I was wet anyway with the surrounding water but I was slick as he pushed a finger inside me and then back out, over and over again, as my breathing came faster and faster. I felt him hard against my thigh so I moved his finger away so that I could capture the whole of him inside of me. As the waves of the bath lapped against our skin, spilling over onto the floor, the waves of our orgasms mingled together and joined us as one.

Neither of us said a word as we climbed out and wrapped ourselves in large towels. We put our comfy clothes on and decided to walk to the chip shop. The snow had already stopped falling and you could guess that by tomorrow it would have melted and disappeared. The sweet smell of the hot oil got my taste buds working and once we reached home, we just opened up the wrappers and ate out of the paper on our laps. James lit the fire and I made us both a mug of hot chocolate as we sat cuddled up together, just happy to be in each other's company.

That night we made love once more, a gentle heartfelt moment that bonded us even further as I fell asleep in his embrace.

Sunday 13th November, 1988
I awoke to the phone ringing yet again. James also heard it so he jumped

out of bed and put his dressing gown on.

"I'll bring us back a coffee," he promised.

I quickly snuck a look out of the window but it was raining and almost all of the snow had vanished. I reached over and put the stereo on, finding a copy of the mix tape James had done for me. I lay back and listened to all the familiar songs on it, smiling as I remembered the various events that had taken place during different moments in our relationship.

After about ten minutes I started to get restless. This was a long conversation for nine in the morning and I hoped that nothing serious had happened. I shrugged on his shirt and stepped out onto the landing, making my way to the bathroom. I couldn't make out any of the conversation, just James saying "yes" or "no" and "I will soon". I padded downstairs and as I passed him in the hallway, he looked surprised and shocked as I ducked into the kitchen and gave a signal that I would make the coffee. He finished the conversation with, "Speak to you soon, bye," and then he entered the kitchen.

Once again for a brief second he looked troubled and there was a strange sadness that flitted across his eyes before a smile broke on his lips and he advanced towards me. I held my arms open to him as he quickly lifted me up and placed me on the worktop so that I could wrap my legs around him. It felt cold on my bare bottom for a brief moment before his lips captured mine in a kiss so long and sensual, I surrendered completely to him as he fucked me in the kitchen. It was short, sweet and satisfying.

As we ate breakfast together I turned to James and said, "Who was on the phone?"

"Just Aunt Sue wanting Mum but having a general catch up," he replied. "It's ok, it hasn't ruined our morning. Sex in the kitchen is just as much fun as sex in the bedroom," he insisted, grinning at me.

"So what shall we do with the rest of the day before you have to take me home?"

"How about a swim? My parents have just got membership to this nearby health spa and said I could use it with you this weekend."

We spent an enjoyable few hours at the health spa, the pool almost deserted. I had never been in a Jacuzzi before and discovered that bubbles could reach places that had never been reached before.

When he drove me home to Ross after that, we chatted and sang along to music but as always, a heavy cloud of despair hung over us. It was late when we left James' place so when we got to Ross, he declined the offer of a final coffee because he needed to get back as he was starting early on Monday.

The clouds overhead hid most of the stars as he wrapped his arms around me.

"I've had the most wonderful time this weekend," I declared, choking slightly on the words as tears started to kiss my eyelashes.

"Me too Stephanie, you are the best thing that has ever happened to me and I will love you till the end of time," he replied, his voice thick with emotion. In the dim light, I saw tears glittering on his cheeks so I reached up to wipe them away.

"Till the end of time," I replied, and we kissed for a final time before I reluctantly released him from my arms.

♫

Charlotte's phone tinged and she looked down to see a text from Mitchell. Quickly she wiped her eyes as the last diary entries had really tugged at her heart and made her realise how much her mum had been in love with James.

Hi Charlie, I am safely home and in bed already. It feels too big without your sexy body beside me!! Keep in touch this week and I will be down as soon as possible on Friday, let me know what time you finish college and I'll come and fetch you on the bike. Love Mitch x

Charlie smiled before she replied:

Hi Mitch, I am in bed too, wish you were here or I was back there!!!! Been busy reading the diary and will speak to you tomorrow. Night, night. Love Charlie x

-38-

In the studio I was live on air with the usual lunchtime request show, answering calls, texts and emails. All of a sudden on the computer screen came a request for me. Someone asked for 'Hunting High and Low' by A-Ha – it was my secret admirer again. I giggled as I searched the database and found the track as I announced, "This next song is for me from my secret admirer."

As the song played, I searched through the text for any further clues. My initial guess was Jack from the hospital so I dropped him a text saying: **Very funny**.

He replied back saying: **What are you talking about?**

I responded with: **My secret admirer?** and he finished by saying: **It's not me! You really do have a secret admirer.**

I spent the rest of the show pondering who it might be. He could easily find out what I looked like and that my favourite artists were George Michael and A-Ha due to the profile on the radio website. Ian poked his head in towards the end of the show.

"So Steph, who is this secret admirer of yours?" he asked, grinning.

"I really don't know, I thought it was Jack playing a joke but he has denied it," I admitted, before I queued up the next song. "It's not you or Paul winding me up is it?"

"No, it's not us," Ian replied. "We'll have to get our heads together later in the pub and see if we can't work out who your mystery man might be."

I wrapped up the show and then Ian took over for the afternoon.

I took the time to do a quick shop and then returned to the studio to find Paul and Ian waiting for me. As we walked to the nearby pub, Jack caught us up and the four of us soon found a table and ordered drinks and some nachos to pick at. Rock On the River was progressing well, with only six weeks to go until the date. All the bands had confirmed, tickets would be on sale by the weekend, and our advertising was already up and around the area. It was going to be an event to remember.

Then the conversation turned to my secret admirer.

"Have you no idea who it could be?" Jack asked, leaning forward slightly with interest.

"Nope, not a clue."

"He could be a real weirdo, you know? We do get obsessive fans sometimes," Ian said, looking over at Paul who laughed.

"Yes, I remember Mary," Paul replied. We all remembered her, the super fan that waited for him outside the studio every morning with a box of doughnuts. I shuddered at the thought that a strange man might be obsessing about me.

"Or it could be a genuine guy? He seems to have cheered you up," Jack said.

"Yes, I like his taste in music so far and it might be a bit of fun if I can counteract his songs with others," I mused.

"Yes that could be good, it will determine if he is serious or just mad," Paul said, draining his pint.

We parted on high spirits and I walked back to my car, keeping alert to any strange guys lurking around. I reached the driveway just before seven and had just put the house lights on when Charlotte breezed in, hot and sweaty from her dancing.

"How's it going?" I asked, passing her a bottle of coke.

"Great Mum, costumes look fantastic, and I need to talk to Mitch about what he will wear for his short appearance at the end," she said, heading upstairs for a shower.

"How's work?" Charlotte asked later, between slices of pizza.

"Good thanks, Rock on the River is shaping up to be a fantastic event."

"Yes, our group are looking forward to dancing at it. I am phoning Mitch later so I'll ask him," Charlotte said, peering at me. "So, you still look happier than usual?"

"Do I?" I asked, startled, but Charlotte seemed suspicious. Had she never seen me happy before? That was a sad thought. "I'm keeping my secrets... seeing as though you're keeping yours," I challenged her, and she looked down at the table, her intrigue at bay for now. It was clear she had something on her mind and I wondered if it had anything to do with the diaries, which she still seemed to be engrossed in.

I still wasn't at all sure a secret admirer was a good thing but it had certainly perked me up, she was right.

-39-

Upstairs in her room Charlotte rang Mitch. He must have been waiting as the phone hardly rang before he picked up.

"Hi Charlie," he said, and she smiled as his lovely deep voice filled her ears. It had been less than twenty-four hours since they had parted but she was already counting down the hours until Friday.

"Hi Mitch, how are you?"

"Fine thanks and you?"

"Yes, just been at dance practice. We're rehearsing every evening this week and next until the competition to make sure we are as perfect as we can get."

"Yeah, we're doing the same up here, I'm aching already and it's only Monday night."

"Me too, I have discovered muscles I never knew I had that could ache so much," Charlie said, imagining Mitch's fingers spreading massage oil all over her body.

"Yes, I could just do with you giving me a massage," Mitch replied, and she gasped, his words perfectly matching her thoughts.

"I was just thinking the same thing."

"So the video clip is in your emails now and I have sent if off to the organisers who are hoping to make a decision by Friday. So, we'll have to keep our phones handy," Mitchell said, excitement bubbling in his voice.

Holding her phone, Charlie got up so she could check her emails.

"So what's the plan this weekend?" Mitch asked.

"Lots of dance practice but I'm sure we could fit in something a bit more relaxing and fun."

"And did you have anything in mind?" Mitchell replied, and she guessed he was grinning and thinking of getting her naked.

"Cinema perhaps or a club?" Charlie replied. "Oh, and by the way, Mum said you can sleep in my room." Her mind shot off in the direction of what they had got up to the previous weekend.

"Excellent news, that spare room was a bit cold without your body pressed against mine," he murmured.

She clicked on the email attachment and images started to fill the screen and with it memories of all the hard work they had put in, as well as feelings of elation when they nailed the lift the first time.

"I'm watching it now," she gasped, tears brimming on her lashes at the beauty of the two of them dancing together on screen. "It's perfect," she sighed.

"Yes I'm pretty pleased with it, I hope we get picked," Mitch said. "So what time shall I aim to get to your college?"

"About 3.30 as we have practice in the hall at four so it will give us half an hour together before that."

As Charlotte dived under the covers later that night, she yawned but was determined to read a bit more of the diaries before the weekend so that she could discuss everything with Mitchell. She scanned through the next few entries and found one of the letters marking a page, stopping there and starting to read.

Dear Diary,

Thursday 24th November, 1988
As I returned from college, I hoped that there would be a letter waiting for me from James, the wait between replies seeming to stretch a bit longer – but I put it down to his new job being much more demanding. I smiled as I entered the hallway and saw the familiar cream envelope and spiky writing that could only belong to my love. Lying down on my bed, I couldn't wait to hear his silent words talking to me from the page in my hands…

Dear Stephanie,
In the past few weeks I have been thinking very deeply about our relationship and have come to the conclusion that it would be best if we split up. I was trying to work up the courage to tell you the last time we were together so it could be face to face as I feel I owe you that, but there hasn't been the right moment or if there was I was too much of a coward.

The tears that fell when I left you standing in the driveway were genuine tears of anger that I had failed to do this and have had to resort to words in a letter and tears of regret that we can no longer be together.

You have been the best girlfriend a man could ever hope to find in a lifetime but I feel that I have made you grow up too quickly and therefore have not given you the chance to date a few more boys of your own age as I was your first. I am also aware that you have hopes and dreams of our relationship becoming more permanent in the next year as you talk of learning to drive, colleges in Warwickshire and of a daughter called Charlotte. This scared me to death as there are so many more things that can be accomplished before talk of marriage and children should ever be considered, even between two adults who love each other.

Finally the distance between us is proving to be a big problem especially now you are studying media and enjoying your shifts on

Hospital Radio. My job in the Fire Service is extremely demanding and working around your study and my shifts means we are seeing each other less and less. Keeping our relationship growing under these difficult circumstances would take a lot of hard work and effort on both our parts. I also know how much our parting each time we are together makes you crumble, I have seen your tears and I want to stop them so much but I know I can't.

I hope that you are mature enough to understand my reasons for breaking things off between us and that perhaps we can remain friends?

Fondest regards
James

I held the letter as tears streamed down my cheeks and dropped slowly onto his words. Perhaps if I cried enough they would disappear and it would all be a bad dream that I could wake up from. Then I felt anger so I picked up the phone and dialled his number, my hand shaking so much as I tried to choke back the sobs that were coming from deep within me. Pam answered the phone.

"Hi Pam... can I... can I speak to James?"

"Yes I'll just shout him for you... are you ok?" Pam said, worry in her voice.

"Yes, I just need to speak to James," I stammered, holding back the tears. I waited a few seconds and then I heard his voice.

"Hi Stephanie, I guess you got my letter?" he answered, a hint of nervousness tingeing his voice.

"Yes," I whispered as tears engulfed me and I started to cry heavily down the line.

"Steph... Steph, please don't cry... I'm really sorry that I had to tell you like that."

"But why?" I mumbled.

"I've told you why in the letter."

"I know... but I love you... I will always love you... till the end of time, remember?" I managed to say before I let the tears take over.

"You'll find someone else, you're very attractive, intelligent and sexy," his voice trailed off into the distance.

"But I don't want anyone else, I WANT YOU!" I shouted, trying desperately to make my words change his mind.

There was silence and I worried that he had hung up the phone, but I could still hear him breathing as he waited.

"Are you still coming down this weekend?" I stuttered.

"Well, I don't really know."

"Please come... I need to talk to you in person, face to face, you at least owe me that." I hoped that once he saw me again, and was in my arms, these thoughts would leave him and he would once more be mine.

"Well," he paused. "Ok then, I'll come and see you and we can sort everything out. Bye."

I was about to say *I love you* but the line had already died. I replaced the receiver and picked up the letter, reading it once more and then laying on my bed, crying for all I was worth.

I cried until no more tears came and then I just sobbed, dry hollow coughs that hurt my chest. I just about managed to shout down to Mum and tell her that I wasn't feeling well and was just going to sleep it off. I changed for bed and then before I climbed beneath the covers, I put my stereo on and let the music on the mix tape waft quietly around the room. It didn't calm me as slowly, the real hot tears of my grief trickled down my cheeks and landed silently on the pillow.

As dreams eventually captured me, I recalled the moment we first met at the pool, and our first kiss beneath the water. The first time he had touched me, and the perfect gift I had bestowed on him for his 21st. All the amazing times we had spent together haunted me. I was once again standing in his garden in the moonlight, except this time, I was naked and alone. I searched for him between the branches of the trees; they reached out for me, trying to hold me tight as they turned into the hands and fingernails of a witch, a witch called Felicity. Her face twisted as she claimed James from my outstretched arms.

I woke in a cold sweat and realised that it was just a bad dream. I climbed out of bed and crossed the room to my drawers, looking inside to find a shirt James had left behind when he last stayed. I had forgotten to take it over the last time I had seen him but I was glad now as I shrugged it over my shoulders. Once my hands slipped through the cuffs, I pulled it up and breathed in. The faint scent of him clung to the collar as I went over to my window seat and looked out into the sky. The stars still shone there, but they were so far away. How was I going to carry on? What was the point of living without James in my life?

Friday 25th November, 1988
I woke with a start to discover I had fallen asleep on the window seat, my head resting on the cold window pane. It was still dark outside so I crossed back to my bed and pulled my pink elephant toy close. I kept James' shirt on and then drifted back off until my alarm woke me. I stepped out of bed and looked in my mirror, realising I couldn't face college today, especially as James was going to be coming over as he had

promised on the phone last night.

I wandered downstairs and discovered Mum had already left for work so I only had to see Dad.

"College today?" he asked, as I poured a cup of coffee and sat down at the table.

"Not today," I lied. "I'm going to do some work at the hospital before James arrives this evening." I thought this would be a great way to take my mind off what was possibly going to be the second worst day of my life. I had already experienced the worst day yesterday.

On the bus I tried to take my mind off James, but the words in the letter continued to float around endlessly. The white corridors of the hospital seemed to calm me a little as I wandered along towards the studio. I was so closed off in my mind that I realised, I was lost. As I felt panic rising inside me, I saw a bench and took the time to sit down and try to think calmly. It was no good because tears started to bubble up under my eyelids and as I scoured through my bag for a tissue, I didn't notice Mark striding down the corridor until he sat down.

"Here, you can have my hankie," Mark said.

"Mark," I said, looking up through tears. "Thank goodness it's you."

"Are you ok Steph?"

"Yes, I got lost," I mumbled, as I wiped back the tears.

"Is that all?" he probed.

"No, but I can't really talk about it yet," I replied. "I thought some time in the studio with Jack would help." I offered Mark his hankie back.

"No you keep it, I think you might need it more than me today," he said, and I looked up into his kind, green eyes.

"Thanks Mark," I replied as I stood up and we walked along the corridor, taking a left turn back into familiar territory.

"I'll be ok now," I said as we paused by the double doors.

"See you soon Steph," Mark said, reaching out to give my hand a squeeze. "If you get lost again, don't worry I'll find you."

I smiled weakly and pushed open the doors to the studio.

Jack smiled up at me and I seemed to lose my tears as the music brought me back to life. In the end I didn't say anything to Jack about James and just threw myself into the work that needed to be done. It was only on the way back to Ross that I started to think about the weekend ahead and what I was going to do when I saw James again. As I opened the door, Mum was the first to pop her head through the kitchen door.

"James phoned and said he won't be able to get here until tomorrow."

"Oh," I replied, wondering if he was going to be a coward and not turn up at all. I put on a brave face and sat through tea and some television with my parents before turning in early.

In the safety of my room I put George Michael's 'Faith' album on the turntable and lay in bed. Hardly any tears fell, except during 'Father Figure' when the lyrics *till the end of time* set me off. Those had been the words we had used throughout our relationship. When sleep claimed me there were no dreams or nightmares, just emptiness.

♫

Charlotte yawned and put the diary down, replacing it with her mobile phone. She quickly tapped a goodnight message to Mitch and was rewarded with one back. It was emotionally hard work reading the diaries but Charlotte knew she had to finish them, no matter how difficult it was as it might lead to her mum finally being happy again – and the same for Mitchell's dad. Closing her eyes, she dreamed of being in the same garden, apple blossom on the trees, as she danced through them with Mitchell.

-40-

I woke up to hear the familiar strains of 'Take My Breath Away' echoing from Charlotte's room and looked over at the clock. It was only 6.30a.m. but she was already practising. I knew the group were determined to be their absolute best for the competition in ten days' time. This reminded me that I had to book some hotel rooms, so I put my dressing gown on and knocked Charlotte's door, poking my head in.

"Coffee?" I asked.

"Yes please Mum, I'm going to do another run-through of 'Skyfall' and 'Umbrella' first though, and then I'll be down."

"Ok," I replied, as I padded downstairs. I turned on the radio and made coffee and toast to the breakfast show.

Paul announced that he had received another request from my secret admirer. I reached over and turned the volume up slightly as the song, 'The Most Beautiful Girl in the World' by Prince started up. I smiled and reached for my mobile phone to give Paul a call. He answered immediately.

"Hi Stephanie, your secret admirer is up early this morning," he said.

"Good job I was or I would have missed it."

"Do you want to send a response in song?"

"Yes can you play, 'Who Are You' by The Who and see if you get a text or anything back."

"Will do Steph, I've got to go now so I'll see you later."

"Bye Paul," I replied, enjoying the final strains of Prince. Then I listened to his spiel before the song I responded with played.

By the time Charlotte appeared I was on my second cup of coffee and had my laptop out as I planned my lunchtime show, a secret smile playing over my face. It felt great to be flirting over the airwaves and even if I never got to meet my mystery man, he was certainly speaking to me in my language. Charlie grabbed her mug and some toast and sat down.

"So what's on your agenda today?" I asked.

"Usual at college and then more dance practice. We're getting our costumes fitted tonight and I can't wait."

"Sounds good, do you know which hotel Mitchell and his family are staying in for the finals so we can book in at the same one?"

"I'll check," Charlie said, reaching for her mobile to send a text. Moments later a reply appeared on the screen and I watched a smile spread over her face. "They are booked into the Ibis and Mitch asked if it's ok with you, can I stay in his room?"

"Well it will save me some money," I replied. "Yes that's fine with me."

I watched as she sent a text back and waited for the reply which was almost instant. I noticed the blush spread over her face and smiled. I found the hotel online and booked a room for Sarah and Chris, and one for me.

"Do you want to see the routine we did to '(I've Had) The Time of My Life'?" she asked, hopping off the stool and coming round the kitchen island to where I was sitting.

"Yes please," I replied, and while she pulled up her emails, I poured us both another coffee. When I had watched it through, I pulled her close.

"That was fabulous, almost like watching the real thing," I said, dropping a kiss on her forehead.

"I know, I just hope we get chosen to perform it while the judges are making their decision."

"When will you find out?"

"Friday night, so if we get chosen we will be able to practice this weekend," she said, and as it played again, she studied it intently. "There are some bits I know I can improve on."

♪

Charlie breezed through the door at six that evening, brandishing her three different outfits for the competition, including a wig.

"Would you like to see them on?" she asked.

I shook my head. "I'd rather wait till the big event now, keep something as a surprise," I said, smiling. "Hungry?"

"Yes, famished," Charlie said, heading for the stairs and the shower.

"Ok I'll heat us up some of the chilli I made the other weekend."

Later, Charlie abandoned me for her bedroom so I gave Sarah a call and we arranged to meet for late lunch the next day, after my radio show. I was desperate to talk to her about my secret admirer just in case she knew who it was.

Upstairs, the unusual quiet made me wonder if Charlie had her head stuck in my diaries again. I didn't know why she seemed so desperate to reach the end of my love affair with James, but I'd seen where her bookmark was earlier and she was racing through my recollections of happier, and then sadder, times.

Dear Diary,

Saturday 26th November, 1988

I woke up to the patter of rain on my window and considered how apt this was as it matched my mood. I had breakfast and then cleaned my room, listening to Wham!, but even their cheery tunes didn't lighten the mood. I wore my favourite dress and made sure that I looked as lovely as possible so that James would not be able to resist.

When I heard his car pull up in the driveway and went downstairs to meet him, I felt suddenly nervous and afraid. Yet as soon as our eyes met, I was sure his feelings for me had not changed and he even managed a small smile.

After making us a coffee, we went up to my room and I put George Michael on the record player, both as background music and to hopefully remind James of all the good times we had shared. He stood looking out of my window into the dark sky beyond, so I walked over to him and wrapped my arms around his waist. He remained motionless so I went up on tiptoes so that I could softly breathe on his neck.

"I don't think I should be here," he said softly.

"But you are and I need you," I replied, as he turned to face me at last. I saw the sorrow and regret in his blue eyes, turning them from vibrant and bright to dull and clouded. Tears had already started to form in mine and the first one made its way over the skin of my cheek.

James reached out and wiped it away with his finger.

"Please don't cry, this is hard enough as it is," he whispered, his voice breaking as more tears stained his fingertips. I didn't let him say anymore as my lips found his and kissed him until he gave in and kissed me back. His lips were hard and urgent as they pressed into my softness and he soon had me pinned against the bedroom wall, his breath ragged with desire. My hands pulled his jumper off and then his t-shirt so that I could drag my nails gently over his chest. He shuddered and moaned under my touch and I reached for his belt buckle, releasing it so that I could pull his jeans to the ground.

Looking up at him from my kneeling position, I saw tears falling from his eyes. Did this mean he was sorry? Would this mean we were back together? I didn't stop as my hands ran up his firm thighs and to his boxer shorts. There, his hands grabbed mine and pulled me all the way up before he let go and grabbed the hem of my dress, pulling it off in a single move. I had deliberately worn the black underwear from the night of the dance and our first night as lovers. His hands ran over the satin fabric, catching my nipples beneath that had already sprung up to meet his touch. He reached round to release the catch and as my bra fell from my shoulders, he bent his head and his mouth was on me, teasing, pulling, and sucking. I arched my head backwards and shook my hair out so that it fell loose and tickled my back.

Running my hands down his back, I went below the waistband of his boxer shorts and edged them lower so they fell to the floor. My hand found his cock and I longed to take him in my mouth but he was now in charge. He picked me up and carried me the short distance to the bed, laying me down. I tried to reach out and pull him with me but he stepped beyond my grasp, his fingers running down my waist and over my hips to the satin knickers I wore. He pulled them off so I was naked and knelt down, his tongue capturing my wetness. I shuddered and came quickly before he lay on top of me, suddenly pushing his raging desire into me. As he pounded me deeper into the covers of the bed, I held him tight and gasped out his name as he came, my climax following his. Tears still fell down my face as I held him close and whispered, "I love you, till the end of time."

James remained silent and before I could say anything else, he pulled away and sat slumped on the edge of my bed. I sat up, unsure what I should do, but he turned to me and said, "I'm so sorry, I shouldn't have done that."

"Don't apologise, I'm not sorry. I know you still love me and you still desire me, so why can't we still be together?" I implored, reaching out my hands to him but then stopping and instead wrapping them around my shivering body.

"I've told you why, it's just not working for me."

"But we just made love together?"

"No Steph, we just had sex."

"Is there someone else?" I asked.

"No," he replied, but he looked down as he said this so I couldn't see the emotion on his face.

"I can move to be closer to you, we don't have to live together or anything, we can take things slow, I just want to be with you… together forever." My voice trailed off as sobs racked my body.

"Stephanie, I do love you but things are too complicated to explain. I will always hold a place in my heart for you but we can't be together any longer."

He stood up and I watched as he pulled his clothes back on.

"I'm sorry I shouldn't have come," he said, walking towards the door. He paused and looked back at me, naked and cold on the bed. "You take my breath away," he said, sadness haunting his features before he was gone forever. I listened to the sound of his footsteps on the stairs and then the roar of the engine. I jumped off the bed and crossed to my window to see the red Mini disappearing into the distance – and with it my whole life.

I looked around my room but all it held was memories, so I grabbed my personal stereo and left the house. I turned and saw Mum's puzzled face at the window but she let me go. I walked into town and although it was busy I still felt alone. Passing the swimming pool just made me cry even more and then along the riverbank, it was deserted as I found the bench we had shared when James had traced the heart on the palm of my hand. Sitting down I stared at all the other names written or engraved into the back of the bench. Our heart was still there, just like the day James had drawn it. I reached into my pocket and found the hankie that Mark had given me, trying to stem the tears that would not stop.

On the way back home I stopped in the churchyard and looked out over the horseshoe bend of the River Wye. I wished that I could just jump in the river and float off and away from my shattered dreams. I really didn't know how I was going to fare alone, after all the time we had spent together.

I didn't want to be alone, I just wanted James, but he didn't seem to want me.

Tears rolled down Charlotte's cheeks from reading her mother's words. She hoped that when her mum set eyes on James again next weekend, sparks would fly and reunite them. Charlie flicked through a few more pages of entries – some dates were left blank – and some had a miserable face drawn on them…

Dear Diary,

Saturday 24th December, 1988
It's Christmas Eve and usually a time of year I enjoy, but not now that I am alone. After a lie-in, I went to Hereford for my radio show, realising that at least I would be at home with my family unlike the many children who were spending it on a ward. Jack was still trying to cheer me up, unsuccessfully. Once I let him know I had split up from James, he seemed to be trying so hard to fix me up with various friends and acquaintances. Even though I told him I needed space and time, in my mind I knew I might never recover – this was terminal.

Before my show ended, Mark popped his head in. "Hi Jack, fancy a pint after work? You can come too if you like, Stephanie?"

"Sounds like a great idea," Jack said.

"I'll pass thanks, I need to get home," I replied, knowing my company would hardly be cheerful.

"Ok catch you later Jack, have a good Christmas Steph," Mark said.

"You know I believe that Mark quite likes you," Jack said, turning to me.

"Get out, anyone would think you were cupid!" I scoffed.

"I might ask him later in the pub."

"Well carry on as you know my answer will be no."

Once I was home, I walked in to find an envelope on the hallway table for me; it looked like James' handwriting so I opened it to find a Christmas card inside – nothing special, no girlfriend emblazoned on it. Not even a *Love, James* at the bottom, just *Fond regards*. What was fond regards supposed to mean? They were nothing but words on a page. I ripped it up and put it in the bin.

Even under the stream of water I couldn't let go of my memories as I remembered the times we had spent soaping each other, giggling and laughing until the suds were everywhere. His fingers on my body, mine on his. I shook as emotions filled my body and I wished again that my life had turned out differently. Perhaps one day he would change his mind and come running back into my arms?

As the shower spray fell on my face it was joined by more tears. Trying to be cheerful and normal all the time was really exhausting, because all I wanted to do was climb into bed and go to sleep and wake up when everything felt better. Or better still, not wake up at all. The darkness of my depression was like a stormy sea threatening to drown me at any moment if I stopped treading water.

Sunday 25th December, 1988 (Christmas Day)
My grandparents were staying so it was great to wander down into the kitchen in the morning and find Nan making coffee and Gramps reading the newspaper.

"Morning love," Nan said. "Merry Christmas." She reached over and dropped a kiss on my cheek. "Is that gorgeous boyfriend of yours going to be here?"

"No Nan, we split up, I thought Mum had told you?"

"He was such a nice young man," Nan said.

Gramps looked up and smiled. "It's ok Steph, your mum did tell her but she seems to forget things really quickly these days," he said, returning to his paper.

The day passed in the usual manner; large roast dinner, the Queen's speech, followed by presents, a walk down the road and back before more food and a game of monopoly. Whenever I could, I left the rest of them downstairs and headed for the security of my room. I sat down on my bed and put the mix tape into the stereo which was kind of comforting and at the same time painful to listen to, too. But listen I did as the memories of the past year filled my head and I lay down and gave into them. I took his letters from my drawer and re-read all of them, except the last one he had sent.

Saturday 31st December, 1988
The last day of the year. In most parts it had been the best year of my life and I should have been looking forward but all I could do was remember the past and what I lost. I was going out with Sarah, Chris, Jack and his new boyfriend Simon and also Mark. These guys had kept me going since my break-up with James in November. Everyone had been so kind so even though I didn't really feel like partying, I was going to try my best to enjoy the day and night – and move on.

I went down for breakfast and saw a familiar cream envelope on the hallway desk, addressed to me. The writing looked like James'. We had agreed to stay friends but we had only managed a couple of letters since. I struggled not to continually write the same things; I still loved him, I wanted him to come back to me – but all to no avail. I still felt that excited buzz of anticipation that maybe he had changed his mind as I raced to my bedroom.

I opened the envelope and pulled out the thick card. As I did, the St. Christopher I had given him slipped out and fell to the floor. It glinted in the weak sunlight shining through the curtains and then I turned the card over and sank to the floor, my legs crumpling beneath me. In my hand was a wedding invitation to the marriage of Felicity and James. I felt dizzy with grief as I just let go of my emotions and howled from the pain. I thought my heart had already been torn apart, the moment that James had driven away, but the hole left now ached so much it was unbearable.

I must have laid on the floor of my bedroom for over an hour, pain disabling me, tears continually rolling down my face as they soaked the carpet. Mum shouted that Sarah had arrived so I quickly gathered up the invitation and the necklace and pushed them under the pillow. I just had to get through tonight and then tomorrow, I could break apart.

"Hi Sarah," I said, trying to hide my red, puffy eyes. Being a true friend she pulled me close and hugged me, letting me cry some more.

"I know tonight is going to be hard for you but you never know, it's the start of a new year and perhaps you will be able to move on?" she murmured softly.

"I know," I mumbled, clinging to my best friend like she was the only piece of driftwood in the swollen river of my tears.

When she let me go, I headed for the bathroom to shower and wash my hair. Sarah put the radio on and filled the room with happy sounds and waited for me to return. I let Sarah tie my hair up and apply my make-up as I had no feelings left in me at all. I was just an empty shell to be painted upon. *Who would want me ever again?* I thought as I looked into the mirror in front of me, seeing my lifeless eyes staring back, my make-up a mask that I could hide behind all night. I slipped into a new dress Mum had bought me for Christmas as it held no previous memories and then I sat on the bed whilst Sarah sorted out her own hair, dress and make-up.

"Steph, what's it like when you don't see someone every day?" she asked, sitting down next to me on the bed.

"It fucking hurts like hell," I said. "Why?"

"Chris is going into the Army and leaves for basic training on the second of January," Sarah said. "How am I going to cope?"

I bit my lip and wanted to be sympathetic, telling her it would be ok, but how could I? I was so jealous because she still had someone to love and care about whilst I was alone. Lost and abandoned.

But Sarah was my best friend and I knew that good friends were hard to find.

"It will be difficult but just write letters and make plans for when you are together and believe me, the times when you are together keep you going through the times when you are apart," I said, reaching over and squeezing her hand.

"We're going to have a great time tonight," she said.

"The best," I said, trying to inject some enthusiasm into my lifeless voice.

"Come on then," she said, pulling me up as Wham!'s 'Wake Me Up Before You Go-Go' came over the speakers and we danced around the room. For a brief moment, I felt alive.

We heard Chris's car pull up in the driveway and after a final application of lipstick, we were on our way into town to meet the others for drinks before we hit the club. The town was buzzing and I tried to hide my pain behind a smile. Jack grabbed my hand as soon as we joined them and propelled me off to meet his new man, Simon. Mark soon joined us and offered a round at the bar as we all got infected with the end-of-year vibe. Then after a few different bars, we met up with other friends who tagged onto our group, finally heading to the club.

Once inside I ducked into the ladies and spent ten minutes sat in a cubicle so that the tears I had been holding back could fall.

"Steph, Steph are you ok?" I heard Sarah calling.

"Yes I'm ok," I sniffed. "I'll be out in a second." I wiped the tears away.

"This club is pumping tonight," Sarah said, grabbing my hand and propelling me through the crowds and onto the dance floor. I let the beat flow through my body and closed my eyes, dancing until I was exhausted. After a quick break, Jack pulled me back onto the floor with him as we giggled and laughed together.

Then as the clock ticked down to midnight, it was impossible for our group to be on the dance floor so we joined hands around our table and did the count down, then 'Auld Lang Syne'. After a few more pumping tunes, the DJ changed to slower songs and I was left at the table with Mark.

"Would you like to dance?" he asked, offering his hand.

"Ok," I replied, and he led me onto the floor and pulled me close. As he held me in his arms, I thought about all the differences between Mark and James. Mark was shorter so my head came to his shoulder and he had green eyes. He just felt different.

Then the familiar strains of 'Take My Breath Away' surrounded me and I started to shake. Looking up into Mark's face, he must have mistaken my trembling for something else as I watched in slow motion, his lips heading towards mine. As they touched, it was all that I needed to realise that I couldn't do this, not now, not ever, it was too soon, it was too much.

I pushed him away, turned and fled. I grabbed my coat from the cloakroom attendant as the lyrics hunted me down and seemed to echo through the cold night air.

I slipped out of my heels and picked them up, running barefoot down the street. I pushed my way through revellers already homeward bound as the hurt inside me thumped in time with my heart. All the way home I ran and cried. The tears would not stop and I knew that at home, all that awaited me was the invitation and the returned St. Christopher. I fumbled with the key in the door as my parents were out for the evening, pushing my way through.

Stopping for a moment, I leaned against the door and made my way through to the dining room to the drinks cabinet. Momentarily I was distracted by the Christmas tree that stood resplendent in its glory. The baubles twinkled under the fairly lights and I walked over towards it and reached out for one of the glass ones. I plucked it from the tree and held it in my hands, noticing the fragility of it, just like my life at the moment. I was the bauble and James the hand, and slowly I crushed it, and it shattered into a million pieces that twinkled even more vibrantly as I threw them back into the tree. Looking down my palm was scattered with red dots of blood and I knew what I had to do.

I found a bottle of vodka and took that up to my room, thinking I might need it to numb the pain, hurt and anger inside of me. I put some music on and took a long slug. I wasn't much of a drinker so it burned as it went down and I almost threw it back up, but by the third mouthful it was starting to take effect as my room swam around me. I listened to George singing 'Where Did Your Heart Go?', such a mournful lament but so true of the way I was feeling. When it finished I stood up and replaced the needle so it started again and again and again. All the time I was staring at the invitation, the necklace hanging between my fingers.

Standing up, I staggered over to my mirror and stared into it. My life had gone wrong and I had no other option. Turning around slowly, I headed for the bathroom and started to fill the bathtub with warm water before I returned to my room. The words George was singing played over and over in my mind, even though the record had ended and the house lay silent.

I grabbed the phone receiver and instinctively tapped in James' home number, even though it was the early hours of the morning. I longed to hear his voice one, last time, but it rang and rang until I let it drop from my fingers. He must have been out with her and I fucking hated her for what she had done to me – what she had done to us – because we had been perfect together.

I picked up my paperweight from the desk and slammed it into my mirror, obliterating my tear-stained face as it shattered around me, spilling sharp shards across the carpet. Removing my dress I found his shirt and once more wrapped myself in its fabric. I placed the St. Christopher around my neck and picked up the sharpest shard that lay at my feet. With invitation in hand, I crossed the room and stumbled to the bathroom.

The tub was full so I closed off the tap and stood there for a moment. Then without any more thought, I drew the jagged edge across my wrist.

I didn't feel anything at first so I quickly did it again and then switched hands and slashed across my other wrist. I held my hands out over the steaming water and watched in fascination as droplets of blood hit the surface and spread out in ripples, fading further and further away. That's where I wanted to be – further away from the pain that would just not leave. After a final slug of vodka, I dropped the bottle on the tiles and that shattered too. I stepped over the rim and sat down, a stain of pink creeping up from the hem of his shirt.

Somehow I ripped up the invitation that I still held in my fingertips and scattered it over the surface of the water that was now a wonderful pink colour. My hearing started to fade in and out as I closed my eyes and saw James standing before me. His beautiful face shining as he reached out his arms towards me, I started to recite all the beautiful lyrics that made up our love affair.

"I'm waiting for a star to fall and carry my heart into your arms, we can be together forever and never to part, you are the desert and I'll be the sea," my voice trailed off and then everything started to become numb, including my heart. I had found escape from the pain of living without James.

♪

Charlotte realised tears were streaming down her cheeks and she wiped them away. That was the real reason behind the faded scars on her Mum's wrists? She had tried to commit suicide? Who had saved her? Why had James sent the invitation? No wait, it must have been Felicity who had sent it but using an envelope written by James. How would Mitchell's Dad deal with this information? How was this all going to work out?

January 1989 was included at the end of the diary so she wiped her eyes and looked through a few further pages, hoping to put the final pieces of the jigsaw into place.

-42-

Dear Diary,

Wednesday 4th January, 1989
I woke up under the bright, artificial light of a hospital room and stared around in disbelief. It hadn't worked, I was still alive. The room swam a bit so I closed my eyes again and started to hear a voice.

"Stephanie, Stephanie, can you hear me?" Mark said.

"James, James is that you, sorry I'm so sorry," I mumbled, my lips so dry and my tongue, thick.

"Stephanie it's me Mark," he replied. I shook my head trying to clear the muddle of thoughts that were there.

"Mark?"

"Yes Mark, you're in hospital..." His voice trailed off.

I started to cry again until I heard other familiar voices, trying to blink and open my eyes again.

"Stephanie, it's Mum," the voice said, as I looked out again and saw her face and Dad's next to it. Their features were etched with sorrow and guilt but also happiness that I was still alive. I reached out and Mum managed to hug me close before Dad joined in.

"Sorry," I said again, my voice faint but audible.

"Don't be sorry, you should have talked to us, told us how you were feeling," Dad said, no reproach in his voice, only love.

"We could have helped," Mum chimed in, her voice broken as she cried.

Sarah sat on the other side of my bed, tears spilling down her cheeks. I reached out and tried to grasp her hand in mine, but I was bandaged so well, I couldn't so she reached out and stroked my arm.

"I'm here for you," she said.

I was just about to close my eyes when Mark walked through the doors and ushered everyone out of the room, picking the chart up from the end of the bed.

"How are you feeling?" Mark asked, popping a thermometer in my mouth before I could even reply.

"Stupid," I replied, once he had removed it. "But it was the only way I could get rid of the sadness inside of me." It was easy to be truthful with Mark in his doctor's coat.

"Ok, I'll see what I can sort out. You'll be going home tomorrow," he said and was about to turn and walk away, when I stopped him.

"So how did I get here?" I asked.

Sitting down on the chair next to the bed, Mark began to tell me.

"Well, once you had run from the club I managed to signal to Sarah and Chris that you were rather upset so we grabbed our coats and started to walk towards your house. When we got there the front door was shut and the house was in darkness apart from the light in your attic room that we could see from the driveway." Mark paused, noticing the pain of the memories flit across my face.

"As it was so quiet we decided to try the door and found it was unlocked so we all walked in and Sarah started to shout your name. We ran upstairs and realised that the light was on in the bathroom and as you still hadn't responded to our shouts, we tried that door and pushed it open to find you unconscious in the bathtub. Chris pulled you out and wrapped you in a towel and then as I started to do CPR, Sarah called for the ambulance." He paused, noticing tears slowly falling down my cheeks.

"It was bad then," I whispered.

"It was close; we nearly lost you," he said, looking away.

"Thanks for saving me," I muttered, although in my heart I wasn't so sure that I wanted to be saved. I would still have the hurt and pain to deal with as well as scars, now. I still didn't know how I was going to cope, but I owed it to my friends to try.

♪

Charlotte closed the diary on what seemed to be the last entry. It was painful to read how her mum's world had crumbled and broken apart due to a bitch that happened to be Mitchell's mother. She hoped never to have to meet this woman as knowing her own quick temper, she'd be in line for a slap. She looked at the clock and dropped Mitch a text to see if he was still awake. He was so she phoned him.

"Hi Mitch."

"Hi Charlotte, are you ok?" he replied, noticing the slight catch in her voice.

"Yes, I've just finished the diary and it's not good news."

"Go on, tell me what makes you think this?" he asked. "Don't worry, I'm sitting on the bed in my room."

"Ok, so your dad sent her the letter, then came down to see her and they had break-up sex and he walked away. Then she tried to get on with her life but on New Year's Eve, she received an envelope in the post with your dad's handwriting on it, so she opened it to find the St. Christopher she had given him and an invitation to their wedding."

"Oh fuck, my dad wouldn't have been that harsh surely?" Mitchell gasped.

"No, my guess is that your mother sent it in an envelope addressed by your dad to really make sure my mum never wanted to speak to James again."

Silence reigned as they both thought about their parent's messed-up lives.

"Well, my mum went out dancing with her friends at new year, including my dad-to-be, who tried to kiss her on the dance floor. She bolted home and decided to commit suicide by slitting her wrists."

Charlotte sobbed this last sentence out, trying to imagine how lost and alone her mum had felt at that time.

"Baby, don't cry," Mitchell soothed.

"Sorry, it's just such a raw thing, such a cry for help that no one heard."

"But someone did hear as she's alive and you are here in this world," Mitchell said.

"Yes, but will she really want to see James again? Will it only serve to open old wounds that have healed?" Charlotte asked.

"Do you think I should tell my dad?" Mitch asked.

"No, let's talk about it a bit more when you come over on Friday and in the meantime, I'll pop and see Aunt Sarah as she was there at the time and she might be able to advise me," Charlotte said, blowing her nose.

"Sounds good to me, I can't wait to see you again," Mitchell said, his husky voice sending shivers down her spine.

"Me too, it can't come soon enough," she replied, thinking about flying into his arms the moment she caught sight of him.

"Well, try your best to sleep and dream of me," Mitch said. "I'll be waiting for you there."

"Dream of me too Mitch," Charlie replied. "Goodnight."

"Night babe, I love you."

"I love you," she said, and the phone line went dead. Charlotte thought that being truly in love was the best feeling on earth as she tapped the light switch and fell asleep.

-43-

I was already buzzing around the kitchen when Charlotte walked through the door.

"Morning Mum," Charlie said, as I passed her a mug of coffee.

"Morning Charlie, you were up late last night?"

"Yeah, was on the phone to Mitch," she replied. "Are you ok, Mum. You seem really happy this morning?"

"I am Charlotte, life is good," I replied, not wanting to share my secret admirer with my daughter as I eagerly awaited his next request.

"Usual for me today, college, and dance practice and then I thought I might go and see Auntie Rah on my way home," Charlotte said.

"Ok, I'll mention that you might do that as she is meeting me after my lunchtime show for a gossip."

I drove into Hereford early so that I could prepare my show but I felt a tiny bit disappointed that no song had come through for me, yet. However once I started my show and the text lines started to reel in, I saw the next one from my secret admirer and after a quick search through the archives, I found the song.

"Well listeners it appears that my secret admirer is listening in again today and this is his song – 'Secret Garden' by T'Pau. Perhaps he's telling me that he's a gardener? Or just enjoys spending time in the garden?"

As the song played I pondered what I could play in return and decided that my response would be very tongue-in-cheek.

"Hope you enjoyed that Mystery Man but this is what I'm looking for it's, 'Holding Out for a Hero' by Bonnie Tyler. Can you be my hero?" I announced and then sat back, keeping an eye on the text.

♪

Over in Warwickshire James listened with a smile on his face. He couldn't believe she had no idea. Or perhaps she did with the hero response, but she was flirting well and enjoying it. He had chosen the song as it always reminded him of their night under the stars between the apple trees. He spent a few moments wondering if he should respond but then decided that there was always tomorrow's song to have some fun with. He would have to get his thinking cap on for that. As the second song ended he paused and listened once more as Stephanie moved on to her next request. Her voice still sounding the same, it tugged at his heart and memories of how she had been when they were together. He was determined to get her back, regain her love and her trust – so that his life might finally make sense.

♪

As my shift came to an end, I handed over to Ian and after a few quick replies to corporate emails, I was out of the door and into the heat of the early afternoon. I had arranged to meet Sarah on the green by the cathedral and as I scanned the crowd, I found her sat on a blanket with a fine spread of a picnic and a cold bottle of crisp white and some lemonade.

"Hey Stephanie, great show," Sarah said, standing up and pulling her earphones out, stopping her radio app on the phone.

"Hey Sarah," I replied, pulling her in for a hug. "Good to see you and what a wonderful surprise."

"So tell me more about Mystery Man," Sarah said, as we both sat down in the sun and tucked into some French bread and cheese.

"Well, there's not much to tell really, he first sent a request on Sunday morning whilst Charlotte was away and it was 'Father Figure', but I thought it was either Paul or Ian playing a joke on me or even Jack from the hospital cheering me up."

"Well, it seems to have worked," Sarah said, "you look radiant, the best I've seen you look in a long time," the warmth of her strong friendship tingeing her voice.

"But they have all denied it, so I really do have a secret admirer who is trying to communicate with me through song." I grinned and blushed at the thought.

"So you have no idea who it could be then?" Sarah asked.

"Nope but it's good fun trying to figure it out, like for example, today's song was 'Secret Garden' by T'Pau. Does it mean he likes gardening or visiting gardens or is a gardener? I really don't know but I'm looking forward to tomorrow's song as he seems to manage to send one every day, but not always directly to my show. He sometimes uses Ian or Paul."

"Perhaps he works shifts?" Sarah surmised.

"Maybe, I just hope he's not a weirdo or stalker, just perhaps a genuine guy."

"Would you meet him?" Sarah said, leaning forward slightly.

"Maybe, I don't know if I'm ready for all that," I said, popping a succulent strawberry in my mouth.

"For goodness sake, it's about time you got back out there; how long have you been single now?" Sarah asked as she poured us another glass of wine and lemonade.

"About seventeen years," I replied, remembering the night I lost Mark.

"Well I think it's time you tried again," Sarah said. "And if your mystery man is awful then I'm sure Chris has some seriously good-looking single friends we can introduce you to." She leaned over and gave me a hug and we lay back and enjoyed the sunshine on our faces.

Eventually I looked at my watch and realised I had to get home.

"Did you come in your car?" I asked Sarah.

"Lisa dropped me off as she was shopping so if I can get a lift back with you?"

"Sure, I think Charlotte wanted to call in on you on her way home from dance practice so I'd better make sure you're there in time."

"It will be nice to see Charlie, how is she?" Sarah asked as we packed everything up and took the short walk to my car.

"In love."

"With that charming boy we met in Birmingham?" Sarah asked.

"Yes, he's called Mitchell. They have sent in a separate dance as the organisers of the competition need a fill-in whilst they make their final decision on the Sunday afternoon. They've recreated the final dance from *Dirty Dancing* and I have to admit it takes your breath away to watch them together."

"We are really looking forward to seeing her dance and also a weekend in the capital," Sarah said. "Chris gets home tomorrow so I can't wait to see him." I watched a faraway look cross her eyes, the anticipation of a loved one back in her arms, wishing I had that.

Once I'd dropped Sarah off, I returned home and switched the stereo system on and plugged in my iPod, finding the mellow tunes of Savage Garden. I had discovered them in the mid Nineties with a whole host of songs that didn't remind me of anything or anyone, just the emotions of being in love. Gathering up the ironing I went upstairs with a pile of clothes for Charlotte's room and after placing them on the end of the bed, I noticed my diary lying open on her pillow and a pile of tissues on the floor. Picking it up I glanced down at the page and realised she had finished it and therefore knew about my suicide attempt. Sitting down heavily on the bed, I turned back the pages and read again what I had written there in my childish script. Once again, I was propelled back to that black moment. I still had times now when I had to reach for a tablet to stem the darkness that would creep over me; certain songs, or an unknown voice that sounded like James', maybe a woman with long, dark hair even – was all it took for me to be right back to 1988.

I now knew the reason why Charlie wanted see Sarah, so I reached for my mobile phone and hesitated over the number to warn her, but as I looked at the time, I guessed my daughter was already there. Standing up I bent down to pick up the tissues from the floor and saw the pink cover of my photo album. I pulled it out, it was open on the last page, the only picture I still had of James. I stared at the image in front of me, my hands trembling as I looked into my innocent, happy eyes and his beside me. How long ago that was, yet my heart started to beat faster and emotions threatened to engulf me like a tidal wave upon the rocks.

I ran my hand over the surface of the protective covering as a single tear hit it and spread beneath my finger. My James, how could I ever forget him? He had been my whole world, the light in my darkness, the moon in the starry sky that I had spent so many nights gazing up at. The sun on my face when we were together, burning under the heat of each other's bodies. Quickly I shut the cover and pushed it back where I had found it, walking to the bathroom. In the mirror I looked at my face and saw a single tear balancing precariously on one of my eyelashes, wiping it away. How could a photograph take me down in an instant? I reached for my tablets and took one to head off the darkness looming in my reflection.

-44-

Charlie wandered up the path, rang the bell and waited for Sarah to appear. All the while she hummed the tune to 'Take My Breath Away' because in her mind, her feet were still dancing the steps.

"Hi Charlotte," Sarah said. "Your Mum said you were going to pop in."

"Yes, I kind of need to talk to you about something," Charlotte said, stepping into her second home.

"Go through to the garden and I'll get you a drink," Sarah said, following her god-daughter through and pausing in the kitchen to grab some glasses of orange juice. The wine in the afternoon had given her a headache.

Sarah gave Charlotte the juice and sat down opposite.

"Mum lent me her diary from 1988, about the time she spent with James. When I was upset about Craig she thought it might help for me to read her experiences but now I've finished it, I need to know a few things."

"About what?" Sarah asked, breathing in deeply.

"Well about New Year's Eve really?"

"Ok, I'll try my best but it's hard to talk about this stuff as I felt at the time I had let your mum down badly. I wish she had talked more about how she was feeling and especially about the wedding invitation when I was with her that afternoon, getting ready for our night out," Sarah paused. "Your dad was the first to alert us that she had run out of the club so I grabbed Chris and the three of us ran to the house."

"Go on," Charlotte urged, even though tears were already falling down her cheeks as she remembered the words in the diary.

"Well we found your mum in the bathtub, Chris managed to pull her out and wrap her in a towel so that Mark could start to revive her. We had no idea how long she had been unconscious or whether she would make it but Mark was so calm and ordered me and Chris about."

Sarah passed a tissue to her god-daughter and paused for a moment, reliving that night again as if it was yesterday.

"Did it take Mum long to recover?" Charlotte asked, as she blew her nose.

"Well, she was in hospital for about a week and then just had to wait for the scars to heal and she had to have some physio to get her wrists working again."

"No I kind of meant in her mind? I need to know before the dance competition next weekend."

"Why?" Sarah asked, her curiosity piqued by this turn of conversation.

She watched as Charlotte wrestled with her revelation

"Well Mitchell's dad is called James Cooke," she declared, watching the colour drain from her aunt's face.

"Fucking hell, how on earth did that happen?" Sarah said, amazed by the slim odds of this happening.

"I know it makes your brain reel if you think about it too much," Charlotte said.

"So I'm guessing James will be at the dance competition next weekend?"

"Yes and they are staying in the same hotel as us and I just don't know whether to tell Mum or just let her meet him there?"

"Christ, I don't know what to advise but I guess that in answer to your previous question, I don't think your mum ever truly got over James, even when she was married to your dad. Sorry I had to say that to you but I guess honesty in the best policy here."

"I was hoping you might say that," Charlotte said. "James knows who my mum is, he guessed when I stayed there last weekend and he is single now and he said that he made a mistake in ever letting her go and I think he still loves her," Charlotte explained, draining the last drops of juice from her glass. She looked over at her aunt who was still in shock with the news. It seemed they were both thinking the same thing – how would James react to finding out Steph nearly died because of him?

"Thanks Auntie Rah, I'm going to speak to Mitch this weekend and see what he thinks we should do."

"Ok Charlie, I'll think on it too and let you know."

"Can you keep it secret?" Charlie begged.

"Yes, mum's the word," Sarah said, giving Charlie a hug and kiss.

"I'd better get going, I'm starving, all this dancing makes you hungry," she grinned

"You know where I am if you need me, don't hesitate," Sarah said.

"Thanks again, you're the best," Charlie shouted, as she walked through the gate and home.

Music was playing as Charlotte let herself in and past the kitchen towards the stairs. She saw her mum dancing around the island to some Savage Garden track and smiled; she really did look happy. Upstairs under the shower, Charlotte considered her aunt's words. It was good to know Sarah still thought her mum had feelings for James but the whole suicide business was the curved ball and Charlotte just didn't know what was for the best.

After a lovely supper together, Charlie went upstairs to ponder all the repurcussions of a reunion between James and Steph – and also to text Mitchell before she went to bed. It had become a lovely habit to exchange a couple of texts with Mitch before drifting off and it always meant that Charlie had good dreams to fall into.

♪

The rest of the week seemed to fly by in the usual state of home life versus work life. I was enjoying work more than I ever had before. My Wednesday song from my secret admirer was 'Kokomo' by The Beach Boys so I joined in and played 'Holiday' by Madonna. I also commented that the song was included in one of my favourite films *Cocktail* as I remembered sitting in the cinema with James and dreaming about making love on the beach and under the waterfall.

The Thursday song was 'I Want Your Sex' by George Michael, so I had a giggle with the guys in the studio and in return I played 'We Don't Have to Take Our Clothes Off' by Jermaine Stewart. Even Jack sent me over a text for that one saying it was a class flirting rebuttal.

As the sun shone on Friday morning, Charlotte burst into the kitchen early, bags flying.

"You do remember Mitchell is coming over today and he's meeting me at college so he can join in with practice, and then bringing me home on his bike?" she said, hardly stopping for breath.

"Yes I hadn't forgotten, you've been reminding me all week. Do you want a lift this morning?"

"Yes please, I never realised how heavy bike helmets were," Charlotte said, gulping down her coffee and ending up with the hiccups, much to my amusement. In the background Paul was on and he had today's song choice from my secret admirer. I moved to turn the volume up and grabbed my phone so that I could reply.

"Morning Stephanie, your song from your mystery man today is 'She Wants to Dance With Me' by Rick Astley, so give us a call or text and let me know if you want to send one in reply," Paul said, as the familiar tune started to fill the kitchen.

"Hi Paul, can you reply with 'Dancing On the Ceiling' by Lionel Richie?"

"Ok Steph, I've had an idea to ask our listeners if they think you should meet your secret admirer at the Rock On the River event?"

I paused to digest this information; the scared part of me wanted to say no because if we never met, I would be saving myself getting hurt again, but on the other hand maybe this was the time to be bold and go for it.

"Ok Paul, you have my permission to do a text vote on this," I replied, with a certain amount of trepidation.

"Cool Steph, gotta go now as the song's nearly finished, see you later..." He hung up and his voice returned to the airwaves, "So listeners, Stephanie's song back today is 'Dancing On the Ceiling' by Lionel Richie and I think we should decide whether Steph takes the plunge and meets her mystery man at our fabulous Rock On the River event. Drop us a text with a yes and at the end of my show, we'll announce the results," Paul said as the song started to play.

I gathered up my car keys and shouted to Charlotte, "It's time to go, are you ready?"

Charlie wore her cut-off denims and a tight, checked shirt with her red mules and red lipstick, obviously to impress Mitchell, I thought privately.

After dropping her off, the smell of her perfume still lingered in the car as I drove home to do a quick spot of cleaning before Mitchell arrived. My mind was still trying to work out who my mystery man could be and hoping that now I had agreed to a possible meeting, he wouldn't turn out to be awful. As I turned into my driveway, I saw a florist van and driver standing on the doorstep with a large bouquet of white carnations.

"Are you Mrs. Stephanie Eden?"

"Yes, wow, what a nice surprise," I replied, signing the slip before the driver left. Juggling an armful of flowers and the door key, I managed to get inside and into the kitchen. I soon located the card and opened it to read the message enclosed.

Stephanie,
Search your heart, search your soul
and when you find me there,
you'll search no more.
Your secret admirer x

I read it through and knew that the lines were from the Bryan Adams' song 'Everything I Do, I Do It For You'. Quickly I searched through my cupboards and found a couple of vases to distribute the large bouquet. With some on the kitchen table, in the lounge and even on the hallway table, my house still looked full to brimming. The worrying thing was that my secret admirer had somehow found out my address – so I needed to make sure there was no one lurking around outside.

Getting ready for work, I remembered the last flowers that had been delivered were for Mark's funeral which had passed in a blur for me at the time. I decided I would take a small posy of the carnations up to his grave on my way to work. I thought about the way Mark smiled and was always full of laughter, despite the pressures of his job at the hospital. I wished now that I could make amends for not loving him as much as he loved me. It seemed my heart was waking up to the possibility of a new love as I made up my mind that this time, I would allow my feelings to flow; twenty-four years was too long a time to keep my fragile heart boarded up.

As I stood by the headstone, I ran my fingers over the cold stone, wishing Charlotte could have known her dad before he had been taken from us. No one had ever been caught for the stabbing and since then, I had never been back to the hospital even though the radio and the wards held such happy memories for me. I turned away and took a quick glance at the winding river below, serene and peaceful in the sunshine. I looked up into the blue sky hoping that Mark was looking down and wishing me the best for the future.

-45-

Charlotte struggled to concentrate through her classes and the hands on her watch refused to tick by fast enough. However the bell rang and after promising Julia she would see her in the hall, Charlie bolted out of class. She had left all her bags in her locker so she unlocked it and pulled out her make-up bag and body spray for a quick touch up. She didn't notice Craig approaching until he was directly behind her, too close for comfort.

"Hi Charlie, you're looking hot today," he said, reaching out and running a hand casually down her arm.

"Thanks Craig," she replied, trying to shake him off, but his hand gripped her and pushed her against the lockers.

"I should never have let you go," he murmured, danger lurking behind his deep voice. "With your tight top and shorts, teasing all us guys with your sexy body," he sneered, his eyes looking directly down to take in the hint of her breasts.

"Just let me go Craig, it's over. I have a new boyfriend," Charlie said, struggling under his tightening grasp. She could see the indents from his fingers marking her pale skin.

"Well I don't see him, where is he, this fictional boyfriend of yours?" he said, bringing his face so close, she could feel droplets of his spit hit her cheeks.

"I'm right here," said a familiar, deep voice and Charlie saw Mitchell looming over Craig's shoulder. "I think you need to take your hands off my girlfriend right this minute, otherwise I will not be responsible for my actions."

A look of shock passed over Craig's features as he turned to stare up into Mitchell's stormy face, his grip on Charlotte's arms slipping away.

"Sorry mate," he mumbled, sloping off away, like the coward he was. Charlotte was still shaking as Mitchell pulled her tight against his chest, the smell of his leathers and aftershave awakening her senses as the shake of fear turned to desire.

"Are you ok, baby?" Mitch murmured, running his hands through her hair, looking down into her face.

"Yes, that was good timing," Charlie replied, looking up into his beautiful eyes, licking her lips slightly.

"You look good enough to eat," he whispered, his lips reaching down to capture hers in an endless kiss that allowed their tongues to explore. When they broke apart Charlie was breathing heavily and her white skin was a blush pink from the heat, the marks from Craig's touch having disappeared.

"So what's the plan then?" he asked.

"Dance practice for about an hour and then we can go home," Charlie said. "Do you want to put your bags in my locker and we'll head to the hall?"

"Sure, sounds good to me," Mitch said, shrugging out of his jacket and trousers to reveal his normal sweat pants and t-shirt.

Walking down the college corridor, several girls did a double take when they saw Mitchell. Being tall and gorgeous, he was hard to miss. Charlotte couldn't stop smiling as she held his hand tight. There were some toilets opposite so Charlie ducked into the ladies to get changed whilst Mitch leaned against the wall opposite and waited for her.

Charlie didn't want to leave Mitch alone; she had seen the way his eyes had swept down her body and back up when he rescued her. She could hardly wait until he was in her room later this evening as it might stop the intense throbbing that was sweeping through all her nerve endings. Once in her leotard and leggings, she grabbed her bag and was once more in his presence. How on earth she was going to be able to concentrate through all three routines with Mitch, she didn't know.

Just before she pushed open the door to the hall, Mitch caught her arms and pulled her against him.

"I just want to take you home," he said in a breathy voice. "Now."

Charlie nodded as they kissed for a final time before composing themselves and entering the hall. After warming up, the group went through their other two dances to 'Umbrella' and 'Skyfall'.

Mitchell noticed they had added some changes to both routines which showed off even more of Charlotte's stunning moves.

"Come on Mitch, we need you." Charlotte's voice shook him out of his thoughts and he stepped onto the floor.

The girls quickly talked him through their routine and they started to dance. Mitch watched in awe as the haunting melody filled the room, one girl seeming to dance alone, telling the tragic story. He almost forgot his cue but as he stood and then caught Charlie, moving her down to the floor, it felt so right – he was meant to dance with her.

After three more attempts, they all felt satisfied and called it a day, after all they would be doing another two hours tomorrow afternoon with full dress rehearsal to check everything fitted with the routines. Mrs. Grantley shook Mitch's hand at the end and was about to say something when they heard a phone ring.

"Sorry, that's mine," Mitch apologised, reaching for his phone. Charlotte watched as he answered and then a look of shock crossed his face, followed by a huge smile as he hung up.

"So?" Charlotte said.

"We've been chosen," he said, picking her up and spinning her round until she felt dizzy.

"You mean the *Dirty Dancing* routine?" Charlotte asked. When he set her down, all the girls who had been about to leave turned round to see what the excitement was.

"Yes," he said, planting a large kiss on her lips.

Julia stood beside them and implored, "Tell us?"

"We did it, we've been chosen to dance in the interval before the judge's decision!" Charlotte exclaimed, reaching over to grab Julia's hand in hers.

"Fantastic news!" Mrs. Grantley said, coming over to congratulate them. "Any chance we could see the routine tomorrow at practice?"

"Sure," Mitch grinned. "We could do with a couple of practice runs before next weekend."

"Well, the hall will be open from eleven tomorrow and main practice starts at noon so see you all then," Mrs. Grantley said, everyone starting to gather their bags and head home.

They were alone at the lockers and before she had chance to turn the key, Mitchell pushed her against them. His hands swept down over her curves and pushed her even tighter into his body.

"I love watching you dance," he said softly.

"I love watching you dance, but I prefer it when we dance together," Charlotte said. Looking up into his eyes, she watched his lips head down and capture hers, softly at first and then with a fierceness that shook her to the core. She was glad of the solidity of the lockers against her back as her legs turned to jelly from the feelings flowing through her body.

In the car park, a few of the girls from the dance group were still there talking and almost didn't recognise Charlotte as she strolled past them and jumped up on the bike behind Mitchell. She waved as they sped off down the road and then she enjoyed the short drive home, her arms tightly around Mitchell's firm body.

At home, the first thing that was noticeable were the lovely carnations on the hallway table.

"Mum, we're home."

"Hi Charlie, hi Mitchell. Cold drink?"

"Yes please."

"We'll go and get out of our leathers," Charlie said, heading for the stairs. "And maybe have a quick shower, too."

"Ok, thought we would have takeaway for tea so I can order when you are both ready," Steph said, her voice joyful, her nose in the air smelling the scent of the flowers.

Upstairs Charlie noticed there were more carnations in a small vase on her dressing table. Her mother must have splurged on her flower purchasing to have enough for her room, too. Once they were alone, Charlie simply lay down on her bed and stuck her legs out.

"Help," she said, smiling up at Mitch as he approached the bed and swiftly pulled her leathers off. Charlie sat up and unzipped the jacket, flinging it over the end of the bed as Mitchell shrugged his jacket off. She sat up on the bed and unzipped his leather trousers, working them down to the floor so that he could step out of them.

"Do you need a hand with any of your other clothes?" Mitch breathed, his fingers touching the strap of her leotard. Charlie nodded as just the barest touch of his fingers on her hot skin made it impossible to think, let alone talk.

She stood as the straps fell down her arms and Mitch bent down to pull the whole thing off at her feet. He ran his hands back up her legs to the waistband of her leggings and then pulled them down as she stood before him, clad only in her white bra and barely there panties. Her hands rested on his shoulders and she could feel him shaking slightly as his eyes drank her in. His hands once more ran up across the smooth skin of her legs and hips before wrapping around her to pull her close so that he could reach her lips with his. She trembled in his arms as she kissed him back and time ticked by slowly as they rediscovered each other. Before they went too far, she pulled back, "Definitely need a cold shower now."

"Don't be too long," he murmured as she grabbed her dressing gown and left.

Under the water Charlie started to breathe normally and thought about the way she felt when he held her. When he danced with her, it was like they were two halves of the same person. She couldn't wait for later and also for tomorrow and the chance to fly above his head again.

Back in her room, she passed a clean towel to Mitch and as he headed out, she watched the muscles of his back and his cute tight ass as he left the room. He was too gorgeous for words and she still couldn't quite believe how lucky they had been to find each other. She pulled a fresh set of knickers on but no bra and just flung her long sun dress on before drying her hair. She was still applying lip gloss when he walked back in, the towel slung round his hips so she could stare at his chest and the small line of hair that ran down from below his belly button to beneath the towel.

"You look so sexy," Charlie said, her voice husky. She walked over and grabbed his towel, pulling it away from his body. She sneaked a look lower and felt a blush creeping over her skin as she averted his gaze.

"It's all yours," he said, catching her hands in his and placing them on his hips. His finger moved to her chin and he brought his mouth down to hers again, before they broke apart and he pulled on jeans and a t-shirt. She noticed he didn't put any underwear on at all.

"You tease," she said, softly. "I'll be thinking of you naked all evening now."

"I think of you naked all the time, well except when we are dancing. If I did that, I'd forget all the steps because you are so distracting. Now let's head down, I'm starving and need a drink."

♫

I heard them come through the door, giggling and I walked through from the patio where I had been enjoying the sun and thinking once again about my mystery man. Earlier, I got to work to discover that an amazing proportion of our radio listeners wanted me to meet my secret admirer at Rock On the River and ticket sales to the event had almost doubled in the hours following the announcement. I told Paul and Ian about my delivery of flowers and both said they had not given out my home address. I dropped Jack a text and he said exactly the same thing, so I still had no idea who my mystery man was.

"Nice flowers Mum," Charlie said, handing Mitch a beer from the fridge and then pouring herself a glass of Pimms, ready mixed.

"Yes they were delivered today," I replied and then quickly changed the subject. "So what would you like to eat tonight?"

"Pizza," Charlie replied and Mitch agreed.

"Shall we sit in the garden as it's nice?" I asked and they both followed me out. "So how was practice?"

"Great Mum, we're going in for more tomorrow," Charlie said. "And we will be dancing in the interval before the judges' decision."

"Congratulations!"

"Yeah it's fantastic. I can't wait to dance with Charlotte again," he said, exchanging a look with Charlotte that was hotter than the evening sun.

I heard the doorbell so I went inside to sort out the food. Glancing out of the window, I noticed Charlie had turned on the music system and she was swaying to the sounds that filled the garden with happiness. Mitchell never took his eyes off her. I picked up the card that came with the flowers but there was no clue in the writing as to who he was, my mystery man, but I would be finding out in a few weeks. I was about to drift off into my thoughts when Mitchell walked in.

"Can I give you a hand?"

"Thanks Mitchell," I replied, handing him some plates of pizza, wedges and coleslaw.

"Would you like another beer?" I asked.

"Yes, don't worry I'll help myself," he said, helping to lay out the food and then disappearing back into the kitchen.

We spent a pleasant evening chatting as the sun went down and as I cleared up, I left them alone in the moonlight. The music was still on low and as I loaded the dishwasher, I realised it was 'Careless Whisper' by George Michael. I paused and closed my eyes, remembering a time when I was young and dancing with the one I loved under a moonlit sky. Mitch stood up and held out his hand to Charlie and as they moved across the grass, it felt as though I was staring into a mirror that was reflecting back a scene from my memories. A single tear balanced on my cheek for a split second and then fell onto the worktop.

"I'm going to bed now," I called from the doorway, "I'm filling in for Paul on the breakfast show so if I don't see you in the morning, I'll catch you later."

"Ok Mum, night," Charlie managed over the music.

"Night Stephanie," Mitchell replied, turning towards me and raising his hand slightly.

I could hardly breathe as the gesture and the way he looked in the moonlight reminded me distinctly of James, who seemed to have returned from my dreams into a new reality with my lovely daughter. I sighed and turned towards the stairs, the scent of flowers filling the hallway. I lay in bed with the window slightly open and I could still hear the faint sound of music coming from the garden. Then as sleep claimed me, I dreamed about my mystery man. In my dreams, he looked a lot like James.

-46-

In the back garden, Charlotte said, "I never get tired of listening to the soundtrack from *Dirty Dancing*." The familiar strains of 'She's Like the Wind' floated out into the calm, warm night air.

"Dance with me," she asked Mitchell, turning to him as moonlight lit up her soft smile, casting long shadows around her on the pale grass. He stood up and pulled her close, their hearts beating in time to the rhythm of the song and each other. Her arms ran down his back to rest on the firm roundness of his ass. She pushed him into her tighter and felt his lips brush her forehead and cheeks, on the way to her lips.

They were lost in the music until Charlie had to stifle a yawn and they realised it was almost two in the morning. After locking up, Charlie sagged against the strength of Mitchell, who silently picked her up and carried her upstairs to bed. She pulled her dress off and slid under the duvet, waiting for Mitchell to join her. Then after some more loving kisses, she curled up in his arms and slept. Mitch looked down at the top of her head, and whispered, "Goodnight," softly into her hair.

When the sun started to shine through the curtains, they stirred and Mitchell carefully moved his arm from underneath Charlie's head. She opened her eyes and stared up at him.

"Morning baby."

"Morning Mitch," she replied, licking her lips and reaching up to pull him close.

"So what are we going to do this morning?" he asked with a mischievous grin on his face.

"Well, Mum's not here so whatever we like," Charlie replied, with an equally cheeky grin.

"I'm sure something was rubbing on my feet last night so I'll pop down and check," Mitch replied as he ducked beneath the covers. Charlie lay still, giggling softly as she waited for his first touch with eager anticipation.

Mitchell located her feet and carefully tested the water by running his fingers over her toes. She started to laugh until he bent down and ran his tongue over them instead. Her laughter turned to sighs of pleasure as he kissed and licked his way up her lower leg, knee and thighs. He could feel her fingers scraping through his hair and gripping tightly when he got closer to the lace of her panties.

Carefully, he ran his tongue lightly against the skin of her inner thigh and paused to see if she pulled away. Charlotte breathed heavy at the feel of his closeness but stayed still and let him continue as it felt too good to stop. His breath tickled her skin and she realised he had paused in case she wanted to stop.

He stroked the outside of the lace and continued upwards, over her smooth stomach and then to the hollow between her breasts. She longed to pull him further up so she could kiss him. But once again, she paused and ran her hands down his neck and onto his back where she traced spirals with her nails. His tongue delicately travelled in a loop towards each nipple, sucking them until she trembled beneath him, working up her throat and then to her lips. She hungrily matched his kisses and in a short lull, she moved from beneath him and let him lie in her place.

"It's my turn now," she purred, and with a kiss on his lips she dived underneath the covers.

Mitchell let his fingers stroke her hair, mirroring what she had done to him, her butterfly kisses on his feet. Her hot hand reached up and touched him for the first time and they both drew in breath. Charlotte peeped up from under the covers and as it was getting rather warm, Mitch threw them off so that he could watch her. She knelt up and paused for a second.

"How do you like it?" she asked.

He reached down and covered her hand with his.

"Like this," he breathed, as both their hands moved together.

As she continued, he let go of her and was able to run his fingers over the curve of her waist and hips. He closed his eyes, letting go of all his pent-up frustrations in the feel of her skin on his.

Pulling her hand away, Charlotte reached for some tissues and lay back down next to Mitchell. He turned so that their bodies lay touching from head to toe, as close as they could get.

"I love you," Charlie said, kissing him.

"I love you too," Mitch replied, kissing her back. "I could stay here all day."

"Yes, me too but I'm starving," Charlie said, pulling away to find his t-shirt on the floor from last night. She pulled it on and it just covered her bum. She turned to look at Mitchell, lying on her bed and looking utterly delectable. Picking up his jogging trousers and throwing them in his direction, she asked, "Are you coming?"

"Already did thanks," he laughed and stood up to pull them on as he watched a light blush appear all over her body. In the kitchen Charlie put the coffee machine on and then turned to Mitch.

"It's gone nine so shall we have something that will pass as brunch to get us through all the dancing?" she asked.

"Sounds good, how about scrambled eggs on toast with baked beans?" Mitch suggested. "I can help cook."

"Good, 'cos I'm a bit rubbish and burn things," Charlie said, laughing as he caught her round the waist and pulled her close for a kiss.

"You're very distracting in just my t-shirt and your pants," he murmured.

When they sat down to eat, Charlotte turned the radio on and they listened to her mum.

"Your mum is great," Mitch said.

"Yeah, so is your dad," Charlie said, between mouthfuls.

"I hope they can sort things out when they meet next weekend."

"I'm really scared about it, after all my mum nearly wasn't here; what if it goes horribly wrong and she gets depressed again?" Charlotte mused, putting her fork down as the seriousness of the situation hit her. "She's been so happy recently, happier than I have ever seen her," she said, reaching out for Mitch's hand.

"I'm sure it will be fine, now come over here, I'm getting withdrawal symptoms."

She slipped off the stool and into his arms.

They reached the college just after eleven. Only Mrs. Grantley was there, so they walked in and were soon warming up.

"Do you need any help with anything?" she asked.

"Well, I do have a suggestion," Mitch said.

"Go on."

"As we are doing the end routine from *Dirty Dancing*, there is a point in the film where the rest of the staff join in and I thought it might be nice if the guys in my group could hook up with the girls in yours."

"I'll ask everyone else when they get here later, but can't see why not... we can try and get a quick run-through on the Saturday after our main dancing?"

Charlotte stood and waited as the familiar strains of '(I've Had) The Time of My Life' poured out and she turned to see Mitchell, his finger beckoning her. Even though they hadn't danced together for a week, their first attempt was not too bad, although Charlie forgot some of the steps and the lift had to be aborted as Mitch wasn't ready. They stopped the music and returned to their starting positions again. The second attempt went a lot better but still not perfectly. As they walked back again, Charlie reached out for Mitchell's hand and pulled him close to whisper.

"Can't wait to get you naked later."

She watched him smile and visibly relax and this time as the music flowed, so did their bodies.

As Charlie ran towards Mitch for the lift, she knew it was going to be perfect and then as her feet left the ground, she soared above his head. Slowly she was lowered to the ground and still holding tight to Mitch, she watched his lips meet hers before they finished the routine. When the music faded away Charlotte heard clapping and turned to see Mrs. Grantley walking towards them.

"That was breathtaking," she said. "I just couldn't take my eyes off you both, you have something very special when you dance."

"You think so?" Charlie replied, looking from her dance teacher back to Mitchell, who still held her tight.

"Yes, don't ever stop dancing," Mrs. Grantley advised.

Mitchell held Charlotte even tighter when he heard the comments and as she turned to look at him, he nodded and whispered softly, "I will never let you go," his lips tenderly brushing over hers.

With Mitchell watching from the sidelines, the girls went through their dance to 'Umbrella' and then changed into their costumes for a dress rehearsal. Mitchell took the chance to admire Charlie's body in the tight red shorts and bra tops that they all wore as they moved with ease, despite the use of the umbrellas as props. Then after a quick change into their suits, they were the female equivalent of Bond, their sharp shooting in complete contrast to the melodic 'Skyfall'. It worked brilliantly and Mitch admired the skill in Mrs. Grantley's choreography.

As Charlie walked over to her bag, she pulled her final costume out and then another and handed it to Mitchell.

"We got you a costume, I hope it fits ok?"

"I'll soon let you know," Mitch replied, as he took the aviation style jumpsuit and held it up.

His jumpsuit was perfectly intact but looking across at the girls and especially Charlotte, he saw they all wore identical jumpsuits but with rips and tears in various places. The wigs they wore completed the whole look, with ragged edges and a darkened fringe. The darkness of the hair only heightened the paleness of Charlie's skin but she still managed to stand out from the rest.

Once in place, the haunting melody of 'Take My Breath Away' flooded the hall and Charlie was lost once more in the lyrics and the dance. She almost floated across the wooden floor and made the final leap into Mitchell's arms, her body lowered gently back to earth. Their first run-through had been perfect and they all took a moment to realise this before breaking into huge smiles.

"Let's leave it there girls, if we practise anymore today it will only end up getting worse," Mrs. Grantley said.

"Now, if you want to take a break, Charlie and Mitchell are happy to show you their dance."

The girls quickly headed out to change from their costumes into their normal dance clothes, while in the hallway, Mitch reached for Charlie and pulled her close.

"Let's be perfect," he said.

"Yes," she replied, his lips catching hers in a perfectly wonderful kiss.

They walked back in to find all the girls sat waiting on the chairs at the back of the room. Taking their positions, the music started and once again the performance exceeded even their expectations.

As they finished, the hall erupted under applause from the very critical audience. Breathing heavily they collapsed on the floor together.

"That was even better than earlier!" Mrs. Grantley said, over the applause.

"Thanks," they both said, catching their breath.

"Gather round girls. Mitchell has a proposal for you," Mrs. Grantley said.

Even though his heart was still racing, Mitchell cleared his throat. "We thought it might be a great idea for you to join up with the guys in my group, and after we have done the lift, you pour in from either side of the stage just like in the film."

"Cool," replied Julia, "Count me in."

"Yes and me," chimed in Lucy and then all the rest.

"Great that's decided then, we'll probably have to sneak a practice in on the Saturday at some point," Mitchell said, smiling over at Charlie.

As the rest of the group gathered their bags and belongings together, Charlie and Mitchell stood up and held each other tight.

"This is my dream come true," Charlie whispered as she hugged Mitch tight. "Thanks for finding me."

"I think you found me too," he said, his eyes full of love and desire. "Shall we go home now?"

"Yes, I really need a shower and to lie in the sun in the garden," Charlie said as they headed for the bike.

-47-

Driving back from Hereford I once again had the top down on my convertible and the music on loud. Today it was George Michael as I sang along to all my favourite songs and enjoyed the happiness that the sun and my secret admirer had brought into my life. I was going to fire up the barbecue, it had hardly been touched over the last few years but if today's weather didn't merit another evening in the garden, then it was a bad job. I had bought some burgers, sausages, French bread and salad.

Pulling into the driveway I noticed the bike was not back yet so I walked into the house and started to open the windows to let fresh air in. I changed into my shorts and was about to head out into the garden when the phone rang. I answered it but after just the hint of someone breathing, the line went dead. Perhaps it was just a wrong number? Or maybe my secret admirer was turning into a stalker? Instead I picked the phone up again and gave Sarah a call, asking if she wanted to come over later with Chris. She agreed and as I flitted through the kitchen, I put some music on and went out to discover what sort of mess the barbecue was in.

"Mum, Mum," Charlie shouted as they found me scrubbing away at the grill.

"Hi guys, thought I would fire up the barbecue for tea. Sarah and Chris are coming over."

"Cool," Charlie replied, grabbing some cold drinks.

"We're just going to get changed and sunbathe in the garden after all our dancing" she said, pulling Mitch towards the hallway and stairs.

As I started to assemble the food the doorbell rang and I opened it to find Sarah and Chris.

"Come in," I said, opening my arms for a hug from both of them.

"Good to see you back in one piece," I said, engulfed in a tight hug from Chris.

"Yes it's great to be back, I'm thinking it might be time to consider retiring and finding a job closer to home," he said, glancing at Sarah and smiling.

"Go on through, drinks are in the fridge, just help yourself as I'm about to light the barbecue."

"Perhaps I'd better help with that?" Chris offered. "I firmly believe that when it comes to alfresco cooking, men are better."

I held up my hands in defeat.

"Carry on, I'll bring the food out," I said, Sarah linking her arm through mine as we headed through to the kitchen.

"Nice flowers," Sarah said, noticing the carnations on the kitchen table.

"Yes, they're from my mystery man but keep it quiet, I haven't said anything to Charlie yet."

"Oh, that's so romantic," Sarah cooed, "but how does he know where you live?"

"Yes, that's the only worrying bit but I'm being careful and there is no sign of anyone lurking around," I told her, pouring wine before we strolled outside.

"Auntie Rah," Charlie said, getting up off the blanket she was lying next to Mitchell on. "Uncle Chris, too."

"You're getting too grown up," Chris said, hugging her and waiting to be introduced to the young man who was standing a little way back.

"Aunt Sarah, you remember Mitchell? Uncle Chris, this is Mitchell my boyfriend," Charlie said proudly. The men shook hands and Mitchell said, "Hi."

I noticed Chris examining Mitchell, seeing a familiarity there I'd noticed, too.

We enjoyed lively conversation as we all ate and drank and then as dusk fell, I went inside with Sarah and Chris to clear up. Mitch and Charlie helped and then disappeared to her bedroom, leaving the three of us alone.

"So what's the plan for next weekend?" Sarah asked.

"I've booked us all into the Ibis Hotel and I think we need to be leaving at around seven in the morning as the competition starts at eleven. Better to be early."

"Would you like me to drive?" Chris offered.

"That would be brilliant thanks," I replied. "I'm sure the traffic in London will scare me to death."

"Good that's sorted then, really looking forward to seeing Charlie dance," Sarah said.

"Yes, Charlie and Mitch are even dancing together in the interval before the results on the Sunday. I've seen the routine on camera… it will blow you away! I'm also meeting Mitch's dad which should be interesting." I watched as a slight flicker of panic seemed to cross Sarah's face before she smiled.

"We'd better be off now," she said standing up, leaving me wondering what that was all about.

Watching their car leave the driveway soon later, I paused and scanned the surrounding area, but there was no sign of anyone else around as I turned and locked the door.

♪

James walked back across the garden after tea with his parents and took a moment to breathe in the cool night air and look at the sky. Then once back in his house, he turned the radio on. He wondered what she was doing right now. Already in bed? Out with friends? He could only hope she might still spare a thought for him. He turned the radio up and listened to the words of 'Waiting For a Star to Fall'. Was she listening, too?

James sighed and thought of the time when this song was in the charts; it was that one perfect year of his life. With his eyes closed, he pictured Stephanie and the way she used to look up into his eyes, a mixture of innocence, pure love and trust in them being together forever. He couldn't forget the way her hand felt in his. The way her skin turned pink when she blushed. The way her lips felt when they touched his. Somehow she had known then what he hadn't. He remembered how she begged him to stay when he made love to her for the final time. The sight of her scared and tear-stained face as he walked out of her life had haunted him. He wished now he had been brave and stood his ground and not given her up. Looking up, he stared at his favourite picture of his boys together in the garden. What would have been the right thing to do?

In her bedroom Charlie put the radio on. "So, what shall we do?"

"I think I need to say thank you properly for this morning," Mitch said, leading her towards the bed. Turning her around he untied the string of her bikini top and it fell to the floor, his hands reaching round to cup her breasts as she leaned back against his body. His hands slipped to her shorts and pulled them off. He felt her trembling as his hands ran back up and turned her around.

Their lips met and they walked backwards towards the edge of the bed. Parting, he gently pushed her back onto the soft duvet. Charlotte breathed in as he knelt down, his hands running to the edge of her bikini bottoms. He hesitated for a moment and looked up into her face, about to ask permission, when he saw her smile and nod. He hooked his fingers under the fabric and slid them down her legs to the floor. Kissing his way back up he breathed in her unique, musky scent and ran his fingers over her small line of hair, lightly easing a digit into her wetness.

Charlotte closed her eyes and gave herself to the feelings of his finger and then they shot open again when she felt his hot breath, lips and tongue there instead. She looked down at his dark hair between her thighs and as the sensations started to bubble up and spread throughout her body, she closed her eyes and tried to stay quiet when she really wanted to moan and cry.

Mitchell found the right spot and she wriggled beneath him, the pure pleasure of his tongue flooding her body as she sighed and let it flow. Grabbing his shoulders she started to sit up, really wanting to feel all of him inside of her – but Mitch pushed her back.

"I want you," she begged.

"Not today Charlie, I seem to remember you said you wanted your first time to be special and I have plans for that," Mitch assured, smiling down at her, seeing the look of desire on her face.

"But I want you now," she pouted, trying to convince him to give in as her hands snaked their way over his hips to pull him closer.

"You'll just have to be patient," he replied, even though his breathing was rapid as he felt her hands on him.

Lying down next to her, they continued to kiss and in between, they talked about the dance competition next weekend and all the things they wanted to do whilst they were in the capital, a city neither of them had visited before.

When Charlotte stirred, she was greeted by the sight of Mitchell lying next to her. Last night had been fantastic and she blushed even thinking about what he had done to her with his tongue. Turning, she kissed him softly and he opened his eyes, staring sleepily into hers.

"Morning," she whispered.

"Is it? I was still dreaming about last night." Smiling back at her, his sexy smile dazzled.

She moved so that she was tightly wrapped in his arms and they listened to the rain falling outside. Eventually the smell of bacon drifted up the stairs and they followed it into the kitchen.

"Morning guys," said Charlie's mum as they appeared with tousled hair and smiles on their faces.

"Morning Mum, that smells nice," Charlie said, pouring some coffee as they hopped up onto the stools by the kitchen island.

"Morning Stephanie. Thanks for a lovely evening last night," Mitchell enthused, looking across at Charlie, a secret smile lighting up their features.

"So what are your plans for the day?" Steph asked.

"Not sure really," Charlie said, looking across at Mitch.

"Think we might rehearse our dance but otherwise I'm in Charlotte's capable hands," he replied, grinning, his mind clearly absorbed by thoughts of Charlie.

Charlotte picked up the florist's card from the table and read it.

"Oh Mum, who is this secret admirer then?" she asked, curiosity brimming over.

"I've no idea," Steph replied, blushing slightly. "But he has good taste in flowers."

Steph placed their breakfast down and joined them, but Mitchell and Charlie failed to hide their worry. Was this new admirer going to be a challenge James would have to overcome? They didn't know.

After eating and helping to clear the kitchen, the young couple headed for the lounge and started dancing again. As the music changed to 'Take My Breath Away', Mitchell watched Charlie dance her solo and made some comments, hoping it would help her even more with the lovely lines and shapes she already created with her body.

They swapped over and Charlie watched as Mitch ran through 'Thriller' again, also making some objective comments of her own that he was happy to take onboard before they finished.

After practice, the rain had cleared to leave a warm but cloudy afternoon so they both went out for a walk. Mitchell had the address for his dad's old house and wanted to see that and then the riverside where the Rock On the River event would take place

Holding his hand, Charlie felt like the luckiest girl alive as they passed dog walkers, parents and children and other couples. Then she remembered the bench in her mum's diaries.

"Mitch, we need to check the graffiti on the benches," Charlie said.

"Why?"

"Well if it's still here, your dad drew a heart and their initials onto one of the benches when he told my mum he was falling in love with her." Charlie slowed down when they reached the first bench. There was nothing there so they continued until they found it at last. Sitting down on the slightly damp seat, they found the heart, faded from the sun and weather after twenty-four years, but still there.

Charlie looked through her bag and found a marker pen, giving it to Mitchell. He found a small blank space not far from the heart and he drew one, drawing inside it *MC 4 CE* before handing the pen back to Charlotte. She left the top off and carefully drew over the lines of the original heart and initials, making it stand out once more against the rest of the scribbles. Sitting together it felt strange but comforting to know they were in the same place as their parents had been, so long ago. Then their lips met and they kissed and held each other, knowing that the time they had left together was short.

"Do you think they'll get back together?" Charlotte asked, as they made their way back home.

"I kind of hope so but I guess it's up to them," Mitch replied. "All we can do is wait and see next weekend." Putting his arm over Charlie's shoulders, they walked in step together.

"I wonder who this secret admirer is," Charlotte said, thinking back to the card from the florist.

"My dad will blow him out of the water," Mitch said. "After all, I've inherited his undeniable charm and good looks and it worked on you."

Charlie gave him a playful punch and laughed. She skipped away from him but he caught her and spun her around and back into his arms.

"I love you, Charlotte Eden."

She smiled at his words and the seriousness that lay underneath the green of his eyes

"I love you too, Mitchell Cooke," she replied, pressing her body close to his.

They entered the house to be welcomed by the smell of roast dinner.

"Where have you been?" Steph asked, as they flopped down on the sofa.

"Along by the river, we found your heart there," Charlie said, but the light left Steph's eyes.

"And we drew one on the bench too," Mitch said, joining in.

"I'll go and check on food, why not watch a film or something?" Steph suggested, leaving them alone. Charlie noticed her mum was disturbed to discover they had been following the footsteps of her past. It was clear Steph needed a minute for herself.

"Hey let's watch that film your final song comes from, what is it called?" Mitch asked.

"*Top Gun*. You mean your dad has never made you watch this? Mum tells me it used to be his favourite," Charlie said in amazement.

She located it on the shelves and put the DVD in to play. Pulling her close, they cuddled up on the sofa and started to watch until suddenly Mitch turned to her.

"Had you realised, our parents have named us after the lead characters?"

"The first time I watched it, was when mum helped me pick the song our group is dancing to… but I hadn't made the connection with your name," she said, laughing. "It could have been worse, he could have called you Maverick!"

"Or Pete," Mitch said. "I like my name, I've never met anyone else called it yet."

As the film ended, Charlie wiped her eyes and he kissed the rest of her tears away, knowing how involved she had been watching it. They went through to the kitchen as Steph had finished cooking and was just plating up dinner.

"So we'll be seeing you again next weekend," Steph said.

"Yes, my dad and grandparents are coming to watch so I'll introduce you to them," he said.

"Well, you've met my guests already. Sarah and Chris are coming down with Mum," Charlie announced.

"Shall we meet at the venue, as it might be difficult to arrange something at the hotel?" Mitch said.

Mitchell was soon dressed in his leathers for the ride home. Charlie felt her mum watching from the doorstep, no doubt reminded of times when she was separated from James in a similar manner to this – living in different towns, separated by commitments that could end up splitting them up…

As Charlie wandered in once Mitchell had left, Steph smiled weakly and handed over a mug of hot chocolate.

"Thanks Mum," she said.

"I know how it feels honey," said Steph, pulling her daughter close, "I've been there."

Her mum read her mind. "Yes, I know, but at least I can keep in touch with Mitchell every day, it was much harder for you just waiting for letters and a weekly phone call."

"Life changes," Steph shrugged, heading for the stairs.

"Night Mum."

"Night, sweetheart."

After a good night's sleep, it was Monday again and a normal working week until the dance competition finals in London. I was really looking forward to spending some time in the capital with my daughter and my two best friends. Sitting in the kitchen, I made a coffee and waited for Charlotte to appear. It was their last week before the summer holidays and I hoped that we would be able to spend some quality time together, if she wasn't too wrapped up in Mitchell. I thought about how the two of them were together and it felt like I was watching a mirror image of myself.

With the radio on in the background I made some toast.

"Charlotte, breakfast is ready," I shouted, and waited to hear the sound of her feet on the stairs.

"Morning Mum," Charlie said, sitting down and tucking into her toast and coffee. "I'm already feeling nervous about the weekend and it's only Monday."

"You'll be fine on the day when the music starts. I just know you will."

"Thanks Mum, hope you'll be ok to meet Mitchell's dad and grandparents on Saturday?"

"Of course I will, well unless they're awful?" I joked, and we both laughed, although I noticed that Charlotte's voice had a slight edge to it.

"I've got two hours of practice after school so should be home at around six," she said, finishing her toast.

When she came down she handed me my diary. "I've finished it," she announced, placing it down on the counter. "It really helped me focus on my life after Craig and has made me realise that true love rarely comes along."

I reached out and pulled her into a hug as she whispered, "I'm glad you didn't die."

"I'm glad too," I murmured, choking back a lump that had formed in my throat, dropping a kiss on her forehead.

"Bye Mum, see you later," she said, the moment over as she ran down the road to meet Julia. I looked at the diary and ran my fingers over the front cover. Was I ready to throw it away and move on? As I couldn't answer that question, I picked it up and took it back upstairs to my bedroom.

At work I thought long and hard about the diary, almost so much that I was surprised when a text from my secret admirer filled the screen with today's request. I sighed to think about this mystery man thinking of me and trying to seduce me with song. It was definitely working as I queued up 'I Can't Help Falling in Love With You' by Elvis Presley and sent it out over the airwaves to the listening ears of my admirer.

In return I played him, 'When I Fall in Love' by Nat King Cole. As my song played, I thought about the sentiments in the words. Did a person only ever fall in love once or could it happen twice? Once again I closed my eyes and an image of James was there, his arms open wide.

♪

As they walked to college, Julia turned to Charlotte. "Wow, the way you dance with Mitchell is awesome."

"I know, we just seem to fit together perfectly," Charlotte replied, a smile on her face as she pulled out her phone, a text message having just arrived.

She paused and read it: **Hi baby, am counting down the days, hours and minutes until I see you again on Saturday, Love Mitchell**

She quickly typed back: **You and me both, can't wait to dance with you again along with other things. Love Charlie**

Julia saw the pink blush spread over her friend's cheeks and asked, "So have you done it yet?"

"No, but we have done lots of other things," Charlie replied, grinning as she remembered where his tongue had been. As her mind connected with her body she felt a quick spike of desire roll through her.

They continued walking as Charlie looked at the next text: **You turn me on so much and I can't wait until we are in that hotel room. I have a big surprise for you.**

I love big surprises! she flirted, blushing even harder at the thought of what he might have in mind. She knew the natural adrenaline high produced when she danced could only be topped by the desire she felt when Mitchell touched and kissed her.

Practice later on went smoothly and Charlotte was really pleased with the props the art department had turned out for all their performances. There was a lot riding on this competition as first prize was £100,000 for the school or college and the possibility of going forward into the European competition. Second prize was £50,000 and third was £10,000. She also knew the judges were involved in recruiting dancers for musicals and music videos, so if you stood out the possibilities were endless.

On the walk home Julia chatted away about things but Charlotte found she wasn't listening as she thought about her Mum seeing James again after all these years. She really hoped that it would all go ok and that they might perhaps get back together. Although she missed her real dad, she had never even known him so having a dad like James was quite a cool compromise, especially when it might mean her and Mitchell sharing a house a lot sooner than she could have hoped.

♪

Tuesday and Wednesday passed pretty quickly for all of us. I continued to flirt over the airwaves and Charlotte was either at practice, in college or in her room. I worried that she was going to burn herself out before the weekend so on Thursday, I took her to the cinema to watch *Rock of Ages* which was great as it was musical and had plenty of dancing in it. Also I had the opportunity to enjoy the sight of Tom Cruise who was still looking fit for his age.

When Friday dawned and I woke early, I heard music coming from Charlotte's room, poking my head in as I passed by for the kitchen, promising some scrambled egg on toast before college. When she appeared in the doorway I looked at her pale face.

"Is everything ok?" I asked.

"No Mum, I had an awful dream last night that Mitchell dropped me during the lift and it all went wrong," she paused. "We've hardly practised it enough and I don't want to let him down or go wrong."

Walking round I pulled her into my arms. "I have complete faith in the two of you, I know you will be perfect on the night and nothing bad is going to happen," I soothed. "Anyway, you can find some time to practise on Saturday evening or Sunday morning."

I felt her shaking stop and went back to finish making her breakfast. I heard her reach for her phone and drop a text, followed by a quick reply. As I put the plate down in front of her, a smile returned to her face.

"Are you dancing tonight?" I asked.

"Yes but just for an hour as Mrs. Grantley doesn't want to overwork us and knows we all need an early night."

"Ok, takeaway for tea, your choice."

Reaching the studio I gave Mark a wave as he was filling in for Paul and would also be doing my Saturday show while I was away. I made us both a coffee and looked through the emails and found one from my secret admirer. This was a change from his normal texts: **Morning Stephanie, can you play 'I Just Called to Say I Love You' by Stevie Wonder? I hope you have a great weekend in London. From your secret admirer.**

I read through it again and again. How did he know I would be in London this weekend? This guy seemed to know an awful lot of private things about me. I reached for my phone and quickly rang Jack.

"Hi Jack."

"Hi Steph, how's things?"

"Fine but my secret admirer seems to know that I will be in London this weekend and I'm pretty sure I haven't said anything on the radio about the dance competition."

"Well, I've already told you, I don't know who he is," Jack replied.

"Ok, I believe you."

"Wish Charlotte luck for me," Jack said.

"Thanks Jack I will," I replied as we hung up.

When Mark came out of the studio, I passed him a coffee.

"Morning Mark."

"Morning Steph, you're looking well, so who's your secret admirer then?"

"I have no idea and it's really bugging me as he seems to know where I live and that I'm going to be in London for the weekend."

"Oh that might be my fault as your daughter texted in and asked to give her group a good luck wish and play them a song," Mark replied. "The email must have come in after that as she mentioned you were her mum in the text."

At least that helped to calm my nerves as I started my show and played the song he requested, following it up with 'Hello' by Lionel Richie. I also played 'Lucky Star' by Madonna for my daughter and her group and asked all the listeners to keep their fingers crossed for their local dance group.

After tea, Sarah gave me a call and checked everything was all ok for the morning. We had a quick discussion about eating out on the Saturday night as Chris knew a good restaurant so I agreed. Suddenly Charlotte flew into my room, holding her phone tightly in her hand.

"Mitch has booked us a ride on the London Eye, isn't that exciting?" she exclaimed.

"That's lovely. Aunt Sarah just phoned to say that they would book us a meal in a restaurant. I said to book it for five but if you guys want to be by yourselves, I'll understand."

"Cool Mum, I can't wait!" she said, running back out of the room, a huge smile on her face and all the worries from the morning gone.

When we finished packing, we called it a night. In my room I glanced over at the diary that still lay on my bedside cabinet. I reached out for it, opened it again and started to read. As I closed the last page I looked across at my clock and realised that it was one in the morning. I got up and went down to the kitchen for a glass of water, stood looking out over the garden, bathed in moonlight. All the memories flooded back through my mind as I felt like a sixteen year old again, sure but uncertain, brave but scared, in love but devastated. I hoped that Mitchell would not hurt my baby, sleeping soundly in her bed. I wished James had never hurt me all those years ago, his words a poisoned chalice that I drank from, his promises shattering me like my broken mirror on New Year's Day.

I crept into the lounge and put the stereo on, listening to all the songs that had made up my relationship, finishing with 'Father Figure' and 'Take My Breath Away'. I cried until no more tears would fall down my cheeks. Had my diary taught Charlotte that life was a cruel mistress, one that would crush dreams in her fist, as I thought again of the bitch that ruined my love. I slowly turned and walked back to my lonely, empty bed, taking one of my tablets until sleep finally claimed me from my dark thoughts.

♪

In her room, Charlotte slept fitfully, tossing and turning as her mind went over all the different steps, turns and lifts in the three routines. Then she was stood, waiting for the music to start for her dance with Mitchell. She dreamed that as she stood there, her mum saw James across the auditorium and stood up. As she did, Charlotte saw the piece of jagged glass in her hand and she drew it across her wrists once more. The blood was spraying the people all around her as she fell to the floor. Charlotte remained motionless on the stage as Mitchell walked towards her and they started to dance. The mayhem in the audience seemed to continue around them as they danced the perfect routine. Charlotte woke in a sweat and went to top up her glass of water.

On the landing she heard music coming from downstairs and she tiptoed quietly down, peering into the lounge. She saw her mum sitting on the sofa, the diary in her hands as tears ran down her cheeks. Charlotte hesitated and wondered if she should go in and comfort her. But something stopped her and she rushed back to her room, reaching for her phone to tap out a quick text to Mitchell: **Mitch, I'm scared about tomorrow, Charlie x**

She lay there in the darkness as the image of her mum in tears haunted her. Her phone rang a few moments later as she lay back against her pillow.

"Hi baby, what's wrong?" he asked.

"Mum's downstairs crying over the song that I'm dancing to tomorrow," Charlie replied, trying to choke back her own fears and nightmares. "I'm worried that it's all going to go wrong tomorrow when she realises who your dad is… and then what happens if she tells me I can never see you again?"

"Hush, now, I'm sure it will be fine and if it's not, we'll find a way through it," Mitch soothed, "I just wish I was there to hold you."

"God, me too. At least Sarah knows and she will be there."

"Try and get some sleep, we've got a long two days in London," he said. "And I need you to have some energy left after all the dancing."

"Ok, night Mitch."

"Night Charlie."

♪

Mitch got up and went down to the kitchen for a drink and to ponder all the possible scenarios that Charlie had obviously been through in her mind. As he stepped through the door, Jester walked over to him and offered his head, as if he wanted to help share the load. Grabbing a glass of water, he went through to his studio and quietly put some music on, starting to dance as it always helped to clear his mind. When he finished, he turned to find his dad leaning in the doorway.

"Can't sleep either?" he said.

"No, guess it must be the nerves," Mitch replied.

"Yes, me too. I'm nervous for you guys dancing and I'm really nervous about meeting Stephanie again. Every time I think about her, I panic and I won't blame her if she blows me out, I just need to explain everything and tell her the truth," James admitted.

"Come on, let's just sleep on it," Mitch said, not wanting to take on his dad's problems as well as his own and Charlie's. Why was life so complicated?

-50-

At 5.30, I pressed snooze for that extra ten minutes, jumping under the shower before my daughter could beat me there. Standing under the warm water, I wondered what this weekend would bring. I had to admit to feeling nervous about meeting Mitchell's family; after all this was the first parent of a boyfriend I had met and it normally meant that things were pretty serious.

I knocked on Charlie's bedroom door at six and she emerged, heading for the shower while I made us some early breakfast.

I watched as Charlie pushed her cereal around the bowl and then threw most of it away. I grabbed some cereal bars and fruit from the cupboard and put them in my bag for the journey, as I knew that she would need something before she started to dance. At ten to seven, Sarah and Chris pulled up into the driveway and we were soon on the road.

Charlotte handed over her CD for the music system and sitting next to me in the back of the car, she closed her eyes and I guessed she was visualising her way through all of the routines in preparation. In between, she was on her phone texting Julia and Mitchell in equal measure. I spent the time gazing out as the various different counties passed by the window, trying not to think of James every time the one song looped around again and took me back in time.

We began to see the city of London crowding into the windows as traffic around us built up.

"Shall we go straight to the venue and leave the hotel until later?" I said, as I watched my daughter staring at her watch.

Chris nodded and continued to weave his way through traffic, nearing the O2. Pulling into the parking area, we got out of the car and I spotted Julia's mum pulling in a little way back. We hung back so that the girls could walk in together.

While Charlie and Julia managed to locate their practice area and the rest of the girls, Sarah found a coffee bar and we waited until we could take our seats. There were twelve different groups competing for the title from all over the country and I guessed that just being here amongst the twelve was an honour. I looked at all the people walking through to the auditorium as I sipped my coffee and then looked at Sarah and Chris sitting in front of me.

"You look as nervous as I feel," I said, trying to lighten the mood.

"I'm glad I'm not dancing," Sarah replied, as I watched her look away and scan the crowd. Chris remained quiet and seemed to be doing the same thing.

As we walked in to take our seats, I looked at the programme and realised that Mitchell's group was on first and then Charlotte was about halfway through with their first dance. Then there would be a break for lunch at around 1.30 before the second dances.

Looking around at all the other people watching, I saw a tall, slim bloke with short blond hair taking his seat a few rows below us, next to an elderly couple who looked so familiar, but I just couldn't think why. Shaking my head I reached across and gave Sarah's hand a squeeze. She smiled at me and the house lights went down. Then I saw Mitchell and the guys walking onto the centre of the stage. Their first dance was to a Justin Timberlake track which I vaguely remembered Charlie playing a few times on her iPod. I was blown away at the way he moved and at how the group as a whole controlled the dance floor and took the audience with them through the tricky steps and turns, somersaults and incredible acrobatics. As the music faded, the audience were immediately on their feet and I joined in, though worried about how Charlie was feeling backstage.

As the next few groups came and went, some with great applause and some not so great, I waited with baited breath for my daughter.

"Charlotte's next," Sarah whispered into my ear.

"Yes I know, I feel sick."

"She'll be great, I just know it," Sarah reassured me as the start of 'Umbrella' filled the hall and the backdrop onstage depicted falling rain. I held my breath all the way through and at the end, I knew from their faces they had been practically perfect. Another standing ovation and I spotted Mitch standing just in the wings as they left the stage. By the time the tenth group were performing, Charlie had appeared and found the spare seat next to us.

"That was fantastic," I told her. "You were definitely the best group."

"Stop it Mum, you're just saying that," she said, smiling. "Mitch and his group were better."

"So, when do we get to meet his family then?" I asked and couldn't help but notice a strange look of panic cross her features, which seemed to be mirrored by Sarah.

"I've spoken to Mitch and we're going to meet after the final dance today, in the foyer if that's ok?"

"Sure."

Charlie headed off again to change and get ready for their second dance. I saw her down at the front near the stage talking to Mitchell.

"I'm just off to the ladies," I said.

"I'll come too," Sarah replied.

All the way, Sarah seemed to be nervously checking all the people that were buzzing around. As we joined the queue, the elderly lady I had seen earlier passed by and seemed to start and then smile at me. Perhaps she thought she knew me too, perhaps it was one of the other girl's grandparents who had maybe seen me at some of the previous dance events.

"Do you have any lipstick?" I asked Sarah, as we stood at the mirror. "I think I packed all mine in my other bag."

"Sure," she replied, handing me some light-coloured gloss.

"How do you think they're doing?"

"Well, I would say it was close between them, Mitchell's group and that mixed group from London," Sarah decided. "But hey, what do I know about dancing?"

The second half seemed to fly by even quicker. I enjoyed Charlie's Bond-themed dance to 'Skyfall' and once again, the crowd did too as the roof lifted to the sound of applause. I was secretly pleased that the London group were slightly out of sync with their music and I think they knew that too as they filed silently off stage. As the final two performed, I turned to see Charlie and Mitch. He slipped into the row of seats a bit further down and Charlie next to me.

"We nailed that one," she said, her face flushed from the exertions.

"It was fantastic, the best in this half," I replied. "So what's the plan for later?"

"Well, once you've met Mitchell's family, our two groups are just going to have an hour's run-through for tomorrow as we decided it would be great for the girls in mine and the guys in Mitchell's to be like the end of the scene in the movie and just join in from each side of the stage. We've checked with the organisers and they are going to let us do a couple of practises once the place is empty… so I'm afraid you'll have to hang around a bit before we go to the hotel."

"That's no problem," I replied as the last group took the stage. "I'm sure we can have a chat with Mitchell's family as we'll all be waiting," I said, noticing worry flit across my daughter's face, draining the colour away.

With the last group finished, the lights came back on and we started to move and stand up.

"I'll just go and get Mitchell," Charlotte said, weaving through the crowds in the aisles. I stood up and stretched my legs, waiting for people to disperse until there were just a few groups still hanging around.

I stepped into the aisle with Sarah and Chris behind me and saw Charlie and Mitch. Then as if in slow motion, the tall, blond guy who I had seen earlier stood up and turned around so that I could see him. My heart leapt in my chest as he smiled that all too familiar smile that I had never forgotten. He started to close the gap between us but I closed my eyes and then opened them again, my world starting to spin and my legs buckling. The last thing I remembered was hearing the sounds around me fade in my ears, memories from twenty-four years ago spilling over like a waterfall as I fell.

I came to and as I opened my eyes, I found I was staring into the worried green gaze of my daughter. I tried to sit up but felt dizzy again and I fell back into the arms that cradled me. I couldn't see who held me but as I blinked a couple more times and then sat up, I saw Sarah, Chris, Charlie, Mitchell and of course the elderly couple who I now knew to be Pam and Peter, James' parents. A couple of stewards were stood to the side.

"I'm ok," I said quietly as I tried to move, but the arms that held me against his firm body wouldn't let go. I looked down and saw the arms were connected to the only man I had ever loved completely. My mind tried to clear a path through my thoughts that linked today with the past, a past that had somehow collided with the present.

"Mum, are you ok?" Charlie asked. "You fainted."

One of the stewards stepped forward.

"Are you ok to stand as we need to clear the arena?" he said.

"I'll help her," a deep voice said from behind me and once again, I felt my whole body trembling from the sound that had not changed in all these years. I looked across to Sarah and she just looked sheepish and then smiled at me.

"Thanks," I said, as James pulled me up and I was standing again, his body so close behind me that we were almost touching.

"I think I need some air." Sarah and Chris appeared either side of me and we started to make our way to the exit.

"We'll see you in a little while," Mitchell said, standing with his arms around Charlotte, both their faces pale with shock at my reaction.

Sarah motioned to the café we had stopped at earlier which had a small outside seating area and she left Chris to escort me to a seat in the evening air. I watched what happened next from afar but it was clear to me what was going on – they all knew about this and I was the only one left out of it. Sarah was ordering at the counter and saw James heading in my direction, but seemed to give him short shrift, heading him off at the pass. Before he headed off somewhere else with his parents, he gave her a piece of paper.

"It's a shame the bar is not open, I could do with something stronger," Chris said, as he watched them all depart. Sarah rejoined us and as she passed me the coffee, she also gave me a small slip of paper.

"It's from James, he said he would like to talk to you," she said, taking a long sip of her coffee and smiling over at Chris. I carefully opened it and once again, I was sucked back into the past, his writing so familiar, so remembered. I could see my fingers shaking as I tried to concentrate on the words:

Dearest Stephanie,
I know it's been a long time, too long really, but I need to talk to you and tell you what really happened. I know I must have broken your heart and for that I am truly sorry but if you'll hear me out, maybe I can start to mend it. Mitchell knows which room I am in at the hotel and I will be there all evening waiting for you... till the end of time.
Yours, James

Breathing out and in again, I read it once more and then a final time, closing my eyes as panic started to rise. My one hand reached for my wrist and I started to rub my scar as I felt my emotions spiralling out of control. Chris noticed and reached over to stop me.

"I'll tell him to leave you alone if you want me to," he said, adding, "I could kill him for what he did to you," the anger rising in his voice. Sarah reached for my other hand.

"You must do what you feel you must. Just remember, you are not alone this time," she said, her voice choked with emotion as she watched the tears fall slowly down my cheeks.

I excused myself for the nearest restrooms so that I could clear my head. I needed to be alone. I needed to think about what had just happened. Leaning against the cool tiles, tears ran in a torrent down my face. I thought I had cried them all last night but yet, they still kept coming like constant rain. Eventually they slowed and I splashed some water onto my face, looking down at the red lines on my wrists. What was I going to do? Half of me just wanted to turn around in his arms and never let him go again. Half of me wanted to hit him for the hurt he had caused when he had walked out of my life. I just didn't know what the best thing to do was.

Walking back into the foyer, I heard music coming from the hall as Charlotte and Mitchell practised their dance for tomorrow, their two worlds having combined to make one. I smiled and walked back to where Sarah and Chris were sat talking. They looked up as I sat down.

"I'm going to go and hear him out," I said. "I owe it to him and as long as you are here, I am strong enough now to decide." My mind was made up.

"So, is it just going to be us at this fancy restaurant later?" Chris said to Sarah.

"I think so as Charlie told me that Mitch is taking her up in the London Eye and I don't think they want to hang out with us old ones," she replied.

"Thanks guys, for everything, but can I just ask, did you know?"

"When Charlotte spoke to me the other week, she told me who Mitchell's dad was and I was so shocked, but she swore me to secrecy. Then at the barbecue, Chris sort of guessed. Sorry I should have told you," she said.

"It's alright, I understand. I always thought that Mitchell reminded me of someone but I talked myself out of imagining my thoughts could be right."

The music finished and after another ten minutes, Charlie and Mitch appeared, their faces shining with sweat and love. I saw Charlie hesitate as she reached the table.

"Sorry Mum," she said. "I should have told you."

Mitch looked around as Sarah stood up.

"Your dad took your grandparents back to the hotel so we'll give you a lift," Sarah said.

We gathered up our bags and with Charlotte tucking her arm through mine, we headed to the hotel. In the lift I turned to Mitchell.

"James gave me a note and said you would know which room he's in?"

"He's in Room 306, just give it a knock. He still loves you."

I paused at the door of my room and turned to Charlotte.

"Have fun but don't stay out late."

"I will, Mum but if you need me, just give me a call or text on my mobile," she replied, then she stepped forward and filled my arms, whispering, "I love you, Mum."

"I love you too sweetheart," I replied and then I watched them walk further along the corridor. Sarah and Chris were in the room next door to me and in a hurry to get ready and go out.

"Are you sure you won't come out and eat with us, you know, make him wait?" Sarah said. I shook my head.

"I don't think I can eat, I'm too nervous and I just need to get this over with."

Turning the handle I entered my room and crossed to look out of the window.

Pacing around I thought of all the things that James might say to me. Did he really still love me? How did I feel about him now? Did I still love him or just the memory of him? Could I forgive him? As thoughts whirled around my mind, I decided to jump in the shower and change before I took the short walk to his room. As the water soothed me, I shut my eyes and remembered all the times we had spent together under the water, right back to that very first kiss in the cool of the swimming pool. My stomach fluttered with nerves as I wrapped a towel around me and then rummaged through my bag for something to wear.

I pulled the dress out I had been planning to wear to the restaurant and held it up against my body. Dropping it onto the bed, I let my towel fall and looked at my reflection. I ran my hands down over my still slim build and hips and looked at my small breasts which were still in the right place, the nipples suddenly springing to life under my fingertips. It was as if my body knew where I was going and reliving all the feelings his fingers had brought to life in me when we were together. I pulled on my underwear and dress and started to do my hair and make-up. Enough to hide some of my wrinkles, but not too much, as I didn't want him to think I had made any special effort.

In the end, I pulled the dress off and stepped into my jeans and shirt which looked a lot better. With my hair in a simple ponytail and a small amount of lip-gloss on, I felt as ready as I was going to be. The butterflies in my stomach made me feel sick.

I grabbed my bag, phone and room key and walked out of safety and into the hotel corridor. As I was in Room 342, I had a bit of a walk to find his room. In my head I listened to George Michael singing 'Faith' as that's what I needed. I paused outside his door, my heart hammering. When I held my hand up to knock I noticed how badly it was shaking as I connected it with the wood and waited.

♫

James had sat in his room ever since he had returned to the hotel. He had tried to watch some television but he kept seeing Stephanie in every scene. She still looked beautiful and so young, as if the years had hardly touched her since the last moment he had. He took a shower and then stared at himself in the mirror. Would she come? Would she give him the chance? Would she still love him? So many questions to answer and he just had to wait and hope. Mitchell was taking Charlotte up in the London Eye and then out for a meal before who knew what they would be up to in their room. He knew his son, he knew from the look in his eyes the desire he felt for Charlie and he hoped the best for their future. A future which might hang in the balance depending on how things went with Stephanie today. Then he heard her hesitant knock and he turned away from the view, his heart pounding, nervous butterflies banging against his ribcage…

-51-

Mitch held the door open and Charlie walked in, immediately dropping her bag to spin around.

"It's fantastic," she breathed, walking towards the window and looking out at the city surrounding them. She felt Mitchell standing behind her and he wrapped his arms around her waist, pulling her tight against him.

"You are the best view I've seen in ages," he whispered as his lips brushed her neck and his hands reached up to caress her breasts. She turned to face him and flung her arms around his neck as he picked her up and walked the short distance to the large bed. He pushed her down and lay on top of her, their mouths meeting. When they parted, Charlie sat up.

"Well, what a day that was," she exclaimed.

"You looked amazing onstage. I managed to watch you perform," Mitch said, stroking his finger up and down her arm as if he was joining up all her freckles in a large dot to dot pattern.

"I didn't get the chance to see you but Mum said you were brilliant and she thinks our main competition is the college from London," Charlie told him, shivering under his touch.

"Yes they are pretty formidable, but we still have tomorrow to go." He glanced at his watch. "Enough chat, we'd better get ready." He started to pull off her top and then her leggings until she was just in her underwear.

"Shower?" he asked.

"What, with you?" she squeaked.

"Yes I can do your back for you," he replied, the cheeky grin she loved lighting up his face.

"See you in there," she said, as she undid her bra and pulled down her knickers, Mitch not far behind her.

Under the water, their hands explored each other's bodies and Charlotte wished they weren't going out now, desire bubbling inside her as the soap bubbles ran down over her skin.

"I've got the taxi booked for 6.30 and our trip on The Eye is booked for seven. I don't want to be late," he said, even though they kept stopping to kiss, as they danced around each other pulling on clothes. Charlie was pleased she had packed her long black sundress and silver heels as she dried her hair and fastened it up. She twirled around for Mitchell and he didn't say a word, just smiled and pulled her close.

In the foyer the receptionist told them that their taxi was waiting and Charlotte felt honoured to be holding Mitchell's hand as they strolled out of the hotel. As the sights and sounds of London passed the cab windows, Charlie couldn't stop smiling and gazing at Mitchell, who looked so smart in his shirt and trousers.

"So where are we going after the London Eye?" she asked.

"That's a surprise," he said, as he put his arm around her shoulders and dropped a kiss onto her cheek. Stepping out in front of the big wheel, Charlie looked up and realised it was much bigger than she imagined. They stepped into the large glass capsule and it was quiet which meant they didn't have to share the space as they slowly ascended into the darkening sky above the capital.

Looking over London was a spectacle and they both spent the ascent looking at all the places they had both only seen on the television. When they reached the top, Mitchell pulled her close and tipped her chin up to him so that their lips could meet in a kiss that far eclipsed the view, her eyes closing, surrendering to his touch. When they parted they were on the way down. As they alighted at the bottom, Mitch hailed another cab and whispered to the driver their surprise destination. Then they drove into the West End and were dropped off outside a theatre showing *Rock You*, the musical based around the music of Queen.

"This is amazing Mitchell, how did you afford all this?" Charlie exclaimed as they found their seats.

"I borrowed some money off Dad, I'll pay him back so don't worry," Mitch replied. "You are worth it."

It was a fantastic show and after standing for the final song and singing and dancing along, they agreed it was a wonderful evening.

"They are always holding auditions for dancers to these shows and I thought I might try out later in the year," Mitch said, as they walked out into the street and looked for somewhere to eat.

"Wow, that would be amazing. I'm not sure Mum will let me."

"Well, you won't know if you don't ask her, maybe she will?"

They ended up grabbing a burger before Mitch hailed another cab and they returned to the hotel. As they walked along the corridor to their room, they both wondered how their parents were getting on. They opened the door to their room and there were more important things on their mind.

"So is this special enough?" Mitch asked, reaching out to push a loose tendril of hair from her face. She shivered just from the slightest touch of his fingertip as she moved into his embrace and nodded.

"I love you so much Charlotte Eden," Mitch said, kissing her forehead and brushing his lips ever closer to hers.

"I love you too, Mitchell Cooke," she replied, before their lips collided in a kiss that blew her away.

Slowly he removed her dress and drank in the sight of her body in just underwear; she was truly beautiful in his eyes as she started to remove his shirt. He helped her with the buckle on his trousers as he saw that her hands were shaking so much that they kept slipping. Then he led her to the bed and they fell upon the cool covers as the moonlight poured in through the gap in the curtains. As they kissed and caressed each other's skin they gently removed the final barriers between their bodies. Mitchell immediately trailed kisses down over her hot, smooth skin and then to her clit, intending to get her almost to the point of orgasm before he entered her for the very first time.

He gently kissed, licked and nibbled his way around her and felt her body arch and respond under his touch as she wriggled beneath him. Then her hands tugged him to come back up and reclaim her lips.

"Are you ready?" he whispered, as he kissed her cheek and neck.

"Yes I think so," she whispered.

He reached for a condom and then started to nudge his way inside of her. She felt full of him as she started to move in rhythm with his body. It felt like they were dancing on a different plane as the stars filled the room above and she disappeared under the swell of passion that lifted them.

When they floated back down to earth, they were bathed in sweat and clinging to each other, unable to move. Charlie looked into Mitchell's bright green eyes and he looked straight back at her as love passed between them as brilliant as the city lights. He leaned over and turned the lights out and then they closed their eyes and went to sleep, each dreaming of the other and their dance tomorrow.

-52-

I watched as the handle dropped and released the catch. I took a deep breath as the door opened and I was staring into the face of my first love, my only love. James moved aside as I stepped past him into the room. I felt sick with nerves but something stirred inside me. There were a couple of sofas over by the window with a table between them, a wine bottle and two glasses in the middle of it, so I passed the end of the bed and settled down on the nearest one.

James shut the door and took the seat opposite me.

"I'm glad you came. Would you like a glass of wine?"

"Yes that would be nice," I managed, hoping he wouldn't notice the tremble in my voice. He handed me the glass and I took a quick sip before placing it on the table. My hands were shaking so much that I feared I would drop it. Then I waited, wondering if I had to speak first or would he. The room was so silent that a car alarm sounding from the car park startled us both. He placed his glass next to mine and cleared his throat.

"Well I guess I'd better go first," he said.

I nodded and gave him a tentative smile.

"I never thought I would be lucky enough to see you again, let alone be sitting here talking to you. You can imagine how shocked I was when I found out your daughter Charlotte was my son's new girlfriend," he paused.

"Yes, at least you found out earlier than me," I said, remembering the moment in the auditorium.

"I knew that this was the best chance I would ever have of meeting you again and being able to explain why I did what I did," James said.

Sorrow and pain tinged his blue eyes. I thought back to the moment he walked out of the door. A teardrop started to form under my eyelid so I blinked it away.

"I didn't really tell you the truth back then," James said. "And for that I am truly sorry but I thought at the time, it was for the best."

"But how could lies be for the best?" I exclaimed, feeling angry and confused.

"I wanted to stop you from seeing my indiscretion and weakness," James confessed. I looked up again and saw a tear trembling on his eyelash. He reached and refilled his glass so that he could take a gulp.

"I had a one-night stand with Felicity," he admitted.

"How could you? With her," I spat, my anger now evident.

"It happened on the night of my leaving do. Felicity offered to drive me home and I was drunk. So she pulled into a lay-by and jumped on me."

"So you were overpowered by a woman?" I retorted.

"Well, I was missing you and, and..." his voice trailed off. I watched as he put his head in his hands and sobbed.

Silence reigned for what seemed like an age, but was probably only a few minutes. I took another sip of my wine and found a pack of tissues in my bag. I slid the packet across the table and as James reached for it, our fingers touched. I felt a shock pass between us as we pulled away and looked up into each other's eyes.

"I tried to forget it and Felicity didn't say anything until a couple of months later when she told me she was pregnant and that it was mine."

"Was that the night I saw you together in the nightclub?" I asked.

"Yes it was."

"So why didn't you tell me the truth then?"

"I didn't want to hurt you and at that stage, I thought that I could work things out and still be with you and that perhaps the baby wasn't mine. I told her I would support her and my baby but that I didn't love her. But she told me that if I didn't finish with you, she would tell you that we had been having an affair for months. She then said that if I stayed with you, I would never see my child."

He let the words sink in with me as I realised that he had been placed in an impossible situation.

"I can't say that I am sorry to have chosen my eldest son over you. It was the hardest decision of my life and one I still have to look at every day," he murmured. "We tried to make things work between us for the sake of Darren, but it was awful and I tried to leave her a couple of times and then Mitchell came along," he paused again. "I thought I'd broken up with you as gently as possible so that you could move on and be happy without me. I also wanted to make sure that Felicity never hurt you as you deserved better than that, than me," he struggled to get the words out.

"But you did hurt me and yes, so did Felicity. You hurt me so much that I thought my life was over, especially when you sent the invitation to your wedding," I said, letting my words sink in.

"But I never wanted you to know about the wedding as I knew it would kill you. She must have sent that. You must believe that it wasn't me!" James implored. I looked into his eyes and saw tears falling, mine joining. He pushed the tissues back and I dabbed at my eyes.

"It arrived on New Year's Eve as I was trying to get over you as best as I could. Sarah and Chris took me out to a nightclub and I tried to forget about the invitation that was at home, taunting me, telling me that you never really cared for me," I stuttered. "Well, after midnight I was dancing with Mark and our song started to play and I realised that I could never forget you and I ran away from the club. I reached the house and something broke inside me, the darkness I had been battling overwhelmed me and I just wanted to escape all my feelings of despair."

I reached down as tears fell unchecked down my cheeks. Slowly, I pulled up the sleeves on my shirt and held out my hands to him, palms upwards. I watched as he slowly looked down and realised what the scars on my wrists meant. I heard him choke on his sob as he reached out to take my hands in his. His fingers gently ran over the raised scar tissue.

James looked up into my eyes and I saw the anger there, anger at himself and at his ex-wife. We both continued to cry as he held my hands in his. As he slowly stroked his fingertips over my wrists I started to feel a tingle rising within me. It was a tingle I hadn't felt in years and I knew that he was re-awakening my deep desire for him. He must have felt the heat starting to spread through my skin as he stood up and briefly let go of my hands to shorten the distance between us. Before I knew it he was kneeling beside the sofa, reaching out for my hands once more.

"Words can't start to express how I feel right now. I feel like I let you down really badly. I feel like I should have known and I should have stopped her from ruining not just my life, but yours. You should have told me what she had sent you, perhaps I could have helped you then before this," he paused and again ran his fingertips ever so lightly across the faded scars.

"Please believe me when I say that I still loved you when we broke up, I loved you throughout my short marriage and I still do."

I watched as he scanned my face, my skin betraying my true feelings. I could feel a pink flush spreading right through from my hands and arms, up to my neck and staining my face.

Once again the silence stretched between us but this time the nervous tinge had faded. There was a different edge to the air around us.

"So where do we go from here?" he asked. His voice shook slightly and I knew that he was nervous at what my answer would be. I shook my head not knowing which way I wanted to go. It had been good to hear his explanation but it also meant that he had both lied and cheated when we were together. My mind was telling me that I needed to think things through and try to make a rational decision. My body on the other hand had started to recollect the feelings that lay dormant in me. It felt like they didn't want to go back to sleep.

"I know you still feel something for me. I knew that when I turned around and saw you earlier today. I knew it when I heard your knock on the door. I know it now as I feel you trembling, as I stroke your wrist and see the pink flush on your skin," he murmured.

He stood up and taking my hands in his, he pulled me up so that we stood only inches apart. Heat flamed in my cheeks, my whole body on fire. Pulling me closer I was back in his arms, so alien now but so familiar. Our bodies touched and again I felt a lightning shock pass through me. James must have felt it because he paused ever so slightly before his hands ran up my spine and reached my neck. We were now skin on skin. He traced the line of my jaw round to my chin and then inclined it so that I was staring up into his face as I watched him lean in.

Closing my eyes I felt the room start to spin as his lips brushed mine ever so softly. I hesitated, wondering if they had or if I had imagined it, but then I felt their touch again. I felt my body start to respond to him as my lips parted and our tongues greeted each other like old friends. I could feel his hands reach up into my hair like they always used to. I was seventeen again in his arms and I opened my eyes and saw James as he once was at twenty-one. Then my mind woke up and it felt like I had been slapped across the face. I pushed him away and stood shaking as tears started to form.

"I need some time," I whispered. I could see confusion clouding James' eyes at my statement. Especially as moments earlier, I had been re-igniting dormant passions through our kiss.

"I'm sorry," I mumbled, as I fled.

He reached for me but I moved out of his grasp.

"Let me sleep on things," I said, as I paused at the door. "It's a lot to take in on one day."

As a solitary tear trickled down my cheek, I reached to wipe it away, but I missed it and it fell and hit the floor. I watched the droplet breaking apart and remembered the shattered glass of my mirror. Could he really erase all the hurt and pain with a simple confession that he was wrong and was sorry?

"Will you have dinner with me tomorrow night after the competition has finished?" he asked, crossing the room to stand by the door.

"I'll let you know tomorrow." I needed to flee to the safety of my room before I changed my mind and allowed my body to take charge. I could feel the pull of desire begging me to close the door and stay.

He nodded and smiled.

"Thank you for hearing me out and I look forward to seeing you again tomorrow," he said, smiling shyly at me.

"Goodnight James."

"Goodnight Steph," he replied, as he watched me walk down the corridor. I could feel tears streaming down my cheeks as I headed for the safety of my room. Once inside, I leaned back against the solid door. I ran my finger over my lips where his had been only moments earlier. My breath was ragged as the final tears fell from my eyes. Why was life so confusing? If I had listened to my body, I would still be in his room, wrapped in his arms.

    I looked across at my mobile phone which I had left on the bedside table. There was a text from Sarah and also one from Charlotte. Both were asking how I was. I removed my clothes and crept under the cool sheets, laying there looking up at the ceiling and trying to figure out what was best. After all, it was not just my life but that of my daughter. Could I risk going back and facing heartache once more? My body seemed to be telling me that he was the only one for me. He was the only one who could scratch that itch. He was the only one who could turn the key and unlock my sealed heart.

-53-

Charlotte looked at the clock; it was only 5.30 in the morning. Weak sunlight poured in through the curtains as she sat up and tried to contain her breathing. She had been having another nightmare; this time she forgot all the steps to their song and just stood on the stage with everyone laughing. Her stomach heaved with the thought and she leapt out of bed and into the bathroom, throwing up the remains of last night's burger. Rinsing her face and cleaning her teeth, she started to feel a little better as she leaned against the cool tiles. Her heart was still beating and the fear still there that maybe they hadn't practised enough.

"Charlotte, are you ok?" Mitch asked. She pulled open the door and fell into his arms. He held her shaking body and felt the slight sheen of sweat on her forehead, which rested against his chest.

"Just a nightmare and nerves," Charlie replied, glad to feel his solid frame holding her. He pulled her over to the bed and they sat down.

"Come on, tell me about it," he coaxed.

"I dreamt that I forgot all the steps to our dance and just stood on the stage and everyone was laughing," Charlotte replied, thinking how silly that sounded.

"Perhaps we need to have a quick practise then." He reached for the phone and rang down to reception.

Charlie listened in to his side of the conversation with a puzzled look on her face.

"Get dressed then, we have a half-hour slot downstairs in the dining room before they lay up for breakfast." Dropping a quick kiss on her forehead, they dressed in their dancing clothes. As they reached the foyer, the girl on reception stood up and came round the desk.

"Morning, Mr. Cooke, would you like to follow me?"

Charlie watched her looking at Mitch, so she held onto his hand tightly. She pulled open some double doors into a large room with chairs and tables stacked at the one end and a small stage at the other.

"The staff will need to be in here by quarter past six to sort out the tables for breakfast."

"No problem," Mitch said. "Do you have a music system?"

"There's one beside the stage."

In the large room Charlie still felt the butterflies inside her as they walked across to the stage and she handed him the disc with their music on it. They stretched to warm up and then as the first strains came through the speakers, Charlie let the music flow through her, calming her. She smiled as Mitch walked to her and crooked his finger, taking her in his arms. The first couple of attempts they aborted due to either mistakes with the steps or not being quite ready for the lift. They paused for breath and checked the clock. They only had time for one more run-through before the staff would arrive. Taking a deep breath, Mitch gave Charlie a large hug.

"We can do it," he whispered, squeezing her hand.

This time Charlie forgot her dreams as the magic started to flow and she became Baby in the film. As she ran towards Mitch and he lifted her, she flung her arms out and remembered the view of the lake. Sliding down his body they were enjoying a brief kiss when applause started to ring out from the far end of the room. They turned to find the waiting staff and receptionist watching them and enjoying the spectacle.

"That was amazing, Mr. Cooke, would you be free to speak to our manager this evening as he is looking for possible evening entertainers?"

"Thanks Samantha," he said, reading her badge and letting go of Charlie to shake her hand.

"Feeling better now?" he asked, pulling her close.

"Definitely," Charlie assured him, on tiptoes so that her lips could touch his.

"Come on, shall we get showered and dressed and maybe some breakfast?" She nodded as they weaved between the staff setting up tables. Charlotte was aware of all the women looking at Mitchell as they passed; Mitchell saw the eyes of the guys on Charlie and pulled her closer.

"Mitch, is it ok if I just give Mum's door a knock after last night?" she asked.

"Of course you can, I'll jump in the shower, so take the key and let yourself in." Before they parted, he pulled her close and kissed her slowly.

"Don't be too long," he whispered.

As Charlotte walked along the corridor to her mum's room, she wondered how last night had been for her. Then her mind went back to her night with Mitchell and she blushed at the memory. After all, it's not every night a girl loses her virginity. She paused at the door, knocked lightly and waited.

"Hi Mum."

"Morning Charlie, is everything ok?"

"Yes Mum, just been rehearsing downstairs as I was feeling the nerves."

"Come in," Steph said, opening the door wider.

"So?" Charlotte asked.

"Well, we talked and we will talk again later today," Steph told her daughter, running her hands through her knotted hair.

Charlotte looked disappointed.

"I'm not unhappy about meeting James again but twenty-four years is a long time and I'm sure we have both changed as people."

"Ok, Mum," Charlotte said, noticing her mother didn't seem to have had much sleep. "Just wanted to check you were ok?"

"I'll see you at breakfast," Steph replied.

Charlotte opened the door to her room and could still hear the shower running. She stepped out of her clothes and crept in through the bathroom door. It was hard to move the shower curtain quietly but it didn't matter because Mitch had heard the door to the room open. As she stepped under the warm jets of water, Mitch held her against his slick body and she felt a spike of desire course through her. Mitchell ran his hands over her silky body and pressed tight against her.

"Do we have time?" she whispered, running her hands over his chest and then downwards to his hips.

"I think we do," he replied, hooking his hands under her bum and lifting her into position. In his arms she felt as light as air, floating with him on the waves of emotion.

With water running down their hot bodies, Mitchell pushed her against the cooler tiles to steady them. Then they rocked together to the invisible music that seemed to bind them. As the orgasm rocked through her, she called his name and was greeted with the same in return. She knew that they belonged together and that whatever happened today, she was really looking forward to their dance.

♪

I knocked on the door to Sarah and Chris's room and wondered what I would tell them about last night. I really needed some time with Sarah so that she could help me talk through the cloudiness in my mind. Perhaps that would have to wait until we were back at home. The restaurant was fairly busy despite the early hour and I guessed that many of the guests were participants and family members in the dance finals. I saw Charlie and Mitch seated at a table for two over in the corner. They both glowed with youth and I guess love if you could visibly see it. As we passed by James and his parents, they all smiled and said hello. I could see the haunted look in his eyes as if imploring me to make my decision quickly. The butterflies in my stomach were still fluttering. Even though I had eaten nothing yesterday evening, I was not remotely hungry.

The venue seemed an even busier hive of activity as we made our way to get some refreshments whilst Charlie and Mitch headed off to their rehearsal rooms to practise and get ready. I picked up a programme and saw the running order had changed slightly and Charlie's group were second on and then Mitch further back at around the halfway mark. As Chris excused himself, I grabbed a coffee with Sarah.

"So how did it go last night?"

"Ok, I think," I replied. "I'm just so confused and I don't know whether to listen to my head or my heart."

"Well let me try and help if I can?"

"James confessed to cheating on me with Felicity," I explained, "but it was only a one-night stand and she got pregnant with Mitchell's older brother. The bitch threatened James with two options to either stay and see his child or leave and have no contact at all. I can't really blame him for choosing his child in such a cruel choice. She also threatened to tell me that they had been having an affair for months and James didn't want her to hurt me any further."

"But somehow she did with that invitation to their wedding. What a complete bitch. So, what else happened?" she asked.

"I told him a little about New Year's Eve and showed him my scars. I watched him break apart in front of me. Then, he kissed me." I could feel a blush staining my cheeks with heat at my admission.

Sarah leaned forward and took my hand in hers. "If you still love him then I think you should give him a second chance. It will just depend on whether the trust has been broken with his infidelity and if you can overcome that."

"Thanks Sarah, I've told him I need time to think about everything."

"So girls, are you ready to take your seats, the show is about to start?" Chris grinned, holding out both his arms for us.

Walking into the auditorium, I could feel nervous tension permeating the air. Everyone was in the same seats as yesterday and I saw James just in front of us. He turned to scan the audience and gave me the fingers crossed sign for our respective children. I returned the gesture and felt myself smiling and blushing again like a teenager. I knew it was no good denying my feelings for him, they were still there and they were still strong. I just needed to be sure that his for me were the same. The lights dimmed and everyone sat expectant in the darkness, waiting for the stage lights to illuminate the arena. I spotted the judges filing in to their seats at the front and realised that one was Arlene Phillips from *Strictly Come Dancing*. I pointed this out to Sarah as we tried to contain our excitement against our jangling nerves.

The first group dropped one of their dancers at the wrong moment and I heard the collective groan from their supporters in the audience. They carried on regardless and for that they still received loud applause as they bowed. I found that I was on the edge of my seat as the curtains fell and after a few moments, they rose again to reveal a set that was breathtaking. Derelict planes painted onto the backdrop and what looked like a plane wing at an angle. I knew that this hid the steps that Charlotte would climb near the end before throwing herself into Mitchell's arms for the finale. It was so similar to the set of the video that I had to keep checking that I was not watching a television screen but the real thing.

Sarah squeezed my hand and told me breathlessly, "It looks fabulous," before the music started to fill the space around us. Its haunting melody made me close my eyes briefly as I remembered a time that this song meant everything. It was our song. In the darkness, I couldn't see James, but I somehow knew he had turned to try and find me in the crowd. Watching my daughter and her group weave, leap and dance their way through the song gave it new poignancy. Charlie always stood out despite the fact that the group wore identical outfits and were so in sync with each other that they flowed as one. I gasped as the audience did when a male figure appeared onstage as Charlotte fled up the steps.

There was a brief pause as Charlie fell backwards off the platform and Mitchell caught her below as she snaked down his body for the finishing pose. It felt as if the whole auditorium needed time to take it all in as the pause seemed to stretch into forever. Then slowly there was applause as everyone around us stood up and clapped and cheered. Tears streamed down my face, tears and joy and pride for my daughter up there. The applause went on for so long that the group had left the stage but then returned for a second bow. I could see Charlotte's face shining with happiness as they all bowed again, Mitchell still with them, holding her hand tight.

As the judges asked for quiet the next couple of groups came and went. I enjoyed the eclectic choice of Eighties music that each had chosen but none received as big applause as my daughter's group. Then it was the turn of Mitchell's group and the stage lighting turned red. They had kept the 'Thriller' theme with their zombie costumes but I gasped in amazement at the different interpretation of the music and the skill of the group. Once again Mitchell was the stand-out dancer among them all with his acrobatic skills that left the crowd gasping in shock and surprise. Everyone was on their feet clapping and cheering for a second encore. I saw Charlie standing in the wings smiling and cheering them on. The final group were the ones from London and they blew everyone away, so it seemed clear that the three in line for the prizes looked certain to be

Charlie's, Mitchell's and the London group.

The judges called for a brief refreshment break and then for everyone to return for their decision and a further performance. We filed out and I watched as people either scurried for refreshments or the conveniences. Sarah, Chris and I did the same and then went back in as we knew what was to come. As I made my way up the aisle I saw Pam, Peter and James, all smiles again. By the time I reached my seat my heart was racing once more at thoughts of our kiss last night. Then the lights started to dim and we were in darkness. A spotlight illuminated my daughter standing alone in the centre of the stage.

I knew that Julia had put some curlers in her hair so that it looked similar to Baby's in the film. Her black dress was the same style and only served to highlight her pale skin. Then the first few notes of '(I've Had) The Time of My Life' floated out and the audience gasped and some applauded as Mitchell walked onto the stage and motioned with his finger to her. I felt the first tear trying to squeeze its way out from the side of my eye. It was a tear of joy that my daughter was up there on the stage and I knew she was dancing to her favourite song of all time. I glanced across at Sarah and Chris.

"Nobody puts our baby in the corner," I heard Chris say to Sarah, and I watched her squeeze his hand.

Watching Charlotte and Mitchell dance so perfectly in time to the music, it was again as if the film had come to life. I could see that even with little practise, they were meant to dance with each other. Then as Mitchell leapt off the stage and danced up our aisle, I watched Charlotte gazing at him with so much longing and love. Then from either side of the stage, two of the guys from Mitchell's group appeared and lifted Charlotte off the stage. The spotlight was trained on her as she ran the short distance and leapt into the air, Mitchell held her high and they were frozen in time. The audience erupted and gave them a standing ovation as Mitchell gently lowered Charlotte to the ground. Filling the aisle and stage were the rest of Charlie and Mitchell's groups in pairs.

Charlie and Mitch made their way back up onto the stage as the audience remained standing and some started to filter into the aisle and dance. Chris and Sarah slipped into the aisle and started to dance and I saw James heading towards me. He held out his hand to me and I took it as he held me in his arms.

"Our children are magical when they dance together," he said.

"Yes they are." I could feel my heart racing as he held me close. My breathing had quickened and we swayed together until the music faded.

When the applause finally ceased, the people in the aisles returned to their seats. As there was a free seat next to me, James sat down in it as the stage cleared and the judges appeared.

"First of all I would like to say a special thank you to Charlotte and Mitchell for that stunning rendition of such a well-known dance," Arlene said, applause once again echoing around us.

"So, it's time to announce the winners of our competition and I have to admit it has been a hard decision to make. The standard of dancing has been of the highest quality we have ever seen as judges."

As she paused there were hushed whispers, and James leaned towards me.

"I am so nervous for them," he said. I looked down to see his hand outstretched to me. I took it and nodded back.

"We were unable to separate two of the groups so we have decided to award a joint second place to the Ross Rhythmics and Footloose Freestyle from Rugby."

James pulled me up as the crowd started to shout and cheer, the two groups appearing onstage. I saw them scanning the crowds and I held my hand up to try and highlight us in the audience.

I saw a brief look of shock cross their faces as they both realised that we were standing together. Then smiles crossed their faces as they held each other's hand tight.

"The winners of this year's competition are The London Beats!" The crowd erupted as the group took to the stage and acknowledged the crowd's applause.

"We would like to ask for quiet so that we can watch The London Beats perform their final dance for us again," Arlene said. The crowd stayed on their feet as the group danced for us all once again. I turned to Sarah and Chris.

"Fantastic result."

"Yes, I wish Charlie had won but joint second is brilliant," Sarah said.

After the final dance the lights came back on and everyone sat down.

"I think this calls for a big celebration," James said, turning to me.

"What did you have in mind?"

"All of us should have dinner together, well if our kids don't think it's terribly uncool to hang out their parents."

"We'll just have to ask them when they appear," I added. I was still aware of his hand holding mine. His finger gently rubbed over my scar and for once I didn't feel ashamed of it. In fact it was igniting feelings I hadn't felt in years. I sat silently next to James, just aware of his finger and my nerve endings and all the unspoken feelings and words that still needed to be shared.

When I saw Charlie and Mitch heading towards us, I pulled my hand away from James.

"Well done, sweetheart," I said, as she flung her arms around me.

"It was fantastic Mum, I flew," she gasped, her eyes catching Mitch in their gaze. She broke away from my arms as she was enveloped between Sarah and Chris who were both hugging and kissing her. Then she turned to Pam and Peter who did the same. Finally Mitch pulled her close again and I reached out and hugged them both and then James was hugging all of us. His arms felt so strong and sure and ultimately so right.

When we broke apart, we looked at each other and I drank him all in once more. My feelings had never died, I had just locked them away to protect myself. I turned to find Pam and Peter smiling at me, with the same warmth that they had always shown. Peter held open his arms.

"You have a beautiful and gifted daughter," he said, hugging me tight.

"You have a talented grandson," I replied, him kissing me on the cheek.

"It was so magical watching them dance," Pam said and I nodded as we exchanged kisses.

The auditorium was almost empty when we all broke apart.

"I would like to take all of you to dinner later to celebrate Mitchell and Charlotte's success," James said.

"Thanks Dad, that would be fantastic," Mitch answered.

The rest of us all nodded. Emerging into the sunlight, still early afternoon, it seemed like a shock to the system. This time Charlie went back with Mitchell, James and his parents. Sitting in the back of Chris's car, I leaned against the window and closed my eyes. I knew that I wanted to follow my heart but I still had the issue of my blind date in a fortnight's time. Also I knew that James and I would have to take things slowly as it wasn't just the two of us now. We both had our families to think about.

Back at the hotel, Sarah and Chris decided to go shopping and sightseeing while I wandered to my room. Charlie had sent me a text saying that she would see me later for dinner. In the corridor I paused outside James' room. I still needed to speak to him and I realised that this was probably the best moment. I saw the surprise on his face when he opened the door.

"Hi Stephanie, would you like to come in?"

"Thanks James," I replied, stepping past him. I stood awkwardly again, aware of the electricity that crackled in the air between us.

"What a fantastic day," James said, breaking the silence and moving towards me.

"Yes it was," I replied, my voice soft and barely audible.

"So what shall we do between now and dinner later?"

"I guess we have some more talking to do."

"Shall we stay here, or would you rather go for a drink somewhere?"

"A drink sounds good," I said.

As we left the room I felt his hand on the small of my back, guiding me, and it felt comfortable. In the back of the taxi we were silent again, but this time it wasn't from nerves. I slowly reached across and placed my hand on his knee, remembering how it used to feel in his car. Glancing across at him shyly, he covered my hand with his and smiled back at me. The views from the window flashed by and again, our eyes focused on each other and I started to fall. The taxi driver dropped us off and we wandered along the West Bank and found a corner table in a small café bar.

Taking a sip of the wine, I hesitated and then jumped into the void.

"I think I would like to give things another go with you but there is a problem."

"And what would that be?" James asked, leaning forward.

"I think we need to try to be friends first and get to know each other again, after all we have probably changed as people over the years."

James nodded.

"We also have Charlotte, Mitchell and Darren to consider, it's not just the two of us."

Again James nodded and reached out for my hand across the table. I let him take it as I swallowed.

"I've also promised to go on a blind date in a fortnight's time. It's a bit of a long story that one." I watched as his eyes crinkled up and he glanced at his watch.

"I have plenty of time. Let's start getting to know each other again."

Over a bottle of wine and some olives, I told James all about my secret admirer who had popped up out of the blue only a couple of weeks ago. I also confessed that I had no idea who it might be.

"So you still like George Michael then?" he asked.

"Of course, there is no one better, it's just a shame he's gay otherwise I would be chasing him right now," I said, laughing at the suggestion.

"And if he were straight, how could he resist?" James joked, and I saw desire flicker over his pupils. I blushed and looked away, aware that I too felt the same desire for him now as I did back then.

On the journey back James turned to me. "So how shall we do this whole friends thing then?"

"I'm not sure yet but I guess as we are still living miles apart; we will have to chat on the phone and email as I try to sort everything out in my mind."

"What, no letters this time?" James said, grinning at his suggestion.

"Well we could if you want to but it's so slow these days, technology is making the miles between people seem very small. And at least this time I can travel to see you instead of having to wait for you to pick me up all the time."

"What car do you drive?" James asked.

"A convertible. And you?"

"I have a 4x4 as I have a dog that needs transport from time to time."

I watched as he fished in his pocket and removed his phone to flick through the photographs it held. He passed it to me and I was staring into the sweet, lovable face of a black Labrador.

"What's his name?" I asked.

"Jester," James replied. He hesitated as if to explain but I just shook my head and laughed as we both said, "*Top Gun*," at the same time.

"I hadn't watched that film for years until Charlotte decided that was the song her group wanted to dance to and we watched it together."

"I watched it the other week when I realised that Mitchell's new girlfriend was your daughter," James said. "It reminds me of us and how much we were in love back then." His voice softened as emotions bubbled to the surface. I turned away; I couldn't speak, my throat tightening up with tears that threatened to break the surface.

"Don't deny that you can't still feel it between us," he asked, his finger turning my head towards him. My whole body shook as I was paralysed under his touch. His face came closer and before I knew it, his lips were once more on mine in a kiss that transcended time. It was as if I was floating and looking down at the two of us but as we once were, young and in love.

When the cab pulled to a halt outside the hotel, we broke apart. I looked away as a single tear seeped out from the corner of my eye.

We walked back into the hotel together and hesitated for a brief moment.

"So, dinner at eight?" I said.

"Yes, but I'll be in the bar from seven if you fancy a drink before?"

"I'll see," I said.

We walked along the corridor together and paused as we reached the door to James' room.

"Today has been great," James said.

"Yes, our children were fantastic and deserved their second place."

"Yes I agree but it's been more than that, it's knowing that you are back in my life again." He reached out to take both my hands in his. "You can't start to understand how much I have missed you over the years." Then with a quick kiss on my cheek, we broke apart. I held the words tight to my heart, which expanded to catch them and keep them there as I entered my room.

I sat down for a moment on my bed and once again thought long and hard about what I was doing. The words that James had just given me were so precious. I looked down at my hands and then turned them over. My scars would always be with me and I hoped that he would make them better. His mistake would always be with him and I knew that at some point, I would have to talk to him about the bitch and how much contact she had with her sons – if I did decide to take the next step.

How did Mitchell and Darren feel about their mother and what part did she still play in their lives?

I looked through my case and found the other dress I had brought with me, a simple black number I knew I looked good in. Placing it on the bed, I turned towards the bathroom and checked my watch. I had plenty of time for a long soak in the bath and to get ready for the evening celebrations. I wanted to look as gorgeous as possible even though there was only one person I wanted to impress.

♪

In his room down the corridor, James pulled a shirt and some trousers out to wear that evening. The afternoon had been almost perfect; the only thing that would have made it more so would be for Stephanie to be standing right here with him now. He had tried to search her soul through her eyes but he had found them cloudy and guarded. It was going to take him some time to break through the barrier that held her heart, the barrier that in a way he had helped to build.

-55-

On the way back to the hotel, Charlie leaned against Mitch on the backseat and closed her eyes, reliving the lift once more. He held her tight as she soared above him and when she opened her eyes, he was still holding her tight. When they reached the hotel, Charlotte and Mitchell crossed the lobby and went up to their room. They both needed a shower amongst other things and they had some time before dinner that evening. Mitchell also had to go and see the manager regarding the possibility of work following that morning's dance session.

Mitchell shut the door and watched as Charlotte flopped onto the bed. He crossed the room and paused to take a moment to gaze at her. A slight hint of sweat still lay on her smooth skin as she reached out to him and he could linger no longer from her touch. Removing his top and kicking off his shoes he watched her watching him, drinking in the shape of his body as he crossed to the bed and she sat up to receive him. Pushing her back down, his body covered hers and their lips joined them together. When they pulled apart Charlie felt her whole body flushed beneath her clothes and she knew she had to get out of them, crawling out from beneath Mitch to hop off the bed.

She saw him looking quizzically at her as she stood in front of him and slowly started to remove her dress. Charlotte saw him start to get up to help but she stepped backwards and shook her finger at him. Mitch grinned at her boldness as the straps fell away from her body and the dress pooled at her feet. Stepping out, she wore just a strapless bra and lace panties, black against her pale skin, which was lightly tinged pink. Mitchell could wait no longer and he was off the bed as he shrugged out of his trousers and stood in his underwear.

"I want you now," he said, drawing her into his arms.

"Me too," she replied as her fingers touched his warm skin, a charge crackling between them.

They danced backwards to the bed and fell onto its softness, Charlie beneath him as he kissed his way down her skin and removed her silver shoes. As his lips travelled back up, he hooked his fingers under her panties and she arched her hips so that he could pull them off. Her hands were in his hair as his fingers and tongue set to work on her already quivering body. Leaving her wanting, he moved further up to her nipples and then back to her lips, rolling over so she could lay on top of him.

Charlotte smiled down at him and her eyes sparkled with love and lust as she moved down his body in return and released him from the tight confines of his underwear. Mitch leaned up slightly to watch as her lips followed her hands and took him into her mouth for the first time. Lying back he surrendered to her tongue as she flicked it over him until he could take it no longer. Pulling her up Mitchell was about to roll her back over again but she pushed him down and stayed on top. Easing onto him she sighed and almost came instantly but she pushed on through the first wave and started to move slowly against him. He held her hips close and moved with her, rocking and rocking as their breath got faster and faster, their kisses longer and stronger. Looking directly into each other's eyes, they reached the brink and then toppled over together.

Mitchell held her tight, watching her eyes close and drift off to sleep, still locked onto his body. He kissed her gently on the lips and closed his eyes, their adrenaline departed, leaving them limp after the dancing and lovemaking.

When Charlie woke she tried to move out of his grasp but he still held her tight. She kissed him and was rewarded as his eyes opened and drank her in once more.

"I'm starving," she said, rolling off him and leaning back against the pillows.

"Mmmmh me too, shall we get dressed and go out or should we get room service?" Mitch asked.

"I feel too tired to go out, and I don't really want to get dressed," she said, a wicked grin lighting up her face.

Leaning over, Mitchell picked up the phone and ordered.

"Shall we have a quick shower before the food arrives?"

"Yes."

Under the water they were still unable to take their hands off each other. Charlie wondered if sex could be addictive because at the moment, she was under its powerful spell. Wrapped up in the hotel robes, they sat on the bed and tucked into their steak sandwiches.

"So how do you think things are going with our parents?" Charlie asked, between mouthfuls.

"It's hard to say really, perhaps we will see how they are at dinner tonight?"

They laid back on the bed together, appetites satisfied.

"So do you fancy coming over to mine next weekend?" Mitch asked.

"Yes, no college now so I'm kind of free anytime."

"Are we still going to dance at the Rock On the River event the following weekend?"

"You bet. Mum won't tell me who the headline act is yet as they are making a big announcement at the end of next week on the radio."

"The guys are all up for coming down and Dad said he would sort out a minibus and drive them."

"Great, as I think Julia is quite taken with Simon," Charlie said, smiling over at Mitch.

"Oh no, not more matchmaking," Mitch groaned, in a light-hearted way and pulled her close.

Mitch had another shower, a shave, got dressed quickly and phoned reception again to find out where he needed to be.

"Will you be ok to meet me in the bar?" he asked.

She gazed at him in his dark trousers and floral shirt; he looked amazing and so sexy.

"Yes, it will give me time to paint my nails," Charlie replied, wishing she could rip off his shirt and jump on him again. Running the bath, she slipped out of her robe and sauntered past Mitch who slid a hand down her spine as she passed.

"God I wish I didn't have to go," he said, pausing at the bathroom door. He watched Charlie slip under the bubbles and smile seductively up at him. He had unleashed a monster but he loved it.

"Off you go Mitch, I'll see you later. I'll be the sexy one at the bar," she said.

"If you're not down in an hour, I'm coming up to find you," he joked, blowing her a kiss. "Don't open the door to any strange men." She blew him a kiss back and watched as he left.

Alone in the water she shaved everywhere and felt the feelings of desire coursing through her as she closed her eyes and relived all their lovemaking to date. For a virgin yesterday, she was more than making up for lost time today. Looking in the mirror, she tried to decide if she looked any different as she certainly felt it. Opening the wardrobe, she found her new floral dress, short with a jagged hemline that rose. She wore no bra underneath as it held her snug under the bust. With nails, hair and make-up done, she surveyed the result in the mirror.

Feeling nervous about going downstairs alone she grabbed her phone and rang her mum.

"Hi Mum."

"Hi Charlie, are you ok?"

"Yes thanks, Mitch has gone for a meeting with the hotel manager and wants me to meet him downstairs in about ten minutes… but I don't want to go on my own."

"Ok, I'm nearly ready so do you want to come to my room?"

"Cool Mum, I'll be there in a bit."

-56-

It was a little after seven and I could already feel butterflies coming to life inside of me. I had originally wanted to keep James waiting a bit longer, but I kept up with Charlie's fast pace. I knew she was eager to find out how the meeting had gone between Mitchell and the hotel manager. As we dropped down into the lobby of the hotel, Charlie kept staring at me. I guessed that she was trying to ascertain what my feelings were towards James and the reunion of yesterday. I couldn't begin to talk to her about it all as I still didn't know how I felt yet. My mood kept swinging wildly from happiness and light that he was back in my life to worry and darkness that it could all go wrong again.

We alighted in the reception area and looked about to see which way the bar was. I stole myself and took a deep breath as we walked through the doors together. There at the bar stood father and son, identical in physique, just different colouring. Mitchell was dark-haired, his father blond. Charlotte skipped away from me and flew into Mitch's arms, as if they had been apart for an age.

I could feel my heart pounding out of control in my chest. I reached up to push aside a tendril of hair that had fallen across my face and I could see the visible shake to my hand. How did he still manage to make me feel this way even from this distance?

I watched a smile break across his face as he looked me up and down, so slowly it felt as if he was peeling away the layers with his eyes. I could feel the blush creeping up on my cheeks as I smiled back and stepped towards him. Aware that our children were watching, James moved aside and I stepped into the gap between him, Mitchell and Charlotte.

"Evening Steph, you look gorgeous this evening," James said.

"Thanks. I like your shirt," I replied, feeling my tongue stumbling over the words.

"Would you like a glass of champagne, we are celebrating tonight?"

"Yes, that would be lovely." I watched as James pulled a bottle from the ice bucket on the bar. Blushing even more, I remembered the time we had spent playing with ice cubes. James arched his eyebrows and grinned back at me, as if he knew exactly what I was thinking.

James handed glasses of champagne to all of us and raised his. "To Mitchell and Charlotte for the most fabulous dancing I have ever seen."

As we clinked glasses I watched my daughter smiling. Mitchell had his arm protectively around her and it was clear their relationship had progressed to another level.

Putting my glass down on the bar, I pulled out my phone.

"Stay there," I said.

I snapped a couple of shots of them and then one of the bar staff came over.

"Would you like me to take one of all of you?" she asked. I looked across at the three of them and they all nodded.

"Ok, that's very kind of you," I replied, handing the girl my phone. I started to head towards Charlie but James stood aside and I found I was standing between James and Mitchell. Standing next to James, I felt his hand resting on my shoulder, the imprint of his fingers burning through the fabric of my dress.

He let his finger run slowly down the sleeve and onto my bare skin and I tried not to jump at the touch. At that moment, with champagne tickling my throat with its bubbles, I just wanted to lean back into James' embrace as if we had never been apart. Then we saw Sarah and Chris at the door of the bar and I beckoned them over.

"Champagne?" James asked, as he motioned for some more glasses and another bottle. Mitchell and Charlotte moved aside slightly so they could talk privately as I handed Sarah a glass.

"Thanks James," she said, noticing immediately how his hand had dropped from my arm. James handed the other glass to Chris and there was a moment of silence between them.

I knew how angry Chris had been when James finished with me and had not spoken to him since the New Year incident. I watched Sarah pause as if to diffuse a situation before anything started.

"Thanks man, but I'd rather have a beer," Chris said. "I'm sure Charlie won't mind if I toast her with a pint." Charlie smiled across at Chris.

I knew Chris still wanted to have words with James, but even he knew that now was not the time. As soon as Peter and Pam appeared, we were shown to our table. Charlie wanted to sit next to Mitch so they took up the one side next to Pam and Peter. Across from my daughter Sarah and Chris took the seats, which left James and I to sit opposite his parents.

Being so close to James meant I was constantly aware of his body. How was I going to get through a whole meal when I knew my appetite had deserted me? Scanning the menu, I let my daughter lead the conversation as she talked about the dance competition, Mitchell joining in here and there. We all made our choices from the menu and James ordered a couple of bottles of red and white wine for the table.

"So how is Ross-on-Wye these days?" Peter asked.

"Nothing changes there, in fact the town is quietly dying on its feet.

There are even plans to close the library and the swimming pool," I replied.

"That's awful news," James said. "I have such fond memories of the pool."

I blushed again at his reference to the place where it all began.

"Closing libraries, that's barbaric," Pam responded. "How can people not care about important services?"

"It's not the people Pam, they are campaigning hard to save both places, it's the council," I replied.

Sarah added, "Don't get me started Pam, it's not as if I need my job to survive but many of my colleagues do, and it's not just Ross… it's the whole county." I could see her anger bubbling to the surface, along with sadness at what the loss would mean to their loyal customers.

"So Stephanie, what do you do for a living?" Pam asked.

"I'm a radio DJ on Love Shack Radio, it's a local station and we tend to stick to music from the Sixties through to the Nineties," I explained, as our starters arrived at the table.

"Yes it's really good," James said. I turned to look at him. "Mitchell told me so I tuned in."

Now I understood his wry smile when I had mentioned my secret admirer, as he had possibly caught some of the requests that had been made on air. The conversation died a little as we all tucked into the food. My appetite which I thought had deserted me, returned at the sight of scallops in a cheese sauce. James started to pass the wine around and I poured myself a glass of red for a change.

"So Mitchell, how did your meeting with the hotel manager go?" I asked.

"Ok, I need to give it a bit more consideration but he would like to run weekend breaks on certain themes and one of them is *Dirty Dancing*."

"Yes, we made an impression this morning," Charlie added.

"You made an impression on a lot of people today," Sarah said, "a standing ovation no less!"

"People were dancing in the aisles, just like the film," Pam said, joining in. "You two look great together when you dance."

"They look great together even when they're not dancing," Peter joked. I watched Charlotte lean over and give him a peck on the cheek.

"Like mother, like daughter," Peter said, looking directly at me.

"I'm just not as good a dancer," I replied.

"Give over," James replied, taking a sip of his wine. "Steph and I can do a passable waltz."

The waiters arrived with the main courses and once again I was happy to tuck in as conversation flowed around the table.

"So when did you learn to waltz?" Pam asked.

"When we were away for my birthday," James said. "A lovely couple in the ballroom of the Blackpool Tower gave us a lesson."

"Jack and May," I replied, recollecting their names. We exchanged a brief look as we recalled what else had happened that long weekend.

"If you'll excuse me," I said, getting up from the table. Memories threatened to engulf me so I headed for the bathroom. Sarah followed and as I leaned on the counter by the mirrors, she tapped me on the shoulder.

"Are you ok?"

"Yes, just so many memories keep surfacing. Everything just feels so surreal, I am still struggling to get my head around it all."

"I know this won't help much, but I can see from the way James keeps glancing at you that he still cares, cares very deeply," she said. She passed me a tissue as a solitary tear slipped out and kissed my hot cheek.

"I know and I guess deep down inside, I still love him but I am so scared of getting hurt again." I finally acknowledged aloud my true feelings.

"Well no one can answer that one for you, you may just have to find the courage to take the chance," Sarah replied, squeezing my shoulders as I fell into her arms for a hug.

Returning to the table, the plates had been cleared and everyone was trying to decide if they could squeeze in a dessert. As I sat back down next to James, he turned to smile at me.

"Is everything ok?" he asked.

"Yes," I replied and hid behind the menu.

Charlie and Mitch were the only ones who could squeeze any more food down so the rest of us ordered coffee. There was a commotion at the restaurant entrance and we all turned to see what was happening. I noticed it was Arlene Phillips and one of the other judges from the competition and they were heading in our direction. Stopping at the end of the table where Mitchell and Charlotte sat, I saw them drop their spoons in shock.

"Mitchell, Charlotte, sorry to interrupt your meal, but I was wondering if I could have a moment to talk to you?"

Mitchell stood up and reached out to shake her hand and that of the other judge.

"Yes that will be fine," he stammered.

"Oh my god," said Sarah after they disappeared. "I can't believe I just saw that."

"Wow, it's so exciting," Pam said, joining in. "I wonder what they want to talk to them about?"

As I sat and joined in the conversation, I felt a soft touch on my knee beneath the table. I glanced across at James who was still talking to his mum and dad and feeling courageous, I placed my hand on top of his. He jumped slightly but carried on as if nothing was going on, a sparkle winking in the corner of his eyes. He turned his hand over and linked his fingers through mine.

Charlotte and Mitchell had been gone for a while so James decided to order some more drinks from the bar. His parents excused themselves and went back to their room, leaving just the four of us. We left the table and found a couple of comfy sofas in the corner.

"So what would you like to drink?" James asked.

"I'll get these," Chris said, standing up.

"Gin and tonic," Sarah said.

"Same for me thanks."

"I'll come and help," James said, leaving the two of us alone on the sofa.

"So, have you decided what to do yet?" Sarah asked as we both watched James and Chris exchanging heated words at the bar.

"No."

Sarah and I watched as they both returned from the bar. Sitting together, it almost felt like old times again except for the slight atmosphere that lingered in the air of all things unspoken. I watched as Chris put his arm around Sarah's shoulders opposite us, whilst I sat slightly apart from James on the other and sipped my drink. Before the silence became uncomfortable, we heard laughter and saw Charlie and Mitch re-enter the bar. I held my hand up so that they would see us and after stopping at the bar to get a drink, they came over. Chris pulled up a large armchair and Mitch dropped gracefully into it whilst Charlie perched on the arm.

-57-

All the other diners in the restaurant were looking at them and some were other competitors from the competition. Charlie wondered what Arlene was going to say and hoped it would be good. She held Mitch's hand tightly and could feel his nerves tremble through her fingers. They went through to the reception area and the girl on the desk came forward, leading them into the conference room, which was huge and empty.

Arlene and the other judge sat down and Charlie and Mitch followed suit and waited.

"Thank you for letting me interrupt your celebrations," Arlene said.

"No problem," Mitch replied.

"Watching you both dance together transported me to another world and I would have loved you to have had the chance to perform your dance again at the end of the competition. Ken here is currently working on a version of the *Dirty Dancing* film for release on the stage, some time next year, and we wanted to give the two of you the first chance to audition for the lead roles."

There was a long pause as Charlie and Mitch took in the staggering offer they had just received. It made the one from the hotel pale into insignificance. A chance for them to tour the country and dance for everyone and earn a living, it was a remarkable offer!

"Now, you don't have to say anything yet," Arlene continued. "We'd just like to take your contact details and give you ours so that we can get in touch nearer the time." They watched as she fished in her handbag and produced her business card and Ken did the same.

"Do you have a pen and paper?" Mitch asked.

"Yes," Arlene said. He turned to the edge of the table and at the same time looked across at Charlotte.

"Are you ok?" he whispered, as he wrote his name, phone number and email address down on the paper and slid it across to Charlie. She almost dropped the pen as her hand was shaking so much.

"Fine, more than fine," she whispered back. She did the same and pushed the sheet of paper back to Arlene.

"Can I ask how old you are?" Arlene asked.

"I'm seventeen," Charlotte replied.

"I'm twenty," Mitch said.

"How long have you been dancing together?" she asked them.

As they exchanged a glance, Mitchell replied, "About six weeks."

Charlie and Mitch watched as she swallowed hard to hide the shock.

"Well, I would never have imagined that," she replied. "Just don't stop, as you have a lot to offer already and I'm sure you will have even more as you grow together." Standing up, she pushed the chair in and Ken followed her lead.

"Once again, thank you for talking to us both and we will be in touch shortly," Arlene said, extending her hand as they all took turns to shake. Once in the corridor, Charlie and Mitch watched them walk away as they remained rooted to the spot. When they were finally alone, Charlotte let out a scream and flung her arms around Mitchell. He lifted her up and spun her around, grinning like a maniac. Then his lips found hers and they were kissing again, until they broke apart needing to breathe.

"Oh my god, did I really hear that right or am I dreaming?" Charlie asked, still out of breath.

"Well, if you were dreaming then I was too," Mitch replied. He held up the business cards that had been handed over and read them through. Charlotte touched them.

"Yes they are real alright," she exclaimed.

"I just can't believe it, firstly the hotel offering us work and now the possibility of parts in a show that will tour the country." Mitch shook his head.

"I told you we were great together," Charlie exclaimed.

"I so love you Charlie."

"I love you too, Mr. Cooke," Charlie replied, putting on her best impression of Arlene. Mitch laughed and pulled her close once more, and as the laughter faded, desire reignited.

Returning to the restaurant, they noticed Pam and Peter had already gone up to their room and in the corner of the bar sat their parents with Sarah and Chris. Eagerly, they went over after stopping to get a drink at the bar. Mitch put the drinks down and sat in an armchair and Charlie perched next to him on the arm. Eager faces waited, wanting to know what had happened. Mitch turned to speak but Charlie beat him.

"Arlene has taken our details and the other guy is planning to turn *Dirty Dancing* into a stage show and would like us both to audition for the lead roles early next year," Charlie stopped, finally taking a breath.

Everyone sat, shocked.

"Isn't that amazing news?" she asked, looking around at all the stunned faces.

James was the first to respond. "Well, what a day it has been, runners-up in the competition and now the possibility of work in the new year."

"Thanks Dad, it is wonderful. Arlene nearly fell over when we told her how long we had been dancing together," Mitch revealed.

"Yes, she's got our contact details and we have hers," Charlie said.

"Congratulations both of you, I knew it was special when I saw the video recording that you submitted," Steph said, raising a glass to the two of them.

"Hey, you won't forget your aunt and uncle when you're rich and famous?" Sarah added, raising her glass.

♪

As we finished our drinks, Sarah started to yawn and nudging Chris, they excused themselves. Charlotte looked far too bright-eyed for sleep but she faked a yawn and grabbed Mitchell's hand.

"We're going to head up too," she said. "Night Mum, James."

"Night Dad, Stephanie. See you in the morning for breakfast," Mitch said.

I noticed Mitchell place his arm around Charlie's waist as they walked out together, perfectly in step as if their whole life was one, long dance. Smiling, I was about to reach for my drink when James grasped my arm and pulled me to him.

"At last we are alone again," he said, breathy. I hesitated as once again my mind tried to warn me against anything foolish. Then I remembered the words Sarah had shared with me in the restroom. I closed my eyes and surrendered to his embrace.

I felt his breath catch my cheek as he grazed his lips over my skin and to my earlobe.

"Stephanie, you mean the world to me and I want to be with you again," he murmured.

His lips travelled down my throat and then to the place where the fabric hit skin. I could feel my heart beating rapidly as I tried to control my breathing at his measured advances. I knew he was hitting all the right buttons, after all he had been the first to find them. I ran my hand up the back of his neck and into his hair as our lips collided in a kiss so passionate, yet so tender, I wanted to cry out his name. The bar staff called last orders so we broke apart and just gazed into each other's eyes.

"Would you like another drink?" he asked.

"I think I've had enough thanks and should be going up. Thanks for this evening, it's been one hell of a day all round."

He nodded and put his arm around me as we left the bar and took the lift. Once inside, James pressed the button and smiled across at me.

"Does this remind you of anything?" he asked.

"Of course," I replied, as the image of Maverick and Charlie in the lift in *Top Gun* sprung to mind. Stepping out, we walked in silence until reaching James' door.

"Would you like to come in?" he asked.

"I don't think that's a good idea," I said, smiling.

"But we need to exchange emails, phone numbers, if we're going to start getting to know each other again?"

"Oh yes, ok I'll come in for a few minutes and we can do that."

Opening the door he ushered me inside. I sat down on the sofa and waited as he found a piece of paper and pen for us. He plugged his iPod into the television and selected some music. I instantly recognised it as the exact playlist that had been on the mix tape he had given me. I sank back against the cushions, kicked off my heels and closed my eyes briefly, giving in to the tiredness.

"So where do we start?" James asked, as he sat down next to me.

I opened my eyes and looked down on the piece of paper at his email address, phone numbers and his home address. I started when I read it.

"So you're living in your parent's house?"

He nodded. "They have a small chalet-style bungalow at the bottom of the garden. I lost my house to Felicity when we broke up," he said, shrugging his shoulders.

I took the pen and wrote down my details, passing it over to James.

"So I think we also need to talk to Charlotte and Mitchell... and is your other son called Darren?"

"Yes, I think we ought to tell them something," he agreed. "Perhaps that we are renewing our friendship but at this stage we don't know where it will lead."

"That sounds like a good idea," I replied, stifling a yawn. I closed my eyes again and let the lilting melody of 'Father Figure' wash over me, lifting my spirits. The words were healing and making me fall back in love with love. As the music faded, I sank into sleep.

I awoke to weak sunlight pouring through the curtains and blinked a couple of times, trying to adjust. Then I realised where I was and it was not in my hotel room. Looking across in a panic, I saw James sleeping beside me, his arm stretched out towards me. I slipped out from the duvet and found my dress lying over the arm of the sofa and pulled it back on. He must have undressed me! Picking up my shoes, I grabbed my handbag and the slip of paper which I folded and placed inside. Then I tore another slip of paper up and wrote a quick message, leaving it folded on the pillow before I crept from the room.

Dear James
This weekend has been surprising for many reasons. I have enjoyed starting to get to know you again and I look forward to more

*conversation over the next couple of weeks as we rekindle our friendship.
Who knows where it will lead?
Fondest regards,
Stephanie*

-58-

Leaving their parents, Charlotte and Mitchell went back to their room. As they stood in the lift Mitch pulled her close.

"I just can't seem to keep my hands off you," he murmured.

"Do you hear me complaining?" Charlie replied, pushing her body even closer to his.

"Tomorrow is going to be so awful when we're not together," she said.

"Well, let's live for today then," Mitch replied, kissing her gently on her upturned lips. They ran along the corridor and almost fell through the door of their room. Mitchell had Charlie in his arms before the door closed behind them, staggering and falling onto the bed together in a jumble of limbs.

Their lips joined in a kiss so long and passionate, it felt as though time was frozen. Charlotte lay back as Mitch gently peeled down the straps of her dress, revealing her naked breasts as her nipples sprang to attention under his touch. He worked his way down and pulled off her knickers, throwing them behind him. Charlie laughed for a second and then it changed to a gasp as his tongue went to work. Her hands ran through his hair as she arched under his touch and surrendered completely to the sensations racing through her body. She shuddered and came. Mitch paused and looked up at her, smiling before he continued again to bring her to the very pinnacle of pleasure. Then he pulled away, aware that he was teasing her but enjoying it.

Charlie undid the buttons on his shirt and threw that over her shoulder. Her hands fumbled at his belt buckle but it came free and she pulled his trousers off. Mitch tried to pull her straight on top of him but she pushed him back against the duvet. He felt her loose hair tickle his body as her lips travelled down to his cock. She paused and playfully ran down his thighs and up again, coming close but not going for the target until she felt his hands trying to push her that way. Then she let her tongue play over the tip and felt him quiver with excitement. She played with him as if he were a lovely ice lolly to be savoured.

He could take it no longer as he hoisted her up to capture her lips with his, his hands guiding her into position as she sank down on top of him. It was like a horizontal dance, neither of them was in control as they flew together, soaring towards the peak of their passion, before crashing down.

"That was the best yet," Mitch gasped.

"I wish we'd started earlier," Charlie whispered, kissing him tenderly on the lips. She snuggled into his arms as they started to cool down. Mitch leaned up and looked deep into Charlie's eyes.

"I can't believe how in love I am with you," he said.

"Neither can I," Charlie replied, fighting the tiredness that was trying to whisk her away from this precious moment.

"Hold me and don't ever let me go," she said, reaching up to pull him close.

"With pleasure," Mitch said.

During the night Charlie woke occasionally and in the moonlight, turned and stared at the handsome man that lay next to her. She still wondered how they shared so much in common especially the links with the past. She brushed a light kiss onto his lips before falling asleep again.

The alarm woke them in the morning, their last morning together for a week. Still sleepy, they kissed and shared their bodies again before heading for the shower.

"I wish we didn't live so far apart," she said.

"I know, but who knows what might happen between our parents in the future?"

"I'm keeping my fingers crossed for them," Charlie said. She held them up for him to see and he grabbed them and kissed them lightly.

"Don't start that, I think I'm a sex addict already," Charlie moaned, as he reeled her in.

"Just as long as it's with me," Mitch replied.

Once dressed and packed, they went down for breakfast. They saw their parents sitting together on a table for four and decided they should join them.

"Hi Mum, James," Charlie said, sitting down opposite her mum.

"Morning Dad, Stephanie," Mitch said.

♪

I watched the two of them sitting next to each other, almost a mirror image of how James and I had looked all those years ago. While they went to choose some breakfast, I turned to James.

"Do you think we should talk to them now?"

"Yes might be a good idea," he replied. "Do you want to do it, or shall I?"

"I will but feel free to butt in at any point."

Once they had sat down I hesitated and felt James' hand on my knee beneath the table.

"So guys, I'm guessing you might be wondering what has happened between the two of us this weekend?"

Pausing, Charlotte and Mitchell looked up and stared across the table.

"We've had a long talk about things and have decided that it would be foolish for us to imagine that we could go straight back to how it was twenty-four years ago." I turned to James who took my cue.

"Yes, so we're going to renew our friendship and see how things go over the next couple of weeks," he said, smiling back at me.

"Are you still going to come down for the Rock On the River event in a fortnight?" Charlotte asked.

"Yes, I believe I'm driving the minibus. That's a point, can you recommend anywhere for us to stay?" James asked, turning to me.

"I'll ask around but I believe the Premier Inn at the end of the M50 is fairly cheap and good."

Once we all packed and settled up the hotel bills, we paused in the foyer.

"It's been lovely to see you again Stephanie," Peter said, reaching out and pulling me into an embrace. I then turned to Pam who didn't need to say anymore as she hugged me. Then I stood looking at James, wondering what to do as I felt my body start to come alive.

"Bye James," I said, as he pulled me into his embrace.

"Bye Steph," he whispered into my ear, and in passing, he brushed my cheek with a light kiss.

Charlie and Mitch disappeared outside so we followed suit and headed towards the cars. We found them at the side of the one car, both so wrapped up in each other that they didn't notice us until we blipped the cars open. They sprang apart but then Mitch pulled Charlie back against his body.

"Ready to go?" I asked.

I could see tears starting to sparkle in Charlie's eyes. She nodded and reached up for a final kiss from Mitchell, who looked just as distraught at letting her go.

As Chris drove off, they followed us for some of the journey out of London. Then due to the traffic, the tiny convoy was separated. Charlie stared out of the window, her earphones transporting her to another time and place. I could just make out that she was listening to the *Dirty Dancing* soundtrack and an occasional tear would slip down her cheek, which she wiped away with a soggy piece of tissue. I reached out and squeezed her shoulder light. She turned to me, a knowing look on her face, acknowledging that I understood how she felt.

I was glad to reach home after such an emotional rollercoaster of a weekend. Pulling our bags out of the car we carried them in.

"Do you want to stay for a bite to eat?" I asked Sarah and Chris.

"Thanks but we'll head home if that's ok?" Sarah said.

"Ok, thanks for driving us Chris," I said, stepping into his strong arms to hug him tight.

"I warned him not to hurt you again or he will have me to deal with," Chris whispered in my ear.

"Thanks Chris, that means a lot."

We waved them off and then walked inside to a flashing answer phone filled with junk calls.

"What do you fancy for tea?" I asked.

"Can we just get some chips Mum, I'm not very hungry."

"Ok, shall we walk in and get them?"

"Sure Mum," she said.

With her phone tucked into her pocket, I grabbed my handbag and closed the house again. Arm in arm, we walked into town in the early evening sunshine.

"You can talk to me Mum, I am old enough to understand," Charlie said.

"Thanks Charlie. My thoughts are all in a bit of a muddle right now."

"But you look so good together, perfect. James is so nice, I wouldn't hate him being my step dad, I think I would quite like it," she said and I smiled at the sentiment.

"We'll have to wait and see."

It was back to work for me, as the good weather broke and I woke up to the light patter of rain on the window. I had slept really well now that I was back in my own bed. My phone beeped and I saw a message from a strange number. Opening it I realised that it was James:

Morning Steph, hope it's not too early for us to start getting to know each other again. So first question is, what do you like for breakfast these days? James x

I replied: **Yes I am awake. I still like toast and coffee for breakfast, although I do remember that you make a mean fish finger sandwich when breakfast gets missed. Steph x**

I pulled my dressing gown on and went downstairs, still clutching my phone as it beeped again.

Oh yes, how I could forget the fish finger sandwich. Are you working today, as I'll tune in and listen?

Yes, I will be on air between 10 and 2. Drop me a text later and I might play a song for you.

You bet I will, take care and can I give you a call this evening?

Ok, anytime after eight will be fine for a chat.

As I made coffee I thought back to when we had first been together. Writing and posting a letter and then the long wait until the reply arrived was torture. It was so slow in comparison to texts and emails but perhaps it had made the whole process more precious. As I ate breakfast alone, I fired up my laptop and started to check my emails. I saw a couple from Paul and Ian and clicked on them and then sat back in amazement. Somehow they had managed to land Rick Astley as the headline act. I was stunned. Ok, it wasn't George but Rick was definitely up there for me. Ticket sales would fly when I announced this at twelve noon.

Upstairs I knocked the door of Charlie's room.

"I'm off to work in half an hour," I called.

"Ok Mum," she replied, "I'll see you later."

I could hear music from behind the door so I pushed it ajar and spotted her swaying along to 'She's Like the Wind'. She looked such a solitary figure without Mitchell.

I crept away to my room and got dressed. In the car, I listened to Paul starting the build-up to the announcement. Christ, Rick Astley, I could hardly believe it and I was just as excited that I hadn't realised that my secret admirer had been silent so far today. Pulling into the car park in Hereford, I walked to the studio, calling in to grab some doughnuts on the way. In the studio Paul raised his hand to me and I noticed that Mark was in too so I put the kettle on and made everyone a cuppa.

"Hi Steph, had a good weekend in the capital?"

"Yes thanks Mark; it was a weekend of surprises and good news."

Paul ducked out of the studio while the adverts ran.

"How did your daughter get on?" he asked, grabbing a doughnut.

"They came joint second but even better, Arlene Phillips was one of the judges and has hinted that she would like Charlie to audition for a part in the stage version of *Dirty Dancing*."

"Crikey, *Dirty Dancing*… still haven't watched that film," Paul replied, before disappearing back behind his desk.

As the time ticked down towards noon, I kept an eye on my phone for a text from James. Then after the news, I made the announcement.

"Well, have we pulled a great one-off for all you guys who have already bought your tickets for Rock On the River in a fortnight's time…? The one and only Rick Astley will be performing his classic hits from the late Eighties as our headline act," I announced. I watched the message board start to go mad as I played, 'Never Gonna Give You Up'. Paul popped his head round the door.

"The ticket line is going bonkers," he exclaimed in amazement.

"I knew it would," I replied. "If I wasn't helping to organise, run and part present the event, I would be buying my ticket now. I have been a fan of his for a long time."

My personal phone beeped and I looked at the message and smiled. Paul noticed but didn't have time to say anything as I flicked through the computer screen and queued up the song.

"This first request is for an old friend of mine called James, here's your song, 'Waiting For a Star to Fall' by Boy Meets Girl."

"Old friend?" Paul asked, as my phone beeped again and I blushed. Then it beeped again with a text from Jack saying: **Do you mean THE JAMES?**

Yes, if you're free after three for a drink, let me know and meet me at the studio.

"Is there something going on I should know about?" Paul asked.

"All in good time," I replied, enjoying the music as it took me back to the past.

By the end of the show, I realised I had still not heard from my secret admirer but I didn't really feel worried.

Outside the rain had been replaced with drizzle. Jack put his arm through mine and steered me to the nearest coffee shop. After ordering some drinks, he sat down opposite me.

"So tell all," he said, leaning forward, "I'm all ears."

"It's a bit of a long story really."

"I've got time," Jack said, sitting back and taking in my flushed cheeks and bright smile.

"Well to cut a long story short, Charlie's new boyfriend Mitchell is the son of James," I paused to allow him time to take in the information. "We met again at the dance competition over the weekend and spent quite a lot of time talking," I said, taking a sip of my coffee.

"And are you back together then?" he asked.

"We're being friends first as it's a big step for me to take after all that happened."

"Steph, don't be a fucking idiot and let him go again, just go for it, that's what I always do," Jack said.

"Part of me wants to just fall back into his arms, but it's not that easy to just pick up where we left off twenty-odd years ago." I sighed.

We were both silent for a moment and drank our coffee.

"But I haven't seen you this happy in a long time. How about doing what's right for you?" Jack said.

"I guess," I replied. "I've got a fortnight before I see him again as he's coming to Rock On the River."

"Shit, what about your blind date with the mystery man?" Jack asked.

"Well, I don't think I can back out of that now but at least I have someone in reserve."

"You could always have a threesome," he laughed.

Checking my watch I realised that an hour had passed by and I needed to get home.

"Well, I'd better get going now," I said, standing up. "Thanks for your input."

"You know me, always happy to help, I'm like a regular agony aunt," he said, pulling me in for a hug.

"See you soon Jack," I said.

"Will do, and… if you ever decide you don't want James, and if he's as gorgeous now as he was back then, I'll have him."

"Yes Jack, he's still gorgeous," I admitted. A picture of him sprang into my mind and made me blush again at the kisses we had shared since our reunion.

Arriving home just before five I heard music and laughter coming from upstairs.

"Charlotte, I'm home."

"Ok Mum, Julia's here, we're just hanging out."

"I'll do some pizza and chips then."

I turned the radio on to catch the end of Ian's show. Then sitting in the conservatory, I thought about James again. I wondered what he was doing this evening.

♪

Upstairs Charlie and Julia were lying together on the bed.

"So what did the two of you get up to when you weren't dancing?" she asked.

A blush spread over Charlie's pale skin and she hesitated, trying to decide exactly what to tell her best friend.

"Well I'm not a virgin anymore," Charlie replied. Her mind started to replay the first time and then the rest in succession.

"Is he as good in the bedroom as he is on the dance floor?"

"Better," she replied, smugly. "Mitchell is the perfect man for me."

"I'm looking forward to seeing Simon again next weekend, I really like him and I think he likes me," Julia said, rolling over onto her back and staring at the ceiling.

"We've also got the chance to audition for Arlene Phillips for a part in *Dirty Dancing* the stage production next year. She's going to contact us and let us know the dates," Charlie said beaming at the thought.

"O.M.G. that's fabulous news!" Julia exclaimed. "You two would make the absolute best Baby and Johnny!"

Her text beeped and she grabbed her phone and saw it was Mitch:

Hi baby, what are you doing right now?

Hi Mitch, just hanging with Julia and talking about you, are your ears burning?

Something is burning but it's not my ears.

Wish I was there to cool you down, honey.

If you were here, you would only be making me feel hotter.

I'll talk to you later when Julia has gone, how about eight?

Eight will be fine, shall we Skype and see each other too?

Yeah, speak later, love you Mitchell x

Love you, Charlie

As the last text disappeared, Charlie heard her mum calling them down for tea.

♪

After tea, Julia went home and Charlie back to her room, which was great as I needed some privacy for my phone call with James. Taking a large glass of wine with me to the lounge, I turned on the music system and put Rick on as some background music. His cheerful pop songs put me in a good mood as the phone rang. Just hearing his voice started butterflies off in my stomach.

"How was your day?"

"Great, thanks to the news about Rick Astley headlining Rock On the River."

"Christ, now I will have to compete with a pop star for your affections next time I see you," he laughed.

"Who knows?" I replied and joined in the laughter. It was amazing that we seemed to fall into conversation so easily despite the time we had been apart.

"Mitchell has been moping around here like a wet weekend," James said.

"So has Charlie, although Julia called over so that helped a bit."

"I will have a chat with Darren at some point. Didn't manage it yesterday as he came home with his own exciting news."

"Do tell," I replied, settling back into the cushions on the sofa and taking a sip of wine.

"He and his girlfriend got offered jobs at the BBC and they're moving to Manchester…"

James filled me in about his eldest son, and although I knew he was the reason for our split, I couldn't blame him. The person I blamed was the bitch that came between us, the bitch who split us up and called the shots. I hated her with a passion and she still made me angry now. After some more wine I mellowed and enjoyed the rest of our conversation. An hour had passed in a blink of an eye as we called it a night.

"So I guess I'd better go now," he said.

"Yeah, but we can talk some more tomorrow night if you like. I can call you."

"Unfortunately I'm on nights for the next couple of days but you can always text me and I'll try and answer when I can."

"Oh, ok then. Shall I call you on Friday night then?"

"Great, that's a date," he said. "Well, sort of."

We both laughed a little more as each of us tried to decide who would say goodbye first.

"So goodbye then," he said.

"Bye James, I've enjoyed talking to you."

"Me too, it's almost like old times," he murmured. "I still love you." His voice trailed off as I paused, not sure if I was ready for the love word yet.

"Take care," I replied.

Finishing my wine I lay back and closed my eyes. My heart and body were telling me that I had to go back. My mind was still trying to put the brakes on and remind me of how it all ended last time.

-60-

In her room Charlie set up her Skype connection. She checked her hair and make-up in the mirror before settling down and waiting for him to come online. Then his face filled the screen in front of her.

"Hi baby," he said.

"Hi Mitch," she replied. "How are you?"

"Missing you like crazy, what about you?"

"Same here," she replied, watching him on the screen and wishing she could reach out and run her fingers down his face.

"You're looking hot."

"You too, what have you been doing all day?"

"Last couple of days at college, will be finished on Thursday. How about I come down Thursday night and then we head back up here on Friday?"

"Yes that sounds better than waiting until Friday morning," Charlie replied.

"It means we get another night together," he murmured, a naughty grin spreading across his features.

Charlie grinned back and licked her lips while she tried to decide what to say next.

"Will you stop doing that?" Mitch said.

"What?" she replied.

"Licking your lips, it's driving me crazy here."

"Sorry. Just watching you on the screen is turning me on," she replied. She could feel the tingle starting to spread through her body.

"I just want to stay online all night until you go to bed," Charlie murmured.

"Yes me too, that weekend spoilt us," he said.

"Yes, my bed feels so empty without you," she responded.

"My whole life feels empty without you," he replied.

They both paused for a second and drank each other in. Charlie even reached out and touched his face on her screen. Mitchell noticed and did the same too.

"Well there are plenty more dances for us to learn," Mitch said.

"I'm your willing pupil," she replied, smiling. He watched it light up the screen.

"I'm going to have to go now, just heard Dad get back with some food for tea."

"Ok Mitch, drop me a text when you get to bed?"

"I will, how could I forget?"

"Catch you later, honey."

"You too, baby," he said, blowing her a kiss. She pretended to catch it and then blew him one back before the screen went blank.

Slowly she undressed the sheets which felt cool on her hot skin. Grabbing the pillow, she pulled it close as if it was Mitchell, but it was no substitute for the real thing. Later on her phone beeped and woke her from the light sleep that she had fallen into. It was a screen filled with kisses. She sent him one back but finished her last line with zzzs.

♫

Tuesday, Wednesday and Thursday passed as normal. My secret admirer had disappeared from the radio station text machine and I wondered whether he would still turn up for our blind date in just over a week's time. Since the announcement on Monday, ticket sales had doubled and we were almost at the sell-out point. Jack, Paul, Ian and I were due to get together on Saturday afternoon at my place as we needed to meet up with the company providing the stage, lighting and sound on the river and walk through the set-up which was due to begin the following Wednesday. Charlie was hanging around at home in between her dance class as they prepared for Rock On the River, too. They had decided to learn something new in place of 'Umbrella' as they didn't want to tempt fate on the day with the weather. They had chosen 'Troublemaker' by Olly Murs.

As Charlie returned from dance practice on Thursday afternoon, she came straight into the kitchen.

"Hi Mum, is it ok for Mitch to stay tonight, he's riding over once he finishes college?"

"Yes, no problem," I replied, looking up from my laptop as I continued to finalise plans for the event.

"What are you up to?" Charlotte said, peering over my shoulder.

"Just the line-up and running order for the event," I said.

"Oh, I can see we're going to be doing *Dirty Dancing* before Rick is on," she exclaimed.

"Yes I've tried to space the dancing out in between the bands as it gives the stage time to clear and the next band to set up. There will be a dance floor set up just in front of the stage for you guys."

"I'm really looking forward to it, our new dance is going well. Just jumping in the shower, Mitch should be here at around 6.30," she said, "and I'd better tidy up my room a bit."

I watched her disappear from view and head upstairs. James and I had sent each other a couple of texts each day, but with him working nights, they had been very sporadic. I had to admit that I was looking forward to talking to him on the phone on Friday night. Leaving my laptop, I headed for the fridge and popped some lager in and pulled out the salad, chicken and jacket potatoes that I was going to do for tea. Looking up at the clock, I heard Charlotte returning downstairs looking pretty in one of her sundresses, even though there was no sign of any sun outside. Just then the sound of an engine coming to a halt outside in the driveway startled us. I watched my daughter race through the front door like a bolt of lightning.

When they appeared in the kitchen, Mitchell was carrying a present.

"Hi Stephanie, my dad sent these over for you," he said.

I put it down on the side.

"Do you want a drink?" I asked.

"Sounds good, but I'll go and get out of these leathers first," he said, looking across at Charlie and grinning.

"I'll help you with your bag," she said. "We'll be down in a bit, what's for tea?"

"Chicken, jacket potato and salad," I replied as they left the room.

I turned to the wrapped box and pulled off the bow. Inside was a selection of old fashioned sweets including Love Hearts. I smiled as I found a note slipped into the base.

Steph, I hope you still prefer sweets to chocolates? Managed to find the Love Hearts and they reminded me of the Valentine Card you sent me. I still remember the way you asked me to consider going out with you. I loved your honesty and courage in expressing your true feelings for me back then. This time it's my turn to ask you to reconsider and take me back into your heart and your life?
Love you more than you know.
James x

I smiled and re-read the note. James was trying very hard to seduce me. I pulled out the roll of love heart sweets and opened up the packet to look at the words on the first one. It said *Be Mine* and I smiled before popping it into my mouth. Could I be his again? My heart was already telling me yes, but I just needed to be sure I could trust it. I picked my phone up off the side and typed out a quick message: **Love the present very much and believe me, I'm still reconsidering your proposal x**

I pulled another sweet out of the wrapper and looked at its message and it said *Take A Chance*. I used my camera on the phone and took a picture of it and sent it over to James with a further message:

I think the sweets are talking to me. The first one in the packet said be mine and the second one says take a chance, how strange is that!!

Returning to my cooking I waited and sure enough my phone bleeped.

Perhaps they are Steph, I hope they are x

"Tea's ready!" I shouted up the stairs as I waited for them to surface.

"So what was in the parcel?" Charlie asked when they came down.

I motioned across to the box of sweets on the side.

"Ooooh sweets," she said, peeping inside, "I've never heard of some of these," she said, holding up a tube of Love Hearts and a couple of drumstick lollies. "Can I try them?"

"After tea," I replied, looking over. "But the love hearts are all mine." I felt my cheeks colour with a faint hint of blush so I turned back to the pan.

"I wondered why dad looked so happy the other day when he was ordering them online, they must bring back happy memories," Mitch said.

I turned round and smiled at both of them. "Yes they do," I admitted.

Serving up the food, we all sat and ate. I gave them the rundown for Rock On the River the following Saturday.

"Yes, we're going to have to find some time to rehearse," Mitch said. "Our group are doing a new dance as well as 'Thriller'."

"What song?" Charlie asked, between mouthfuls.

"'Suit and Tie' by Justin Timberlake. In fact I might need a female dancer for part of it, do you know anyone?" he asked.

"Me of course, I'll do it," Charlie said, beaming at him. "It's a fantastic tune."

"Well I guess I had better cancel auditions tomorrow evening then," he joked.

"You bet," Charlie replied. I smiled at their infectious enthusiasm.

"There's some ice cream in the freezer," I said, as I cleared the table.

"Thanks Mum, maybe later," she replied, standing up and grabbing Mitchell's hand. "I think Mitch needs to tell me about this new dance I'm going to have to learn in just over a week."

"Thanks for dinner Stephanie, can I help clear up?" Mitch asked.

"Thanks but I can manage," I replied, knowing they would much rather spend time with each other than with me.

-61-

In her room Charlie found her iPod and looked for Justin Timberlake and the track. Sitting next to Mitch on the bed, they listened together. As they did, Mitch talked her through what he was planning. Repeating the track, Mitch stood up and started to show her the steps and general feel of the piece he was working on. By the third run-through, Charlie had joined him as they started to work together on both the moves and the feel of the dance, becoming emotionally connected to the music. They would have continued except Mitch paused at the end of the track and turned to her.

"Let's have a look in your wardrobe and see if you already have the clothes I think you'll need."

Charlie crossed the room in front of Mitch and opened the doors wide for him, standing back. He pulled out a couple of different dresses including the one she had worn in London.

"Shall I try them on for you?" Charlie asked.

"Yes please, I'll know it when I see it," Mitch said, lounging back on the bed and keeping the track on repeat.

"Which one first?" Charlie asked, looking at the four dresses he had chosen.

"The red one first, then the lilac, the white and finally the one you wore last weekend."

Charlotte shrugged her sundress off to reveal a set of plain white underwear. The recent sunshine had given her pale skin a light tan. She pulled her red dress on and pranced up and down the room like a model, twirling in front of him. He reached out and pulled her close. Shaking his head, he slipped the straps down and the material slithered to the floor.

"Next one please," he said.

Turning away she slid the next dress over her body. This whole scenario was slowly turning her on. As the lilac dress only had one strap, she removed her bra to avoid spoiling the effect. She watched him reflected in her mirror. Once again she paraded up and down in front of him before he pulled her close.

"It's still not quite right," Mitch murmured and he gently eased it off her body. This time his fingers lingered long enough on her skin to take in a passing glance across her nearest nipple. Pushing her away again she turned to try on the white dress, which was one of her favourites. Once again she put on a show for him until he beckoned her closer.

"Nope," he said, shaking his head but grinning. "I do like it though."

He turned her around and undid the zip down the back and it fell to her feet. As he did this his fingers slid down her spine and over her ass, lighting up even more of her nerve endings. Her skin now had a rosy tint to it as the burning flames of desire ignited.

She slowly pulled on her floral dress and turned around to find Mitch standing right there in front of her.

"It's perfect," he said, pulling her close. She reached her arms around his neck as their lips came together, crushing the breath from their bodies.

His hands ran down her back and beneath her hemline and in a swift move, her knickers were gone. Charlie pulled his t-shirt off and felt his smooth hot skin under her fingertips. Placing her palm flat against it she felt his heart beating in perfect time with hers. Before long they were naked and entwined. He lifted her up and balancing her against the wall, thrust inside of her. Biting down on her lip to stop her screams, they came quietly together. Mitch just had enough strength to carry her to the bed as they lay down.

Leaning up on her elbow, Charlie looked down into Mitchell's green eyes and sighed.

"Perfect," she murmured, "I needed that."

"Yeah," he replied, pulling her down for another kiss.

"I'm enjoying this new dance," she said, giggling.

"No, it won't be quite like that I'm afraid," he laughed.

They let the song finish this time and lay in silence. As the moonlight bathed their bodies in its silver sheen, they whispered together about the weekend to come and their plans for the summer.

Charlie didn't hesitate as he moved back on top of her, the pair making lazy love before sleep claimed them.

♪

I woke up at the usual time and crept downstairs for some breakfast, shocked to find Charlie and Mitch were up and the coffee machine already on.

"Mitch is doing scrambled eggs for us, do you want some Mum?" she asked.

"Thanks guys that would be great. Can I help at all?" My daughter passed me a mug of coffee.

"It's ok thanks, we've got everything under control," Mitch replied, whisk in hand. Charlie was loading the toaster. Before I sat down, I put the radio on and poured everyone a glass of orange juice.

"What time are you off?" I asked.

"Probably about ten, by the time I've got my bag packed," Charlie said.

"Ok, just drop me a text and let me know you have arrived safely," I asked.

Saying goodbye to the two of them as I left for work, I watched Charlie standing and waving to me on the doorstep.

"See you on Sunday night," she called.

"Have fun," I called back as I pulled out of the driveway.

The sun had returned so I enjoyed the pleasant drive into Hereford. Parking up, I made the short walk across the old bridge, blinded by the sparkle of the sun as it glinted on the river. It was going to be a busy weekend of work, preparing for the following weekend. Pausing as I came to the cathedral, I pulled my phone out and snapped a picture, sending it off to James.

Morning James, remember that day when we stood at the top of the cathedral and looked out across the city? Just heading in to work, text me when you can and I'll play you a song x

Pushing open the door of the studio I was amazed to see a hive of activity in what was normally a quiet office. The sales team was in and deep in discussion on various phones, trying to fill up the last few spaces of advertising that were left. Mark was in with the large paper plans unfolded on the desk, having a look at the technical side of things ready for our ground level meeting tomorrow.

"Hi all," I said, brandishing a box of biscuits.

"Hi Steph," Mark said. "Can't believe this event is only eight days away now!"

"Yes I know, it's pretty big and scary if you think about it."

My phone beeped in my bag so I pulled it out to read the messages. The first was from Charlie saying they were just leaving for Warwick. The second was from James:

Just woken up to your text, yes I remember that day. I'm off to turn my radio on so just play me a song and surprise me with the choice x

I giggled and replied to both as I poured a coffee and walked back through, ready for the handover from Paul.

"So, what's happened to your secret admirer? He's been noticeably absent this week," Paul said.

"Who knows, perhaps he's got cold feet about meeting me next weekend?"

"You don't look too upset about it."

"I'm not really Paul, I have other things on my mind at the moment."

I slipped into the studio and started my show with some Rick Astley. Then as I dealt with the other requests coming in, I tried to decide which song I should dedicate to James.

In the end I plumped for some Madness and played 'House of Fun', with the message saying I hoped that he still enjoyed listening and dancing to them. As the song played, I fell back in the chair and read the message that had just come through on my phone:

Yes, good choice and yes is the answer to your question. I tried to teach Mitch the dance but for some reason he laughed at me.

I wonder why!! Anyway, they left Ross about an hour ago so should be with you soon. Look after my baby for me.

Will do x

I smiled and looked into the office, seeing all the guys staring at me and the smile that was lighting up my face. I realised I had never looked this happy. Giggling, I stuck my tongue out at them all and went back to my work.

Once home I gave Sarah a call to see if she wanted to come over for tea. Instead I ended up getting showered and changed to visit her and Chris for the evening. I walked the short distance to Sarah's place and pushed open the back door.

"Hey, where are you?" I shouted.

"Down in a minute," Sarah replied from upstairs as I heard the shower click off. I spotted some wine glasses on the table so I opened the fridge and poured one. Chris was the first to appear.

"Hi Steph, see you helped yourself," he said, opening the fridge and grabbing a cold beer. "She'll be down in a second, we weren't expecting you here so quickly."

"Hi Steph," Sarah said, hurrying into the kitchen, her hair still wet.

"Hope I didn't disturb anything?" I grinned, seeing her cheeks colour slightly as she poured her wine.

"So how are things going?" she asked, sitting down.

"Good thanks, loads of work to do tomorrow, ready for next Saturday."

"Can't believe you managed to get Rick Astley here!"

"Neither can I."

"Please spare me," Chris said. "Can I go home when he comes on, as I don't think I want to watch the two of you drooling over him."

"I only have eyes for you honey," Sarah said, reaching over and giving his hand a squeeze.

"James had better watch out if Rick is his competition," Chris joked.

"So how is that all going?" Sarah asked. As if realising this was his cue to leave, Chris stood up and grabbed his jacket and wallet.

"I'll get the food then, guessing you want the usual?" he asked us both. We nodded and watched him leave.

"God Sarah, I have been thinking about it ever since we got back from London and I'm still not sure what to do," I said, taking a sip of the cold, crisp white.

"Well, only you can decide," Sarah said. "Charlie's growing up now and you're not getting any younger," she joked. I laughed at her comment.

"Yes I know but every time I was with him at the weekend, I felt like I was sixteen all over again." I sighed. "A mix of emotions that are tangled together into my past and the years I have tried to forget."

"I'm guessing you told James everything?" Sarah said, glancing down at my wrists.

"Yes I showed him the scars and he broke down in front of me," I replied. For a couple of seconds we were both silent, locked in our own personal memories of that New Year's Eve.

"What about Mystery Man?" Sarah asked, changing the subject.

"Well, I've been back at work since Tuesday and not a single request, perhaps he's backing out?"

"That's a shame as I was getting the feeling that you kind of liked his taste in music."

"Maybe," I replied.

On his return, Chris found us both on the second bottle of wine, the table set and plates warming in the oven. It was lovely to spend the evening with them and at least I wasn't home alone with my muddled thoughts. Sarah had hit the nail on the head, it was my decision to make and I had just over a week to decide.

The walk home helped to sober me up as the moon and streetlights lit the way. Getting in, I put some music on and grabbed my phone, dialling the number. I couldn't believe that after all the time that had passed, I still remembered it by heart. It rang a couple of times and then a slightly deeper voice answered.

"Hi there, can I speak to James?" I asked.

"Sure I'll get him for you," he said, as I heard him shouting. "Dad, phone for you," followed by, "Thanks Darren."

"Hi?" James said.

"It's me."

"Hey Steph, so nice to hear your voice!"

I sank back against the sofa cushions and savoured the sound that could instantly get my heart racing.

"So how was work?" I asked.

"Fairly busy, loved the song you played today, it brought back so many good memories."

I paused, realising it was so true. A single song could make your heart race, tears fall or just plain laughter over a precious moment in time. Music could be your best friend or your worst enemy and it had played such a huge part in my life.

"Are you still there?"

"Sorry I must have drifted off," I apologised. "Think I drank too much wine with Sarah and Chris," I replied, giggling, "I might have to eat some sweets to help sober me up again."

"You liked them then?"

"Of course I did, you still know me," I replied.

"Better than you think."

"So what have you got planned for the weekend then?" I asked.

"Well, if you are free tomorrow, I could always drive down and we could spend some time together?" James asked, sounding cautious.

"Unfortunately, due to the event next Saturday, I have a busy day tomorrow onsite with the crews providing the stage, lights and sound, so they know what they're doing on Wednesday when the structure goes up."

"Oh, no problem," James replied. "It was just a thought."

From the tone of his voice, I sensed his disappointment, but in a way I was still not sure I was quite ready to spend a whole day with him.

"I'll see you next Saturday anyway, well for parts anyway, as I'll be presenting different sections of the show," I replied.

"I'm sorry for trying to rush you into making a decision about us, I just don't want to waste any more of my life being alone," he said.

Listening to his plea down the phone, I could feel my numb heart waking up again, the torn and jagged edges that he had pulled apart slowly starting to heal. Would it be so difficult to love him again? For my heart to be returned to its rightful place, beating in time with his?

We promised to keep in touch over the weekend as James was keen to hear about all the plans for the event. As I wandered upstairs, I stopped and gazed at the pictures in the hallway of Mark. If I took James back into my life, would I need to remove these from sight? I knew that if there was any sign of the bitch still at his place, then it would have to be removed, or would that seem unreasonable? Did his sons still see her on family occasions? All these questions spun around my head.

Arriving at the house they opened the door and Charlotte was almost floored by Jester running to meet her. His solid black body bumped her legs before he dropped onto the floor and looked up at her with his soulful eyes. She bent down to give him a rub before James looked out from the kitchen.

"Hi guys, just put the kettle on, would you like one?" he asked.

"Yes please, Dad," Mitch replied. "We'll just pop upstairs and dump the bags."

After a coffee, Mitch was all business as usual. "Let's go and get changed and start practising, I told the guys to come over at two which gives us a couple of hours to try a few things."

As Charlie started to warm up, Mitch sorted out the music system and then did the same.

"Can we start with a quick run-through of '(I've Had) The Time of My Life'," she asked.

"Yeah, why not," Mitch agreed. As he walked back across to the stereo system, he trailed his hand across her rear and tried to keep his mind on the dance. He had a couple of weeks to wait for his exam results to come through and then it was up to him to start building his own business – a daunting proposition. Queuing up the track, he turned to find Charlie waiting in position. She looked across at him and gave him the nod. They breezed through the dance a couple of times with only a handful of mistakes.

Pausing for a bottle of water and quick breather, Mitch found the music for 'Suit and Tie' and they had another listen to it.

"Ok Charlie, you're going to be my sounding board as I show you what I'm thinking of doing. Then we can work on your involvement," he said.

"Yes Boss," she replied.

He laughed at her comment and as the song played for the second time, he part danced and part talked his way through it. Occasionally he would pause and ask Charlie about a step he had just done or she would suggest something and stand up to demonstrate. When they stopped again, Mitch flopped down next to her and looked at the clock.

"We've got time for lunch before the guys show up," Mitch said.

"Yes please," said Charlie, as he pulled her up from the sitting position on the floor. She reached up her arms and pulled him close.

"I think I need a kiss first," she murmured.

"You're insatiable," he replied, laughing as their lips met.

James had gone out so they were alone as Mitch rustled up some tuna salad and a packet of crisps.

"Thanks for the help," Mitch said. "You should seriously consider doing a teaching course in dance when you've finished your current one."

"You think so?" she asked, pleased to hear his praise. "Well, I have learnt from the expert."

"In a few weeks I should get my certificates through and then I'm going to start teaching here in my studio, set up my own business. Dad said he would help where he could," Mitch revealed, sounding nervous about the prospect.

"You'll have a queue to the end of the road," Charlie replied. "You'll be great."

They heard a knock at the front door and Mitch went through to open it for Simon and a couple of the other guys. Charlie felt a little overwhelmed at being the only girl in a room full of testosterone but the guys were soon laughing and joking with her as if she were one of them. The rest of the afternoon passed easily and they soon had a decent routine to continue working on during the week. Charlie filled them all in on the running order of events and promised to send Mitch a photo of the set-up on Wednesday.

"Have you two been inside all day?" James asked as they appeared in the kitchen.

"Pretty much Dad, we're just going to grab a shower," Mitch said.

"How about you take Jester for a walk" James suggested.

"That sounds lovely," Charlie said. "Can we?"

"Sure," Mitch replied.

After a quick shower they called Jester and strolled out into the evening sunshine.

"Can we go to the park, I'd like to see it as it's where my mum and your dad went roller skating together," Charlie asked.

"Yes, it was probably the one across the road," Mitch replied.

As Jester ran loose and chased ducks and pigeons, Charlie walked along beside Mitch, her hand held firmly in his. She felt so happy, she loved dancing with him, she adored making love to him but even a stroll in the park felt special. The whole world somehow looked brighter, like she had just stepped into high definition. All she needed now was her mum to make up with James and they could all be a big happy family. She would at last have a dad, one who just happened to be her boyfriend's dad.

When they went upstairs to bed later, Charlie snuggled into Mitch's embrace. She felt his fingers running up and down the length of her body as she sighed and gave herself up to the deliciously intense feelings. Lying in the afterglow, Charlie held him tight.

"I still can't quite believe how much I love you," she said.

"I can, so you'd better believe it," he said. Playing in the background was the *Dirty Dancing* soundtrack and Charlie realised the lyrics seemed to take on more meaning the more time she spent with Mitchell.

As the sun shone through the windows, Charlie woke up with a smile on her face as she gazed at Mitchell still sleeping beside her. Remembering her mum's diary, she disappeared beneath the duvet until her lips found their target. Slowly she slid her tongue up and down his shaft a couple of times and felt Mitch shudder beneath her touch. Then she took the whole of him in and moved her lips up and down. She knew what she wanted and she wasn't going to stop until she tasted him for the first time. His hands in her hair, guiding her, she ran her fingers up his body. She could hear his breathing quicken as he shuddered and then filled her throat.

It tasted salty as it slipped down and she savoured his unique flavour. She loved it but she also adored the way she held him in thrall of her tongue. The buzz from the power she felt was immense and she couldn't wait to emerge and look into his eyes. As she peeked out from under the covers he smiled broadly and pulled her closer for a kiss.

"That was amazing," he said. "But I believe that I need to return the favour."

Pushing her back against the pillows, he trailed kisses down her body until his lips and tongue found her spot and then, he went about making her body ripple until he tasted the flood in his mouth.

"So what are the plans for today?" Charlie asked.

"Dancing this morning and then we'll go into town for lunch or even to the Bullring again, your choice?"

"If we go to Birmingham, can we go to the salsa club?"

"Yeah, sounds good to me," Mitch replied, smiling as he trailed his fingertips over her lips.

"You are so good for me," Charlie said, smiling up at him.

"You are so bad for me," he replied. "All I can think about all day is you, whether we are together or apart." As they heard footsteps on the stairs, they pulled on their dance clothes and went down for breakfast.

"Hi guys, just making some toast," James said, motioning to the increasing mountain on the table. Darren was already tucking into a couple of slices.

"What are your plans for today?" Darren asked.

"Dancing this morning then Birmingham for the afternoon, should be back later though," Mitch said.

"Great, because we're all going out for dinner to celebrate Darren and Sophie's exciting news about their new jobs," James said, joining them.

"Ok, we'll be back for six," Mitch said.

Their morning in the studio was really productive as they moved forward with 'Suit and Tie' and also had a quick run-through of 'Take My Breath Away' before lunch. Then after a shower and change, they jumped on the bike. As they had plenty of time, they wandered around the shops for a while and Charlie bought a new dress for dinner that night. Then they headed down the street to the club and after a drink, they took to the dance floor. It was really busy but they found enough room and started to move. Their bodies moulded to each other in time with the Latin beat that pulsed through their blood.

When they left, the cool breeze was a blessing as it lightly touched their hot bodies.

"I love that place," Charlie breathed.

"Yeah, it's fantastic," Mitch agreed, placing his arm over her shoulder as they walked back to the bike.

"So what's your brother's new job then?" Charlie asked.

"Working for the BBC, but they'll have to move to Manchester," Mitch replied.

"Wow, that sounds great," Charlie said.

When they pulled back into the driveway, the sun had vanished and been replaced by grey clouds.

"Was thinking about sending out the search party for you," James said, welcoming them back.

"It's ok Dad, it won't take us long to get ready," he said.

"Ok, well how about Sophie, Darren and I take the first taxi and you can follow on with your grandparents?"

Mitch admired Charlie in her new dress as she twirled in front of him, before fastening up her hair.

"Are you ready, the taxi is here," they heard Peter shout from the hallway.

"Down in a minute Gramps," Mitch replied. Winding his arms around Charlie, he breathed into her ear, "You are so beautiful and I love you."

"You are so sexy and I can't wait until later," she replied.

"No more sexy talk now, it's too distracting," Mitch said, laughing as she turned and poked her tongue out at him, a glint of love and desire lighting her eyes up as she stared into his for a brief second.

-63-

As Saturday dawned, I lay in bed and drank in the silence of the house. Then pulling my dressing gown on, I wandered downstairs and waited as the coffee brewed. Checking my emails I found one from James, so after I filled my mug, I put the radio on and sat down.

Dearest Stephanie,
This is a bit like today's version of the letters we used to send to each other, just much quicker! Also, you don't have to decipher my awful writing!!
  It was lovely to talk to you last night. Once again, I am sorry if it felt like I was pushing you to make a decision, which I know is going to be difficult for you in such a short space of time.
  Ever since the night I walked out of your life, I have regretted it every day and I have quite often over the passing years thought about you, wondering what you were doing. And whether you still thought of me. Sadly I must have mislaid the St. Christopher you gave me and believe me, I have searched long and hard for it.

I paused and took a sip of my coffee. It was easier to read typing than his writing and his comment made me smile. Then when he mentioned the St. Christopher, I knew that although he might have thought he had lost it, he probably knew Felicity had removed it. He still didn't know that I knew exactly where it was. I had worn it for a while and then when my relationship with Mark had grown from friendship, I had removed it. It was safely wrapped up in a small piece of material, white with black hearts on it. His letter continued…

  So this Rock On the River event sounds great and a lot of hard work for you for the next week, so I will try my best to back off and keep things friendly. I still work for the Fire and Rescue Service and I still love it, even after all these years. Do you remember that comment you made about 'fires to put out, people to save and cats to rescue' well there have been a lot of all of them and I hope to tell you about the cats some time! I have had a quick chat with Darren, but he has other things on his mind at the moment so not sure whether it has really sunk in.
  Anyway, your wonderful daughter is currently in the garage with my son, dancing as seems usual (the garage has been converted into a studio by the way), but I'm going to drag them out later for a family dinner to celebrate Darren's good news. I do wish that you were here but there I

go again, trying to push too hard.
Take care
All my love, James x

I finished the email and got up to refill my mug and pop some bread in the toaster. Then I read my other emails and turned to the electronic copy of the plan I had ready for this afternoon. Mark, Ian and Paul were coming over as well as Jack and Mr. Ford from the hospital. I had a few hours to kill before we were due to meet down at the pub.

As I cleared up, Paul announced: "This song is from Stephanie's secret admirer who has returned from his absence last week. Today he has chosen 'Valerie' by Steve Winwood, just a substitute for the name Stephanie, from your secret admirer who is counting down the days until Saturday."

As the song played I sat down and listened to the lyrics, trying to see if there was a clue, but the only one I could come up with was, *'I'm the same boy I used to be.'*

Could it be someone from my school days? I still had no idea as I dropped Paul a text asking him to play, 'Too Shy' by Kajagoogoo.

As I dredged my mind, a thought struck me. What if it was James pretending to be my secret admirer? Now that would account for the choice of song and possibly some of the others. But how could I find out for certain? Or should I just start to choose some songs that would hint that I had guessed?

After a quick bite to eat for lunch, I decided to walk through town the long way. I picked up some flowers from the market and ended up in the graveyard. Picking my way along the path, despite the sun I felt a slight shiver run down my spine as I reached the stone. Placing the flowers onto the ground, I moved the dead ones away, ready to drop in the bin on my way out. The inscription etched into the stone read:

Mark Eden
Loving Husband and Father
To Stephanie & Charlotte
Suddenly taken from life
24th November, 1968 - 17th April, 1995

The whole funeral had passed by without me fully taking part. I remember standing there in the church, holding Charlotte tightly, but no tears fell. I guessed that everyone else thought I was still numb with shock, but I had never really cried that much. I had told myself that I needed to get on with my life for Charlie's sake. In truth Mark had been a fantastic friend and I owed him my life in the truest sense of the word. He had deserved better than me, a broken shell of a girl. Standing up, I felt the guilt inside of me like a large stone weighing me down. As I walked away I heard my phone ting.

Hi Steph, it's a lovely morning. Just checking you received my email? Hope you have a good day and I'll give you a call later, just let me know the best time x

Yes thanks, busy already but I'll send you a reply later x

Even in his grave, Mark could not escape the spectre of our marriage.

Walking down to the river, I started to imagine what it was going to look like in a week's time. We were expecting nearly 500 people and with the various bands and performing artists, the numbers would be over 1,000 on the day. I saw Jack sat on one of the benches outside the pub and walked over.

"Hi Jack."

"Hey Steph," he replied, standing up to pull me into a hug. "How are things?"

"Good thanks, really looking forward to next weekend," I replied.

A car pulled into the car park and I saw Mark, Ian and Paul get out and head towards us.

"Is this everyone from our lot?" Ian asked.

"Yes, just waiting for the technical guys and Mr. Ford," I replied.

As Mark talked to the technical guys about power for lighting and sound, I watched them stride around and spoke to the company supplying the stage and dance floor. Jack and Mr. Ford went through all the advertising hoardings with Paul and Ian. After a couple of hours, it seemed that everything was in place. As I lived the closest, I would meet the guys on Wednesday morning for the start of the set-up and also be their contact at the end of the day.

Bidding goodbye to the technical guys and Mr. Ford, I turned to the others.

"Do you want to stay for a drink here or I've got some in at home and I can rustle up some food?" I offered.

"Your place sounds like a great idea, we can have a final look through the running order," Paul said. Jack gave me a lift back in his car and the others followed as we adjourned to the back garden.

"I'm really looking forward to meeting Rick," I said, "he's been an idol of mine for quite a while. Only second to George Michael," I laughed.

"God you and George, I'd stand a better chance with him," Jack joked.

"Yeah, you're more his type," Ian said.

"But are you looking forward to meeting your secret admirer?" Paul asked.

"I guess so," I replied. "I think he's trying to give me clues in the songs as to who he is."

"Any idea yet?" Mark asked.

"I have my suspicions but I'm not one hundred per cent sure yet," I replied, feeling a blush rise to my cheeks.

Eventually the guys went home, except for Jack who decided to have a drink and stay over. Whilst he went out to get us some pizza for supper, I picked up my phone and dropped James a text.

Jack's here at the moment and staying over so I'll give you a call tomorrow morning instead, when I'm alone. You remember Jack; I used to work with him on Hospital Radio?

James replied with:

Ok, I do remember Jack; he's the gay one right, so I don't have anything to worry about?

That's right, he remembers you too, fancies you and all!

I'll bear that it mind if things don't work out with us. LOL

When Jack returned I had changed into my comfy clothes and poured us both another beer as we settled in for a night on the sofa and a film. I was preoccupied with James and in a way, I wished he was sharing this evening with me. Climbing into bed later, I grabbed my tablet and sent a reply to his earlier email:

Dear James,
Sorry for the delay but today has just flown by so quickly. All plans for next Saturday have been finalised so it's just roll on and deal with any last-minute glitches which undoubtedly there will be!!

I have still managed to spend a fair amount of time thinking about us. Your email this morning made me smile. If this technology had been around when we got together, we would have probably sent each other lots more emails and texts!! Yet writing an email is almost the same as a letter and sometimes it's easier to write down in words what you are unable to say in person or over the phone.

Since I gave my diary from 1988 to Charlie, I have been doing quite a lot of soul searching regarding my past. Although with my visible scars, I guess I never really escaped from it, if the truth be told. As you said, when we met, you don't want to be alone again and I can wholeheartedly agree with that sentiment. You have the easy side of things, just falling back in love with me. It is harder for me as I never truly fell out of love with you, I just suppressed my feelings and tried to mask them with happiness, either forced or induced.

Even though Charlotte is a real joy to my life (and I wouldn't be without her now), the circumstances around her being here hold enormous pain and I now need to reconcile myself with the fact that I managed to screw up someone else's chance of true happiness. Unfortunately, I can't just tell Mark I am sorry for never loving him. That is why you need to be patient with me and don't give up if I seem to swing one way and then the other. All I can be certain of is that it's going to take time to un-break my heart.

Keep in touch this week, it brightens my day.
Love Steph

I read it back through and hesitated with the delete button over the last paragraph, but in the end, I just closed my eyes and pressed send. Feeling my eyelids getting heavy, I fell asleep.

This time I dreamed about Mark. I was there as the faceless stranger attacked him and stabbed him over and over again. I tried to run and help but I was glued to the spot as his attacker seemed to sense me in the dark shadows. Turning to remove the Balaklava that hid the identity, long dark hair tumbled loose and I found myself staring at the bitch as she started to walk towards me. She was laughing and telling me that I would never be happy. She had robbed that from my whole life. I woke up with a start as I felt hands on my shoulders. Looking up, it was Jack I saw.

"Steph, wake up," Jack said softly. "You were screaming."

I stared at him, not quite knowing what was going on as reality came into focus.

"Sorry Jack, I must have been having a bad dream," I said, struggling to sit up.

"Do you want to talk about it?" he asked, settling back on the covers.

Sitting silently, I tried to clear the image from my head.

"No, it's ok, I think I can deal with it. Although, you could go and get me a glass of water?"

Jack hurried downstairs which gave me the chance to turn the bedside light on and banish the dark shadows from the room. I found one of my pills and quickly swallowed it before Jack returned. Handing me the glass he sat down.

"If you need me to stay in here I can," he offered.

"Thanks but I think I'll be alright now, I might just read my book before I go back to sleep."

"Cool, just call, I'm only next door." Leaning over he dropped a kiss on my lips, "Night Steph."

"Night Jack, and thank you," I said softly, watching him disappear through the doorway. Then after a few chapters, the pill kicked in and I fell asleep with the light on.

-64-

Charlotte enjoyed a lovely evening with the Cooke family and it was good to talk to Darren's girlfriend, Sophie a little more than she had done when she last met her. She did notice how distant James looked when he thought no one was watching. It reminded her of how her mum looked on occasion and she prayed silently that they would become more than friends again. Having read her diaries, she knew exactly how her mum had felt; the power of first love was immense.

On the way home in the taxi, she lay back in Mitch's arms and hoped they would last longer than a few months. Secretly she hoped it would last forever, but she knew that forever was just a dream.

In bed together, they made love slowly, and she kept her eyes open and focused on Mitchell's, mirroring hers in their passion and intensity as their bodies took control. Charlie was trying to stare into his very soul to see if she could glimpse their future together. Unfortunately, she couldn't, so she settled for the feel of his lips on hers, his hands that covered her body touching her in all the right places, and his skin on her skin as they burned together.

Once they were awake, they had to satisfy their passionate itch before they could even consider leaving the covers. However the next best thing was dancing together and that's where they went after breakfast.

In the kitchen James was listening to Love Shack Radio with a smile on his face.

"Hi James, don't think my mum's working this Sunday," Charlie said, as Mitch passed her a cup of coffee.

"She doesn't need to be, it's a great station," he said, but she could tell he was hiding something, going by the smile on his face.

Once they were alone in the studio, Charlie turned to Mitch.

"Do you think your dad might be this secret admirer sending my mum flowers the other week before they met?"

"Well, come to think about it, he did ask me where you lived, saying that he was trying to picture how Ross looked now in comparison to when he was there," Mitch replied, smiling as he got the music switched on and they started to warm up together. Somehow their warm-up always seemed to finish with them wrapped around each other.

"I think it might be," Charlie replied. "That is such good news."

"I hope so," Mitch replied. "Come on, let's get started."

Charlie gave Mitch a preview of her new dance to 'Troublemaker' and he loved it, especially when she told him about the outfits they would be wearing.

After lunch they decided to head back to Ross early via a quick tour of the local area. Charlie asked to see all his usual haunts and his college. Mitch didn't mind as he loved his bike, especially when he could feel the weight of Charlotte behind him, her body pressed against him as they sped along. He also didn't mind as he was spending Sunday night with her and returning home on the Monday, having promised Ian a hand in his bike shop that week.

"Mum, we're home," Charlie shouted as they both walked into the lounge and found her mum collapsed on the sofa, watching Jack doing his best impression of the Rick Astley dance.

"Hi guys," she said, waving at Jack who seemed to be in a world of his own. He turned to find an audience, one of which he knew but she had certainly grown up since his last visit.

"Hi biker chick, what have you done with my sweet little Charlie?" Jack joked, as he raced over and pulled her into his arms.

"Hey Jack, it's been a long time since I last saw you," Charlie said, as he whisked her off her feet and spun her around. Putting her down he extended a hand to Mitchell.

"And who might you be?"

"Jack, this is my boyfriend Mitchell, Mitchell this is Jack who works on Hospital Radio and taught my mum how to be a DJ," Charlie said, introducing them and watching in amusement as Jack pulled his hand up and kissed it.

"Jack, will you stop flirting for just a second," Steph said, standing up to go get everyone a drink.

The music they had been listening to finished on the radio and was promptly followed by Ian, announcing, "That was for our very own Stephanie, once again from your secret admirer."

♫

I smiled as I began to think that my suspicions were correct. Finding my phone, I typed in my reply as the beat started to a song that never failed to cheer me up. Returning to the lounge, I could see Charlie and Jack clicking their fingers as they started to jive to 'Wake Me Up Before You Go-Go'. Putting the drinks down, Mitchell grabbed my hand in his and we joined.

Jack finally went home soon later and left the three of us together.

"Mum, do you know who your secret admirer is yet?" Charlie asked.

I could see the two of them waiting for my response.

"I think I do and if I am right, then I won't be unhappy," I said, watching them exchange looks.

I left them in the lounge as I went to cool off and give James a quick call from the privacy of the kitchen. I could still hear them laughing together as they kept dancing to whatever came onto the radio. It felt good to have them in the house, their vibrancy chasing the dark shadows away that still lurked in places.

I was still trying to catch my breath when James answered the phone.

"Hi James."

"Hi Steph, are you ok, thought I was listening to one of those heavy breathers," he joked.

"Just been dancing with your son actually," I said. "He certainly got me go-going," I replied, giggling.

"Yes I've been listening to it on the radio, good choice for your secret admirer."

Somehow from his response, I knew that it was him and I sort of hoped that he knew that I knew.

"I've sent you a reply to your email," he said, as the mood changed slightly.

"Ok, I'll read and reply later tonight."

"Cool, so apart from dancing what have you been doing?"

"Catching up with Jack of course, it was fun having him stay last night but I did wish that you were watching the film next to me. What about you?"

"Usual chores really, the meal last night was great though."

There was a natural pause in our conversation.

"With everyone out of the house, I feel kind of lonely here."

"Yes, I get the same feeling when Charlie is up with you and I'm rattling around here all on my own. They're growing up so I guess it's something we'll have to get used to."

"It's a scary thought," he agreed.

I could hear his hesitation and knew he wanted to say something about us being together.

"I hope in time that you will fill that lonely space Stephanie," he whispered.

"I hope that I can," I whispered back, my heart pounding as I said it.

"Well I'm going to go now before I say too much or before I repeat what I have written in the email," he said.

"Thanks James, you are still the boy you used to be."

In my mind I could see him grinning at the use of the words from the song he had requested earlier.

After I had cleared up the house I found my tablet and turned it on to read the email:

Dear Stephanie,
Thanks for your email and your honesty. Although you have only hinted at what happened in your life, I can appreciate why you ended up with the person that you did. I can only guess that perhaps you felt some kind of gratitude towards Mark, the man who saved your life and because of what I did to you, he made you feel safe and secure. Once again I cannot begin to express in simple words how devastated I was to find out that my leaving would cause you to try and take your life, thinking that it was the only way to escape your pain. My ex has an awful lot to answer for because she ruined so many lives, not just ours.

You have raised a beautiful, talented young woman in Charlotte and I am so proud that my son is going out with her. Although it is rather mad that the two of them happened to find each other in the way they did, perhaps it was fate? I also kind of like the way that we somehow named them after characters in our film. Top Gun *will always be our film and until the other week, I had not watched it since we split up as the memories associated still linger in certain scenes. I look forward to us watching it together again soon.*

Anyway, all I'd like to finish with is that I will give you all the time in the world if it means that we become more than friends again.
My heart is yours, till the end of time.
James

Smiling, I pressed reply and started to write. It really did feel like old times.

Dear James,
Thanks for your kind words of encouragement. Having been so open when we were together, I realise that ever since, I have tried to protect myself by closing off from people and even my own thoughts. It is only now that I am facing these realisations and the work that I will need to do to get through this. But enough about me, I wish I could say that I was the same girl I used to be!! I believe that she is inside me somewhere and I am trying to find her as quickly as I can.

How much contact do you still have with Felicity? I have to ask as I will need to consider whether I can manage it if I were to start going out with you in the future. It's important for children to have access to both their parents and it's something I wish Charlie could have had more of with her dad. Chris has been invaluable as her sole father figure for the last seventeen years and he has done a wonderful job. You'll be pleased to know that she has already told me she wouldn't mind you being her step dad if we were to take that large step. You have obviously made a huge impression on her and what more can I say about daughters taking after their mothers!!! Mitchell is a credit to you and I look forward to meeting Darren in the future if things progress.

I agree with you regarding Top Gun, *I had barely watched it until Charlotte chose one of our songs and asked if she could watch it with me. It was a difficult evening; you are right that certain scenes remind me of certain times in our relationship. I would love to watch it with you some day. I have had to listen to the songs because in my job, I can't refuse to play music that reminds me of us as it happens all the time. In a way I find that music has been the only constant through my life and I know without a doubt, I can't live without it.*

Keep listening to the radio and I will keep searching.
Love Steph x

Checking the house was closed, I turned off the music in the kitchen. I could hear faint giggles coming from Charlie's room and I felt both happy and wistful. In my room, I opened the lid of my jewellery box. I didn't own much of value as I spied the tiny slip of white satin, pushed securely into a corner. Carefully I pulled it out and unwrapped the St. Christopher, a symbol of the happiest moment in my life. As I held it up to the light and read the small inscription that had cost me a month's pocket money at the time, I held it tightly and looked out onto the night sky. A single star caught my eye as a tiny tear slid down my cheek and the memories flooded back, so bittersweet.

Under the covers I slipped into sleep and this time, I was back in love and everything was perfect on the soft, slightly damp grass, as James lay me down beneath him and I surrendered to his touch.

-65-

I woke early on Monday and remembered to give Charlie and Mitch a call as I passed on my way downstairs. There was a week to go before the biggest event of my life, in more ways than I could comprehend. As Paul's cheerful voice on the radio spoke to me, I turned and started to make coffee and toast as I heard the shower upstairs.

"Well there's a week to go until Rock On the River and our very own secret admirer is up early this morning with his request for Stephanie. It's the classic track, 'No More Lonely Nights' by Paul McCartney."

Listening to the lyrics of the song, I couldn't help but smile at James' persistence as I absorbed the sentiments behind the words.

Grabbing my phone I called the station.

"Morning Paul."

"Morning Steph, are you excited yet?"

"Oh yes, but I'm here to respond to my secret admirer. Can you play 'First Time' by Robin Beck, I think we've got it on the system?"

"Yes, found it… but it seems a bit of a strange choice. Are you sure you don't know who the mystery man is?" Paul asked.

"Maybe I do, Paul but I'm enjoying the game," I replied, giggling.

The phone line went dead and his voice returned to the radio.

"I've just been talking to Stephanie and in return she would like me to play, 'First Time' by Robin Beck for her mystery date on Saturday."

Charlie and Mitch arrived in the kitchen to find me smiling as the radio played.

"Morning Mum. This is a cool song, I've never heard it before," she said, and I turned it up slightly. I saw her looking at Mitch as the lyrics meant something to her relationship.

Leaving them in the kitchen, I went to get dressed for work. The songs from earlier were filling my head with optimism as I pulled on jeans and t-shirt. I knew this week was going to be fun. Back downstairs, I saw Mitch already dressed in his leathers, ready for the ride home.

"I'm off now," I said. "See you at the weekend, Mitchell."

"Yes, hope this week goes ok with the setting up," he said.

"Mitch is coming down on Thursday afternoon," Charlie said. "Would we be able to go and see the dance floor that evening?"

"Yes, it should be almost set up by the end of the day so they have Friday to make any slight changes. I'll take you both down when I go and check."

In my wing mirror I could see them lingering together on the doorstep before I turned the corner.

The rest of Monday passed as usual and apart from the odd text from James, we kept things light because he still hadn't replied to my email. As the sunshine re-appeared on Tuesday morning, I knew that James was on early shift so I wasn't expecting any requests until later. Sure enough it was as I was driving home...

"Our mystery man is later than usual today, but here is a song for Stephanie, it's 'Sign Your Name Across My Heart' by Terence Trent D'arby."

Pulling over into a nearby lay-by, I found my phone in the bag and dropped Ian a text as the smooth voice of Terence sang.

James had certainly chosen another good song which spoke of our relationship. Racking my brain I sent my reply.

"Stephanie has just sent me a text and her response to today's song is a romantic one from Whitney Houston, 'Where Do Broken Hearts Go'. Hope you enjoy it."

Pulling back onto the road, I turned my stereo up and sang along to the words that were so apt with regards to our break-up. It was almost as if I had written them myself.

At home I turned on my tablet to check on the plans for Wednesday as I needed to be down at the river by eight in the morning. Blinking in my inbox were two messages so I opened the first one which was from Sarah:

Hi Steph, sorry haven't been in touch recently, have been busy with the campaign to Save Herefordshire Libraries and have also managed to catch a cold. Thankfully it's clearing up now so when are you free for a catch-up, coffee before Saturday?

Also I have been listening to the song requests from yesterday and today – is there something going on that I should know about? Have you guessed who your secret admirer is then? Give me a call later.

Please also sign the petition attached and send it on to anyone else who you think will sign it!!

Love Sarah x

As I nursed my coffee and signed the petition, making sure I sent it to everyone else on my contact list, I decided to give Sarah a call later in the evening and tell her the situation. Meanwhile I clicked on the second email from James.

Dear Steph,
Your last letter was another honest one from you and it breaks my heart

that the event I was forced to impose upon you changed the person you were so drastically. I hope that with time and love I can help you find the girl I knew and loved all those years ago. I sense she is still there just beneath the surface. I guess I must have changed in some way but I have yet to discover this!!

With regards to your question about Felicity and her involvement in mine and the boys' lives. Basically when she left me and them, I tried to keep things on a friendly basis as they were only young (Darren – four, Mitchell – two) and she used to have them for a day or two during the week, but this seemed to dwindle as her new relationship heated up. Eventually she would only make time for them at Christmas and their birthdays. Now they are older and able to make the decision to see her, I believe that they rarely do, but I have left that up to them. My parents were a godsend and pretty much helped a lot with bringing them up as I struggled to work and look after them. It was a hard period for me but a relief that she was finally out of my life as much as she could be. I hope that answers your question enough to help with your decision. I guess she loves them but I have to admit that looking back, they were just pawns in her control of us, which is an awful thing to admit. Believe me when I say that if I do ever happen to see her again, then I will not be responsible for my actions after the pain she caused you.

Anyway, enough of the past unless it's remembering the good times of which there were many. Do you realise that we hardly had an argument in the time we were together – that must be some sort of record!!!

Really looking forward to seeing you on Saturday and watching you control the crowds which undoubtedly you will. After all, I remember when you took the reins at my 21st Birthday party.

Till Saturday
Love James

Hearing the front door shut, Charlie appeared, sweaty and warm from rehearsals.

"Hi Mum," she said, grabbing a bottle of water from the fridge.

"Hi Charlie, everything ok?" I asked.

"Great Mum, the new dance is fantastic. Both of the others are just a case of continuing to practise them. How long until tea, as I want to practise my part in Mitch's new dance?"

"Come down when you're ready, I'm just about to put the frozen lasagne in the oven so I'll throw some chips in when you appear."

I turned back to the email and wondered how to reply.

Leaving the screen open I grabbed the phone and tapped in Sarah's number. Perhaps a chat with my best friend would help.

"Hello, who is this?" a deep voice answered.

"Hi Chris, how are you?"

"Hi Steph, fine thanks and you?"

"Good thanks, is your wonderful wife around?"

"Yes, she's just smiling at me now and asking who I'm talking to. I'll pass you over and look forward to seeing you on Saturday for the event of the century."

"I know, I just hope Rick's driver can find us," I replied. Chris laughed. "Here's the other member of the Rick Astley appreciation society."

"Hi Steph," Sarah said, giggling at her husband's last comment.

"Hi Sarah, how's the cold?"

"Better and thanks for signing the petition, the numbers are rising so quickly it warms your heart to know how much the people of Herefordshire value their library service when it is threatened with closure."

"Will your job be ok?" I asked.

"I really don't know at this stage, I am just keeping everything crossed." I could hear the worry in her voice, despite her light-hearted tone.

"Let's cut to the chase then, who is he?"

"Oh you mean, Mystery Man?" I replied, coyly.

"Yes, damn it, I'm your best friend. I have a right to know."

"I believe it's James. He sent me the song 'Valerie' last week and suggested substituting the name with mine and it was the line, *'I'm the same boy I used to be'* that got me thinking. Since then, a couple of songs this week have only confirmed my suspicions."

"So, what will you do on Saturday then?"

"Probably try and act surprised, but I think James may have guessed that I know it's him."

"Have you decided whether to take things further yet?" Sarah asked.

"Almost, we have been exchanging some very frank emails about the subject but deep down I am still scared."

"Well, you know where I am if you need to talk further before Saturday," she finished.

"Thanks and if I need to, I will."

"In the meantime, I'll keep my radio on and if the rest of the listeners are as entranced by this flirting as I am, you have a captive audience," Sarah giggled.

"I'd better go, I think the music has finished upstairs which means Charlie will be down for food."

"Take care Steph and how about a coffee on Friday?"

"I'll let you know, depends how things are moving with the event, if I have time…"

"Ok, speak soon," she replied.

"Bye Sarah."

-66-

When Wednesday morning dawned, I was full of excitement. I was off to get the contractors started on the stage build. Hurrying downstairs, I made a quick cup of coffee and scribbled a note for Charlie, in case she had forgotten where I was. As it was easier to walk, I pulled on my raincoat. I decided to cut through the car park for the swimming pool and as the sun started to poke through the dark clouds, I let my mind wander back in time. How many times had I walked this route? All my hopes and fears jumbled up in a knot of emotions that rolled around my stomach.

I took a look at the tired frontage of the pool as I walked past it. Apart from age and the new steps and ramp at the front, it had remained unaltered by time. It reminded me of such happy memories as I wandered through to the river meadow. Ahead I could see the various vehicles and groups of guys hanging around and enjoying the respite from the earlier rain. The foreman recognised me from Saturday.

"Morning Mrs. Eden," he said, reaching out to shake my hand.

"Call me Stephanie," I replied in response. "Do you have the plans?"

"Yes," he said, unfurling various sheets of paper. A gust of wind tried to remove them from his fingertips but his grip was strong.

"Anything I can help with?" I asked.

"Just a quick clarification on the dance floor area would be good," John said.

"Sure," I replied. We located and pegged the edge of the stage and then walked a couple of metres away from it as I made the decision. Another peg went into the ground and John nodded.

"Here's my card with my contact details on it, if you have any questions please just give me a call," I asked him.

"That's great, this should be a breeze," he said, pocketing the card in his jeans.

Walking back home, I called in at the bakery and bought some croissants for breakfast. All was silent as I turned the radio on and then called up the stairs.

"Charlie, do you want some breakfast, I've got fresh croissants."

"Yeah, thanks Mum, I'll be down in a second." I heard my daughter's muffled voice.

Once I was on air, a text to the studio came through from my mystery man. I smiled as I looked through the catalogue and found the track, thinking about what I might pick as my reply. The deep voice of Lionel

Richie filled the studio as I dedicated 'Destiny' to myself. I could see Paul and Ian in deep discussion in the office area, but they both looked over at me and started to mouth, *Who is he?* Today's words really started to pull at my emotions.

I closed my eyes and squeezed back the tears of happiness that threatened to spill out. All I could see there was the image of James as I always remembered him, at twenty-one. Although it was only the middle of the week, I couldn't wait for the weekend. As I started to play my response, I opened my eyes again and tried not to laugh as the guys in the office were making kissy faces at me.

Then as 'Rain or Shine' by Five Star came on as my response, they started to laugh. I knew they were looking forward to supposedly setting me up with my blind date, but I was going to have the last laugh.

Later, I drove down to the river and was amazed by the sight that greeted me there. The dance floor was down and surrounded by the hoardings ready for the advertising posters. They had started on the stage area, which seemed to look huge as I parked the car and walked onto the field.

"Hi John, wow it's looking amazing already," I said.

"It sure is. I'm bringing the family along for the day as the line-up of local bands looks brilliant," he said.

"That's great news, the more the merrier."

"Yes, just have to hope the weather is ok," John said, casting a glance at the grey sky.

"That's the only thing we can't plan for. I'll have to check out the forecast for Saturday when I get home. Well, I'll let you get finished for the day and I'll be around tomorrow afternoon. I promised I would show my daughter the dance floor area as she is one of the acts performing."

Ticket sales continued to exceed our expectations as I nervously checked the weather forecast for Saturday. On Thursday morning Charlie was up early and offered to clean the house while I was out at work. I could tell she just needed something to do to pass the time before Mitchell arrived.

"When I finish work later, I'll come straight home and then pop down to the site at around five. Will Mitchell be here by then?" I asked.

"I think he's planning to leave home around two so yes, that will be fine. Would you rather we met you down there?" Charlie replied.

"Ok, I'll park in the pub car park and we can walk to the site together. I'll aim to get there for 3.30."

On the way into work Paul had my secret admirer's song for that day.

"Hope you're listening in the car on your way into work, Steph as your admirer would like to seduce you with 'I Just Can't Stop Loving

You' by Michael Jackson. Let me know what I can play him in return," Paul said.

I pulled over and wracked my brain for a suitable song. Early Michael Jackson was a great choice and I listened to the words whilst I sent my text over to Paul in the studio.

Pleased with my reply, I drove into Hereford as 'Miss You Like Crazy' by Natalie Cole filled the car and I sang along.

I heard my phone beep in my bag as I pulled into the car park. It was from James:

Love the song today – I really hope you are.
You'll have to wait until Saturday.

I couldn't hide the huge smile on my face as I entered the office and was surrounded by the hive of activity.

The day passed quickly and after a quick chat with Paul and Ian as I showed them the pictures of the work happening in Ross, I drove home.

Pulling into the car park outside the pub, I grabbed my copy of the plans and walked along the pathway to the site. I was hit with the sight of the stage looking spectacular. Sitting on one of the benches, I saw Charlie and Mitch.

"Mum this looks amazing," Charlie exclaimed.

"I couldn't have put it better," I replied.

John saw us and walked in our direction. Closing the gap, we met just on the far edge of the dance floor. It framed the stage and lighting well and the hoardings were now being coated with various posters. It was just the electricians and the stage equipment that were coming tomorrow.

"So, is it looking ok?" John asked.

"More than ok, you've done a fantastic job," I said, shaking his hand.

As the two of us wandered around, he pointed out the access points and places where the cables from tomorrow could be hidden. Charlie and Mitch walked through the gap and onto the dance floor. I watched them stare up at the stage ahead of them, deep in conversation.

"Is that your daughter?" John asked.

"Yes and her boyfriend, Mitchell. They are both dancing and I promised they could come and check out the dance floor this afternoon."

After looking at the rear of the stage, we walked back around to the front and discovered that checking the dance floor apparently required actual dancing. We both watched as they ran through what was obviously the dance from *Dirty Dancing* and then the famous lift. As Charlie slid back down to earth John and many of the other contractors who had stopped to stare started to clap and cheer. I could see the happiness on their faces, lighting up the cloudy day above. After taking a bow, they left the dance floor and met me.

"Come on you dance freaks, let's get home," I said.

"Any chance I can bring the group down tomorrow for a run-through?" Charlie asked.

I looked across at John but he only nodded.

"Ok, as long as you don't get in the way of the electricians and other contractors who are here to do a job," I replied.

The evening passed by with lots of happy chatter over the dining table before Charlie and Mitch left me to my laptop. I started to quietly panic about everything that needed to be done on the Saturday morning. Then I opened my emails and began to type out a reply to James' last one:

Dear James,
Sorry for the delay in replying but as you can imagine, the closer we get to the big event, the more work I have to do just to stay ahead of the game. I have to admit that at this stage, I am starting to feel very nervous as well as excited. I hope that I will be able to find the time to see and speak to you but honestly, don't count on it if things get chaotic on the day!!

Just been down to check on progress on site and the stage is up and the dance floor has just been tested by Charlie and Mitchell – honestly you can't take them anywhere without them spontaneously breaking into a dance routine!

I will arrange for Charlie to be at our place when you arrive on Saturday. I hope you were able to book some rooms at the nearby Premier Inn for the rest of the lads? Undoubtedly I will be riverside from around 7am in the morning to ensure everything is going to run smoothly. HELP!!!

Thanks for letting me know about your ex, I just needed to know as unfortunately I just don't think I can ever forgive her for what she did to us. Although I am hoping that time will heal and I will be able to forget.

Hope you are well, sorry I haven't had much chance to talk or even to play you a song on the radio. I hope that some of the songs being played are reminding you of us??

If I'm not too frazzled I will give you a quick call on Friday night just to finalise everything and look forward to seeing you on Saturday.

Hectically yours,
Stephanie

At last some sunshine greeted me as my alarm went off just after six. Keeping my fingers crossed that this was a sign of the impending weekend weather, I jumped in the shower. Once again I walked down to the river and saw John and a couple of electricians. They all seemed on top of it so I left them to it. I paused and walked to the prospect to get a better view and snapped a picture on my phone, ready to share with the guys at the station later. I also sent it to James.

Here it is – the event of the century.

Morning you early riser, it looks great. I can't wait, he replied.

I smiled at the early riser mention and blushed as I thought about the many times I had woken to his! The more I thought about the good times, the brighter they seemed and the bad times seemed to be fading. I knew I would never forget that moment, how could I with scars I could still see? Saturday was going to be our moment because I was going to agree to try again.

Back in the kitchen at home, Paul announced that my secret admirer was very early this morning with his request for, 'Nothing's Gonna Stop Us Now' by Starship. Instantly I was transported to the evening we had watched *Mannequin*. I closed my eyes even though I knew that Charlie and Mitch had stopped eating their breakfast and were watching me as I mouthed the lyrics in time with the music.

Grabbing my phone I tapped in my reply, knowing it couldn't be anything other than the song that Paul started to play in reply. Leaning against the worktop, I closed my eyes again as emotions overtook me. I could feel tears of joy and relief starting to sparkle in the corners of my eyes at the wonderful combination of George Michael and Aretha Franklin as they sang, 'I Knew You Were Waiting'.

Perhaps deep down, I had known that somehow by keeping my memories and heart locked up all this time, that this moment of release would appear. Like a knight in shining armour galloping towards me, thundering hooves as my heart drummed. I had waited for so long. I experienced a moment of sheer release from all the darkness, hurt, anger and tears of my past. As the song came to an end, I wanted to hear it over and over again as I felt arms wrap themselves around me. Four arms as I opened my eyes to see my daughter and behind her, Mitchell hugging me tight. Tears of happiness were reflected back at me from the glistening green eyes my wonderful daughter Charlie.

We pulled apart and Mitchell passed me a nearby box of tissues as I watched him wipe the tears from Charlie's cheeks. There was no need for me to say anything so instead I just smiled at both of them. Driving to work I still heard the song playing on a continuous loop all the way in and then throughout the day. The whole office and studio were strung up on nerves as I just floated through the day. After my show, I went out to do some shopping before walking to the pub to meet Jack, Paul, Mark and Ian for our final discussion before the big day.

When I walked in, I saw Jack and Paul already deep in conversation. I grabbed a drink at the bar and went over as we waited for Mark and Ian to arrive.

"Hi guys," I beamed, sitting down next to Jack.

"Hi Steph, you are looking radiant today," Jack said, kissing my cheek.

"Yes, you have been very weird all day," Paul said, grinning at me. "Can't you please tell us why?"

"All will be revealed tomorrow," I said, feeling very smug.

"I'm sure Steph knows who her mystery man is as the requests this week have been odd for people who don't know each other," Paul said.

"Have they?" Jack asked. "Sorry I've been busy and missed them except for the two this morning."

As Paul went to the bar to get some more drinks, Ian and Mark joined him there. Jack leaned over and whispered, "Is it James?"

"Yes it is, but don't tell them," I replied.

We were going to be broadcasting from the site for the whole day so we split it up into different two-hour sessions. As I lived in Ross, I would start in the morning and then do another couple of hours later in the afternoon.

"So, should we do the *Blind Date* thing before your daughter's last dance, which is before Rick?" Paul asked.

"That's fine with me," I said.

"You don't seem very nervous about meeting your mystery man?" Ian said.

"There's too much to worry about for the rest of the day before that one moment. I'll be fine, in fact I'm looking forward to it." Standing up, I reached for my bag. "Well, I'm off home for a final site and sound check before I get an early night."

Checking my phone before I set off, I saw a message from Charlie:

We're practising on the dance floor and they're using our music to check the sound system, it's brilliant!

I'm coming home now, so I'll call by, I texted back.

As I neared the car park, I saw the pub was already busy with people enjoying the late afternoon sunshine. I walked along the path and I could hear the music floating through the air. A few people were walking along the path and many had stopped to take in the spectacle of the stage. I saw Sarah and Chris walking in the same direction and hurried over to meet them.

"Charlie dropped us a text to say they were practising so we decided to come down," she said.

"I'm feeling really nervous now with it literally only being hours away when things get started," I said.

We paused to watch the girls start their new dance to 'Troublemaker' and I saw Mitch lounging on the grass, his eyes firmly rooted on a single dancer.

"Hi Stephanie, Sarah, Chris," Mitchell said, standing up.

"Hi Mitch, how are things going?" I asked.

"I wish the guys were here so we could have a full rehearsal," he said. "Would we get chance to have an early one tomorrow morning if they can make it down for eight?"

"Yes, I'll be here broadcasting from our bus over there," I pointed just to the side of the stage at our large studio on the move.

"Great, I'll let them all know, and Dad of course," he said.

When the music died, Charlie raced over to us all and flopped down on the grass next to Mitch.

"Does it look ok?" she asked.

"Yes, but you need to extend more when you prepare for the splits," Mitch calmly mentioned. He pulled her close and planted a kiss on her forehead.

"From an audience point of view, it was excellent," Chris said. "I'm not as technical as Mitchell but I know what I like."

"Anyone want a drink?" Sarah asked.

Everyone nodded as Mitch pulled Charlie back up and said, "Shall we have another go?"

"Yes," she agreed, and they handed a disc to the sound man and took to the dance floor. I watched as Mitchell danced alone to 'Suit and Tie' before Charlie crossed from the far edge of the flooring, swaying her hips before reaching for an imaginary tie.

My phone started to ring so I walked a little further away.

"Hi James, how are you?"

"Fine Steph, I've just been trying to get hold of Mitchell but he's not answering."

"He's busy on the dance floor at the moment."

"Ok, just let him know that I will have the lads over for eight in the morning. Do I come straight to the river?"

"Yes, there will be plenty of people around and I'll be broadcasting until ten in the large bus."

"Ok. I'll bring coffee and a bacon sandwich."

"Sounds great, I'll tell security to let you in."

"You have security?" he asked in amazement.

"Tomorrow I do, after all, I have a blind date to meet who could be a deranged psychopath or axe murderer." I giggled.

"You never know, he might just turn out to be your hero," James said.

Hanging up, I saw Sarah carrying a large glass of wine.

"I really need that," I said, taking it from her.

"Who was on the phone?"

"Just James trying to leave Mitchell a message."

"Anything else I should know about?"

"I have made up my mind to say yes," I said.

"You're going to start dating again?" She seemed ecstatic, pulling me carefully into a hug as we avoided spilling our wine.

"Do Charlotte and Mitchell know?" she asked.

"I think they may have guessed this morning. I had a rather emotional epiphany in the kitchen as Paul played, 'I Knew You Were Waiting for Me' by George and Aretha."

"Does James know?"

"I think the songs I have been playing for him this week may have hinted at the fact," I replied.

"I'm so excited Mum, I don't think I'll be able to sleep tonight!" Charlie joined us, jumping for joy.

"I'd better get you drunk then," Mitch joked, reaching over to squeeze her hand. "Otherwise, perhaps we'd better stay here and dance all night instead."

"Maybe," she said, a blush tinting her cheeks with a rosy glow.

As it was a nice evening we sat outside the pub and ordered some food and more drinks.

When Charlotte and Mitchell told me they were going to walk home, I suggested, "You should go through the churchyard to the prospect, the view of the set-up looks fantastic from there."

"Sounds good Mum," Charlie agreed. "We'll see you in a little while."

Linking hands, they walked further along the river and then up into town.

-68-

Charlie and Mitchell walked hand in hand along the path that headed into town. Carefully Charlie steered them in the direction of the church, instead of through town so that they could take in the view. Leaning over the railings, they stared down onto the stage and dance floor spread out before them. "That's a fabulous sight," Mitch said in a breathy voice.

"It still looks huge from up here," Charlie said in awe. She felt Mitch's arms around her shoulders and she moved in towards him.

"Let's walk this way," Charlie said, moving down the familiar paths that led to her father.

Silently she paused in front of the headstone. She had only been here a few times over the years, mostly with her mum. Kneeling down she saw a bunch of fresh flowers, running her fingers over the engraved name.

"Hi Dad, this is Mitchell. We're dancing together tomorrow and I hope you'll look down on us and watch," she whispered. Mitch rested his hand on her shoulder and read the inscription. Although he spent very little time with his mum, at least he still could. Standing up she turned to Mitch and he held her in his arms.

"I just felt that I had to come here," Charlie said.

"I know it must be hard for you, as you never really knew him."

"I think it's more to do with the fact my mum is going back to the person she really loved and I don't want Dad to think that I will love him any less," she sighed. "It's kind of hard to explain."

Looking up into his face, she watched his lips head towards hers and he kissed her with a tenderness she had never felt before. As the darkness started to fold its cloak around them, they walked home.

"Mum, we're home," Charlie called when they got back to the house.

"That's good, I really need to get to bed," Steph said, appearing in the hallway.

"Ok Mum, we'll see you in the morning. I'll come down with Mitchell to meet his dad and the guys at eight."

"Night Stephanie," Mitch said.

Charlie filled the kettle and made them hot chocolate, taking them through to the conservatory where they sat down on the sofa.

"Can't wait for tomorrow," Mitch said.

"Me too. I think it's going to be amazing." Leaning across, she planted a kiss on his cheek. Mitch turned his head slightly so he could taste the sweetness of the chocolate on her lips.

"Let's go up to bed," Charlie murmured.

"What happened to being too excited to sleep?"

"I don't think I said anything about sleeping," Charlie teased.

♪

When my alarm sounded at five in the morning, I flicked it to snooze and had a further ten minutes. I grabbed a quick shower and took a look out of the window. The sun was shining in a perfect blue sky, a real rarity. I found my new sundress and fastened my hair up in a loose ponytail, applying a light coloured lip gloss. I didn't need any other make-up as my skin seemed to glow and my eyes were bright with love. After a quick coffee, I was out of the door.

Paul had driven the radio bus down to the site and was sat outside waiting for me to arrive.

"Morning Steph, did you order the weather?" he asked.

"Of course, it's going to be a perfect day," I replied. In fact that was the very song I would start the show with. I checked the set-up and started up the music and the tone for the whole day ahead. My phone beeped.

Driving along the motorway now, listening to some great music, James texted.

The next song was, 'Somewhere Out There' by Linda Ronstadt and James Ingram.

I smiled, feeling my heart starting to beat that little bit faster. My phone went again as James requested the next song. It was 'Waiting For a Star to Fall' by Boy Meets Girl, a favourite, obviously. The words perfectly matched mine and the way we were both feeling as we teetered on the brink of rediscovery.

I was soon playing requests for people preparing for the event. As I watched the clock tick by, I looked up to see Charlie and Mitch standing outside, holding coffees in their hands. Then Paul came in talk to me.

"Steph, there's a guy outside with a coffee and bacon sandwich for you," he said, looking puzzled.

"Send him in," I replied, as I lined up the next song to automatically play and stepped out of the tiny studio. When he walked onto the bus, I could feel my heart already increasing in tempo.

"As promised," James said and I stepped forward, taking them and putting them straight down on the nearby table.

"You look beautiful," he told me, closing the gap between us.

I heard the second song start to play and knew that I would not have much time before I needed to be back behind the desk. Looking down, I saw my hands were shaking from the tension that surrounded us. When I looked up I was staring directly into his blue eyes and I stepped into his open arms. Breathing in, I closed my eyes as my heart hammered in time with his, feeling his hands pulling me in tighter. I looked up again to a sight that took my breath away.

He was here, he was real. James was mine again. His lips captured mine and I struggled to remain in reality as feelings of love exploded inside of me, escaping their years of confinement. I felt like a butterfly emerging from its chrysalis into the warm sunshine, feeling free.

Pulling away I still couldn't speak as I motioned to the song that was starting to fade out. I hurried back behind my desk as James watched with interest. I found my voice and announced the next couple of songs coming up. Then once another three songs were set to go, I felt calm enough to leave the safety of the studio booth.

"Hey," I said, stepping back out and picking up a mug of coffee.

"How long have you got before your session finishes?" James asked.

"An hour. Hope you don't mind waiting just a little bit longer?"

James shook his head. "If that kiss means what I think it means, then I'm more than happy to wait." He was still the gentleman that I remembered, when he had waited for me all those years ago.

Mitch and Charlie peeped round the door.

"Everything looks great and sounds fantastic," Charlie said. "James brought us some breakfast so we're having an early picnic on the grass outside."

"I'll join you when my show finishes in an hour," I said.

"I'll join you in a moment," James said, as we watched them leave.

"I should be able to sneak away for an hour after my show and you can drop your bag off at the house," I said, smiling shyly at the thought of James seeing my place.

"Sounds like a plan, meanwhile how many songs do we have left?" he asked. He took my coffee mug from my hand and reeled me in.

"I'm struggling to let you go," he whispered. "I keep thinking you might be a figment of my imagination."

"I'm real," I said as my lips found his.

The hour passed quickly and when I emerged into the sunshine, I found the riverside already bustling with people. The girls from Charlie's group had appeared and they were already warming up ready for a final run-through of their dances. A number of the local bands had turned up and as I wandered towards James, I saw Jack heading in my direction.

"Hi Jack," I called out.

"Hey Steph. What a glorious day to spend by the river." He pulled me in for a hug and turned to take in the stage and the dance floor.

"It really does look good. Has our big star arrived yet?" he asked.

"Rick's due here at three this afternoon. But I have an hour off and there are a few things I need to get done," I said, smiling as I saw James closing in.

Jack turned to see where my attention had wandered off to. Spotting James, he grabbed my arm. "I hope you're going to give it another chance?"

"I am."

"Hi James, this is Jack. You might remember meeting him some years ago?" James nodded and stuck out his hand.

"Hi Jack, can I possibly whisk Stephanie away from you?" he asked.

"Sure," Jack said. "See you later." We watched him walk towards the dance floor and talk to Charlie.

"At last," James said. "I have you for a whole hour."

We walked to the minibus and James grabbed his bag and then my hand.

"I'm sorry I'm not letting you go," he said.

Walking along the river, we cut through the swimming pool car park.

"God this brings back memories," James said, as we paused to look at where it all began.

"I know, I still swim sometimes, but swimming was never the same without you." James pulled me close and brushed a light kiss on my lips.

"I'm only going to say sorry this one final time, from now on it's a fresh page that we have to write on," he said.

"That sounds like a plan. Like the very first letter I ever sent you."

"Like the very first time I ever kissed you. Although re-visiting that spot might be kind of nice."

"I think that could be arranged," I replied.

Letting us in, I glanced nervously over to James. I was watching for his reaction.

"Lovely house," he told me.

"I'll give you a quick tour if you like," I said, feeling shy.

"Lead on," James said, as we went through to the kitchen. He admired the layout and peeped into the conservatory. Then we went to the dining room and lounge.

"I'm sure you remember my place. It's so much smaller than yours."

"A building doesn't make a home," I murmured. He looked across at the bookshelves and then all the DVDs lined up. Moving closer, he ran his hands over the spines of a couple of books.

"You're still a bookworm then?" he asked. I nodded as he moved on to the DVDs. He pulled one out and turned to me. Before I even saw it, I knew which film it was as I closed the gap between us again. My hands touched the case before he slipped it back onto the shelf.

I was in his arms again, surrendering to his familiar touch, reawakening so many feelings within me. My heart had started to beat again as our tongues met and explored in a pattern that we both knew. Time slipped away as we stood in each other's arms, our eyes wide open, watching each other anew. I heard the grandfather clock in the hall pass the hour and pulled away.

"We'll have to go back I'm afraid. I've got more work to do and a superstar to meet!"

"Come on then," he said. "We'll finish this tour later."

Charlie and Mitch spotted our return and came over to meet us. I left James with them as I returned to the studio. Mark and Ian had arrived and between them, they were organising the bands and explaining the procedure as the first ones started to set up onstage. Charlie briefly interrupted me.

"Mum, we're going to go home and fetch our costumes, can we change here on the bus?" she asked. I watched the guys give my daughter the once over.

"Sure, I'll save you a space," I said, before she turned and ran back to Mitchell.

"Was that Charlotte?" Paul asked.

"Yes, stop being a letch, you're old enough to be her dad!" I laughed.

"I wouldn't stand a chance next to her boyfriend," he replied, as we watched Mitch pick her up and carry her on his back.

As we finalised plans, Paul and Ian prepared to take to the stage ready to kick the event off. I had a look through the running order and saw Sarah and Chris. Waving, I walked over to them and seeing James looking a little lost now that the kids had disappeared, I motioned him over.

"Hey Steph, looking beautiful today," Chris said, pulling me into his arms for a hug.

"Sarah you look great too," I said, as we hugged and kissed. Then James was with us and it almost felt like old times again. The four of us together again.

"Can I get some drinks in before the bar gets busy?" James asked.

"Sure, I'll give you a hand," Chris said, as we watched them walk away together.

"I hope they'll be friends again," Sarah said.

"Me too, as you're going to be seeing a lot more of James from now on," I replied.

"I think you've made the right decision, I've not seen you this happy in such a long time," she said. We paused as the sound system was turned on full blast.

"Welcome to Rock On the River, our amazing fundraising event for the local hospital," Paul announced. Cheers deafened us as the crowd responded.

"So there's plenty to enjoy throughout the day but we're kicking off with an hour of your requests before our first band Rubble are ready to rock us," Ian said.

"Yeah, come and see us over by the bus and tell us what you want to hear," Paul said. "This first song is from us to all you guys, it's Queen with, 'We Will Rock You', so let me see your hands and hear your singing."

The guys returned with our drinks. Jack had also come over to join us as I hovered around and took requests from people. A young girl came up to me.

"Are you Stephanie?" she asked.

"Yes," I replied.

"Can't wait to see who your secret admirer is later, your romance on air has had me hooked!"

"You'll have to wait until just before Rick Astley," I replied, blushing.

"Are you nervous or excited?" she asked. I glanced across at my friends and James.

"Excited, I'm sure he's going to be the man of my dreams," I replied. I saw Jack laughing and trying to hide it from everyone around us.

"I can't wait to see your look of surprise later," Jack said.

"I'm really looking forward to seeing Ian and Paul's faces when they realise."

As the clock crept towards three, I kept an ear on my phone, waiting for the Rick Astley entourage to contact me when they got closer. I twisted a strand of my hair nervously as I watched Charlotte and the girls waiting to perform their first dance of the day. Rubble had just finished their set to rapturous applause from the crowds who loved their high energy rock covers. I waved across and she saw me and waved back. Sarah, Chris and James had moved closer to the dance floor to get a better view and were joined by Mitchell. His group would be dancing straight afterwards before our next run of requested songs and the second live band. I could hardly believe how smoothly things were running with an event this large. The riverside was crowded with people of all ages, having fun and enjoying the warm weather.

Then my phone rang and I wandered a little further away from the crowds to speak.

"Hi, is that Stephanie?" a male voice asked.

"Yes speaking," I replied.

"It's Evan, Rick's manager. We've just reached the end of the M50. Are there any signs for us to follow?" he asked.

"Sure, there should be one just off the roundabout, then just follow those and as you turn into the road that runs parallel to the river, I'll meet you there as I'll need to move the road closed signs."

"Great, we'll be in a large coach," Evan replied, before hanging up.

"Rick's at the end of the M50 so I'm off to meet him at the road closed sign," I said to Ian in the studio.

"Fantastic," he replied. "You know where you're directing them?"

"Yes, I'll get on the walkies and let the stewards know," I replied.

At the thought of meeting Rick Astley, I felt even more like a teenager, as I hurried through the crowds. I could hear the next band really warming up their audience. I even saw Charlie and Mitchell dancing in the centre as he spun her around. I saw the coach approaching and started to move the signs so that they could pull in. Putting them back into place, I saw the door of the coach opening and a guy popped out.

"Thanks Stephanie, do you want to come onboard to direct our driver?" he said.

"Sure," I replied, as I climbed on and shook hands with Evan. Trying to look professional as if meeting superstars was part of my usual working day, I kept my eyes fixed on the windscreen. Slowly we made our way through the crowds and then into position. As the vehicle stopped, I turned around and looked into the back of the coach to see my idol casually sitting there.

"So what's the timescale for setting up before Rick's onstage at 9.30?" Evan asked. I had remembered to pick up my clipboard and located the relevant plans and schedule and passed him a copy.

"In the meantime if you need anything else, I'll be just over by the other bus and then I'm onstage from five, so if you require anything at that point then contact Paul or Ian. All our details are on the bottom of the schedule."

I felt someone standing behind me and I turned to look directly at Rick.

"Hello Mr. Astley, it's lovely to welcome you to Ross-on-Wye," I said, extending my hand.

"Hello Miss..." he paused, as he tried to remember my name.

"Just call me Stephanie," I said, blushing as he shook my hand.

"Just call me Rick," he replied. He was charming me already as I struggled to contain my excitement.

"Will it cause much disruption if I have a wander around outside; I've got security but I don't mind talking to the fans," he said.

"Certainly," I replied. "Perhaps later, I could trouble you to sign my copy of your first album? I've been a huge fan of yours since you started."

"No problem, come and find me later," he said.

He was about to turn away when I remembered my blind date introduction that would take place before he began his set.

"I have a final request," I asked.

"Go ahead," Rick said.

"To cut a long story short, I'm supposed to be meeting a secret admirer onstage just before your set starts, he's been sending me song requests for the past couple of weeks and the guys on the station thought I should meet him in front of the crowds." I paused and tried to imagine how this was sounding to a world-famous singer. "The thing is, the secret admirer is actually my first boyfriend who I went out with in 1988 and one of our favourite songs was 'Together Forever', so if you could dedicate that to us in your set, I would be eternally grateful."

"Wow, how fantastic, certainly Stephanie. Just let Evan know the name of your man and I'll do that for you both," he said, smiling.

Quite literally the stage was set for the finale of the day. I had a quick look around and saw that everything was under control, so I sauntered towards the dance floor and my friends and daughter sitting together in the sun.

"Hi Steph, glad you could join us for a bit," James said.

"Would you like a drink?" Sarah asked, reaching for a glass and the orange juice.

"Great. I'll be onstage at five and introducing your next dances," I said to Charlie and Mitch.

"Is Rick here yet?" Sarah asked.

"Yes, I've just had the pleasure of meeting him. Watch out as he is planning to have a wander round at some point. A true gentleman and still gorgeous," I said, as I felt James give me a nudge on the arm.

Charlotte and Mitchell followed me over to the bus later so that they could change for their next set of dances. I felt slightly nervous as I took to the stage but as the crowd finished applauding the last band, I soon held them captive, in the palm of my hand. I could see Charlotte and her group waiting to start their performance so I let them have the floor to perform their new dance to 'Troublemaker' by Olly Murs. Then as the crowd gave them a standing ovation as they left the dance floor, I saw her racing to the radio bus to change for Mitchell's group dance with her special appearance. I let the crowd chant for more to give her some extra time before Mitch and the guys filled the floor.

I watched the young girls and many women in the audience inhale sharply at the sight of these young men in their smart suits. As Justin Timberlake's 'Suit and Tie' hypnotised the crowd into silence, the dancing began and once again, the crowd stood spellbound. As Charlie walked back across the field ready for her entrance, I saw Rick to the side of the stage and beckoned him up so that he could see the dancing better. Charlotte swayed across the dance floor in her flirty, floral dress.

The seemingly disinterested guys in the crowds started to perk up and I heard a number of wolf whistles.

Standing to the side of the stage with Rick, he turned to me.

"They're fantastic dancers," he whispered.

"Yes, the girl performing now is my daughter and the dark-haired guy that she is leading around by his tie is her boyfriend," I replied.

"They definitely stand out above the others," he murmured, "I might need some dancers for my next tour, would it be ok to contact you on the information that Evan has?"

"They're dancing together just before you take to the stage later," I said.

I watched as the routine finished with all the guys holding Charlie aloft whilst she twirled a loose tie.

Leaving the stage I headed for the small studio on the bus to take over from Ian. As I boarded I saw all the guys in a huddle.

"What's going on?" I asked.

"We need to find your mystery man to let him know when and where we need him for later," Paul said.

"Ok perhaps I'll play him a request and ask him to meet you behind the stage," I said, enjoying their looks of amazement at my calmness.

"Aren't you even a tiny bit nervous?" Ian asked.

"No, I'm sure it will be fine," I replied, as I made my way into the studio and put my headphones on.

I played the first few requests that we hadn't had time for in the last stint while I tried to think of a good song to play. In the end it had to be 'Perfect' by Fairground Attraction, as it summed up the event and the secret fact that I hoped it was going to be perfect when we were together again. As the song faded out, I took to the microphone.

"I hope my secret admirer is here and waiting patiently to meet me later," I paused and I could hear the screams from the crowds outside who had been following the requested songs for a couple of weeks. "I'd like to play you 'Perfect' by Fairground Attraction and if you could make yourself known to Mark and Ian, they will be waiting for you behind the main stage," I said, as the song started to play.

I grinned as I felt my mobile phone buzz in my pocket. As Ian and Paul had left the bus, I pulled it out and read the message from James:

Fantastic choice of song, I'm on my way now. I don't think they've seen me with you at any point during the day, so the game is still on.

The only one who has is Paul and he's still outside the bus at the moment, have fun and I'll look forward to meeting you at about 8.30 onstage.

Time flew by and as my request session came to an end before the last local band kept the crowds entertained, I had time to reflect on the day. On the whole there had been no major hiccups and so far, no one had got drunk enough to cause any fights. I still couldn't quite believe that I had spoken to one of my teenage idols and he was a genuinely nice guy. Sitting back in the studio chair, I nursed a cup of tea as I heard Mark onstage, warming up the crowd for the band. I closed my eyes. It had been such a long day and it still wasn't over yet.

The event had raised over £8,000 through sponsorship and even paying for our big star to perform was reasonable. The guys who had supplied the lighting and stage equipment were getting a small amount coupled with major advertising on the radio station. Overall everyone was happy and the great weather had helped. From outside I could hear the crowd clapping in time to the music and I opened my eyes. I had hardly stopped for food apart from my morning sandwich. Returning to the bus with a portion of chips, I saw Jack walking towards me.

"Hi Steph, how are things going?" he asked.

"Fine, feeling a bit knackered, but there's still a few hours to go," I said, offering him a chip.

We sat down on the grass outside the bus and watched the world go by.

"So are you single at the moment?" I asked.

"Yeah, can't seem to find the right one for me," Jack said, pinching another chip.

"You will. Just look at me for example."

"Yeah, single for years and now you're getting back together with your first boyfriend," he sighed. "So romantic."

"Not sure romantic is quite the right word, these last few weeks have felt like I've been on a rollercoaster of emotions but today it comes to a halt and I get to alight."

"Happily ever after," Jack sighed, as he pulled me close for a hug.

"I'd like to believe that," I replied, as we watched the sky start to shade into pale pink and purple.

"I can't believe it's our last dance already," Charlie said. "Today has flown by."

"I know, but it's not quite over yet," I reminded her, following them onto the bus.

"I've told Dad that I'll drive the minibus up to the hotel later and drop the guys off," Mitch said.

"Just in case you want to go home before the end," Charlie added.

"Are you implying that I'm too old to last until the very end?" I retorted, laughing at the same time.

"No Mum, but the bar further along the river is staying open late and they have a DJ, so we might stay on for a dance."

"I wish I still had your energy," I sighed, as I thought of the times I had danced until two in the morning.

By the time Charlie and Mitch had changed into their costumes for the last dance, I was ready too. Charlie turned to hug me.

"What's that for?" I asked.

"Because I love you and I'm happy about you and James," she said, her eyes shining bright.

"We'll never forget about Dad," I said.

"Never," she replied, before grabbing Mitchell's hand in hers as they made their way to the dance floor. As I crossed to the side of the stage, I saw Sarah and Chris and waved. Sarah gave me a wave and smile and I knew she was happy for me.

Stepping onto the stage to join Mark, Ian and Paul, we all acknowledged the crowds before us. I could feel the excited anticipation in the air at the thought that Rick Astley would be appearing in a matter of moments.

"Thanks everyone for coming and supporting us today," Paul said.

"We've raised over £8,000 for the hospital here and I can't think of a better cause," Ian added, joining in with the claps and cheers that echoed between the trees and the river's edge.

"The night is still young and we still have a couple of things to cover so firstly, let's watch our dancers for one, final time. Charlotte Eden, Mitchell Cooke and their groups will leave you with the iconic dance from *Dirty Dancing*," Mark announced.

"Let's hear it for them, as I can't agree more with the sentiments of the song... today has been the time of our lives," Paul commented.

The spotlight pinpointed Charlotte stood in the centre of the dance floor as the melody started to fill the night air. The light had just started to fade as the sun sank into the surface of the river beyond, casting reds and oranges over the calm ripples of the Wye. Rick Astley stood on the other side of the stage from us and watched the best performance of the day so far. The crowd stood or sat in stunned awe at the sight of Charlotte and Mitchell as they danced together across the floor. Then the spotlight picked Charlie up as a couple of the guys from the group lifted her across part of the floor before she ran the short distance and flew into Mitchell's awaiting arms. The noise from the crowd almost drowned out the music for the moment when she was held aloft. I could feel tears of pride sparkling in my eyes as the guys tried not to get affected by a dance performance which excelled.

When Charlie touched the floor again, the music spoke to the audience as people danced along and the girls and guys joined in to create the final spectacle. After a couple of minutes and a multitude of bows, they cleared the dance floor and Charlotte blew me a kiss into the air. I knew in my heart that I had been lucky enough to witness what was possibly going to be the start of a sparkling career for my daughter and Mitchell.

"For some of you, the wait for Rick Astley is nearly over but we have one thing left to do this evening," Paul said. I realised that Ian had disappeared from the wings of the stage as Paul called me over to the centre. "Stephanie, our favourite female DJ. Come here!"

"Only female DJ!" someone shouted from the crowd. Paul nodded and laughed.

"Yes that too. Well Stephanie has been single for too many years to count and a few weeks ago, our radio station started to get requests for her on a daily basis from a secret admirer."

The audience started to whistle and cheer their approval.

"Well, tonight ladies and gentlemen, boys and girls, we have found the mystery man we hope has started to steal Stephanie's heart with his great choice of music." Paul stopped to take a pause as the clapping and cheering began again.

"Are we ready to meet him?" Paul asked the crowd.

They all screamed, "YES!!"

"Stephanie, are you ready to meet him?" Paul said as he turned to me.

"Yes I think so," I said.

As Mark gave Ian the nod, I watched and waited in silence. It was almost as if the audience were holding their breath. Then I saw James behind Ian and started to grin.

"I think it might be going well," Paul said. "Stephanie is smiling."

With Paul standing between us, I watched as James stepped forward and handed me a bouquet of pink roses. The crowd went wild and Paul had to wait before he could say anything else.

"For those of you who are old enough, I officially feel like Cilla Black on *Blind Date* standing between these two," he said, motioning to each of us. I saw James wink at me and I grinned back. Ian stepped forward and handed Paul a clipboard with some notes scribbled on it.

"So, I think everyone deserves a little background on our blind date couple before they head off into the sunset together," he said, as he turned to James.

"So what's your name and where do you come from and why do you want to go on a date with our Stephanie?" Paul said.

"My name is James and I'm from Warwickshire but originally from Ross-on-Wye about twenty-four years ago," he paused to look at me again. I could see he was trying to decide what to say to the date question. I nodded across at him.

"I first fell in love with Stephanie in early 1988 and I broke her heart on a cold day in November of the same year. I have regretted that day ever since and when I discovered her again, I knew I had to try and win her back."

I heard the women in the audience sigh collectively, and some claps and cheers from the men. Paul was so shocked, I thought his chin was going to hit the floor and at the side of the stage, I saw Mark and Ian replicating his expression.

I was trying desperately not to laugh at their faces as Paul turned to me.

"So Stephanie, same question to you."

"My name is Stephanie and I'm from Ross and I would love to go on a date with James as for the past few weeks, he has been mending my broken heart with music," I replied.

Closing my eyes, I tried to control my breathing as the beat of my heart accelerated to a point where the sounds from the people below seemed to fade beneath the beating. As Paul moved out of the way, I passed him the flowers that filled my arms and waited for the moment to take my breath away. I could feel James' hands on my waist pulling me closer as he reached up and I felt his fingers tangle into my hair. I was trembling in his embrace and it seemed an age for his lips to capture mine in a kiss that eclipsed any I had ever experienced before.

As the sound of applause started to penetrate my ears, we broke apart and looked out across the sea of smiling, happy faces. I scanned the crowds and found my family; Charlotte, Sarah, Chris and now Mitchell. Just behind them, I saw Jack waving frantically at me and I waved back. I turned to see Paul still standing in shock as I reached over and picked up the microphone.

"Once again, thank you everyone for coming today and I'll let you finish your night off with the sensational soul voice of Rick Astley. Come on everyone, relive your past like I just have."

James took my hand and laughed at the comment. "I don't remember us ever doing this in the past," he joked, making our way to the side of the stage. I paused to watch as Rick acknowledged the audience and then stood in front of the microphone.

"Thank you everyone for your wonderful welcome to Ross-on-Wye. It's my first visit but maybe it won't be my last."

The crowd went wild for a few more minutes and then Rick spoke again.

"I am going to start my set tonight with a song from 1988, a year that has already been mentioned this evening."

I turned to James as he squeezed my hand in his.

"I would like to dedicate my first song to the newly reunited couple, James and Stephanie. I believe it played a part in their relationship back then and I hope that hearing it now will be a good omen for the future."

Rick glanced across at us standing in the wings, as the familiar sounds of 'Together Forever' hit the air.

James glanced down at me as I looked up at him.

"You asked him to play this for us didn't you?" James asked. I nodded as we walked down the steps of the stage, Rick's voice floating through the night sky.

I wasn't ready to go back into the crowds and to our various family and friends, so I led James across the grass towards the river's edge and the run of benches. As we neared our bench, it was my turn to squeeze James' hand as the moonlight cast its silver glow over the area. James ran his free hand over the old wood.

"It's still here," he said.

We walked round to the seat and with the glow from the moon overhead, we could just make out our heart. It looked fresher than I remembered it. I looked a little closer and found a second smaller heart not too far away with the initials *MC 4 CE*, realising it could only be Charlie and Mitch who had drawn it there and possibly refreshed our heart at the same time.

Pulling me into his arms, I looked up into the beautiful blue eyes of my true love, my only love. I could see him gazing into mine as I pressed closer into his body with the words of Rick Astley still alive in our ears. Then his lips met mine and I surrendered fully to the feel of our bodies reuniting through the touch of our lips. Our hearts beating in time, I felt I had returned to the safety and warmth of home, escaping from the wilderness I had spent the last twenty-four years of my life in. We sank down onto the bench and James pulled me onto his lap as he took my hand in his. Gently he traced a heart onto my palm and then brought it up to his lips to kiss it.

"Stephanie, I believe I'm falling in love with you," he breathed.

"James, I know I'm falling in love with you," I replied.

Neither of us said another word as we sat together and watched the moon sparkle on the water in front of us. Looking up, we gazed at the stars and I let all the happy memories of our love flood back to fill my heart.

"I guess we'd better go back and speak to Charlotte and Mitchell?" I asked.

James nodded as we stood up and with his arm wrapped around me, we returned to the lights and sound of the stage. It felt like we were back in the Eighties all over again. The only difference was that we were no longer young and inexperienced. We had lived and we were aware of loss and sorrow which only served to make the joy and happiness more poignant. Sarah was the first to see our return as she took in the sight of us together. Chris turned and held out his hand to James.

"Welcome back mate," he said.

James took it and I pulled Sarah in for a hug.

Looking around, I saw Charlie and Mitch in the centre of the dance floor, entwined as Rick Astley sang, 'When I Fall in Love'.

"Shall we join them?" I asked.

"I thought you'd never ask," James replied.

The four of us joined the other dancers on the floor and swayed our way towards Charlotte and Mitchell. My daughter saw us and smiled, Mitch grinned at his dad, and we all enjoyed the finale of a wonderful day.

As Rick Astley took his final bow and encore, Sarah and Chris said goodbye and went home. Charlie and Mitch joined up with the other guys and girls from their dance groups and went to the nearby bar. I could hear the beat of the dance music starting to fill the sudden silence of the air around us.

"I guess I'd better just check on work before we leave," I said.

At the bus I saw Jack, Mark, Paul and Ian sitting on the grass outside, beers in their hands.

"What a day," Paul exclaimed, when we reached them.

"A fantastic day," I replied.

"You had us all fooled," Ian said.

"I only guessed who he was a week ago," I admitted. "But I couldn't resist playing along and keeping you guys in the dark, it was great fun."

"It couldn't have worked out any better though, the crowd loved it,"

Mark said, joining in.

"Yeah, a million hankies filled with tears of joy at the romance of it all," Jack said, dramatically. I nudged him with my foot as he looked up and smiled at me.

"You deserve all the happiness you can find," Jack said.

"Well if it's ok with you guys, I'm going to go home before I fall asleep standing up," I said.

"Sure Steph, we'll finish up here and then sleep in the bus so we can have another couple of brews," Paul said.

After saying goodbye to all of them, I felt James' arm around my shoulders as we wandered across the grass towards home. As we walked together in silence, I couldn't have asked for a better ending to the day. When we reached the car park for the swimming pool, I turned to James.

"I have something for you," I said.

Looking inside my handbag, I found the small scrap of material and pulled it out.

"Hold out your hand," I said.

I carefully coiled the silver chain back into his outstretched hand and closed his fingers around it. Looking up into his eyes, I could see all the questions there about how I had come to have this. James opened his palm and held it up so that he could just make out the inscription on the back of the St. Christopher. The soft moonlight picked up the shine on the small medallion as he handed it back to me.

"You put it on me," he said, bending down so that I could reach. My lips found his at the same time and we kissed as the chain found its way back against his skin.

"This time, it will be till the end of time," he said, breathless, holding me tight.

"I hope so."

James tilted my head as our tongues collided and our hearts melted.

ACKNOWLEDGEMENTS

I would like to thank Vicky Gillespie, Paula Spencer, Simon Holroyd, Kristina Thimm, Anne James, Julie Goodwin and Anne-Marie Dossett from Herefordshire Library Service for all their comments, advice and critiques whilst I was writing this book and putting up with my various musings about how things should develop between the main characters in the book. I must have started to feel like a record with the needle stuck sometimes!!

Thanks also go to R Domingo for giving me a male's point of view on the characters in the novel. Emma Lane a close friend who made me rewrite the start fairly early on to make it flow like the rest of the novel. Valda de Dieu who also gave me a very thorough critique of the work and suggested some useful changes.

I realised that to sell a book you need an amazing Book cover which was supplied by the local Herefordshire designer Simon Hammond, please check out his work at www.shammonddesign.com and by all means name drop me, not sure if it will get you any discount but who knows.

Also to the newest local band in Herefordshire called Rubble, please check them out on Facebook to find out where they are playing locally or at their website www.rubbleband.co.uk

A big thank you to Sunshine Radio who provided me with many of the inspirational song titles, that I was able to use in the storyline and also provided a great soundtrack to write to.

Writing this novel has been a revelation and an awful lot of hard work so I hope that you enjoy it. Please get in touch with your comments as you can find me on Facebook or email me: audrina@audrinalane.co.uk.

Check out my website www.audrinalane.co.uk for details of future books.

ABOUT THE AUTHOR

Audrina Lane lives with her partner Steve and two Labradors in Herefordshire where The Heart Trilogy is set. The first book is based on a diary the author wrote in 1992 and is inspired by her own experiences of first love.

The other books in the series, *Unbreak My Heart* and *Closer to the Heart* are out now. To find out more about Audrina and her books, visit www.audrinalane.co.uk or http://author.to/audrinalane.

Made in the USA
Charleston, SC
09 December 2015